The

KEEPER

of

LOST ART

The

KEEPER
of
LOST ART

A Novel

LAURA MORELLI

wm

WILLIAM MORROW

An Imprint of HarperCollinsPublishers

THE KEEPER OF LOST ART. Copyright © 2025 by Laura Morelli. All rights reserved. Printed in the United States of America. No part of this book may be used or reproduced in any manner whatsoever without written permission except in the case of brief quotations embodied in critical articles and reviews. For information, address HarperCollins Publishers, 195 Broadway, New York, NY 10007.

HarperCollins books may be purchased for educational, business, or sales promotional use. For information, please email the Special Markets Department at SPsales@harpercollins.com.

FIRST EDITION

Interior text design by Diahann Sturge-Campbell

Library of Congress Cataloging-in-Publication Data has been applied for.

ISBN 978-0-06-320601-4

25 26 27 28 29 LBC 5 4 3 2 1

The

KEEPER

of

LOST ART

CHAPTER 1

HIDDEN WONDERS

Autumn 1942

Vision, to an artist, is the guiding light that steers the hand. It is the most central, the most powerful of the senses for any who, in pursuit of beauty, aspires to imitate Divine creation with a pen and brush, to form a bridge connecting the inner soul with the boundless external world. Yet in these perilous times, it seems every lantern in Florence has been extinguished, especially for those of us for whom light is most vital. Instead, there is a shroud of darkness, and it seems the tribulations of Italy have only begun . . .

—FROM THE LOST DIARIES OF SANDRO
BOTTICELLI, FLORENCE, SUMMER 1480

From a distance, Villa Santa Lucia seemed a miniature version of the Palazzo Vecchio in Florence, with its tall, narrow tower surrounded by azure hills and massed cypresses. Before we arrived, the villa shook with the thunderous roar of the cannons the Panzer unit had placed around it. But inside that once-idyllic fortress, in the middle of unspeakable devastation, we discovered a marvel that surpassed the bounds of my wildest imaginings . . .

—FROM THE DIARY OF CAPTAIN WALLACE E.
FOSTER, MONUMENTS OFFICER OF THE
FIFTH ARMY IN TUSCANY, JULY 1944

For Stella Costa, the war in Tuscany begins over a featherbed.
"That's mine."

Stella's cousin Livia pushes her aside and hops onto the flowered coverlet, sending dust motes sparkling in the glow of a sunbeam. Livia is sixteen and has burst from her dusty pubescent cocoon into a colorful creature, old and beautiful enough to secure the mayor's son as a fiancé. But in this moment, Stella watches her nearly grown cousin pout like any five-year-old.

"I got here first!" Stella's younger cousin, Mariasole, scrambles up onto the high bed next to Livia.

"*Peccato*. I'm the oldest." Livia shoves her little sister sideways until her head flops on the bed and her giggles go muffled in the messy quilt.

Stella doesn't know her two cousins well enough to predict what will happen next. But caution isn't Stella's strong suit. Without thinking, she vaults on top of both girls. "I'll fight you both for it!" she cries, pummeling her fists into the soft bedding.

More muffled giggling. Down feathers join the dust, rising and spinning in the light, then landing on the terracotta tiles. Beyond the open shutters, a flock of swifts wheels against the sky's blue canvas, the silhouette of thin cypresses, and the Tuscan countryside beyond.

"Stella. Stellina!" Her aunt's voice, sharp and snake-like, comes from nowhere. "*Smettila. Subito!*"

Stella feels sudden pain stab the left side of her face while her aunt yanks her roughly from the bed by her ear. Immediately, she is on her feet on the cold tiles, cowering under her aunt's grip.

"*Aya!*" Stella presses her palm to her cheek. On the high bed, her two cousins sit up straight and cover their mouths. Their giggles trail off.

Zia Angela's face is suddenly very close to Stella's stinging ear. "Sir Harwell's automobile is barely a speck on the horizon. And you . . . acting like you own this place . . ." She stabs her thumb toward the window as if Stella could see the Englishman's Aston Martin from here. Dust billowing along the winding Tuscan roads, halfway to Switzerland. "And a girl," she continues, "using her fists . . . *Vergogna!*"

Zia Angela flicks her cold hand away, releasing her grip at last. Stella sinks into the closest chair and rubs her throbbing ear.

"None of you will sleep here," her aunt says, shooing the girls off the high bed and smoothing the coverlet. "Your father and I are taking this room. You girls will share the yellow room next door. In the stairwell . . ." From behind, Stella's aunt looks lean and brittle, like a dried tree branch in a flowered dress. One that might snap at the slightest provocation.

Stella's aunt turns and opens her mouth again, poised to resume scolding. But suddenly, Stella's cousins dart out of the room. Stella follows, ducking under Zia Angela's grasp. In the doorway, she nearly trips over Mariasole's abandoned, battered leather shoes. Then she runs after her cousins, newly formed allies, who are already at the far end of the long corridor.

STELLA, AT TWELVE YEARS OLD halfway between Mariasole and Livia, jogs to catch up with her cousins. Her ear still throbs with the dull ache of her aunt's icy hand. She glimpses her cousins' fluttering skirts up ahead, Mariasole spinning and skipping barefoot across the terracotta tiles.

"*Finalmente!* We will be countesses!" Mariasole cries, her voice echoing through the empty corridor. "Contessa Livia! Wait for me! *Aspetta!*" But her sister has already reached the base of the tower stair.

Jogging past the many closed doors, Stella feels tempted to stop chasing her cousins and turn a knob instead. She hasn't entered any of these rooms yet. She's only just arrived from Torino, where her mother bundled her into the back of a big car along with several other children and a Red Cross worker headed to family members to the south. Stella to Tuscany to stay with her uncle and aunt, who she's met for the first time in her life.

It's safer in the countryside, her mother told her for the thousandth time, pressing a warm, wrapped *panino* into her hands.

Stella's cousins are new to the villa, too. They say they've moved their things from the caretaker's cottage beyond the olive grove. The rich English couple who were living here asked Stella's uncle to take care of things when they had to leave. Their father is just a driver, they say, but now he's in charge of the whole place.

Each closed doorway promises hidden wonders. Secret chambers painted with mythical beings on the walls and ceilings. Filled with treasured possessions, forgotten keepsakes, silent histories tucked away in drawers and closets. Stella imagines peering through keyholes, exploring cupboards, under beds, inside the elaborately decorated storage cabinets newly vacated by their owners.

Ahead, Livia and Mariasole disappear up the coiled spine of the narrow watchtower. Stella's slippery leather soles find the hollows of the stone treads, worn away under the weight of three hundred years. Through narrow, deeply splayed slits in the walls, Stella catches fleeting glimpses of spiky cypresses and distant lavender hills. A pink cloud hanging like a tuft of spun sugar in the bright sky.

She's only been here a day. But despite being separated from her mother, and the dire circumstances that have led her to Tuscany and the Villa Santa Lucia in the first place, Stella feels a bud of excitement bloom in her chest. Here, in this magical villa, there is only the prospect of new life. It all seems far away from the shadows and desperation that brought her here.

By THE TIME she reaches the landing at the top of the watchtower, Stella is nearly out of breath, and a gust of cool air whips strands of hair across her cheeks. She sidesteps the pigeon droppings and cobwebs to meet her cousins along the stone parapet.

For a moment, her head spins. She reaches for the ledge, where Livia leans out over a staggering vista. The landscape spreads around them in all directions, like an unfurling carpet of emerald and amber. "Florence is that way," Livia says, pointing, but all Stella sees are hills that turn to gray and violet as they stretch to the horizon.

An olive grove blankets the hillside, unfurling along the edge of the villa. In the trees, the timeless dance of the harvest is underway. Stella spots several men and women with baskets, reaching up to pluck the ripest fruit. Wooden ladders propped against the gnarled trunks. Leaves flashing silver and deep green in the autumn air. Beyond the grove, vineyards hang heavy with purple fruit. In the sties, her other uncle, Zio Stefano, is throwing handfuls of grain to the dark pigs, whose hides look like Stella's cracked leather shoes. Her eyes follow one of the snaking roads, lined with rows of green-black vertical cypresses, to the village below. She spots an ancient stone church and the dark silhouette of the little *canonica* alongside it. Behind the squat church tower, golden light bathes the landscape.

At the base of the tower, Stella watches Livia and Mariasole's father, her zio Tino, circle Sir Harwell's Alfa Romeo roadster. The vehicle is a sleek, black silhouette in the shadowy carriage house, waiting for its master's return. Zio Tino, the loyal driver of ten years, runs a rag over a headlight one last time before dislodging the great wooden door from a rock and heaving it closed. Stella watches him turn an iron key. Stash it in his trouser pocket.

"What's that?" Mariasole asks.

Stella only now realizes she's reached for the locket around her neck. Already, it's become an instinct to reach for the metal oval on a chain, with its tiny, grainy photograph of her mother. During the trip from Torino, the pendant seemed to hold the entirety of Stella's world—her mother's embrace and their small apartment, the only home Stella had ever known. "Even while we are apart," her mother told her while she brushed Stella's hair aside and fastened the locket at the nape of her neck, "you'll know I'm with you." This was before Stella got here, before she met her cousins, her aunt and uncles. Before she knew there was not only newfound family but a whole wondrous world waiting for her in Tuscany.

It's safer in the countryside.

"It's my mamma," Stella says, turning the open locket toward Mariasole, who squints at the tiny sepia image of Stella's mother with growing curiosity. "Your *zia* . . ."

As Mariasole twists the silver locket between her fingers, it's difficult for Stella to imagine the growing threats reported in the newspapers and on the wireless. Instead, Villa Santa Lucia seems a haven—everything her mother promised and so much more. To Stella's eyes, there is only peace here in Tuscany.

Now it feels impossible to picture her mother back in Torino, hunched over an assembly line in a typewriter factory that now makes munitions. Their ragged apartment with its peeling paint and the wailing air raid sirens. All around them, city blocks in ruin, blown to rubble by the constant onslaught from British planes. Here, there are no heaps of smoldering rubble, no sound of roaring engines, no enemies in the sky. No sleeping on make-shift pallets in the underground tunnels. None of the reasons her mother sent her here.

Stella wishes her mamma could see it here, and she wonders why she's never brought her to Tuscany before. It's her family, after all—her mother's own brother along with cousins who have been strangers until now.

"I've never seen her," Mariasole says, letting go of the locket, which falls back into the hollow of Stella's neck. "How come you don't have a picture of your father in there, too?"

Stella shrugs and snaps the locket closed, realizing only now that the empty space on the opposite side of her mother's image might be designed to hold a second photo. She has no memory of her father and has no idea what Daniele Costa looks like, even though she, unlike her mother, bears his surname. The only thing she has to show for him.

"Well, he can't show his face around *here* anymore," Mariasole says.

Stella stands dumbstruck as she tries to make sense of her cousin's offhand comment. Mariasole knows something about her father?

But before she can ask, Livia calls, "*Venite*! Come look!"

FROM THE TOWER, the village below seems a speck on a vast map of undulating hills.

Livia gathers herself into a regal pose, leaning against the stone parapet, hand on her hip. She curtsies deeply in her faded dress. "*Piacere*. I am Contessa Livia."

"*Che bella!*" yells Mariasole, taking her sister's hand and striking a similar pose. "And I am Contessa Mariasole. Now we can do whatever we want! That old *signore inglese* and his smelly wife can't tell us what to do anymore."

Livia laughs. The servants have overthrown their masters. The estate stretches out before them, with its goat pens, olive presses, and woodshed. Its carriage-house-turned-automobile-garage. The caretaker's house where her cousins lived until this week. The creaking well and a carpet of olive and lemon trees, of grapevines sloping down the hillsides as far as the eye can see. With Sir and Lady Harwell gone, Stella's cousins have inherited not only an empty fortress but infinite possibility. A dreamland where anything can happen. Their faces are aglow with raking sun and their own excitement. For a magical moment, Stella sees herself as part of this wondrous new world order.

Mariasole, still posing, says, "You can be Contessa Stella."

Disoriented by her cousin's comment about her father not being able to show his face in the village of Santa Lucia, Stella nonetheless copies her cousins, curtsying over the ragged laces of her single pair of shoes.

She's among strangers and doesn't understand the nuances of relating to her newfound family. And maybe she doesn't belong here at all. But for now, the girls have made her feel a little less alone.

"*Piacere*," Stella says.

Mariasole reaches out to her, and Stella squeezes her cousin's small, sweaty palm.

IN THE AFTERNOON, Stella is kneading dough and warily monitoring her aunt when a fine automobile crunches the gravel outside the villa.

Stella stops pressing the heels of her hands into the pliable mass and looks at her aunt. At the other end of the flour-covered table, Zia Angela frowns in concentration. She cuts small pieces off the end of a long roll of dough and pushes her thumb into each one, curling them up into tiny wisps. It looks effortless, this brief flick of the thumb that turns a shapeless lump into a small marvel that, once cooked, melts in your mouth. Stella has failed at it enough times to know it's harder than it looks. She doesn't believe she'll ever do it so quickly and effortlessly. Stella frowns too, mirroring her aunt's concentration.

"*Vado io!*" Zio Tino's voice echoes from the courtyard.

Stella runs her palms across the floured surface of the table again, then presses the heels of her hands into the supple mass of dough, which yields under her touch. Through the window, the sun warms her cheeks and shines bright rectangles of light across the weathered worktable. She watches Zio Tino escort a well-dressed man from his elegant vehicle into the courtyard.

Stella picks up the rolling pin and presses her weight into it just like her aunt has shown her, flattening the dough. Stella's aunt continues to turn out tiny, perfectly formed shapes. The pasta looks completely different here than in Torino, she rationalizes, and besides, Stella and her mother mostly eat rice or polenta. Her aunt can't expect her to know how to do everything.

Stella hears her zio Tino's voice as he leads the newly arrived visitor into Sir Harwell's dining room, a large hall with a table that might seat twenty or more. Above their heads, rough-hewn beams look as if they were timbered from some ancient forest. Zio Tino scrapes a wooden chair back across the red tiles. The visitor removes his hat to reveal a head of silver curls.

"I'm sure you can understand the rationale," the man is saying. Stella's aunt wipes her hands on her apron and unties it from her waist. Waits in the doorway.

"We decided to disperse our collections across different repositories in the countryside," the man is saying as Zio Tino motions for him to sit. Stella sees him from the back, his charcoal-colored suit jacket stretching across his broad back. He unfolds a handkerchief and dabs beads of sweat from his forehead. "That was the unfortunate lesson we learned from the Great War. It's best if the paintings are not in a single location. It's too risky."

"ANGELINA!" Zio Tino calls from the table. Stella tries to imagine her aunt as a "little angel," and it almost makes her laugh out loud. "Bring Signor Poggi a caffè."

Stella's aunt returns to the kitchen and lights the stove, grumbling to herself. She dumps a few heaping spoonfuls of bitter-smelling grounds into the pot. "What are you waiting for?" she snaps suddenly at Stella. "Get the cups."

Stella stops kneading. She doesn't know what to expect from her aunt. Stella wonders why Zia Angela agreed to let her come if she didn't want her here anyway. Stella collects two small cups and saucers from an ancient cabinet. She carries them to the stove, careful to still their rattling.

"Where are the rest of the paintings going?" Stella hears her uncle ask the gray-haired man. Signor Poggi.

"We've already brought several hundred of them to the Villa Bossi-Pucci at Montagnana," he says. "We have a full-time custodian posted there. The ministry has also requisitioned Poppiano and Oliveto. And a few others."

Zia Angela pours a steaming stream of espresso into each cup until a foam forms on top. "Bring the sugar," she says. "And the water." Stella picks up the glass pitcher with slices of lemons. She follows her aunt into the dining room.

"With all due respect, Signor Poggi," her uncle says as they enter, "I understand the museum's problem . . . the need to disperse the works of art to keep them safe from any unforeseen dangers. But . . . I don't have any way to reach Sir Harwell. To get his approval, you see." He shrugs. "I'm just a driver."

"I'm sure you're loyal to your employer," Signor Poggi says.

Her aunt sets the small shots of espresso in front of the men, then stands by the table with her arms crossed.

"My wife, Angela," Zio Tino says.

"*Grazie*, signora." Signor Poggi acknowledges Zia Angela briefly before turning back to Zio Tino. "Surely you understand, my friend, that Sir Harwell is now considered an enemy of the state, as much as you may be fond of him. The British residents of Florence have mostly left the city . . . Has he returned to England?"

"Switzerland," Zio Tino says, running his hand over his thinning black hair, slicked with *pomata* that smells like pine. "He believes this will be over soon enough. Didn't want to go too far. Hopes to be back here as soon as possible. I don't have to convince you he

loves Santa Lucia. It's been his home for more than ten years."
Zio Tino gestures to the handsome room, with its uneven terracotta tiles and tremendous stone hearth, its hulking beams and
dining table.

Stella hopes what her uncle says isn't true, that the Harwells
might return to Villa Santa Lucia soon. Her cousins have told her
Sir Harwell is an odd man. And anyway, Stella is so delighted with
the elegant bedroom she shares with her cousins and eating in this
very dining room that she hopes they never come back; that her
family never has to return to their little caretaker's house on the
edge of the hill.

Signor Poggi nods. "*Senti*. I have nothing against the English.
Not personally. But I'm afraid your *capo* is overly optimistic. It
seems the *inglesi* don't understand their enemy alien status. Many
of them are still in Florence against their better judgment. Better if
they leave Italy altogether. At least for now."

"Sir Harwell and his family . . ." Zio Tino says. "They can
return easily when the hostilities die down."

The older man pauses, downs his espresso in one shot, then sets
the tiny cup rattling back in the saucer. "I'm afraid Sir Harwell
is no longer the owner of this lovely place, my friend. The Italian
state is."

Without realizing it, Stella has stepped into the dining room,
captivated by the men's conversation, wanting to know more about
the Harwells and the paintings Signor Poggi mentioned. She leans
against the wooden buffet. She feels defensive, protective of this
villa, which—though it seems to have slipped out of Sir Harwell's
hands—feels like it belongs to Stella and her cousins. Stella has
only ever seen it occupied by her own extended family. She never
thought that the Italian state might be the owner instead.

The raw truth of it seems to render Zio Tino speechless.

Signor Poggi garners some compassion. "With the increased British air raids across northern Italy, well . . . Things are uncertain. Not to mention problems with our own local regimes here . . . Anyway, I am old enough to remember what happened to our collections during the Great War, so . . ."

"What are you doing, Stella?" Arms still crossed, Zia Angela sets her hawk-like gaze on her. Stella runs her finger along the chest where the glass water pitcher sweats onto the wood. "You're supposed to be preparing the dough."

"I'm thirsty."

"You know where the well is . . ."

Zio Tino raises his hand and her aunt goes silent. "It's alright, Stella," he says. "Pour yourself a glass."

Stella hesitates, then pours a small glass of water, which goes down cool and tangy in her throat.

"This is my niece, Stella," Zio Tino says. "My sister's child. Her mother is working at a munitions factory in Torino and her father is . . . away."

Zio Tino's voice trails off. Stella finds it strange, hearing her mother and father mentioned together again in the same breath, when Stella and her mother have lived apart from Daniele Costa for most of her life.

"More children than ever heading to the countryside— everything precious is leaving the cities, it seems." Signor Poggi gives Stella a grin that looks at the same time paternal and sad. "Many Florentines have also chosen to send their children out to relatives in the country."

"*Eh, allora.*" Zio Tino scratches the top of his head where the hair has gone sparse. "My wife could use a hand in the kitchen." He gives an equally sad-looking grin to Zia Angela, whose face is like stone. "And they had some space in the village school."

This is the only rub about being here, Stella thinks. The fly in the oil. She doesn't want to go to school.

"Stella, this is Signor Poggi. From the Uffizi Galleries in Florence."

"Signorina." Signor Poggi nods his head toward her gallantly, which makes Stella feel more important than she was before. Like the countess she pretended to be when she curtsied to her cousins in the watchtower. "Who else lives here?"

"Sir Harwell entrusted me with the care of the estate and now we are the only ones left. Myself along with my wife and our two daughters. My wife's brother, Stefano. And Stella."

Signor Poggi records this information in a small notebook, then pulls a stack of paper from a leather case. "Here is the list of what we propose to bring to Villa Santa Lucia," he says. "In my view, you have the ideal situation. The ceilings are high, you have large, open rooms where the shutters can be closed and the doors locked with a key." He gestures to the enclosed courtyard.

Stella decides she would like to count the rooms in the villa. The number of hearths and cabinets. The number of tapestries, frescoes, and chandeliers.

"Of course, you will be compensated for your time and services in guarding the works," Signor Poggi continues. "Ideally, the Uffizi would cover your time from eight in the morning until nineteen hundred in the evening. For this, you would be paid seventeen lire per day. And then we would seek another man to guard them overnight . . . He would be paid at half that rate."

"My brother-in-law can do it," Zio Tino says. "He tends to Sir Harwell's animals and olives." Stella sees her uncle and aunt exchange a nervous, fleeting glance full of words unspoken.

The man from the Uffizi nods. "*Benissimo*. It seems we are in agreement. You have only to sign here and I will see to the rest. Expect the first load of trucks next week."

Zio Tino signs the paper with a careful script.

"You understand there is risk . . ." Signor Poggi says.

Zio Tino's mouth settles into a thin line. Then he shrugs. "That is true for all of us, my friend, no?"

Signor Poggi answers with a grunt of agreement and a firm handshake. He stands and puts on his hat, buckling his briefcase closed.

What risk? Stella thinks as she sets down her glass of water and returns to the kitchen to help her aunt. Things here are *nothing* like they were in Torino. Here, there are only docile goats, waving grass, and spiky trees. Stella and her cousins, suddenly countesses. If it weren't for her mean aunt, the whole thing would be perfect. From Stella's vantage point, war seems impossible here, while other possibilities seem endless, unfurling like a carpet of Tuscan hills.

THEY SPEND THE REST of the afternoon hiding things.

The air cools quickly as the sun sinks behind the distant hills. Stella's aunt lowers herself to her knees in the kitchen garden. The olive leaves turn golden with the late afternoon light, their winding trunks casting long shadows on the caked earth. Stella loiters at the edge of the garden with a trowel while her cousins dart among the gnarled trunks in a lazy game of hide-and-seek it looks like they've played a thousand times. Nearby, Mariasole's orange cat, Luigi, hunkers in the grass like a small tiger.

"Giulia Rossi says Alessio is coming to visit us soon with his father," Livia says, revealing her face from behind a tree trunk. Stella thinks her eyes look radiant and flashing in the golden light.

"I told you he's going to ask her to marry him!" Mariasole bursts from behind another gnarled trunk. "Everyone's talking about it."

Zia Angela exchanges a fleeting, flickering glance with her husband, who leans against a stone wall, watching his wife and daughters with a mixture of fondness and concern as they dig fresh holes in the ground. A shovel is propped alongside him. He cups his hands around a cigarette and lights it, the smoke curling up and dissipating into the air. Stella thinks he looks like he wants to say something. But he stays silent.

"As far as families, you could do worse." Zia Angela begins to dig among the overripe eggplants, a few rotted tomatoes, and tangled masses of thyme and oregano. With a trowel, she pries a hole between two unruly rosemary bushes. Stella watches her aunt's sinewy figure, lean and strong, push the tool into the red dirt caked hard from the sun. The newly upturned earth smells of worms and damp.

Zio Tino finally speaks. "When you marry, you marry the whole family, not just the man, *capito*? And if you have different views on how things should be . . ." His speech trails off and he gazes at the distant hills.

"But marriage can sometimes transcend such differences," Zia Angela says, standing and wiping her brow with her forearm.

Mariasole jogs over to her mother and yanks on her skirt. "If Alessio's family is so important, maybe they could get us some more ration cards!"

Zio Tino's brow wrinkles, but he says nothing more. Stella struggles to imagine Livia as a wife, living in the mayor's house, no less. But there is much Stella doesn't understand about this family and their complicated relations with the villagers who live at the bottom of the Villa Santa Lucia's winding drive.

So, Stella carefully observes without commenting. She has spent the afternoon in the storage pantry off the dining room, where she counted pieces of Lady Harwell's shiny, clanging silver services. In scratchy handwriting, Zia Angela recorded the number of serving spoons, of tea strainers, of pitchers and salt cellars and meat forks in a small, lined journal before wrapping everything in individual sheets of newspaper. Meanwhile, Stella's uncles worked all afternoon to fit Sir Harwell's finest bottles of wine and cherry brandy into hidden crevices of the dank wine cellar.

Suddenly, Mariasole darts behind one of the olive trees, flushing out her older sister by swatting her with a broken olive branch. Livia jogs sideways, holding onto the skirt of her flowered dress. Laughter rings through the air.

"Girls!" Zia Angela turns, her forehead etched with lines. "Help, please."

Zio Tino hands the large shovel to Livia, who frowns but takes the tool from her father and begins digging a little farther away.

Zia Angela produces a tin box large enough to fit a pair of shoes. She nestles it in the hole.

"What's inside?" Mariasole asks.

"It's the *signora*'s jewelry," Livia says. "What she left behind."

"Don't dare tell Giulia Rossi," her aunt says, wagging a finger. "Or any of your friends."

"Won't Signora Harwell be angry to find her jewelry in the dirt?" Mariasole asks.

"The Harwells may be enemies of the state for the moment," Zio Tino says, "but they have been kind to us. When they come back, I want to make sure everything they treasure is still here. Even if it's in the dirt."

Mariasole presses her small hands into the soil. Somber silence overtakes the girls' laughter as the sun dips below the horizon. Zia Angela pats the dirt flat and replants a small rosemary bush to mark the spot.

LIVIA ARRANGES for a village boy to escort Stella to her first day of school. Waiting outside the front door, Fabio is a spindly, olive-skinned boy with a cowlick. He's also the younger brother of Alessio, Livia's supposed fiancé.

"First day," he says as they start down the winding dirt path. "You must be excited."

"Not me," Stella says.

"Why not?" He laughs, even though Stella doesn't think it's funny at all.

"I don't see the point of going to school." Stella kicks up pebbles with the toe of her scuffed shoes as they make their way toward the schoolhouse. Below, Stella can see the entire village in a single glance, with its winding road, mismatched geometry of terracotta roof tiles, dingy stucco, and pockmarked brick. Laundry strung on zigzag lines. It's the opposite of Torino, Stella thinks, which goes on and on, farther than you can even go on the tram.

Fabio kicks up dirt beside her. "Don't you want to be smart?"

"I'm already smart." She shoots him a smug glance. "I know how to read and write. I can add and subtract numbers. What else is there?"

Fabio darts toward a large rock in the road and kicks it like a ball until it falls into the ditch. "You gotta go anyway, *sciocchina*. We have to stay till fourteen now."

Stella pokes out her bottom lip; she doesn't appreciate being called a dummy.

"I would have quit school already by now if I could," Stella says. She's still mad she couldn't stop at twelve so she could start working in one of Torino's factories like her mother. Make some money to help out. But that was before they changed the rule to fourteen. "My cousin Livia is lucky. She's sixteen. Never has to sit in a schoolhouse again. She can even get married soon . . ." Stella stops. Maybe she wasn't supposed to mention it. She shoots a sidelong glance at Fabio, to see if he will confirm that his older brother will ask for Livia's hand in marriage.

But Fabio says nothing of the sort. "Where are your parents?"

he asks instead, stopping to pick up another small stone and dash it into the dust.

"My mamma stayed behind in Torino for work," Stella says.

Behind them, Mariasole breaks into a jog to catch up with them, her too-big leather satchel slapping her skinny hip. "They were living in the sewer!" Mariasole informs him loudly. "That's how come she came to stay with us."

An image flashes across Stella's mind of the life she left behind in Torino, which now seems so far away, it might as well be on the other side of the world. The flickering lanterns casting eerie shadows on the damp walls. The air thick with earth, sweat, fear, and unwashed bodies. The terror that returned every time the low rumbles vibrated the concrete underfoot and made ash fall from the ground overhead.

"Oh," Fabio says, shoving his hands in his pockets.

When they reach the outskirts of the village, sounds of children's chattering and laughter grow. Stella pulls her leather school bag close to her chest. She is wearing an ill-fitting uniform handed down from Livia, a black dress with a sagging white collar, the too-short skirt revealing knees that knock together like a newborn pony. The worn satchel was once Livia's, too, back when she was young enough to still have to go to school.

Other girls emerge from their village homes, their mothers having cleaned and pressed their dresses, their leather bags new and rubbed to a sheen. Stella presses hers under her arm as one girl shoots her a curious glance, then turns back to her friends and whispers. All the girls turn around to look.

Stella knows it was a mistake to come here.

In the village, they pass the workshops of a bricklayer and a man repairing shoes. There is a small clinic that looks closed. The parish and the lichen-covered church. Beyond, on another hill, stands a chapel and a distant cemetery.

The mayor's office and house, where Fabio's father presides, stands in the center of the square, its flags swaying in the gathering heat. Through her careful observation of her aunt and uncle, Stella has gathered that Fabio's father is the village mayor and chief of police, one of the last remaining villagers to put his faith in the Fascists. Stella wonders if this is where Livia will live, too. One day. From the bakery, the smell of freshly baked bread wafts through the air. Beyond, there is a vista to neatly planted vineyards.

When she turns around, Stella glimpses the Villa Santa Lucia perched lonely and high on its own hill, with its tall, thin watch-tower and crenellated battlements. Black-green cypresses anchor the hillside, reaching toward the sky with their pointy silhouettes.

Viewing the villa from this distant perspective, Stella recalls the first time she saw it, after her uncle picked her up from where the Red Cross car stopped in Pisa, and she slid into the slippery passenger seat of Sir Harwell's fine vehicle. That's when Zio Tino told her the car wasn't his; he was only the driver. From here, even with its tall watchtower and fortifications, the villa seems somehow smaller than she thought. Even fragile.

THE ONE-ROOM SCHOOLHOUSE squats along a high stone path between the parish church and the village bakery. Its tile roof and deep windowsills are covered with white deposits of a hundred pigeons. Stella enters the schoolhouse door among a sea of unfamiliar faces.

The children spread across the enormous room, which Stella thinks looks like a place where people might have raised farm animals long ago. It is little more than a single stone chamber with a dark loft made of wooden beams. Stark and ugly, Stella thinks. High windows illuminate a blue sky and tufted clouds. It smells of damp. Of small, sticky children.

A great crucifix hangs above the blank, dusty chalkboard.

On either side of the suffering Christ stand faded portraits of Benito Mussolini and King Vittorio Emanuele. This, at least, is the same as her classroom in Torino. Under the windows stand glass-front cabinets full of leather-bound books. Along the top of the bookcase, under the window, is the dusty clutter of the same kind of gas masks they had back in her old school. At the sight of the masks, with their bug-eyes and respirators, Stella feels a strange mixture of nostalgia for home paired with unease.

"Put this on," Mariasole says. The children grab white smocks from hooks near the door and slip them over their clothing. Mariasole hands one to Stella.

The sound of children's voices grows nearly deafening until the teacher claps her hands in a rhythmic pattern. The children respond in unison by clapping the same pattern. The cacophony calms to a low din as the sound of creaking wooden desks and metal chairs scraping the floor replaces the chatter.

"*Maestra!*" Mariasole yanks on Stella's hand and runs up to her teacher. "*Maestra!* This is my cousin, Stella. It's her first day!"

The teacher is pretty, Stella thinks. Her thick, dark hair is tied back like a horse's tail, her skin as gold as the first press of olives. She wears a white smock that hangs loose across her petite frame, matching the children's.

"Stella Costa! Your uncle told me you were coming. We've saved a place for you." The teacher guides Stella to a desk in a crowded row, just in front of Fabio and under the light of the tall windows. "Don't be shy." She smiles widely, displaying a row of white teeth.

Stella feels all eyes fall on her as the *maestra* steers her with her shoulders as if she is a little kid instead of a big one. She walks past the many children younger than her. She's too old for this, she thinks. Her cheeks turn hot and she desperately wishes to be four-teen instead of twelve, so she could walk out the door and never come back. Stella slides into the cold wooden seat and places her leather bag on the floor beside her.

She opens the scratched lid to the wooden desk. Inside, there are two worn-down pencils and a couple of notebooks. One notebook has a picture of a Madonna and Child and the name "Ghirlandaio" on the front. The other shows a faded image of Il Duce standing in front of the Colosseum as if he were a Roman emperor. She opens the front cover to find pages scribbled with another kid's writing.

A younger girl turns around in the desk in front of Stella. Her two front teeth are missing. "Where'd *you* come from?"

Stella squirms in her squeaking seat and opens the notebook with Il Duce to a blank page. The girl's question claws at Stella.

"Torino."

"Heard it's all blown up," the girl says. Her eyes are wide, green, and mocking. "Everyone's dead."

"Giulia Rossi . . . that's enough. *Ragazzi!*" The teacher's voice rises above the din. She claps her hands again and the children settle. "A project for today . . ." The girl mercifully turns around in her seat and Stella glares at the back of her small head. The teacher's words turn the other kids' attention away from Stella.

From the desk behind, Fabio taps Stella's shoulder. He gestures toward her notebook. "Ha! You got somebody's old stuff," he whispers. His face is sour, like when you suck on a lemon.

"You see?" Stella whispers back to him smugly. "I told you. There was no point in my coming here."

At noon, Stella and Mariasole trudge back up the hill to Villa Santa Lucia for the midday meal. The church bells count the noon hour as the schoolchildren fan out down the village streets to their homes. Fabio veers off near the mayor's house, catching up to an unruly-looking group of boys. Two of the boys climb onto the edge of the fountain in the square, shoving one another.

"Someone needs to teach them some manners," Mariasole says.

"*We* could never get away with that," Stella says, part of her wishing she could climb up and teeter on the edge of the fountain, too.

The walk from the schoolhouse to the villa is a slow, uphill climb. While they've worked on their morning lessons, the sky has turned gray and heavy, bearing down from above.

"How do you know about my father?" Stella says at last. The sense that her cousins know more about her family than she does hangs heavily in the air.

Mariasole shrugs, scrambling to keep up. "How come you don't?"

Stella figures it's a fair question. Apart from her surname, Stella has never felt a connection to Daniele Costa. Has rarely given him a thought. He's never been a presence in her life. She and her mother have been completely fine together, just the two of them. But now, in this village where both her mother and her father grew up, Stella begins to realize there might be more to her parents' story. Mariasole's question dredges up old anxieties that Stella now realizes have lain dormant and unspoken for years. In the end, Stella fails to come up with an answer.

"Mamma says you're the spitting copy of your papà."

Spit.

Stella imagines Zia Angela saying the word *sputo* and she knows it's not a compliment.

As they draw nearer to the villa, Stella glimpses Sir Harwell's prized formal gardens, his lemon trees, his high terrace overlooking a grove of olives that drapes like a gold, green, and silvery carpet over the hillside, now quiet and still in the gathering clouds. Along the edge of the vineyard, Stella sees Zia Angela's older brother, Zio Stefano, wiping his brow and surveying the trees, animals, and vineyards he spends all day tending. Stefano is lean and angular like his sister. A man of the soil, all sinew and sweat. His face is weathered, as bronze as the ancient vines he tends. Stella watches him pick up a shovel and disappear down a row of gnarled grapevines.

"He likes to work outside," Mariasole says. "That way he doesn't have to be near my mamma. She likes to strike him if he gets too close." Mariasole runs ahead. "You know how siblings are." But Stella doesn't know. Stella has never had siblings and has never felt the love and wrath and angst that goes with having sisters and brothers. She's always been alone. Stella thinks again about her father spitting her out and leaving her behind, nothing but saliva. *Lo sputo*.

But as Stella approaches the villa and anticipates putting the midday meal on the table alongside Zia Angela, she feels her initial excitement about arriving at Villa Santa Lucia wane. Now she wonders if it was a mistake not only to go to school but to come here at all. Perhaps she was better off in Torino. Sewers and air raids and all.

Beyond the road, dilapidated, distant farms appear like wrecked ships on the ocean of the rolling landscape. According to Zio Tino, long ago, the owners of Villa Santa Lucia were the masters of this land, as far as the eye could see. There were some fifty farms, each with its own olive presses, dairies, granaries, wine cellars, workshops, and outbuildings. Each farm had to share a portion of their crops with the owners of the villa, human misery and poverty exchanged for the master's power and extravagance.

But then, a generation ago, the villa's owners fell on hard times and sold to the English. Sir Harwell and his family used it as a refuge from their English winters. Instead of working the land, Sir Harwell sat in his study and wrote in his leather-bound journals. Even though the farmers no longer had to share their crops, they felt a sense of affection and relation with the owners of the Villa Santa Lucia. "And we still depend on these close arrangements with our neighbors," Zio Tino told her. "The work of the farms would never be complete otherwise."

As Stella and Mariasole near the villa, the aroma of roasting meat wafts through the air, as if emanating from the walls. Stella's aunt appears at one of the upper-floor windows, snapping sheets over the sill. Stella hears Livia singing and the sound of a metal spoon clanging on a copper pot. Two geese peck at the cracks between the stones.

Mariasole stops abruptly. "*Guarda!*" she says. Look.

There is a large truck parked at the villa's entrance, and the two massive front doors stand open. Just inside, Stella detects a flurry of activity—murmured voices, the scraping of furniture.

Two men stand at the back of the truck. They unload an enormous painting, a sliver of an ornate gilded frame emerging from a blanket. The men move slowly, heaving the giant package up the stairs to the villa's front door.

Signor Poggi's paintings have arrived.

CHAPTER 2

MADONNA, HELP US

Winter 1942–43

*I have undertaken a new commission for His Excellency . . .
a marriage gift. An ambitious endeavor filled with some trepidation, if I am honest. It must encapsulate everything I know
about painting—and many things I do not: myth, legend, allegory. Already, I see it will be like nothing else I have painted.
A daunting responsibility that at the same time fills me with
inspiration, in no small measure thanks to His Excellency's faith
that I am worthy and capable of such a task. And more than
that. It could be a new beginning for me. A spring. A Primavera.
The promise of pulling me out of the darkness that has shadowed
my soul for so long. A chance to begin again.*

—FROM THE LOST DIARIES OF SANDRO
BOTTICELLI, FLORENCE, SUMMER 1480

*No other region of Italy is as significant in artistic patrimony
as Tuscany. It is the cradle of the Renaissance. The home of the
likes of Michelangelo Buonarroti. Leonardo da Vinci. Sandro
Botticelli, whose unique aesthetic is like no other. These great
masters of the past could scarcely have envisioned such horrors
as modern warfare. What can a single individual do to protect
this vast canvas of human achievement from annihilation?
It feels impossible.*

—FROM THE DIARY OF CAPTAIN WALLACE E.
FOSTER, MONUMENTS OFFICER OF THE
FIFTH ARMY IN TUSCANY, JUNE 1945

After the men and the trucks depart, Stella finds the door to a large room off the main courtyard standing ajar.

She pushes it open with a tentative hand. At the far end of the room, Zio Tino's silhouette is framed in the bright window. She sees the back of his balding head, his hands pushed down into the depths of his trouser pockets. His shoulders up near his ears, shrugging in his pinstriped jacket. Elegant in his driver's suit, ready to escort his *capo* anywhere his heart desires—if only he would return from his Swiss exile. Zio Tino rocks back and forth on his heels, watching the now-empty trucks rattling loudly in a cloud of dust, winding down the hillside. The floor tiles, red octagons, reflect the diffuse, cloud-filtered light.

Where this room was once sparse and severe, decorated with a large table and two of Sir Harwell's fancy sofas that Stella and her cousins are not allowed to sit on, it is now filled with what must be several dozen enormous paintings. Most are at least twice as tall as Stella. They dwarf her uncle, who's shorter than his own wife and not much taller than Stella herself.

In the shadows, the paintings are stacked against the walls six and seven deep. Stella steps slowly into the room, surveying the mismatched assemblage of shimmering frames and painted surfaces. A kaleidoscope of frozen stories. There is a man on horseback, wearing an enormous white collar around his face that unfolds like a fan. A woman in an oversized blue dress. A battle scene with a writhing group of armored men clashing with one another on the backs of muscular horses. Each one a gilded window into a painted universe.

One painting looks like it should stand above the high altar of a church. It's a massive panel with a triangular top that nearly reaches the ceiling of the great room. In the center is a gigantic, flat-looking Madonna who seems to float in a sea of gold. Her face is unreadable, her eyes little more than slits. She holds a strange-looking, puffy-eyed Christ child in her lap. To Stella, the baby looks like a frog.

On the other side of the room stands another massive painting in a gilded frame. The surface is covered in painted flowers, its bright colors apparent even in the darkening room as the rain clouds collect and the light begins to fade. On the surface stands a figure of a woman with flowing red hair. Another in a billowing dress. Another woman has a garland of flowers spilling from her mouth. Above it all, a fat winged baby—a blindfolded baby—shoots an arrow from his bow.

Stella takes in the paintings for a few long seconds, mesmerized by their strange beauty. She feels the presence of something ancient and mysterious in the paintings, something that speaks of beauty and possibility. But she can't begin to understand it. She has never seen anything like this in her life.

"You can't tell anyone about this, Stella."

Her uncle doesn't turn from his place at the window. But somehow, he knows she is there. His voice is low and serious. She watches the balding spot on the back of his head, then looks again at the flat Madonna, whose face stares indifferently into the gathering shadows of her new surroundings.

"What are they doing here?" Her voice comes out quiet and small.

Zio Tino turns to her, his face grave, lines running down either side of his mouth. "Signor Poggi—the man from the Uffizi Galleries—has entrusted us with keeping them hidden for the time being. A big responsibility."

Stella pauses, feels the weight of the task, even if she doesn't know what the responsibility entails.

"But you can't tell anyone. You hear me? No one outside this villa can know about this. Especially at the school. This is our family's own secret. You understand?"

At first, Stella feels a thrill that her uncle would trust her to keep a secret so wonderful, so important. But her uncle's expression troubles her. Stella nods.

"*Brava.*"

"But . . . Why would anyone come in here? Those English airmen only come in planes . . . They're too busy dropping bombs, not stealing paintings . . ."

Zio Tino's troubled expression silences Stella's train of thought. His mind seems to search for the many things he might say in explanation. Instead, he only says, "Come now."

Stella follows her uncle out of the room. She watches him pull the heavy door closed behind him, then lock it with an ancient-looking iron key. He hesitates, looking around the courtyard and then double-checking the door. Then he reaches up and places the key up high, wedging it into a crack between two large stones in the wall.

Suddenly, Zia Angela's voice rings out across the courtyard. "*Porca miseria!* You're going to burn the whole thing!"

"It wasn't me!" Stella hears Livia yell back. "You want it done that way, then do it yourself!" Her cousin storms out of the kitchen, yanking her apron from around her neck. She stomps across the courtyard, ignoring her father and Stella.

"Best we go distract your Zia Angela before she finds her wooden spoon," he says, and now his face turns into a conspiratorial grin. He puts his arm around Stella's shoulders and leads her to the kitchen.

THE EVENING RADIO BROADCAST brings news of violence. A new British air raid has hit Genoa, damaging churches, leveling several city blocks, and shutting down the ports. Another one has targeted one of the Fiat plants in Torino, killing several workers. Everyone around the table holds a collective breath as the disembodied voice drones from the hulking wooden machine in the corner of the dining room. Mariasole's orange-striped cat, Luigi, sprawls across the cool floor tiles, unperturbed.

Stella picks over her *ribollita* made with red beans, onions, and carrots, thickened with bread and dressed with a few sprigs of rosemary from the kitchen garden where they buried Lady Harwell's necklaces. She picks at the few curls of discarded pasta bits she's tossed into the stew, frowning. Even though she's tried a lot of times, she thinks she'll never get it right. Her aunt and her cousins roll out the long, narrow *pici* with ease, while Stella's come out sticky and uneven. But no one at the table comments on her weak attempts and they clean their plates all the same.

"You see where the Fascists have led us," Zio Stefano says, listening to the news. He pushes up the dirt-streaked sleeves of his work shirt and rests his elbows on the table, tugging at the roots of his unruly hair.

Zia Angela rises abruptly. "That's enough." She turns the knob on the wireless and retakes her seat. They eat the rest of their dinner in heavy silence. Even Mariasole, usually chattering, remains silent. The adults stare at their plates or send one another furtive glances, the weight of the broadcast lingering over them like a heavy blanket of gloom. Stella sees that even far away from any bombed city, three years of war have made the adults weary and uneasy here, too.

"I'm going to check the coop and make sure everything is locked," Zio Stefano says finally. He scrapes back his wooden chair. He is older than Zia Angela, his beard laced with a few wiry gray hairs that half hide his weathered face. He hobbles away, as if his knee is aching.

"Me too!" Mariasole leaps up and follows her uncle out of the room. Mariasole is Zio Stefano's unofficial assistant, helping to feed and care for the animals on the property. "Come on, Luigi," she says, gathering up her cat. Stella watches Mariasole and the cat, its long striped legs dangling from her grasp, disappear through the doorway and Stella wishes she could disappear from the room, too. She would prefer to go to the animal pens to watch Zio Stefano's silly chickens, with their flicking heads and nervous *co-co-dè*. But she knows she's expected to help Zia Angela in the kitchen instead.

Reluctantly, Stella helps Livia clear the dishes. Only Stella's aunt and uncle are left at the table. Zio Tino swirls the last mouthful of red wine in the bottom of his glass.

When she reaches the door, Stella hears her aunt begin speaking quietly to her husband. Stella hesitates.

"I don't know why you agreed to let them bring those pictures here!" Her aunt's dark hair is pulled back into a bun, coming loose at the edges, tendrils falling around her stern face. Her apron is tied tightly around her waist, cinching her cotton dress. "They will only attract unwanted attention." With nervous energy, her small hands, cracked and worn from the relentless washing of dishes and clothes, pick breadcrumbs from the tablecloth.

"What choice do we have, Angelina?" Zio Tino says. "Signor Poggi is right. The Harwells are now enemies of the state and anyway, this house isn't ours any more than it's theirs. And I'm just a driver. What authority do we have to refuse them?"

"And what authority do we have to take care of such things?" she retorts, her voice growing louder.

"*Boh . . .*" Zio Tino shrugs, a motion that brings his shoulders all the way to his large earlobes. "You heard the man. They have to find somewhere suitable. There aren't so many places like this, no?" He gestures to the high, beamed ceiling.

Stella's aunt squirms in her chair. After a moment, she says more loudly, "How much are those pictures worth?"

Heavy silence.

"They are . . . part of our culture, our collective history," her uncle says finally. "Surely it would be difficult to put a price on them."

Stella sees her aunt's eyes narrow to slits, just like the Madonna's in the gilded altarpiece. "And remind me how much you are being paid per day to guard these supposedly priceless masterpieces?"

This time, a long silence stretches between her aunt and uncle.

"Exactly," her aunt says, even though Zio Tino hasn't answered her question. "And is my brother aware you are being paid twice as much? Did he have any say in the matter? I see you didn't ask him first before signing those papers with Signor Poggi."

Zio Tino has no response to this, but Stella thinks his face looks guilty.

Then, Stella watches Zia Angela swat her husband with a napkin. He ducks.

"Anyway, those treasures will only bring the Germans to our doorstep," Zia Angela says. "Stella forgot to clear the glasses." The glasses clang together as she scrapes back her chair across the tiles and stands. "Stupid girl. I told you it was a mistake to bring her here. After all that girl's parents put us through . . ."

Stella slides away from the door and makes a run for the corridor, leaving Livia alone in the kitchen with her mother.

STELLA IMAGINES that whatever Mariasole knows about her family, she must have learned from her own parents. Stella doesn't feel confident around Zia Angela yet, but she thinks she might approach the more gentle-hearted Zio Tino on the subject.

When Stella thinks of her parents, only her mother comes into sharp focus. Earnest and hardworking. Competent in her factory uniform and her able hands. Quick to pull Stella into a warm embrace and teach her things she wouldn't have known about otherwise.

But when Stella tries to picture her father, he remains remote and dim in spite of her best efforts to claw back any images from the cavern of her memories. She reaches for a glimpse of a time when he might have been a living, breathing presence in her life. But she's never sure if her father's face is an actual memory or the product of her own imagination. His face stays fuzzy and out of focus like a bad photograph—the curve of a strong jaw, large and calloused hands, a mischievous slant to his eyes and expression. Whittling wood between his knees.

Cucciola, he called her. At least she imagines so. Puppy. As if she could be picked up and loved. Then left behind while he went off to do something unknowable. And she, waiting, convinced he may never return.

But the rest fades away in a blur, like a swirl of brushstrokes.

AFTER NIGHTFALL, Stella returns to the villa's main courtyard. Through a doorway, the kitchen stands dark and empty and clean. The air has turned cold and the night sky reveals a sprinkle of stars.

Stella sees a small light coming from the large room where the paintings are stored, little more than a glow at the bottom of the door. Stella opens the door tentatively. If she can catch Zio Tino alone, Stella thinks, she might dare to ask him what he knows about her father. How Zia Angela knows what he looks like and why she might have claimed Stella was the spit of him.

But Zio Tino, his dark silhouette nearly invisible in the shadows, is standing in front of the gigantic golden panel with the strange Madonna and her frog baby. The altarpiece dwarfs him, a small figure in a dark suit. The gold glitters in the light of a lamp on the table in the middle of the room. The docile, almost uncaring face of the Madonna staring out with her hooded eyes. Stella watches her uncle's hands move over the worn wooden beads of a rosary. She would no more interrupt him now than if he were praying before the high altar of the village church. Finally, her uncle lowers himself to his knees with some difficulty, all the way to the tile floor. "Madonna," he says, looking up at the silhouette of the giant Mary in the shadows, "help us."

THE NEXT DAY, Stella's mother manages to get a telephone line through to Villa Santa Lucia.

"I miss you so much, *tesoro.*" Her mother's voice sends a lightning bolt of emotion from Stella's head to her toes, bringing with it a sudden rush of streetlights and trams and train whistles and car horns and midday crowds and the great Mole Antonelliana that towers over Torino. Her mother's anchoring embrace and the smell of onions frying in butter before the rice goes into the pan. The sounds of their noisy apartment building full of neighbors and friends. It's all Stella can do to hold back the dam of tears that threatens to break. She feels the sudden and painful rip from her home as if she herself were torn in two.

"*Dimmi tutto . . .*" her mother says. Tell me everything.

But Stella struggles to know where to begin to tell her mother *one* thing, much less everything. How could she explain her loneliness, her difficulty in finding a friend despite living with cousins who behave like siblings, her unending labor in preparing food and cleaning it up, the precariousness and wonder of being here in this place, with this family who is her own flesh and blood but at the same time so foreign?

"I'm helping in the kitchen," she says.

"*Brava.*" Her mother's voice crackles across the phone lines.

"But mamma . . . Are you safe? You're still in the tunnel?"

For a long moment, Stella hears only distant static and she wonders if the line has dropped. "Yes," her mother says finally. "I'm still there at night, just to be safe, you know. I'm still working at the factory during the day. It's not so bad." A small laugh.

"But we heard on the wireless about the air raids."

"The broadcasts exaggerate things. It only damaged some of the Fiat plant, nothing else. We are following the precautions."

"*Va bene*," Stella says.

"Let me talk to your uncle. Don't worry about me, *tesoro*. I miss you terribly. But it's best if you stay with Zio Tino and Zia Angela for now. You know it's safer in the countryside. You and I will be together again before you know it."

Stella thinks she wants to open the subject of her father again, but she hardly knows where to begin.

"*Ti voglio bene*, Stella. *Ciao ciao*," her mother says, and Stella hands the heavy telephone receiver back to Zio Tino.

Standing next to her uncle, Stella now hears her mother's voice as a sudden and distant tidal wave of words. Only a few intelligible. Something about rioting in the streets. Frequent strikes. Fascist troops with machine guns in the quarter. More people and less food available. No clean water and the frozen air underground. Little hope that help will come from the Germans or the Fascists. Stella watches her uncle's face grow dark, a mass of lines and shadows while he listens. Only small grunts in response to his sister's words across the line.

"You know you can come here if you wish . . ." he says. Then his mouth forms a thin crease.

Don't worry about me, tesoro.

Stella watches Zio Tino finally replace the receiver in its cradle. Now Stella wishes she had told her mamma about the paintings the men from the Uffizi brought into the villa. That her family has been entrusted with a great responsibility and secret.

But then she remembers her uncle has made her promise not to tell anyone.

STELLA AND MARIASOLE RETURN from the schoolhouse one afternoon to find everyone in the attic. It has turned cold outside, but the attic air is stifling and heavy with dust. The winter sun casts a glow through the single low, tiny attic window. Above their heads, cobwebs stretch across the old beams, silvery in the dust-flecked light.

Along the back wall, two men are working with wet mortar and a pile of bricks to create a space that looks to Stella like a small room.

"Papà hired a man from the village to build a hiding place," Livia informs them. "He's making it with bricks and then he'll cover it with stucco so no one knows there is anything there."

"Where's that box with the teapots?" Her aunt has been squatting among the wooden trunks. She straightens with her hands on her hips, surveying the clutter of dark shapes, years of the Harwells' belongings covered with blankets. "Stella!"

Stella flinches.

"Bring me that box near you. Let's not spend one more moment up here than we need to."

When she carries the box across the space, Stella stops to look through the pane of the attic window. In the distance, she spots a group of people walking toward the villa. They are slow and ragged-looking, a grim parade of a few adults and children trudging up the dirt path. A slight woman bundles a child to her chest against the stiff wind, her skirt fluttering. One man pushes a rusty bicycle heavy with bags tied to its handlebars. Another carries a thin, flopping mat on his head.

Behind her, Zia Angela fusses over what to put inside the newly constructed hiding space—silver, bed linens, lace, Lady Harwell's furs. She worries they should have made the hiding space larger. And then that they might need something but won't be able to access it.

"None of it matters, in the end, Angelina," Zio Tino says. He is wrapping a half dozen small bronzes he says Sir Harwell told him came from a dealer in Florence and are valuable.

"There are people coming," Stella says. Mariasole scampers to the window, and Zia Angela steps closer to look at the curious parade.

"Hmph," she says. "I'll go down. You girls stay here and keep wrapping."

Zio Tino reaches up and pulls down an old box from the wooden rafters. Zia Angela has brought blankets and old newspapers to wrap the large china service with gilded rims that Lady Harwell brought all the way from England. She tasks the girls with wrapping intricate forks and spoons in discarded newspaper.

As Stella wraps, the headlines of each newspaper telegraph a chaotic narrative that she fails to weave together in any coherent way. New air raids in Milan that have leveled several blocks of apartment buildings. No prospect of victory. Everyone shackled by their common burdens. No one in charge. Fascism must end, but no one knows what to do. All talk and no action against the decades of Mussolini's rule. A feeling of shame on the international stage.

At the sound of voices downstairs, Zio Tino says, "I'd better see what this is about."

The girls work diligently until her uncle's footsteps have receded down the stairs. Then they run to the window. From here, they can see all the way down to the village, its handful of electric lights tiny pinpoints against the vast panorama of the dusky hills beyond. Just as the last rays of sunlight disappear behind the rolling horizon, the sky turns a vibrant shade of orange-pink.

Another group of a half-dozen people are walking up the long, winding path. Two girls are balancing tied-up bundles on their heads. A man and woman are wearing a few too many layers, even for the cold weather. One woman clangs up the path, a few pots and pans strapped to her leather belt. They all look dirty and exhausted.

"What are they doing?" Mariasole asks.

Stella says, "Looks like they want to come inside."

ZIA ANGELA GIVES each family who appears at the villa a hunk of unsalted bread or another meager offering, then sends them on their way and locks the door behind her. But by the next afternoon, more small bands of ragged-looking travelers arrive at the villa. Stella counts a dozen or more asking for help.

Stella's uncles say Angela should offer them a place to sleep for the night instead. "It's the least we can do," Zio Tino says.

"You'll be sorry!" She wags both hands at her husband. "Refugees will only strip our trees and eat our animals. You'll wake up lucky to have anything left."

"Don't forget our own good fortune to live here," Zio Tino says. "If not for Sir Harwell and God himself, where would we be? And if we ourselves had to leave here and walk across all of Italy, what difficulties would we encounter?"

Stella wonders what it would be like to walk all the way here from Torino, carrying everything she owned on her head.

ON THE DAY BEFORE the feast of the village patron saint, the *maestra* prepares the children for a special trip across the square. In the classroom, there are a few fresh faces among the smaller children, from refugee families now tucked into farms and homes around the area.

Pacing at the front of the classroom, the *maestra* tells students that the town's patron, Santa Lucia, was an early Christian martyr who lived on the island of Sicily. Her parents had money, and she dedicated her life to serving the poor and sick.

"We've heard this story about a thousand times," the girl who sits in front of Stella says. But the story is unfamiliar to Stella and the new children, who listen intently as the *maestra* recounts how Lucia refused to marry. During the persecution of Christians under the Roman emperor Diocletian, they sentenced her to serve in a brothel.

"But when the soldiers tried to pick her up and take her there," the *maestra* continues, "she became so heavy they couldn't budge her."

"Then they stabbed her in the throat!" one of Fabio's friends interjects.

"Don't spoil it, Ciccio," the *maestra* says. "Father Ramondo will show us how the story ends."

The children spill out of the schoolhouse, a chaotic throng of small bodies converging on the parish church. Fabio runs ahead with his usual group of boys. On the way, Mariasole fills in Stella and the new children with more details. "Santa Lucia comes tonight to bring gifts to all good children," she says. "But you can't try to watch her come. If you're watching her, she'll throw ashes in your eyes and you won't be able to see for days! So you'd better keep your eyes closed."

At the portal of the parish church, Father Ramondo awaits, beaming, his bulk partly hidden by a billowing black cassock. Behind him, on the high altar, stands Santa Lucia herself, a gleaming, skewed, and heavy-looking statue of painted wood and metal. The children settle into the ancient wooden church pews and Father Ramondo walks among them, pointing to the old frescoes along the upper walls. Stella thinks the paintings look in terrible shape. The colors have faded and some entire sections are missing, but Father Ramondo talks excitedly about them as he walks up and down the aisle between the pews.

"Santa Lucia lived in the third century after Jesus Christ," he says, his voice echoing. "Nearly a thousand years later, a gifted group of artists painted her life on the walls of this church."

"What were their names?" one boy asks loudly. The children snicker and the *maestra* shushes them.

"The artists?" Father Ramondo says. "Good question. We don't know their names. Some experts call the head of the fresco workshop the Master of Santa Lucia based on his work in this very church. But we don't know who he was. We only know of his legacy. His talent. A distinct memory of himself and his contribution to the history of art. These paintings were here long before you or I were born, and God willing, they will be here long after your grandchildren are gone."

Father Ramondo picks up the story of Santa Lucia, pointing out an image where the saint is hitched to a team of oxen but doesn't budge. Then set upon a pyre that won't ignite. At first, Stella sees the frescoes only as faded remnants of a past that are no longer understandable. But as Father Ramondo continues unfolding the dramatic story scene by scene, Stella becomes engrossed in the unbelievable tale of how a young girl navigated unthinkable hardship all those years ago.

Eventually, the faded images take an even darker turn. Father Ramondo recounts how Lucia's angry suitor reported her as a Christian, and then the horrible ways in which the Roman authorities tried to kill Lucia. But, the priest says, she never renounced her faith, only continued to speak out in spite of all their attempts to silence her—by fire, and by driving a spear through her throat. Stella looks up at the colored walls, her mouth hanging open as she considers Lucia's speared throat and gouged eyes. And finally, the strange-looking eyeballs displayed on a plate.

"But her vision was miraculously restored!" Father Ramondo exclaims. "And Lucia came to be a symbol of divine light."

Stella wonders at the fact that she's been in this church a few times, but she understood none of this before. She only saw a crumbling church with a bunch of old paintings. She had no idea what they meant. Now she sees they tell a dramatic and dark story that ends with hope.

"Long ago, most people didn't know how to read," Father Ramondo says, "and paintings like these served to teach and inspire."

"That's the power of art," the *maestra* adds. "It can tell a story. An official story. But each one of you might also see your own story in it. At a minimum, you might find hope, even when there is darkness."

"*Esatto*," Father Ramondo says. "In the past, this is how people made meaning in their lives. And as your *maestra* says, it gave them hope when people felt things were out of their control."

Stella thinks about all the paintings hidden in the Villa Santa Lucia, and she wonders if they might have served a similar purpose.

"And tonight Santa Lucia comes to bring us gifts!" Mariasole exclaims, her voice echoing in the church. Everyone laughs, even Father Ramondo.

Before she leaves the church, Stella stops in a side chapel, contemplating an image of Santa Lucia holding a spear at her side, peering out bravely from an old painting darkened by the smoke of hundreds of years. Then she plunks a coin in a metal box, and lights a candle for her mother.

WHEN THEY RETURN to the villa that afternoon, Mariasole tells Stella they have to prepare for Santa Lucia's arrival.

"If we want gifts, we have to leave her some coffee! And a carrot for her donkey. And a glass of wine for Castaldo. He's the man who travels with her for protection." Stella watches Mariasole excitedly produce these items and lay them out on the dining table.

The next morning, Stella looks for a gift—even though she expects she might get coal instead. The carrot is gone and the stained wine glass and coffee cup are in the sink. On a plate, there is a small *biscotto* with sugar for Mariasole.

But there is nothing for Stella and Livia, and Stella imagines their enthusiasm for the patron of light must not be as strong as Mariasole's. "It's only for little kids," Mariasole says, licking sugar from her fingers. And no one speaks of it again.

During the procession that day, the villagers parade through the winding street, following the gleaming statue of Santa Lucia with the spear through her throat. Bobbing precariously above their heads.

Two weeks after the Feast of Santa Lucia, when the first snowfall dusts the hills, more refugees arrive at the villa. Zio Tino convinces his wife to let some of the uninvited visitors stay overnight.

"Have some compassion, Angelina," he says, sitting outside in a patch of sun with the family, sharpening the blade of an ax they use to chop firewood. The smell of wood smoke fills the air among the metallic scraping of the file. Tino pauses and squints at his wife. "Think of what it would be like if you were the one walking in this weather, carrying everything you own on your back. Some roads between Florence and Arezzo are impassable."

Stella has spent the past hour collecting twigs and shriveled branches for kindling. She sets down a tangle of dead weeds into a pile and watches her aunt waver. *The countryside is a safe place.* Stella hears her mother's voice in her head.

"Besides," Zio Tino says. "The *tramontana* is coming."

"Yes it is," Zio Stefano echoes, coming up the hillside in coveralls that have gone stiff with a freshly tilled coat of red dirt. "The hens are producing fewer eggs and two of them won't even come off their roosts. The weather is about to take a turn for the worse. It is only a matter of when."

"And where are you going to put these people?" Zia Angela crosses her arms and draws the collar of her wool wrap around her neck.

"They can stay in the cantina," Zio Tino says, resuming his scraping.

"The wine cellar? *Dio!*" she cries. "It's designed to store wine, not to live in . . . First, priceless paintings. Now, these helpless people. What do we have to take care of next?" Her aunt throws up her hands in exasperation. "At least we locked up the silverware. But we've already given out most of our bread supply and we only have a certain amount of food stored for the cold months. Soon we will have used up our ration cards."

"But there's plenty of room in the cantina, mamma," Livia says. Her mother ignores her.

"Plus," Zia Angela says, "there are risks. Now, with so many strangers on the property . . . What would your Sir Harwell say about that?"

For a moment, Zio Tino hesitates. "You've already locked up the silver and the furs, *cara*. Even Lady Harwell's jewelry. These poor people are not here for jewelry. They just need a roof over their heads and something to eat . . ."

"Where are they coming from?" Livia asks her father.

"A few from the north, but mostly south of here," Zio Tino says. "We are in the middle. That old man with his daughter and the baby?" He gestures to a newly arrived family who are bundling themselves around a small bonfire they've made on the edge of the property. "He says they walked all the way from south of Naples. They have come a very long way." Zio Tino stops sharpening and hands the ax to his brother-in-law. "I'm going to check on the paintings . . ."

Stella perks up. She wants to go with him to where the paintings are stored.

"I suppose you didn't think of those paintings before you told them they could stay?" Zia Angela says, pinching her fingers together like a bird's beak and then wagging her hand forcefully before her husband's face. "Eh? A bunch of filthy people in the cantina with nothing but what they can carry . . . Best be careful one of them doesn't disappear with the treasures of the Uffizi in the bottom of their carts."

Zio Tino only shrugs and heads back inside the villa.

"I want to see!" Mariasole yells. Stella sets down the last of the dried twigs and catches up with Mariasole.

"I'll get some extra blankets from the cabinet in the corridor," Zia Angela says, walking off, frowning.

When they go into the room where the paintings are stored, the shutters are closed and the room is cold and dark as night. Zio Tino picks up a small oil lantern he fished out of the attic days ago and lights it with a match. In the glow of the flame, the paintings take on a new aspect. Zio Tino holds up the lantern to the giant gilded altarpiece and it suddenly sparkles like magic. "Probably how it was meant to be seen originally," he says, "back when it was painted." All of them stand in silence, admiring the beautiful and mysterious effect.

Stella imagines one of the *rifugiati* putting the gilded Madonna in the back of their rickety cart. She knows her aunt is worried, but even if they did take something from this room, Stella can't envision how they would carry something this large and what they would do with it even if they managed to take it.

In the momentary peace that has taken over the room, Stella sees an opportunity.

"Zio," Stella says, still watching the wavering gilded surfaces in the lantern light, "do you think my mother will come soon?"

Zio Tino contemplates for a long time, his palm running across the stubble of his chin. "She can always come to us, of course," he says finally. "For now, she thought it best to send you on but stay in Torino . . . well, until things improve."

"And . . . Do you know . . . where my father is?" The question has always felt heavy as lead in her gut. But now that she's given it voice, the question seems so obvious, so basic that Stella can hardly believe she hasn't asked it out loud before.

Zio Tino lowers the light and looks at Stella. "I do. Well, I did . . ." His face turns shadowed and haggard. "My understanding is he's been living in Rome for some years."

"Rome? Why?"

Zio Tino shrugs. "Always more work in the city than here. People selling things. Working in the streets and shops and hotels. In the train station."

"Maybe he'll jump on a train and come find you!" Mariasole interjects, ducking out from behind her father's trouser leg.

Stella hasn't considered before that her father might want to come looking for her. Or instead, perhaps worse, that he might not. Stella's mind spins with the idea of her father out in the world, living a regular life in Rome without the slightest thought of Stella and her mother. Perhaps he has a whole new family now, a new wife and children while Stella and her mother have carried on all these years in Torino. These fractured ideas make Stella freeze, spawning more questions than answers.

But Zio Tino only runs his palm across Mariasole's head and frowns. "I don't imagine it's possible to travel right now, *patatina*. Especially from the south."

Stella struggles to formulate another question, but Zio Tino is finished with his rounds. He heads for the door and Stella follows the weak lantern light reluctantly. He locks the door and grasps the lever, double-checking its security. Then he replaces the key above the stone just as Zio Stefano appears, having exchanged his dirty work clothes for plain trousers and a wool jacket. Zio Stefano ruffles Stella's messy hair as she passes, a momentary gesture of fondness that contrasts with his stoic exterior. Zio Tino ends his shift guarding the paintings from the Uffizi and Zio Stefano begins his vigil with his usual pacing in the shadows of the courtyard. Stella lingers there, feeling like she ought to spend a while pacing back and forth like Zio Stefano, wallowing in her double longing for both her mother and her mysterious father, whose presence has suddenly loomed large out of the dark void of his absence. One parent carrying on with life north of here, the other doing the same in the south. And Stella, marooned in the middle, left wondering about both.

As night falls, Stella watches her aunt close the door that leads to the wine cellar from the kitchen so the newly settled *rifugiati* can't come up into the house.

ZIO STEFANO'S CHICKEN WEATHER PREDICTION COMES TRUE.

After dark, the wind gathers. It sweeps down over the hills surrounding the Villa Santa Lucia, spilling biting air across the hills and valleys. Sharp and cutting, it turns the normally sunny landscape into a harsh and unforgiving place. The grapevines shudder under its gusts, their bare vines like skeletons.

Stella lies in the bed she shares with Mariasole. The girl is in the habit of putting her cold feet under Stella's legs. Stella lies awake, listening to the wind rattle the panes. On the single bed wedged under the window, Livia snores softly, oblivious to the maelstrom. The wind brings the smell of alpine forests, tinged with chimney smoke and frozen earth. It brings a reminder of the impermanence that governs their lives on the farms, the relentless, eternal dance of warmth and cold, light and dark.

Stella thinks about the paintings, so old and fragile, hidden away in their darkened room. "Your papà talks to the pictures," Stella whispers to Mariasole.

"He talks to the geese, too," Mariasole whispers back.

The two girls giggle.

But the heaviness has returned to Stella's gut. She turns the new information about her father over in her mind. The idea of

Daniele Costa out there, maybe eking out his living in Rome. That he might even be thinking of her. Might even have had the ability to come looking for her but didn't. She had never considered it before. Would her mother and her father both come here to find her in Tuscany? Meet here at Santa Lucia? Stella hardly dares to hope for such a thing. Struggles to imagine them together under the same roof.

Unable to settle, Stella's mind turns to the ragged-looking refugees who have begun to collect in the wine cellar, clearing spots for their children, lying on their thin pallets. Among the ancient, dust-covered wine bottles; storage boxes; and long-forgotten, moth-eaten blankets hulking in the damp shadows. About the possibility of bullets or bombs falling from the sky instead of rain. Stella thinks about the dozens of paintings from Florence, safe from the storm, in the dark hall, her other uncle standing vigil in the dark, windswept courtyard. The villa as a safe place. A haven for both paintings and people.

Thinking of the overwhelming dampness and humanity in the cellar brings with it a deep-seated memory of the sewer-turned-shelter in Torino where Stella and her mother stayed. Stella recognizes the same uneasy pair of collective resolve mixed with desperation. For a moment, Stella thinks she might belong in the cellar rather than upstairs with her aunt, uncles, and cousins. Stella knows what it's like to leave everything behind, to go forward into the unknown. She thinks it could easily have been her living in that wine cellar, if not for the fortune of her mother having a brother, an unlikely guardian of an Englishman's villa.

Filthy people, Zia Angela had called them.

If not, where else would she be? Her uncle's words echo in her head. Refugees. *Rifugiati*. People seeking refuge from something bad.

When she thinks about it, Stella realizes the word describes her, too. That's what brought her to Villa Santa Lucia. Even though she is alone, at least she has her newfound family. Stella is a kind of refugee, too. A lucky one.

WHEN CHRISTMAS EVE COMES, the haggard guests lodged in the wine cellar follow Stella's family to the village church. Stella watches Father Ramondo's radiant, rosy face as he stands below his frescoes and celebrates mass, just as his predecessors have for seven hundred years.

Crowded together in the creaking pews, the locals and refugees exchange Christmas wishes, and Stella feels a sense of solidarity that she hasn't experienced in the village before. The air vibrates with a feeling of common struggle, of worry, of apprehension for what may come. At the end, together they sing "*Tu Scendi Dalle Stelle*" and for a moment it feels like everyone in Santa Lucia is singing with one voice.

When they return to the villa's courtyard, Stella's aunt and uncles share boiled chestnuts with the guests. Afterward, Zio Stefano lights a fire in the dining hall hearth and Mariasole stretches her arms across the table, turning over an orange, looking bored. The adults crowd around the wireless to hear the pope's homily.

Stella hopes the warm feeling of unity stoked in the church pews will echo across the airwaves, all the way from Rome. But Papa Pio XII's scratchy voice sounds on the edge of despair rather than hope. Stella thinks that when he appeals for better international understanding and human solidarity, the speech sounds like something another person wrote for him. Around the dinner table, Stella watches the shadows return to the adults' faces.

THE NEW YEAR TURNS and on the coldest day of 1943, a Royal Air Force bomb levels several city blocks in the center of Torino. On the radio, they announce the section of the city where Stella and her mother's apartment lies.

Zio Tino tries to get a phone line through to Torino but fails. Over the following days, he tries again. And again. He sends letters. Eventually, he stops.

More people come looking for refuge in the villa and the ones who were already there make room.

The spring comes.

Then summer.

There is still no word from Stella's mother.

CHAPTER 3

THE ARTIST

Summer–Autumn 1943

The artist faces a battle each time he comes to the page. A great struggle between inspiration and intimidation. Each preparatory sketch, each figure and line loaded with the gravity of a stone added to an already teetering scale. All of it stacked against him. Each day threatening the successful completion of the work. This Primavera, on which I have started and then started again, is both a field of dreams and a battlefield strewn with the carcasses of my own abandoned aspirations. Another work that exists perfectly formed in my head; seemingly impossible to achieve. Only His Excellency's faith in me, and my signature on our agreement, bring me back to my sketches. I awake the next day and try again.

*—*FROM THE LOST DIARIES OF SANDRO BOTTICELLI, FLORENCE, SUMMER 1480

Before we arrived in Tuscany, of course we already knew of the widespread destruction in the northern cities like Milan and Turin. The mistakes of our own forces that destroyed irreplaceable historic monuments and cost innocent human lives. We vowed things might be different in the preservation of cultural heritage as we moved into Tuscany. But there, we had a different set of problems to deal with. In some ways, more daunting.

*—*FROM THE DIARY OF CAPTAIN WALLACE E. FOSTER, MONUMENTS OFFICER OF THE FIFTH ARMY IN TUSCANY, AUGUST 1944

The summer comes, the wine cellar grows crowded, and lice break out among the refugees. Stella's uncles hand out chores to any women, children, and old men physically capable enough to work. They collect mushrooms and truffles from the woods. Chop logs and stack firewood. Sharpen blades and repair plows. Boil water to sanitize the bedding and hang things on the line. Make soap from olive oil and tree ash. Milk goats and harvest olives. Prune the vines and climb ladders to pick ripe fruits from the top branches of the fruit trees. Search the edges of the fields for rabbits and birds. The children bond together, inventing games and doing whatever they can to slip out of the adults' reach.

Stella's job, for the most part, is to work with her aunt to keep the supply of food coming. Her workload multiplies along with the increasing number of mouths to feed. The good news, she thinks, is that her skills in making pasta have improved. Now she can form the dough into a perfectly round mass with no cracks, can roll the *pici* into long, even strands that are no longer a tangled mess. She knows how to dress them with stale breadcrumbs, plus a drizzle of olive oil and salt with a dash of grated pecorino. Between the cracks of her relentless chores, her mother's absence looms like a giant hole in the universe.

One evening, near the lemon grove, Stella watches Signora Romano, a mother who has walked with three small girls all the way from a village near Benevento, shave her daughters' hair with a razor. Her suntanned face is a picture of weary determination. The girls watch their dark hair fall around them on the hard-caked dirt.

Looking through the window over the sink, Stella thinks the newly shaved girls look smaller and more pitiful. But then they spring to their feet and dart down the hillside, giggling and free from their mother's task, oblivious to how they look, like freshly shorn sheep whose sprightly, ungainly bodies have been revealed for what they are. Their laughter cuts through the silent evening air. The girls play *nascondino* in Zio Stefano's lemon grove, hiding their waiflike bodies behind trees and dusty farm equipment while the light fades behind hills that turn purple in the dusk.

When Zio Stefano comes in after a hot day of working the fields, he is holding a ragged copy of *La Nazione* in his suntanned, dirt-stained hands. "Il Duce has resigned!" he announces.

"Madonna!" Zia Angela exclaims, wiping her hands on her apron. "Is it true? After twenty years?!"

The family assembles at the table as Zio Stefano spreads the newspaper out and reads the article with some difficulty. In Mussolini's place, he says, the king has appointed Marshal Badoglio, who vows that "the war goes on."

The news is confirmed on the evening radio broadcast. The announcer's voice crackles across the air waves, stating that Mussolini has resigned "on account of his health."

After dinner, when Stella brings a fresh loaf of bread down to the cantina, she finds everyone huddled around a small radio someone has brought with them. The cool air is a respite from the incessant heat. Frail light comes from the glow of a few light bulbs tucked behind the stones. Carlotta Bianchi, who has walked from her village outside Rome with a group of a dozen women whose husbands and brothers have gone to fight, has discovered how to tune in to the BBC. She claims she can understand some of the English-language broadcast. She tells everyone the British announcer states the Italians must actively work to expel the Germans.

"As a rabbit might rid itself of a fox," a man they call Old Giuseppe says, leaning against a great oak barrel in the shadows. Stella has seen the man play a mandolin he brought along with his scant belongings. He stands on the hillside at dusk, eking out soulful and sad-sounding tunes she imagines might remind him of home.

"They say if we don't," Signora Bianchi continues, "then the war continues and the Allies will sweep across Italy from end to end. Either way," she says, her eyes large and shining in the weak light, "the BBC says all of Italy will become a battlefield."

THE NEXT DAY, Stella turns thirteen. She almost forgot it was her birthday.

No one notices.

STELLA IS PULLING warm figs from an ancient tree clinging to the hillside when she notices a skinny boy, newly arrived, sitting on a boulder. He holds a pencil and a scrap of paper and is drawing something with intense concentration. He uses his bony knee to balance the wrinkled page, dragging his pencil across it.

Stella plunks the figs one by one into her apron pockets. In her palm, they are plump and warm from the sun. Zia Angela has told her to pick only the ones that feel the slightest bit of give under your thumb, so each one can be wrapped with a thin slice of prosciutto and enjoyed in a single mouthful.

"I saw them take your *rosmarino*." The boy addresses Stella without turning his head. He continues to watch his hand make a line on the paper.

"*Cosa . . . ?*"

Beyond the hillside, a vast patchwork of emerald and jade stretches out as far as the eye can see. From here, an ancient farm structure with the roof caved in is barely visible between the massed cypresses and tangled thornbushes. A chorus of cicadas fills the air with their harsh vibrato, sending up their song like a shimmering heat wave rising from the parched earth.

"Just now," he says. "I saw that *ragazzo* pick rosemary from your kitchen garden and take it inside." He turns his face toward her now. Fine features. Two piercing eyes, the color of espresso, among wisps of dark hair. He gestures toward the barn door that forms the entrance to the villa's wine cellar. Stella thinks about Lady Harwell's jewels buried just below this very rosemary bush.

Nearby, a group of small children has collected to kick a worn leather ball through the dust. Stella watches a boy repeatedly kick it against the stone wall and the wooden cellar door, where it makes a loud thunk.

Stella knows this is exactly what her aunt fears, that the families hiding in the cantina will strip everything from the villa and leave them with nothing. That they might stash one of Sir and Lady Harwell's valuables into their carts and leave. Still, Stella feels sorry for them.

"You didn't want to play with them?" she says to the boy on the rock.

"I don't play with rosemary thieves," he says. One side of his mouth turns up in a half-smile.

"They aren't thieves," Stella says, taking a few steps closer to the boy. Trying to see what's on his paper. "They're just trying to get by. Aren't *you*?"

Stella has heard her uncles say the refugees are stuck here now. Many of them want to go north to the mountains to escape the heat and the soldiers, whether German or Allied. But some say they have seen German tanks in the area already, so it's too late to move now. The Germans are collecting here in case the Allies decide to land in Grosseto, Piombino, or Livorno.

The boy shrugs off Stella's prodding and turns back to his drawing. She steps back and watches him ignore her, feeling a surge of indignation mixed with pity. She doesn't know how to reconcile her compassion for their plight along with this particular boy's disinterest in her.

"Can I see?" Suddenly, she's intent on seeing what's on his paper. Something about the boy's calm self-assurance and his seeming indifference about being moored here at all makes her desperate to know him.

At last, the boy holds out the paper, and she takes it between her hands. With a few quick strokes, he has captured the lines of the landscape before them—the dip of the hillside, the winding dirt road, the half-collapsed rooftop of the nearby farm, the spiky pencil cypresses reaching toward the sky. Stella has been looking at this very view for months, but has never really *seen* it. Not in the way he's captured it on this discarded page.

"How'd you do that?"

He shrugs his bony shoulders. "I just do it." His gaze turns toward the village. "You go to school?"

She nods and returns the wrinkled page to him. "Down the hill. Next to the church. But I won't be there for a day longer than they make me."

"Why not?"

"I don't see the point."

He squints at her. "Well, *I'd* like to go. I miss my school. Back home."

Stella thinks about sitting on the rock next to him, but somehow it seems presumptuous. "I can take you. Even tomorrow, if you like. I know the *maestra*." Stella imagines the boy slinking into one of the cold wooden seats, the eyes of two dozen strangers on him.

Suddenly, the leather ball crashes into the boulder and bounces off, rolling down the dirt hill. Stella darts out to kick its frayed stitching, volleying it back to the refugee boys, who laugh and make a comment about not letting girls in their game.

"*Vieni*, Alessandro!" one boy calls out.

But the boy on the rock only shakes his head and turns back to his page.

Stella thinks this is strange. What boy doesn't like to play ball? What boy doesn't like to beat another one? One boy kicks the ball back down the hill and Stella runs toward it, giving it a harder kick this time, volleying it back up the hill to the tallest boy, hair falling to his jawline. A cloud of red dirt blooms around her shoes and bare legs. She feels the figs bounce inside her apron pockets. The boys cheer.

Suddenly, there is the sound of an airplane engine. The distant hum and rattle expands, and the children stop. One boy raises his hand over his eyes and looks into the sky.

"Stella!" Zia Angela's voice rings out from an upper window. Stella sees her aunt's bony frame lean out over the sill. "*Madonna!*" She gestures with one hand. "Come inside!"

Stella reaches into her apron and produces a ripe fig, warm and purple-black in her palm. "I have to go." She hands it to the boy on the rock.

"Stella," he says, and she watches a grin break across his face. "*Stellina*. Little Star. This your house?"

She laughs. "No. I'm just staying here. Like you."

"Stella!" Her aunt's voice bursts again from the open window.

"Your mother's calling," he says.

When he says the word "mother," Stella feels a pressure emerge behind her ribs, sharp and aching. It hurts to take a deep breath. Her mind swirls with an image of her mother hanging her factory uniform on the line strung across the alley; emptying her bag on the kitchen table, a smattering of lipstick, of crumpled lire and ration cards; washing the stinging aroma of garlic from her hands after making *bagna cauda*. All these months, her mother's absence has felt like a bottomless hole. Stella cannot see a way in which her mother might still be there, might still be a living and breathing presence, even if far away.

Stella's mother couldn't be any more different from Zia Angela, leaning over the windowsill in her apron. But Stella doesn't correct him.

"Coming!" She takes a few backward steps. "And you're called Alessandro?"

But the boy doesn't answer. He's placed the fig on the rock beside him. He's already picked up his paper and turned his gaze back to the horizon.

When the black outline of a plane appears between the clouds, it seems to swoop closer to the ground than it should. The boys playing ball disband. The worn leather ball rolls slowly and comes to a stop alongside a tree trunk while the boys scatter.

As the engine grows to a shuddering roar, Stella feels a deep vibration well up in her chest. She runs inside the villa, leaving the boy-artist on the rock.

But with the mention of her mother and the sudden and close roar of the plane, something inside Stella snaps. Like a fragile twig that's been bent past its breaking point.

As soon as she's inside the cellar corridor of the villa, she leans over, hands on her knees, breathing loudly. Her mind becomes a sudden battlefield. Images of being in the underground air raid shelter come flooding back, ravaging her senses. She can almost smell the dank sewer; hear the sirens wail; feel her mother's arms firm around her while the engines roar and the dust rains down on them from the ceiling of the shelter.

For months, Stella has done her best to believe that her life here in Tuscany is the only one; that the chapter of her life in Torino has been a surreal, distant vision. A nightmare. She knows now why she hasn't probed further into her mother's silence. It would mean having to face the truth that her mother is gone.

OUTSIDE HER WINDOW the next morning, the air is filled with chittering birds and the glow of sun-bathed light through the gnarled olive branches. It's as if the swooping plane is a distant dream. When Stella opens the wooden shutter, she sees Old Giuseppe holding the butt of a cigarette, leaning over a stone wall and looking out over the vineyard. A few of the refugees have moved their pallets out to the edge of the hillside, taking in the fresh air before the day turns sweltering.

Before leaving for school, Stella clutches her worn leather bag to her chest. It now contains the half-used notebook with a portrait of Il Duce, along with a few pencils with someone else's teeth marks in them. The small act of packing up brings a fresh wave of dread to the pit of her stomach as she recalls her own first day in the unfriendly classroom.

The only thing luring her to the schoolhouse now, she realizes, is the prospect of bringing Alessandro the artist with her. In the kitchen, Stella turns the thumb lock on the cellar door and steps down into the gathering darkness.

She pauses to let her eyes adjust to the dark. The air tastes stale and damp. She hesitates at the overwhelming smell of humanity—sweat, food, desperation. Her mind registers the strange paradox: Upstairs, dozens of paintings stand silently in the fanciest room in the house. In the dank cellar, dozens of human beings eke out their days in the frail light and thin, subterranean air.

Halfway down the stairs, she sits and surveys the cellar crowded with women and children. A young woman who looks not much older than Livia holds a baby against her shoulder as she paces back and forth, bouncing. There is a table with discarded cigarette butts and a scattering of playing cards from a game continued late into the night. An old man with weathered hands is leaning against the doorway, looking out at the countryside.

Suddenly, at the base of the stairs, Alessandro appears from the shadows. A ragged-looking stack of papers and a pencil in his hands, his brown eyes glowing.

"*Andiamo?*"

He looks so eager.

IN THE SCHOOLHOUSE, curious stares and whispers greet Alessandro, just as they had Stella. Stella knows what it's like to be the new student in a room full of children whose histories intertwine in the same way that generations of families train their grapevines to lace together in a complicated web that can never be untangled.

"*Bella questa camicia*," one boy says, picking at Alessandro's frayed sleeve. Snickering erupts behind them.

Alessandro pulls his arm away. "Thanks. I was going to get it tailored before coming here, but I didn't want you to feel out of style." The snickering turns into outright laughter. Stella stands there, stunned and impressed. Most of the boys let Fabio have the last word. But now they are as happy to laugh at the mayor's son instead of the newcomer.

"Put this on," Stella says, handing Alessandro one of the white smocks from the hooks on the wall.

They walk down the rows of desks where the low din of conversation among the children focuses on repeating snippets of their parents' conversations after last night's broadcast. Each comparing their own information with that of their friends. No one knowing what the truth is. *But we're winning . . . My papà says the Germans are the real enemies, not the British . . . His older brother got thrown out of the bar . . . German soldiers could be here by next week . . . The Germans imposed the war on us and we never wanted a war to begin with . . . Giulia Rossi's goat had two babies . . . There are German Panzers in Pienza . . .*

At the front of the room, the *maestra* claps her hands in the now-familiar pattern, like a predictable cadence of a well-worn song. The children repeat it and settle into their creaking desks while the rumors die down. Alessandro follows Stella down one of the narrow aisles.

When they pass Fabio's desk, Stella feels his eyes sear their backs. Is Fabio jealous? Stella wonders. Has he assumed some possession of Stella, as his older brother has of her cousin Livia? She steers Alessandro to the *maestra*'s hulking wooden desk at the front of the class, still feeling the glare.

"*Benvenuto*," the *maestra* says matter-of-factly. "What's your name?"

"Alessandro Baldini, *maestra*." Stella hears a quaver in his voice that wasn't there before. "I'm thirteen. I've finished fifth."

"Like Stella." The *maestra* shakes Alessandro's hand. "A pleasure to know you. We'll need to assess your reading level."

"He should be on the same level with the six-year-olds. Right, *terrone*?" Fabio asks. A few of the children snicker.

Stella butts in. "He's an artist! *Capito?*"

"That's enough, Fabio. An artist?" The *maestra*'s eyebrows fly up. "Let's see. What have you got there?"

Reluctantly, Alessandro pulls a page from his stack. At first, Stella thinks it's the same drawing she saw Alessandro working on that day on the boulder, but it's a different view. She sees the same delicate outlines of the cypresses and the crest of the hills. In the sky, Alessandro has drawn what looks at first like birds, but then the shapes reveal themselves as distant warplanes.

"*Ma che bravo!*" the *maestra* exclaims, inspecting it in the light streaming in through the tall window. "You have a natural talent, Alessandro."

"He is so good!" Stella interrupts again, as if she knows more than only having seen one drawing. "He draws lots of these!" She knows she has over-exaggerated her familiarity with his work. "Doesn't it look real?"

The *maestra* hands the drawing back and gives Stella a warm smile. "You want to show Alessandro the desk behind Marina?"

Alessandro and Stella make their way down the aisle. Two dozen sets of eyes pierce through them.

When they pass Fabio's desk, Stella sees his leg extend out into the aisle. A split second too late for her to act.

Alessandro stumbles.

He lets out a cry and falls to his knees, his beautiful drawings scattering across the stone floor. Stella catches fleeting, fluttering glimpses of landscapes, of an old woman with a lined face, a German tank, a man in a uniform. Each image a testament to Alessandro's gift, to things he's seen or imagines, now splayed across the classroom floor for the children to ogle, appreciate, ridicule.

Around them, a mocking symphony of laughter fills the air. Alessandro is on all fours, scrambling to gather his dignity along with the scattered scraps of paper.

"Are you alright?" Stella kneels.

"I just didn't see his foot," Alessandro mumbles amid the bursts of laughter around him.

Stella is in front of Fabio's face before she can think. Around the edges of her vision, the classroom and the symphony of giggling—everything but her own indignation—becomes a blur.

"*Stronzoooooo!*" Stella yells. The expletive rings through the air, echoing as if a film reel slowing in speed, silencing everything around her.

For a moment, Stella doesn't know if Fabio or she will be in bigger trouble with the *maestra*. She doesn't dare turn around, only stares at Fabio's surprised face, his eyes wide and locked on hers. His mouth hanging half open. Frozen in time.

STELLA AND ALESSANDRO walk out of the school together into the hot, dusty noon. They start up the hill toward the villa, a distant mirage that shimmers along with the chorus of cicadas.

As she had for Stella, the *maestra* has outfitted Alessandro with an assortment of worn notebooks and pencils. Recognizing his artistic talent, she's added a few fresh sheets of drawing paper from her desk drawer.

Stella feels relieved that her lapse in judgment was met only with a momentary intervention. To Stella's relief, their teacher was more angry with Fabio for tripping Alessandro than she was with Stella for her slipped expletive.

Suddenly, Fabio swoops by, followed by his usual followers and a rush of laughter. The boys run ahead toward the mayor's house.

In their wake, Alessandro only shakes his head. "Thanks for sticking up for me."

"Well, Fabio is—a *stronzo*, I mean," Stella says. "Just because his father is the mayor, he thinks he's better than the rest of us and can boss people around." She makes a sour face at the big *municipio* with its tricolor flags sagging in the heat.

As they walk, Stella sneaks a glance at Alessandro's profile. His dark hair hanging over his forehead, eyes on the street, hands deep inside his pockets. "Well?" she says. "Do you?"

"Do I what?" he says.

"*Do* you know how to read?"

Alessandro pauses as if considering whether to say more. "If you want to know the truth, Fabio was half right. I don't know how to read very well."

Stella nods, letting the understanding sink in, buoyed by his willingness to share a secret weakness with her.

He shrugs. "Or maybe it's just that . . . I need to sit closer to the *lavagna*. Like I used to do back home."

"Then you should tell the *maestra* to move you to the front," Stella says. "Or just forget about school altogether. No one's keeping track of the people hiding in the cellars," she says.

"But I want to stay in school," he says. "At least till I get better at reading. Anyway, I like it."

"So, where'd you come from?" Stella asks as they trudge up the hill. Immediately, Stella regrets the question, the same one that made her feel like an outsider at school instead of someone who belongs.

"I promise you've never heard of it," Alessandro smirks. "*Piccolo paese.*"

"Somewhere far south of here," she says, noting his accent, which sounds strange and charming at the same time.

"*Sì.* A village outside of Napoli. Near Vesuvius."

"The volcano?"

He nods.

"Aren't you afraid it will erupt and destroy everything?"

"That hasn't happened for a long time."

"But it could still happen. Who knows?"

"Who knows?" he echoes, smiling at Stella.

"Where's your family?"

He kicks a pebble up the dirt road. "My parents have been gone for a long time."

"What happened?"

"An accident in the car. I don't really remember them; I was very little. And then my older brothers had to report for duty."

"And they're coming back for you . . ." Stella wonders if this is a question or a statement.

Alessandro only shrugs. "I was worried when they got called up, but I guess it saved them—and me—in the end. At least so far."

"Why is that?"

"Because we weren't there when the Germans came to our village."

"What did they do?"

"I heard from the others that they ransacked everything. Set fire to our church and the *municipio.* By that time I had already left to come here."

Stella falls silent for a while, letting the gravity of Alessandro's situation sink into her mind. "Who brought you here, then?"

"One of the nuns from school organized things so I could travel with a family coming here. A man and woman plus their five children. They came from a different village. I didn't really know them. Anyway, they're gone already. They went with the others to the Apennines a few weeks ago."

"You mean they just *left* you here? And . . . you're here *all alone*?" Stella stops walking, stunned. Now she realizes how fortunate she is not only to live in the Villa Santa Lucia but to have any family left at all. No matter what has happened to her mother, at least she is not completely alone, and she has a few people who care what happens to her. Suddenly, she sees Alessandro not just as a skinny boy from the south but one with wisdom, talent, and experience beyond his years. She has a new respect for him.

"I'm not alone in that wine cellar." Alessandro grins. "You know that." Stella thinks of the scores of people piling up inside, eking out their days until they can go home to ruined villages like Alessandro's.

Stella considers everything Alessandro has gone through—losing his parents, being separated from his brothers, grieving the loss of his home and village, and now being abandoned by the people who brought him to safety . . . By instinct, Stella takes the silver locket around her neck between her thumb and finger, sliding it back and forth on its chain, and thinks Alessandro must be the toughest and bravest *ragazzo* she knows. It makes her feel fortunate and, most of all, ashamed to have snapped like she did. She wishes she had half his strength.

"What about you? You were born here?" he asks.

"No, my mother and I were living in Torino," she says, feeling the familiar pang well up in her gut. "I came here like you did, to escape the fighting."

"And your papà?" he asks.

"My papà . . ." It feels strange to say the word, when she doesn't know him at all. "He's fighting at the front lines." Stella knows it's a lie and she immediately regrets it. But she has begun to imagine a story in which her father has donned a uniform and rushed into the heat of battle. She imagines a man who might resemble her father ducking into a foxhole with the sound of artillery fire in the air. If she keeps imagining him this way, she figures, it seems both heroic and a good excuse for why he couldn't come looking for her. A better story than that he left Stella and her mother behind, and might have no intention of coming back.

"Called to the colors," Alessandro says. "Like so many. I guess he'll come for you after this is all over."

"I guess," she says. Now Stella regrets having invented the story at all, much less having said it out loud. Suddenly, Fabio and his roving band of friends run by again in a flash. "Something wrong with your eyes, *bifolco*?" Fabio whizzes by, knocking Alessandro's sketchbook from under his arm. His new pencils scatter across the dust.

"*Stronzooooo!*" Stella yells again, this time louder than before, confident both in her assessment of Fabio and the fact that she won't face consequences out here on the dusty lane, where the children have their own rules out of the adults' view and they have to stick up for themselves.

But before Stella has time to stick up for her new friend again, Alessandro himself has already pounced.

Alessandro pummels Fabio, punching him across the shoulder. Fabio staggers, then the two boys roll together in the dirt, turning over and over toward the edge of the path.

Fabio manages to scramble to his feet. "Never heard of a blind artist! Ha!" Alessandro presses the back of his hand to his face, which is covered in dirt and a small trickle of blood.

Fabio makes another move toward Alessandro, but before he gets there, Stella runs at Fabio with all her force and hits him with her satchel full of books and papers. Then with her fists.

That evening, Stella's aunt beats the *caca* out of her.

"Who's ever heard of a girl giving a boy a black eye?!" her aunt yells, pummeling Stella with repeated open-handed slaps across the top of her head.

Stella cowers on the floor near the flowered skirt that hangs around the large sink, her arms crossed above her head, trying not to sob out loud. Her aunt lashes out, hitting Stella about the head until she believes she may not make it out of this situation without a black eye of her own. Each blow harder than the last. A frenzy.

"Fabio's mother is a pillar of our community. She's been one of my best customers! Now I won't see any more of her mending. And then she will tell her friends. Eh?! What shall I do then?" Zia Angela's brown eyes have turned black with rage. "You will ruin our own daughter's chances to marry their son? You will ruin all of us! You will ruin everything!"

Would Fabio or Alessandro be getting the same punishment? Stella wonders. But boys rarely get punished for fighting. And even if Alessandro has done something worthy of punishment, no one is here to punish him anyway. These thoughts spin through Stella's mind as she tries to avoid her aunt's small, stinging hands.

Then, for a moment, Zia Angela miraculously pauses, and the world falls silent. Stella dares to look up. Has the harsh beating stopped? But Zia Angela only reaches for the wooden spoon. "Pull up your skirt, girl!" Her face contorts with anger and shame at the damage Stella has done to their family's reputation.

"Listen!" Livia comes running into the room. "Mamma, stop!" she yells. "Stop it! *Vieni!* Listen to the radio! It's Badoglio!"

At the mention of the prime minister's name, for a long merciful moment, Zia Angela stops her tirade and there is silence. Stella lets go of the breath she was holding, bracing herself against the anticipation of the lashing of a wooden spoon against her bare thighs.

Then the voice of an announcer grows louder as Livia turns up the volume on the radio in the dining hall. Zia Angela lowers her arm, her left hand still gripping the handle of the wooden spoon, veins trailing over white knuckles, and she follows her daughter into the dining room. Stella's uncles appear now in the dining hall and come to stand before the wireless.

A man's booming voice rings through the air, crackling across the airwaves.

> *The Italian government, recognizing the impossibility of continuing the unequal struggle against an overwhelming enemy force, in order to avoid further and graver disasters for the Nation, sought an armistice from general Eisenhower, commander-in-chief of the Anglo-American Allied forces. The request was granted . . .*

"*Ma che . . .* ?!" Stella's aunt cries. "We've surrendered?"

"Sh . . . *Chiudi il becco!*" Zio Tino says. Stella thinks he is brave to tell his wife to shut her beak, especially with that wooden spoon in her hand.

Prime Minister Badoglio continues.

> *. . . Consequently, all acts of hostility against the Anglo-American force by Italian forces must cease.*

The broadcast goes on to explain something about an armistice that's been signed on Sicily, along with more details about how relations have unfolded between Italy and the Anglo-Americans. Stella struggles to follow.

Within minutes of the broadcast, while Stella and her family are still standing in front of the radio, trying to make sense of it all, the clangorous blare of dozens of car horns rises from the village below.

Livia and Mariasole suddenly dart from the dining room. Stella follows, thankful for the excuse to escape the room and her aunt's merciless wrath. The girls race up to the stair landing, where there is a view of the village clinging to the hillside. Below their window, lured by the commotion, dozens of refugees step out from the wine cellar door onto the grassy terrace. Stella sees the small cluster of Signora Romano with her three shorn daughters, and Old Giuseppe with his hobbling gait. Stella searches the small crowd. At last, she spies Alessandro, standing all alone on the hillside with his swollen eye.

IN THE WAKE of the prime minister's evening radio broadcast, villagers emerge from their homes. Over the next hour, everyone in Santa Lucia pours into the square. Even families from nearby farms walk or hitch their wagons to come into town.

Zio Tino takes his wife's hand and Angela leaves her wooden spoon forgotten on the dining table. Stella follows her cousins and the stream of refugees down the dirt path toward the jumble of tile rooftops and the beacon of the church's squat bell tower. Beyond, the sun sinks behind hills turned to lavender and black undulations. The sky becomes brazen and glowing. The smoke of a dozen bonfires from distant farms rises against the orange sky.

The car horns and cheering grow louder as they wind through the street that leads toward the square. On the upper floors of their apartments, people have opened their shutters, leaning over iron balcony railings. Others have climbed to their jagged rooftops.

In the square, Stella watches an old man steer his tiny, rusty car in slow circles around the fountain, pressing the horn with the heel of his hand. In his lap, a round-faced baby flutters his small arms in delight. A group of Stella's classmates follows behind the car, laughing. One boy hops up and clings to the back of the vehicle as it goes around in circles. Other children have climbed on top of parked cars.

At the Bar dell'Angolo on the square, the proprietor has flung open his doors and turned on the lights. Immediately, he is overcome with the newly exuberant crowd. He ignores the old metal cash register, and Stella watches him pour free drinks for the people streaming into his bar. "*Viva l'Italia!*" a few people yell in unison. One man hands Father Ramondo a drink and clinks his glass with his own.

Outside the bar, Stella watches a man plant a deep kiss on his wife's lips while holding a small child up on his shoulders. On the balcony above, an old woman in a housedress waves a dirty rag above the heads of the people in the square and displays a wide, toothless smile. Young children dart across the square, taking advantage of a moment when their parents are not paying attention.

From another balcony, a man has pushed back the blackout curtains from his window. With a booming voice, he begins singing a familiar refrain from "*Fratelli d'Italia.*" Soon, the song spreads across the square as everyone joins one another in a cacophonous rendition. When the song ends, everyone cheers. Afterward, Stella presses her bulk into Livia's side. "The war is really over?" Stella asks her older cousin. She wonders if it means she can go back to Torino now to look for her mother.

"That's what they said on the broadcast," Livia says, distracted. Her eyes search the crowd and Stella thinks she might be looking for Alessio. But the mayor's house stands somber in the sea of gaiety, shutters locked tight.

Zia Angela has suddenly turned into a different person, hugging some of the village women with joy. An old man clasps hands with Zio Tino, kissing him on each cheek. "Our boy is coming home," the old man sobs. "*Grazie a Dio! Grazie a Dio!*" Stella has never seen an old man sob with such tears of relief and joy.

But while Stella watches Zio Tino pat his friend on the shoulder, she's never seen his face look more somber. While he hugs the sobbing man, he quietly observes the others, his face grave and drawn. Like a statue.

Long into the night, the celebrations reverberate from the village below. Stella lies awake in bed, watching Mariasole's small back rise and fall with slumber. She wonders how the girl can sleep between the horn blaring and drunken singing from the village. Some time before dawn, Stella sleeps fitfully.

When she comes down for a hard *biscotto* and warm milk the next morning, the countryside has returned to its normal rhythm. Fog blankets the air around the villa. The village and the distant farms and hillsides disappear into the white void. The fog lingers over the wheat stubble in the valley until the morning sun burns it away. The mist is tinted with the color of the sunrise, the rays of golden light shining through it like shards of glass. It won't be long before the sun turns everything hot and the smell of ripening wheat fills the air.

Stella finds her aunt and uncles huddled around the table in a sober mood. Stained coffee cups and crumbs litter the table.

"And so we have switched sides. All for the better, eh? *Vabbè.*" Zio Tino says to his brother-in-law, gesturing animatedly. "But Badoglio has only spoken for us—for Italians. Not for *them*. Not for the Germans."

"What will we be, then?" Zio Stefano asks, stirring a small lump of sugar into his cup of espresso, his calloused hands pinching a tiny brass spoon. "Reluctant participants or collateral damage? Trust me. There is no winning for us, whoever is in charge— I don't care if it's Fascists, Germans, or Americans."

Stella enters the room, tying the strands of her apron at the small of her back. "*Buongiorno*," she says, yawning.

"*Ciao, Stellina.*" Zio Tino's tone sounds friendly, but Stella thinks his face still looks shadowed. Grave. Zio Tino has dressed as usual in one of the elegant suits he used to wear to drive Sir Harwell. Stella picks up the discarded plates. "I'm afraid you're correct," Zio Tino says to his brother-in-law. "How many new ones have come over the Brenner Pass to Italy in recent weeks? No one's told *them* the war is over. And even if it is, what about the millions of German soldiers who are still on Italian soil? Where are they to go now? They won't give up so easily."

"Maybe now they will go home," Zia Angela says with a dismissive wave of her hand. She stands and collects the remaining cups from the table. "And good riddance. *Auf weidersehen!*"

"Exactly the problem," Zio Tino says. "What horrors will they cause on their way home? I don't expect them to tuck their tails. They won't give up so easily. Why would they?" Stella thinks of what Alessandro told her about what the Germans did to his little village far south of here.

Stella keeps her distance from her aunt—and watches out for the wooden spoons, but Zia Angela seems to have forgotten all about yesterday's beating. She is like *Vesuvio*, Stella thinks, the great volcano near Naples where Alessandro came from. The one that occasionally spews fire and then goes dormant. And who knows when it might erupt?

AFTER STELLA FINISHES cleaning the figs she's brought in from the tree along with her other chores, she goes to look for Alessandro. She winds down a narrow path through the olive trees to the edge of the hillside, where there is a vista over the neighboring farms and the swell of the hills beyond.

She finds him sitting on the same boulder where she first encountered him, with his pages and one of the new pencils the *maestra* has given him.

"*Tutt'apposto?*" he says, looking warily at her face. Stella thinks it's a wonder her aunt's beating didn't leave any bruising. She wonders if Alessandro has heard the beating all the way from the wine cellar, and if she should consider herself lucky she doesn't have an eye as swollen as his.

"I'm fine."

His tentative smile reveals a row of crooked teeth. "Your mother?"

Stella shakes her head. "That's not my mother. This is." Stella opens the silver locket around her neck and turns it toward Alessandro. She can see the whole of the tiny picture in her mind's eye—the lively eyes, the fresh face, the flip of her hair just below the chin line. "That's my aunt," she says, closing the locket and letting it fall against her breastbone. "She doesn't like me."

"Why not?"

He waits for her to answer, but Stella only shrugs and picks at a twig that's fallen from one of the sturdy maples at the edge of the villa. How could she begin to explain when she hardly understands the mysteries of her family's relations herself?

"Anyway, *grazie*," he says finally, when she fails to come up with an answer.

"For what?" Stella gathers her skirt under her legs and sits next to him.

"For sticking up for me. Again."

Stella grins at him, taking note of his freckles. "*Niente*. You really think the war is over?"

Alessandro shrugs. "Some people in the cellar think so. Others . . . no."

"Maybe you'll get to go back home soon . . ."

"I got nowhere to go," he says, and Stella realizes she has

blundered again. Then it dawns on her that she is in the same situation, at least for the moment.

"Me neither. My *zio* says maybe the Germans won't give up so easily. They won't just turn around and go home. And even if they do, they might be in a bad mood on their way there."

He nods. "The *tedeschi* might burn stuff like they did in my village. Or at least take anything valuable with them."

"Well, they won't do that here," Stella says. "We locked everything up before you got here. Even buried some stuff in the . . ." But Stella thinks maybe she shouldn't give away the location in case word spreads among the people in the wine cellar.

"Good idea," he says. But Stella thinks he looks unconvinced.

The talk of locked-up things gives Stella an idea.

"*Senti*, you want to see something amazing?" she says. "Follow me."

CHAPTER 4

THE TREASURE ROOM

Summer–Autumn 1943

The aim of every artist is to find within himself a way to unlock the beauty of the mind and the divine spirit. But in spite of my best efforts and the encouragement of my steadfast workshop assistants, the Primavera eludes my grasp.

—FROM THE LOST DIARIES OF SANDRO
BOTTICELLI, FLORENCE, SUMMER 1480

The Italian superintendents did everything they could to hide and protect the works of art in their care. But after we saw the devastation at Allied hands in the north, and devastation at German hands from the south, I waited with extreme anxiety until it was safe enough to get to the towns I was assigned. What kept me awake at night was realizing that Tuscany was right in the middle, right in the center of the crosshairs, where it would be squeezed like a vise from forces north and south. A perilous standoff was inevitable, and only a matter of time.

—FROM THE DIARY OF CAPTAIN WALLACE E.
FOSTER, MONUMENTS OFFICER OF THE
FIFTH ARMY IN TUSCANY, JUNE 1944

Stella makes sure no one is in the courtyard when she leads Alessandro through the villa's giant wooden front doors. He resists at first, standing frozen, looking up at the grand proportions of the courtyard, the multi-story conglomeration of buildings, and the skinny watchtower looming overhead. As if someone is watching from up there. He's only been in the wine cellar and on the grounds of the villa. Never inside.

Now Stella wonders if she's made a mistake, remembering her uncle's warning not to tell anyone about the paintings. But she *won't* tell anyone else, she reasons. Only Alessandro. Her inexplicable urge to make friends with this boy on the rock with his paper and pencil makes her want to let him in on the secret. "It's alright," she whispers, tugging on his wrist. "Come on."

They cross the courtyard and Stella fishes the key from where she's seen Zio Tino hide it, in a crack between two rough stones in the wall. She fits it into the lock, then opens the door and pulls Alessandro into the room with the hidden paintings, careful to close the door softly behind them.

At first, there is only darkness. Stella picks her way across the red octagonal tiles to the shuttered windows on the opposite side of the great room. She raises the latch on one of the shutters and folds it back on its hinge.

Suddenly, the autumn Tuscan light illuminates the shapes of the dozens of frames, of the pictures stacked six and seven deep along the walls.

"*Caspita!*" Stella watches Alessandro turn in a slow circle, round and round, looking at everything as he spins. Finally, he bursts into laughter.

"Shhh! We're not supposed to be in here," she whispers loudly.

They take their time, moving slowly from painting to painting. Alessandro gawks, his jaw open, as they look at a large painting showing people lifting the dead Christ down from the cross, bleeding holes in his hands and feet. In another gilded panel, haloed saints strive upward, seeking redemption among craggy rocks and twisted trees that look like the ones outside the villa. The trees float against the gold, a dreamlike wilderness. It's the same surreal beauty that struck Stella on her first vista of the landscape around Santa Lucia. Surprising and nearly heart-stopping in its beauty.

When they get to the enormous Madonna and Child, Stella watches Alessandro's eyes search the gilded surface. The angels with their decorative haloes, the Virgin Mary with her crown and blue cloak, staring down at them from her throne with half-closed eyes, as if she is skeptical of the two thirteen-year-olds standing there. As if she knows they're not allowed to be in the room.

"My zio Tino talks to this one," Stella says. "That baby looks like a frog."

Alessandro bursts out laughing. "That's *Gesù Cristo*," he says, punching her lightly on the arm.

"I know that." She laughs and punches him back.

Alessandro moves on to the picture of the bearded man on horseback, the one with the armor and flowing cape, with the chin that protrudes outward, looking as if he has tried hard to grow a thin reddish beard. "*Cavaliere*," Alessandro says, bowing deeply to the man on the horse.

When Alessandro finally turns to face Stella, his expression is full of light, even with his bruised cheek. "To think . . . I've been sleeping in the dark under these pictures ever since I got here and I had no idea."

When they stop before the giant picture with the thousands of flowers and the beautiful floating women, Alessandro looks for a long time at the sinuous figure in the white flowing gown, a halo of flowers around her reddish-blond hair. He runs his fingers lightly over the surface of the paint and the hairline cracks in the pigment, bringing his face close to it. He touches the string of flowers emerging from the woman's mouth. When his fingers get to the three nude women dancing in a circle, Stella feels heat rise to her cheeks.

"What does it mean?" she asks.

He shrugs. "Who knows?"

He bends over and squints at the gilded scroll at the bottom of the frame. "Sandro," he reads. "Sandro Botticelli."

"Like you!" Stella says, giggling. "An artist like you. From now on," she announces, hands on her hips, "I shall call you *Sandro*."

Alessandro—now Sandro—turns away from the giant picture to face Stella. His face glows, beams with an expression of wonder like she has never witnessed.

Suddenly, Sandro takes Stella by the shoulders. She feels his strong, squeezing grip on her narrow frame. She notices they are exactly the same height. From the light of the window, she can see the gold flecks in the depths of his brown eyes, along with a crackle of red in the white. For a long, strange, and unprecedented span of time, they are frozen like that, like the kind of timelessness that stretches out just before a fistfight begins. Then the idea crosses Stella's mind that instead, they might kiss. Her face suddenly blossoms with heat.

"Stella!" he whispers loudly, shaking her a little. "This is a treasure room. It is the best thing I've seen in my whole life."

Sandro's words don't break the spell; they make it grow larger. Stella feels her chest expand with joy to have been the one to bring this light to his eyes.

THE ADULTS SAY the harvest will come, whether the Germans or Americans come with it.

Every person in the villa, young and old, is put to work. Even the smallest children from the cantina are corralled into digging up potatoes. Their mothers grind wheat, milk goats, and stomp grapes until their feet turn black. Two old men who say they are brick masons from Bari make a new hidden wall inside the outbuilding where the pigs come in to eat. The skin of the pigs and the men are crinkled and creased like ancient parchments. The animals' deep grunting makes Stella and Mariasole laugh. In the evening, she watches Zio Tino hide some of the harvest behind the wall.

Beyond the olive grove, Zio Stefano paces up and down each lane between the grapevines, pinching the burgeoning purple fruits between his thumb and finger, testing their readiness. His hands are stained purple no matter how much he washes them at the spigot near the feeding trough.

Signora Donati is a strapping, elderly widow with wax-like skin. She says she grew up in Santa Lucia but her ancient home is barely habitable now. Stella watches her scatter grain for the chickens, who hop and stumble over one another, clucking in a frenzy to get to it, pecking violently at the ground. Signora Donati's son Filippo, the youngest of ten, is handsome, helpful, and strong-looking. Stella's uncles give him the hardest chores that involve carrying heavy loads. In the garden shed, two of the older refugee men have been corralled into sharpening the scythes used to harvest the wheat. Other men walk the fence line, mending places where sheep—or people avoiding the main roads—have trampled the wire.

Following her aunt's instructions, Stella gathers more figs from the tree, picking the ones that give under her thumb. They pick black kale that seems to grow everywhere and in any conditions. She and Mariasole fill the baskets and bring them to the kitchen. Zia Angela is wiping out the glass jars, preparing to can for the winter. "We will need more than usual," she says gravely.

In the afternoon, an older couple arrives, asking to stay for one night; they say they will keep moving until they get to a relative's farm near Prato. Livia brings them a plate of cheese and bread, listening to them recount how many German Panzers they have seen between Siena and here.

In the carriage house, Stella watches Zio Tino and another man remove the wheels from Sir Harwell's elegant Alfa Romeo. Then they bury the tires and a large tin vat of gasoline in a freshly dug hole in the ground. Wipe their brows with a cloth and look out to the purple hills. Sweating.

STELLA IS PULLING a tangle of dead weeds from the kitchen garden when she hears the distant hum of an engine.

An orange glow appears over the horizon. Mariasole and her mother are rinsing out buckets in the old stone *lavatoio*, where a few other women are washing clothes, their arms in the soapy water up to their elbows. Mariasole's hands are already dry and cracked like an old woman's because she helps with the washing. At the sound, one of the refugee women lifts her hand to her brow and looks to the horizon.

The sound turns from a low hum to a roar. Suddenly, the form of a plane appears in the sky. Stella sees her aunt grasp Mariasole by the waist and pick her up as if she is a toddler. She runs for the villa. The other women run for the lower door of the cantina. Stella stands frozen for a few seconds as two more planes appear. They swoop low, and the high-pitched roar grows louder. Stella watches what seems a thousand *rondini* wheel in formation, then scatter crazily in loops above the pointed cypresses. Finally, she runs inside the villa.

In the kitchen, Stella crouches under the flowered fabric skirt of the ancient sink, pulling her knees up under her chin. The windowpanes rattle in their wooden casings. Stella feels the floor tiles tremble beneath her feet. The centuries-old stone building, so solid, such a castle, feels suddenly insubstantial.

At last, the sound of the aircraft recedes into the distance, fading until it's nothing but a distant whisper. Stella stays with her knees up under her chin. Outside the window, the sky turns from orange to red.

"Stella!" Zia Angela throws open the door to the kitchen. Behind her, Mariasole and Zio Tino are there.

"I'm here, *zia*," Stella says, standing.

"She's here," her aunt says. "*Dio.*"

THE NIGHTLY BROADCAST reports that Prime Minister Badoglio and King Vittorio Emanuele are collaborating with the Anglo-Americans. German troops have made a ring around Rome and say they will protect the Vatican. There is fighting all around the capital city, but no one knows who is winning.

Zia Angela throws up her hands and says this can only mean that there is no more government in Italy. No one in charge.

"*Boh.*" Zio Tino shrugs his shoulders at the dinner table. Zio Stefano remains silent and pensive, tearing a small hunk of bread between his grape-stained fingers.

To Stella's way of thinking, the adults seem to see their fates tied to the vague missives coming to them in the dining room each evening, disembodied words amid the soft static. But to Stella, it is impossible to know what it means for her, when all anyone can do is prepare for the harvest, along with everyone on the farms as far as the eye can see.

A few families have left the wine cellar in recent days. Stella watches them depart, burdened under the weight of their bundles and layered clothing. Zio Tino says they are going to the mountains because they believe they should move even farther away from Florence, but no one knows if they are right or wrong to do so.

At night, they now have to cover the windows with their shutters or black curtains. They can hear planes roaring overhead amid murmuring of impending departures or decisions to stay put. No one knows which is correct.

All they know is that day by day, Stella, her family, and those holed up in the villa become more isolated. More alone. There is no more mail being delivered. No buses or trains running to and from Florence. And no more newspapers. The phone lines have been down for weeks.

In the village, there are no more celebrations since no one knows what anything means anymore. The shoemaker and tailor keep their doors shuttered and don't bother to open at all. Fewer supplies and food are available. And there is still no news from Stella's mother in Torino.

Outside of school hours, Stella's days are filled with relentless labor. They can fruit and vegetables. They store and hide food in every way and place they can find. They make do with fewer ingredients. They waste nothing.

Each night, they sit at the dinner table and wait for the disembodied words to reach them through the static. Struggle to interpret how it affects them.

Stella doesn't know what any of it means for her. While she works, her only thought is how she and Sandro will find their next moment to sneak back inside the treasure room. How they might find another moment of joy and light in a world where not even the adults have answers.

ONE EVENING, after Stella has eaten everything on her plate and still feels hungry, the broadcast announces that all men formerly conscripted as soldiers or carabinieri must report for a new wave of service to the Republic. Stella watches Livia's shoulders freeze as if gripped by an unseen force.

A few days later, Fabio's older brother Alessio appears in the shade of the olive grove. Neat and skinny in his uniform. From the herb garden, Stella watches Livia go out to meet him. Alessio leans into Livia and talks quietly to her, touching her chin with his thumb and the knuckle of his finger, as if burning her face into his memory for all time. His lanky frame returning down the path to the village. Stella thinks he looks much older than seventeen.

"Nothing bad will happen to him because he's the mayor's son and his father used to be a *carabiniere* in Florence," Mariasole says.

"So they'll get married when he comes back?" Stella asks.

"Yes. He likes Livia more than she likes him. But mamma says she needs to marry into the best family she can, even if they are Fascists." Stella tries to imagine what it would be like if her family expected her to marry Fabio, and it makes her nose wrinkle.

At school the next day, Fabio is sullen and quiet at his desk. Stella thinks of his older brother, now somewhere in his uniform on a train. Maybe heading to Germany. Stella can't help but feel sorry for Fabio, *stronzo* or not.

She knows what it's like to be separated from the ones you love most. And to have a family that sometimes makes you feel a bit ashamed.

IN THE DAYS after Alessio leaves the village, more refugees arrive. From their bedroom window, Stella and Livia lean over the sill, watching them come. At the bottom of the slope, a narrow dirt footpath cuts through the field of silvery grass, like a river carrying a slow tide of exhausted people seeking shelter. Stella sees a man carrying a toddler on his shoulders, the little boy high above the grass, enjoying the ride. A lumbering old woman trails behind them.

"Mamma's not going to like this," Livia says.

At that moment, Zia Angela's voice, stern and scolding, echoes through the corridor, followed by the low mumbling of Zio Tino. Stella can't make out the words.

"What did I tell you?" Livia says. The girls move quietly downstairs. In the courtyard, Stella finds Zia Angela and Zio Tino talking. Her aunt is gesturing wildly.

"And what are we to do with them?" her aunt says.

"Have some charity, Angela. Surely we have some Christian duty to help. At least to provide them shelter, food. Anything they might need. We have plenty of space here. We have vegetables to share. There is fresh water in the well."

"We've already got enough charity cases on our hands here." A fleeting glance. Stella feels in her gut that her aunt is talking about her.

A tentative knock on the door silences everyone.

Zio Tino gives his wife a look. She throws up her hands and walks away, heading toward Stella and Livia. "Go to the attic and bring down more of those blankets," she says. "And fill up the carafes with water from the well."

Zio Tino opens the door. Stella spies the man with the toddler and the old woman, who is huffing heavily and leaning with her hand on the doorframe.

"*Venite*," Zio Tino says. "Come."

Stella thinks the old woman looks as if she might fall to her knees. Stella watches her shake her prayerful hands at him in gratitude. As if she is bowing before Father Ramondo at mass.

MORE DESPERATE PEOPLE ARRIVE.

Haggard women, small children in their arms. Thin, ragged boys and old men, carrying sacks and suitcases. Begging for food. Some are on their way home. Some are fleeing their homes or the Fascist edicts instead. Some stay at the Villa Santa Lucia. Some move on. Over weeks, there is a rotating cast of uninvited guests.

Stella helps her aunt pull blankets and sheets from the upstairs storage closets, each folded into a neat package. From the cabinets in the dining room, they locate a few old metal pitchers and glass carafes used for local wine. "Not so valuable," her aunt says. Stella has already seen her aunt and uncle lock some of Sir Harwell's finer bottles of wine and brandy behind a door in the cellar with a series of complicated metal locks. Others pressed into crevices or buried in the ground.

Stella has stopped trying to count the people in the wine cellar. There are women, old men, and children of all ages. The ones who were there first move over to make way for the new families. They prop the doors open to the outside, but others close them to keep the cool air inside. Women set up small stoves outside, boiling water, stringing together meals, drawing water from the well and a nearby rusty spigot along the main road.

When they walk to school, there is a crowd of children now. The *maestra* pulls them all in, making room on the floor for them among the crowded desks. Stella and Sandro are no longer the new kids.

When Stella's uncles make their morning rounds, there are new families huddled together, sleeping on the stones before the villa's front door, waiting for first light. Some are dressed in tatters, others in fine suits or flowered dresses, the children in white collars. Bundles of blankets are untied to reveal precious belongings from home: photographs, watches, cutlery, food, special heirlooms. Carts and bicycles assemble outside, propped against the blue-black cypresses that flank the broad stairs. Most of the people are dirty and scared-looking, carrying whatever they can in ragged bags, tied to rusty bicycles. The lucky ones pull a cart piled with thin mattresses and clothes, food, and pans.

Stella brings down a few additional sheets they've uncovered in the attic. Livia and Mariasole scrub them with olive oil soap in the ancient stone *lavatoio* on the hillside, with its cold water and sagging wooden roof. Livia pins the sheets on the line, where they dry quickly in the scorching sun. When Stella brings the clean sheets into the cantina, the pungent scents of cold earth and decaying grapes hang heavy in her nostrils. The cantina is a mass of shadows, great oak barrels like hulking beasts among the increasing press of people.

Much like Stella herself, she realizes, the families staying here have no picture of the future. No idea when they will go back home, or if home will still be there when they return. Here in this peaceful place, Stella struggles to imagine what they have left behind.

"That's it," Zia Angela says. "No more. We can't possibly house anyone else. We have nothing else for them."

"We're alright here," Zio Tino counters.

"And who will help *us* when our stores run dry?" she says. "They will have to find somewhere else to go."

"Are you planning to throw them out, Angelina? I'd like to see you try."

Stella sees a sideways grin cross his face, out of view of his wife.

Long ago, Stella tells Sandro, Sir Harwell's villa stood at the center of a system of connected farms. For as far as the eye could see and even beyond the most distant hill, there were dozens of related farms. The farmers shared their crops in a complicated system that ensured there was enough for everyone to eat.

"Zio Tino told me the pacts between the owners and farmers go back to the twelve hundreds," Stella informs him. "The land-lord kept all the farms and buildings in good working order. He supplied everything they needed to cultivate the land. When the harvest arrived, the owner and the farmers shared the profits. The families' fates were all tied together, like one big family."

Suddenly, Stella realizes Sandro is not listening to her history lesson. Instead, he is studying her face intently. "How come your mother didn't come with you from Torino?" he asks.

Stella sighs. An innocent curiosity. But Sandro has given form to the fundamental question, to the thing that remains hidden in the core of her heart out of fear of what the answer might be. After months living with her aunt, uncle, and cousins, she still doesn't have a good answer.

OVER THE NEXT FEW DAYS, heavy silence falls over Santa Lucia. Somber. Only the cicadas dare to utter a few weak shrills into the void.

On the radio and through the towns comes the announcement that any freed British prisoners of war must give themselves up immediately to the nearest German Command. There is a final call for formerly enlisted Italian soldiers and officers to report at once to the nearest town hall or police headquarters where they will get new orders and a train ticket.

At the mayor's office, the windows and doors are flung open. Signor Bagnoli, Fabio and Alessio's father, sits at a large table with his tricolor sash across his Florentine suit jacket. Twirling a heavy silver pen between his thick fingers. Taking account in a giant, leather-bound ledger of who has reported themselves and who is missing.

The *maestra* cancels school for the day. Stella and Sandro watch her stand by bravely, her face like stone, as her husband, the village's only notary, stands before the *sindaco* and signs the ledger. Stella sees some of their farmers in their dirt-caked trousers and worn shoes, including Signor Martinelli's oldest son, who has only just returned home from France. She imagines his wife and children must be very sad to see him go off to fight again so soon.

When she returns to Villa Santa Lucia, Stella finds Zio Stefano at the edge of the vineyard, talking to two men who say they have escaped from a German labor camp near Orvieto. They refuse his offer to let them stay in the wine cellar; they are trying to make their way back home as soon as possible.

"Can't remember the last time I had a toothbrush," one of the men says. Stella feels a pang. His accent is so familiar. "I just want to go home."

Immediately, Stella recognizes the distinctive accent of her home region of Piemonte. Even though the man is a stranger, his voice is so close to her heart. It's the sound of voices that filled her world before she left Torino to come here. *I just want to go home.*

She almost falls to her knees. Instead, she rushes inside to the nearest bathroom so no one can see her come apart.

THE NEWLY RENAMED SANDRO begs Stella to let him back into the treasure room.

"I won't tell anyone," he says. "Promise." This time, he is armed with his mismatched collection of scrap papers and pencils the *maestra* gave him.

Stella knows she'll get in trouble if her uncle finds them in the secret room with the paintings. But then she thinks about the way Sandro held her shoulders in his hands that day, about the light she brought to his eyes. She wants to feel like that again. In a world where she has little control, it's the least she can do. She reaches her hand into the crack between the stones for the key, and lets Sandro in.

The room stands dark except for a few lines of light through the louvers in the shutters. Gilded picture frames stand hulking and silent in the shadows. Stella turns the latch and opens one of the tall shutters as the light reveals their colors, their quiet grandeur.

Sandro sits cross-legged on the floor before the giant picture inscribed "Sandro Botticelli." Stella can't imagine how a thirteen-year-old boy could begin to replicate such a complicated masterpiece with a pencil and a discarded scrap of paper, but soon enough, she sees he doesn't try.

Instead, he focuses only on the figure in the middle, the woman in the draped dress. His hand moves slowly but with confidence across the page. With a few quick strokes of his pencil, he's already sketched the outline of the figure that closely matches what Stella sees in the painting.

"How'd you do that?" She sits next to him, tucking the hem of her worn dress under her mosquito-eaten legs.

"This one's easy. You can see the figures are outlined in black already."

But Stella hasn't seen this. Probably, she thinks, she *wouldn't* have seen this at all if Sandro hadn't pointed it out. But now that he has, it's all she can see—the sinuous, elegant lines outlining the mysterious and beautiful female figures. The strange bluish man on the right, blowing wind from his lips. The three nude women who look like paper dolls, as tall as Stella herself, flat and floating on a carpet of a thousand flowers.

Stella struggles to understand the meaning of these flowing figures. In fact, the entire painting seems overwhelming and important, yet out of reach. Like a foreign language or a Rosetta Stone that must be decoded. All the same, she is entranced. Prompted by Sandro's deep concentration, she draws closer to the massive painting, her face inches away from it, with its bright colors and figures and flowers. Each detail speaks to her, though she can't understand the language at all. She feels the heaviness, the import, the weight of the painting, even though she can't find any words to explain why or how.

"Maybe she is their mother," Stella says, pointing to the large figure in the center of the composition.

"No," Sandro says. "Even though there is kind of a halo of light behind her, she looks different than the Madonna. She's more like . . . a goddess." Looking at the giant Madonna across the room, Stella concedes he is right.

Suddenly, the bell tower in the village church clangs seven, its loud ringing reverberating across the valley.

"*Merda!*" Stella scrambles to standing; she's lost track of time. "I haven't prepped the dough yet, and it still has to rest. My aunt will beat my legs with her spoon."

"Can't you leave me here?" Sandro says.

Stella hesitates.

"I want to finish my drawing." His brown eyes grow big and pitiful. Like a dog's.

"Both of us will be in big trouble if my uncle finds out I left you in here."

"I won't make a sound," he says, pleading with his eyes again. "Promise. They won't even know I'm here."

"Stella!" Her aunt's voice from the kitchen. "*Dov' è sei?*"

Stella flinches. "Alright. I'm going to lock you inside, though, *va bene?* I'll come back to let you out after dinner."

He nods.

"Stella!"

"Coming, *zia*!" Stella locks the door to the treasure room and quietly returns the key to its hiding place. She hesitates. Won't someone from the cantina notice Sandro is missing?

With a sinking heart, Stella realizes there is no one to come looking for him.

THE EVENING MEAL is a patchwork of necessity—a plate of *pici* that Stella has managed at the last minute, some freshly picked basil that is about to go to flower and tastes slightly bitter. A few greens pulled from the garden and a hunk of stale bread. Two overripe tomatoes and some cheese made from the milk of one of their goats.

Zia Angela, a force of nature in a faded apron, brushes crumbs from the flowered tablecloth into her palm while Zio Tino stands and turns the button on the wireless. Watching their father go to the radio, Livia and Mariasole turn sour. Mariasole stretches her arms out and rests her cheek on the table, as if the mere sight of her father turning on the wireless has pulled the plug on her remaining energy.

The atmosphere shifts with an announcement that the whole of Italy north of Rome is now under German martial law. General-feldmarschall Kesselring's edict says that starting today, trains, telephones, and postal services are under German control. Private letters may not be sent. And private phone conversations will be monitored.

"As if we could make a call," Zia Angela says. Their phone lines have been dead for weeks.

After the broadcast, Zio Tino turns off the radio with a flick of his hand. "I told you it was only a matter of time before the Germans were in control of everything."

Stella sees why her uncle was so somber on that night when everyone thought the war was over. Now those preemptive celebrations make the entire population of Santa Lucia seem naïve, maybe even stupid. Without another word, Stella's family scrapes back their chairs and starts their chores. Zio Tino goes to lock up all the doors in the house. Livia heads out to the hillside to unpin dry laundry from the line. Mariasole follows Zio Stefano outside to check the roosts. Mariasole's role will be to pick up all the chickens with motherly roughness, manhandling them into their roosts as if they couldn't do it by themselves.

Stella reluctantly follows Zia Angela into the kitchen with the dirty plates as the sky turns orange and violet.

After the dishes have been washed and put away, Stella returns to the courtyard, which stands pale and gleaming in the moonlight. In the treasure room, the eerie glow creates rectangular panes of stark shadows across the floor.

She finds Sandro in the same place she left him, seated on the tile floor in front of the giant painting by Sandro Botticelli. Like a lonely monk in a great sanctuary. Scraps of paper scattered all around him like the pages of some sacred text.

Stella sits next to him and hands him a dishrag with a piece of leftover bread and a hunk of salty goat cheese. Then she picks up one of the pages, and squints in the darkness to make out the face of the central female figure. With a few strokes of his pencil, he has brought to life the woman's eyes, nose, and mouth.

Sandro tears off a bite of the stale bread with his teeth. Around them, the room fades into darkness. The pooling moonlight has transformed the room into something even more magical.

Sandro whispers, "Your uncle entrusted you with a great secret."

As Stella takes in the beauty of Botticelli's painting in the pale light, she feels honored to have been the one to share this great treasure with her new friend.

At the mention of her uncle, the door opens and Zio Tino is standing there. Stella feels like a rock is sinking to the bottom of her stomach. She left the door open by mistake. Her uncle must have seen the door open as he made his nightly rounds.

"Who's there!?" Zio Tino demands.

Stella scrambles up immediately. "It's me, *zio*."

Zio Tino looks at Stella for a long moment and then his eyes fall on Sandro.

CHAPTER 5

A SECOND HARVEST

Autumn 1943

If done well, painting is more than a play of color and form on the panel. It can be a testimony that transcends the boundaries of perception in a way that words on a page can never achieve. Art has the power to be a repository of shared experiences and dreams unrealized. A mirror reflecting common joys and sorrows. Victories and defeats. Our highest triumphs. It tells us who we are—or at least, who we aspire to be. In my darkest days, painting has been a steadfast companion that draws me from my crucible of despair. Some days, it has given me a reason to rise from my bed.

—FROM THE LOST DIARIES OF SANDRO
BOTTICELLI, FLORENCE, SUMMER 1480

If you take away people's heritage, they are easily conquered. It's why the Italian custodians have worked so hard to preserve theirs. For if no one protected their unequaled treasures, how would they tell their story? How would they remember who they are and why they should keep going? In these dark moments, surely they would lose all hope.

—FROM THE DIARY OF CAPTAIN WALLACE E.
FOSTER, MONUMENTS OFFICER OF THE FIFTH
ARMY IN TUSCANY, AUGUST 1944

S tella! What are you thinking? This door has to stay locked. And I told you not to share this with anyone."

Zio Tino's initial reaction is a swirl of surprise and fear, his voice a thunderclap in the hushed reverence of the treasure room. Stella feels heat rise to her face. She is covered in shame to have betrayed her uncle's trust when all he has shown her is kindness.

"No one can come in here," he continues. "I told you, Stella . . . This is *my* responsibility." In his worried voice, Stella recognizes now that for Zio Tino, the treasure room is at the same time a duty, a privilege, and a liability. It's a secret he carries with an immense burden, one too weighty for young shoulders to bear.

But as Zio Tino stands there, absorbing the scene—the innocence in Stella's eyes, the half-chewed morsel of bread in Sandro's hand, the careful sketches strewn across the floor—Stella watches the lines on his forehead rearrange themselves, smooth out, give way to a reluctant understanding.

"We're just . . . looking at them," she says. Her voice trails off as she finds herself unable to find the right words to convey the magic she and Sandro have found in this room, the sense of being connected to something larger than themselves.

Zio Tino picks up one of Sandro's sketches from the floor and examines it. As Stella watches him run his eyes over the drawing— not just an aimless doodle, but a serious attempt to capture the essence of Sandro Botticelli's painting—a budding realization seems to dawn on him. Perhaps it's Sandro's earnestness—or his talent— that calms Zio Tino's rising emotions. A silent acknowledgment that Stella and Sandro, in their young, eager exploration, have already shown a depth of understanding and a respect for the gravity of the treasures that surround them.

"We were only trying to understand the stories better, sir . . ."

Zio Tino hands the drawing back to Sandro, and a certain sternness returns to his face. Stella only now sees the dangerous situation they've stumbled into: the risk that the secret haven could be exposed to those with ill intentions.

"Art tells stories, yes," Zio Tino says finally. "But these paintings are also very valuable and important. Right now, I'm the one responsible for keeping them safe. That means this door has to stay locked." Zio Tino shoos Stella and Sandro out the door and replaces the key between the stones.

THE LAND KNOWS NO ENEMY. No ally. No war. It only knows the alchemy of sun and soil, the relentless and irreversible turn of the seasons. The days grow shorter and the temperature drops quickly as evening falls. The last remains of green in the valley turn brown and gold, and the harvest comes to Santa Lucia. Late September brings rain and oxcarts piled high with grapes, like translucent purple and green-yellow glass. Everything smells like wet trees. In the evenings, Stella finds Zio Stefano on the high terrace, surveying a tapestry of cultivated wheat, olives, and vines as he removes his hat and wipes his forehead with his sleeve.

At dawn each day, everyone from the cantina, young and old, embarks on the collective labors as if they were living in a medieval village. The women and children walk through the vineyard lanes, cutting the fruits from the twisted vines and collecting them in ancient baskets. The old men chop the ripened wheat and alfalfa as the fields come alive with the rhythmic sways of their scythes. Soon, the hillside to the west lies like a tattered quilt, golden with stubble.

Stella remembers last year's harvest like a dance in successive acts: first the wheat and alfalfa, then the grapes, then the olives. The olives turn from green to red and then purple-black. They pick them and press them. Then press them again. The oil goes into large jars. They reserve the kernels for fuel.

But the stakes are higher than last year, Zio Stefano says, because if they don't store every last olive and grape, with the number of people they're feeding and the dwindling availability of food in the village, they might not have enough to last until the spring. Also different this time: Stella's uncles coordinate with other farms to bury their stores of olive oil; to wrap their hams and sausages and cheeses in white cloth and tuck them into holes in the ground; to take care to retrieve them when needed, but any requisitioning army won't be able to find them if they go looking.

News comes to them, fragmentary and haphazardly, like scattered leaflets. Benito Mussolini returning to power in Salò, thanks to the help of his German friends. German paratroopers touching down in Saint Peter's Square even though the Vatican says it won't take sides. Americans surprising everyone by landing their ungainly amphibious vehicles on the beaches south of Naples.

But for those laboring at Santa Lucia, adults and children alike, all of this seems far away. Instead, they take their carts to a neighboring farm to share weather predictions, bottles of wine, and rumors. Few dare to travel beyond the farthest hill they can see with their own eyes. The residents of Santa Lucia become more self-contained, along with the villagers and peasants beyond, with a bond of common interests and enemies, and a growing sense of solidarity against the threats that may lie beyond their own small world.

In the kitchen, Stella has gotten better at making the pasta shapes and the dishes that have become their staples. Endless varieties of wheat flour and beans and tomatoes and stale crust and olives. She and her aunt work in companionable silence, each moving efficiently to knead and roll, cut and shape, chop and stir. Some days, to her surprise, the entire surface of the floured table is covered in her finished shapes, ready to dry.

For a while, the tide of refugees slows, and the people in the wine cellar get through their day, helping with the harvest, cooking whatever they can find, mending sheets and socks, and writing letters that go nowhere. Then falling into heaps of slumber at the end of the long days.

At school, too, the children fall into a routine. Sandro has moved himself to the front row, where he is the first to raise his hand, the first to give correct answers. There is no doubt among any of the pupils, including Stella, that Sandro is the *maestra*'s favorite. She calls on him for quick responses and solutions to tricky math problems. She praises him for his drawings and his insightful comments. Stella feels a sense of envy mixed with pride for his success. She continues to sit in the back along with Fabio, who is sullen but accepting of the new order. There is no news of his brother, who, for all they know, might be in a work camp in Germany.

One afternoon, walking home from school, Sandro and Stella see two German tanks rumble by along the main road. They duck into the ditch and watch the tank armor glint under the low-lying sun as they pass. From where she crouches in the weeds, Stella sees a man's head emerge from the top of one tank. His helmet looks like a dusty turtle shell.

EVERY EVENING BEFORE RETIRING, Zio Tino makes his rounds of the villa to ensure everything is in order before handing things over to his brother-in-law for the night. Stella thinks he looks ready, expectant, as if Sir Harwell might return at any moment. Zio Tino is dressed as always in his dark suit, ever the devoted custodian. The *pomata* he uses to slick his dark hair across the top of his head has become a comforting aroma for Stella.

Ever since he caught them in the treasure room, Zio Tino lets Sandro and Stella follow him there each evening. Together, they stop and look at each painting, one by one, in the same way that Zio Stefano counts each hen as she makes her first fluttering hops out of the henhouse each morning.

Best of all, Stella's uncle seems to have forgiven her for taking Sandro into the treasure room without asking. Their new routine of making the daily rounds has served not only to forgive but to forget her transgression. Instead, it seems to have fostered a deeper connection between Stella and her uncle, a bond strengthened not in spite of her misadventure but because of it. It marks Stella and Sandro's silent promotion, along with her uncles, into the unofficial keepers of these treasures.

Zio Tino stands not much taller than Sandro. He always begins by counting the first layer of paintings on the right. He then speaks to the pictures, especially to the gigantic Madonna and her frog baby, enthroned against the glittering gold.

When they get to the great painting with the thousand flowers, they stop.

"Who are these figures, *zio*?" Sandro asks, even though Zio Tino isn't his real uncle. "And why so many flowers?"

Zio Tino considers quietly. "Truthfully, I'm not sure," he says. "This one is different from the rest. All I can tell you is this is one of the most famous paintings in the world. People around the globe know of it—and its maker, Sandro Botticelli. Even with so many other valuable and important paintings in the museum, this one was the pride of the Uffizi Galleries."

Stella is dumbfounded to think that something so famous, considered precious and important by people around the world, could be here in this quiet place, held in the possession of her own family. She feels a swell of pride through her chest. Her uncle goes on to enumerate a long list of other artists whose work is represented in the room: Masaccio, Giotto, Bronzino, Raffaello, Pontormo . . .

The names swirl through Stella's head, a mass of old-fashioned-sounding words she thinks she ought to recognize but doesn't.

"You learned about art in school, *zio*?" Sandro asks.

Zio Tino wags his head. "I only went as far as *scuola elementare*, my friend. There were no rules back then about how long you needed to stay. My parents had a farm not so far from here. They needed me."

"*Vedi?*" Stella swats Sandro's arm. "No school. And he turned out fine."

Zio Tino raises his eyebrows. "I never had the *opportunity* to stay in school like the two of you. But that doesn't mean my education didn't continue, *cara*. When I came to work for Sir Harwell . . . that's when I began to learn in earnest."

Stella listens to the way Zio Tino pronounces *Harwell*. She's repeated the name to herself silently. She's seen it written but finds it hard to say in any other way than something that comes out like *Arvella*. But she knows it isn't exactly right.

Zio Tino moves to stand before a large painting of peasants in a landscape of wheat fields and a lake. "Sir Harwell is a great collector of fine things, that is true. But he is more than that. He is fair and has treated all of us—down to his driver and gardener—with the same respect he might afford his peers back in Great Britain. I used to drive Sir and Lady Harwell into Florence often," Zio Tino continues. "Sometimes, after I found a place to park his Aston Martin or his roadster, he would bring me into the Uffizi or the Pitti to see the paintings and sculptures. That's how I learned a little bit about art and history. Not in school."

"Why didn't they just leave the paintings in the museums?" Sandro asks. "Don't they have locks and guards? Wouldn't they be safer there?"

"No, *sciocco*, it's safer in the countryside," Stella says.

Zio Tino points to one of the figures in the landscape, a young man with a basket, a hat, and a bundle of sticks. A basket not unlike the ones they use for the olive harvest.

"You see this man?" Zio Tino says. "He's just a peasant, a farmer. A man collecting wheat. But the artist has transformed an ordinary person into something extraordinary. Something that allows us to see beauty in the world where, perhaps, we didn't see it before."

Stella and Sandro stand there and feel a newfound appreciation and sense of wonder for the paintings in the room.

"That's what Sir Harwell did for me," Zio Tino says. "He treated me with dignity and respect. Helped me see the world—and myself—as something more."

"Will you let me come back in and do some more sketches when it's light outside?" Sandro asks.

"Yes," Zio Tino says. "But you must not tell anyone—or touch anything."

A smile breaks out on Stella's face. She knows Sandro will create something beautiful. Something he hopes will outlast them all.

THE FASCIST-RUN GOVERNMENT gives a final call for all eligible men to report to their nearest mayor's office or police headquarters for military service. It will be up to the German leadership where the men go. They say those who do not report within a fortnight will be shot. Landowners who shelter conscripts in their homes will face severe consequences.

In the golden dusk, outside the wine cellar door, Signora Donati gives her handsome son Filippo a tearful kiss on the cheek. She presses a small sack of food and a tight wad of lire into his hands. Zio Tino gifts him a pair of Sir Harwell's worn leather shoes. "Custom made in Florence," he says. When they fit Filippo's feet perfectly, Stella thinks her uncle looks as if he, too, will cry.

They watch the young man head out into the woods in his shabby shirt and trousers, a small pack on his back. Stella watches him disappear into the dark fold of the tree line. He doesn't tell anyone where he's headed.

Her voice shaking, Signora Donati says it's better if no one knows so they won't be tempted to tell later on.

ON THEIR WAY TO SCHOOL, Sandro and Stella walk past the *municipio*. Its flags stand tattered and quiet in the cool air, and the door stands wide open. Buoyed by the renewed German support, Fabio's father stands more resolute than ever in his authority over the villagers. Stella imagines the mayor sitting inside with his ledger, recording the names of those in town and on surrounding farms eligible for service. Sending his men out to find those who don't willingly report.

In the classroom, quiet rumors circulate. "One of our farmers saw a bunch of carabinieri loaded together on a train," one of their classmates says.

"They're going to Germany," another boy says. "Not as soldiers. As *prisoners*."

"Interned soldiers, they are calling them," another boy says. "They're going to work camps. The Germans already sent all their men to war, so they need people to fill their spots! Half of them are working in factories or camps in Germany by now."

The *maestra* listens warily to the children, her arms crossed, pacing back and forth in front of the classroom. But she says nothing. Her face looks shadowed and pale.

"My papà says those boys have been tricked," one girl says. "They don't know what they have signed up for." The girl's father, a farmer, has just returned to his family from near the French border by stealing a mule for the long trip.

Stella wonders about Alessio, skinny and resolved in his uniform, touching Livia's chin with his knuckle. Has Alessio been tricked? Is he on a train to Germany, even now?

"Mine says the Germans may not even come here at all. And even if they do, they won't be here forever. They will leave eventually."

"Then what will happen to our *sindaco*?" another child asks.

"If the Germans leave Santa Lucia, he will have to go with them," the *maestra* blurts suddenly. But then her face blanches and Stella thinks this slipped out and she didn't mean to comment on the mayor.

At that moment, the door creaks open and Fabio appears. The students stop talking and the air is filled with a sudden and heavy silence. All the students watch Fabio shrug his white smock over his shoulders and make his way to his desk.

He slides into his seat, his eyes scanning the quiet room. "What is it?"

But no one says a word. Not even the *maestra*, who turns toward the chalkboard to write the day's assignment. All the children watch her back and her ponytail in silence.

A FEW DAYS LATER, the mayor himself hikes up to the villa, sweating in a dusty suit and tricolor sash. Stella's family and some of the refugees collect outside the front door to receive him. Stella thinks Signor Bagnoli looks weary and pallid. With him are two armed carabinieri from a nearby town. Stella joins the ragged group of refugees in the shade of the cypresses, listening to the mayor's impassioned final call for recruits while his dark eyes flit from person to person.

First, the *sindaco* tells everyone, they must respect the new curfew and there are to be no lights after sunset. All the windows must remain shuttered. There are to be no public meetings, he says, looking nervously at the refugees who collect as a large group on the hillside.

As he continues his proclamations, Stella thinks he looks increasingly uncomfortable before this tired-looking crowd.

By this time, they all have heard incidental rumors from the nearby farmers. At one farm, a teen refused to register, so they arrested his father instead. Another young man has run off to distant relatives in Montepulciano, and his parents hope the kid will have the good sense to stay hidden. Another boy's family faked a doctor's note and kept him in bed when the carabinieri knocked on their door. Others report to their local mayor, get their papers and ticket for the town where they must board the train, then on the way, they scatter. The families can only say their sons went off to report themselves and they don't know where they are now.

The refugees and Stella's family listen in silence to the mayor's final warning about fathers being imprisoned and families losing their ration cards if they don't flush out their eligible sons. But Stella's uncles are too old and all the other boys in the villa are too young to report. There is no one left here to answer the mayor's call. After a while, he returns with his armed friends to the village.

FOOD SUPPLIES BEGIN to run out in the village. In the main square, a few turnips and onions look lonely in the vegetable sellers' baskets. The fruit sellers have only a few handfuls of figs and plums delivered to them from local farms. There is a queue of weary-looking old women down to the corner by 8:00 a.m. By 8:15, there is nothing left to buy.

Zia Angela announces she told them so.

Inside the cantina at Villa Santa Lucia, there are only a few precious canned things from last year. The saving grace, Zio Stefano says, is that the harvest is upon them. Stella watches her uncle pace back and forth among the vines and olive trees carpeting the hillsides beyond the symmetry of the terrace and Sir Harwell's formal garden. Beyond, wild plums spill down the hillsides where mosquitoes and fireflies float up into the air as the sun drops. Everyone's labor will be necessary for them to harvest enough food to last through the winter, they say. They will do as they have always done; they will live off the land, even if there are so many more mouths to feed.

In the wine cellar, Old Giuseppe, who has brought his daughter and grandson from near Naples, reminds them they are still better off than people in the cities, who don't have the option to live off the land when food supplies dwindle. He sits on the hillside at dusk, playing mournful lines on the old mandolin he's brought with him. Its eerie refrains echo through the evening, silencing even the incessant din of the insects.

Stella's aunt and uncles give over part of the kitchen garden and cultivation area to the people in the cantina so they can begin to fend for themselves and grow their own vegetables.

ONE EVENING, Dario Sabatini, one of their farmers, comes to see them in a horse-drawn cart that looks a hundred years old. Stella cranks the handle on the well and brings him a glass of cold, earthy water. He sits with Stella's uncles on the terrace.

"I wanted to warn you," he says, his eyes haunted. "A handful of soldiers came to our farm looking for food and a roof over their heads. Say they escaped their regiments near Pienza. If they haven't come here yet, they will."

Zio Tino shrugs. "What's a few more? Our cantina is already bursting with displaced people." He manages a weak smile.

"No," he says, his face grave. "This is different. They are soldiers, not civilians. And you've heard the warnings about harboring them. Most of them have simply torn off their uniforms and escaped into the woods."

Stella thinks about Signora Donati's son and wonders where he is now.

He continues. "They told us they jumped from a train headed to Rome with a group of escaped soldiers piled on the roof. They're trying to get away from the German commands and the Fascist recalls in whatever way they can. There's no way they will return to their hometowns and report in again. They are desperate. And having desperate men in your house is not a good thing."

"Understood," Zio Tino says. "Who could blame them for hiding and waiting it out? They would be stupid to trust the German commands—or the hollow promises of our own mayors."

Dario nods. "The good news, I suppose, is that there are not enough carabinieri to go looking for them. And maybe most of them would just as soon turn a blind eye and let them disappear into the trees."

Zio Tino tents his fingers under his chin. "What do you think will happen when the Americans land here? You think the men go sign up with them? Or run from them? Stay hidden? What a mess," he says.

"One of our neighbors was able to get the BBC broadcast on their wireless. They are saying Italian planes and ships are headed to Allied bases on Corsica and ports south of Rome. And no one knows if there might be another Allied landing in Tuscany. Maybe Grosseto. Maybe Pisa. And they say Italian forces should protect any British POWs. They must not know that these so-called Italian forces are hiding in the woods and we have our own problems to deal with. Those British prisoners are on their own, I'm afraid."

THE FASCIST GOVERNMENT blocks the radios. At the evening broadcast, they are only able to hear the Rome or Florence stations. Zio Tino chooses the Florence station, where they nonetheless receive mostly news from Germany and a promise of final Italian victory. The broadcast begins and ends with a rousing rendition of "*Giovinezza.*" While the familiar refrains travel through the air,

Stella watches Zio Tino rub his lined forehead with his fingers and Zia Angela sits in her seat, arms folded across her chest. After that, there is a concert broadcast from Vienna.

In the cantina, Signora Bianchi pulls out her hidden radio and tunes in to the BBC while all the others gather around and eagerly await her rough translation.

MIRACULOUSLY, a letter from Sir Harwell arrives at the villa. Stella watches Zio Tino's hands shake as he fumbles to open the envelope. His shoulders drop in relief when he reads his boss's words, confirming that he made the right decision when he agreed to take in the paintings from Signor Poggi and the Uffizi. "Thanks be to God," he says, wiping his brow with a handkerchief.

At night, the air is silent and suffocating with the new, required blackout curtains over their shuttered windows. In the middle of the night, Stella lies wide awake while Mariasole sleeps through the brief pops of gunshots in the woods.

ONE BRILLIANT AFTERNOON, Mariasole and Stella are weeding the vegetable garden when a pair of men emerge from the underbrush near the edge of the hillside. Something about the men's demeanor makes Stella scramble to standing immediately. She dusts the red dirt off her hands.

One man holds up his hands, palms out, as if capitulating. "*Buongiorno, signorina,*" he says. Stella notices his eyes go to the ripening eggplants in the dirt before returning to her. Both men are disheveled and dirty. The second man has deep lines on his cheeks and oily hair drooping over his forehead. "You have something in your garden to spare for us?" he asks. "It's been a few days since we've been able to find anything to eat."

In spite of their pitiable state, Stella feels a growing sense of unease. These men are different from the men, women, and children in the wine cellar who have run from their homes. She senses a different level of desperation in their eyes.

"Go get your papà," she says to Mariasole, who drops her rusty garden fork and runs toward the stairs leading to the villa's terrace.

At that moment, two refugee men from the wine cellar appear at the hillside, carrying harvest baskets on their backs. One of the men sets his basket on the ground and comes to talk with the newly arrived men.

Zio Tino and Zia Angela rush outside. At the state of the men's appearance, their ragged clothing and the one man's bare feet, Angela's eyes widen. She stops dead in her tracks. "You can't stay here," Zia Angela says.

"Of course, signora," the older man says. "We only are asking for water and whatever food you can spare."

"We have too many mouths to feed as it is," she says, but Stella thinks she looks embarrassed not to take them in.

"See if we have some shoes to spare." Zio Tino nudges his wife and she heads back inside.

The men sit on a stone wall near the garden and talk to Zio Tino while Stella pumps the well and fills their canteens. The man with the greasy hair tells Zio Tino the woods are thickly populated with fleeing Italians and escaped Allied soldiers. They say they have run from their regiments and have been hiding in the woods for weeks. And they are not alone. There are scores of fugitive soldiers, some terrified boys no older than sixteen, who have slipped out of the Germans' grasp. They would have been working already in labor camps north of our border if they hadn't jumped from trains or dashed into a ditch or a wooded path in the nick of time.

Stella thinks of Alessio, neat and skinny in his uniform at seventeen years old, and wonders if he has been put in charge of such youngsters. Or if the Germans have tricked him, too, and he will be little more than a slave looking for the smallest opportunity to slip out of their grasp.

After a while, Zia Angela brings the older man a pair of Sir Harwell's old socks and a pair of leather shoes that must have been expensive and fine at some point long ago. Stella thinks the shoes look old-fashioned, and especially, they look out of place with the man's ragged clothes, but at least they are better than going barefoot. "I know Sir Harwell would gladly give you these himself," Zio Tino says with renewed confidence.

Stella's aunt tells her to pick a few ripe tomatoes while one of the men in the cantina draws them a map of the creek bed that will lead them in the direction of Chiusi. Zia Angela packs a woven sack with the tomatoes and a loaf of bread made from their stores of wheat. The men nearly fall over themselves with gratitude and Stella sees her aunt soften a little around the edges. Stella thinks she may even see a glimmer of compassion.

After the men disappear again into the brush, Stella wonders if her father might be out there somewhere in the woods, struggling for food and warmth like these men. Could he be among those who have left their units behind, who have thrown their uniforms into a ditch and fled into the woods? Men dirty and without shelter or food. Without hope or even shoes.

Stella can't help it. She watches for Daniele Costa.

STELLA IS COVERING the kitchen garden with old sheets to protect it from the frost when the roar of planes returns.

The leaves on the birch trees at the edge of the wood turn rust-colored and fall one by one at the slightest breeze. The weeds in the kitchen garden turn dry and brittle. Above the wheat stubble reaching to the dark silhouette of the hills, the sky is a broad, clear canvas of cerulean.

She recognizes the familiar, distant-then-growing roar. The sense of tightness that begins in the pit of her stomach and rises to her chest. But this time, it's different. It's not one plane. It's many.

The refugees working in the alfalfa fields freeze, hands tented over their eyes. Then they abandon their tools and baskets and start to run toward the villa.

Stella cannot begin to count the planes now. Twelve, then double. Then triple. They are large, sleek and shining, a parade of power slicing the air. When they near Santa Lucia, the sound is deafening, as if it may rattle the ground itself.

But even before anyone can take cover in the villa, just like that, the planes are gone. There is a distant boom and a flash of light in the distance. Then the rumble of an explosion far away. Only whirling dust and stunned faces are left behind. Birds wheel crazily above the trees.

Then the fields turn back to silent.

WHEN STELLA GOES OUT to the henhouse to collect eggs for the pasta later that evening, a swirling wind lifts her skirt, sharp and biting around her bare legs. The wind has turned cold, gusting across the Tuscan landscape with a whirl that carries with it the scent of the north—a smell that brings with it the memory of snow-capped mountains and the frozen embrace of Alpine valleys.

On her way to the coop, Stella passes the woodshed. Its door stands open and flapping, banging against the crumbling stucco. She presses into the wind, hurrying to close it.

At the threshold, there is a flutter of movement in the darkness. Stella freezes and squints into the gloom of the woodshed's interior, her eyes adjusting to the shadows. Even from the threshold, she senses something different in the cold, damp air. A subtle shift in the atmosphere, a tense undertone, a silent buzz of anxiety. She steps inside the building and out of the wind. Hesitates.

In a shadowy corner, a man is cowering on the dirt floor among the grain sacks. His face looks greenish and pallid in the semi-darkness. His wispy hair is greasy and stuck to his head. His left leg extends across the floor, bent at an unnatural angle, a crude, bloody wrapping around it. As Stella approaches, their eyes meet. Through the frail light, she watches a flash of terror cross his face.

"*Signore!*" Stella nearly drops her basket, but gathers her wits and asks the obvious. "You need help . . . ?"

But the man doesn't understand her. He only raises both palms. A silent capitulation. His muddy, ragged tunic looks different from the Italian uniforms like Alessio's, and it has a dark stain across the leg. Stella watches the man's jaw shiver, either from pain or cold or fear, Stella doesn't know. Then a few weak words come out of his mouth but Stella understands nothing.

"Stay here," she says, realizing the man probably couldn't move if he tried. "I'll be back." Then she drops her basket and runs out into the gusty wind.

Three of the refugee men help carry the injured soldier across the garden and into the shelter of the wine cellar. In the light, Stella can now see that the man is tall and fair. One of the women gives up her pallet on the floor. Signora Donati pushes her bulk through the crowd to get a closer look at the man's injured leg.

Stella watches the man's pained, glazed eyes take in the unfamiliar surroundings: the shadows, the great wooden barrels, the damp air, the dozens of curious faces looking back at him.

"He doesn't speak any Italian," Sandro whispers, appearing at Stella's side. "But Signora Bianchi understands some English. She says his name is Sergeant John Cakebread," he reports. "He's from Durham, England. His plane crashed. He was lucky to survive it, but then had the misfortune of stepping too close to a mine on the roadside on the way here."

Stella watches one of the refugee men wad up John Cakebread's bloody paratrooper's uniform then head outside, where there is a small fire burning inside a ring of stones. Stella worries the men will need to extinguish the flames by sundown. She watches them throw the uniform on the fire until it crackles and hisses in the blue flames. Now the British man wears an Italian farmer's shirt and trousers. One of the trouser legs has been cut off to reveal his pale, crooked leg and mine-ravaged foot. He shivers with pain, pushing himself up to sitting on the pallet.

Even if he could walk, Stella realizes, this soldier has no hope of going anywhere now. According to Signora Bianchi, the man's co-pilot has died in the woods. Now his friends are far south of here and he would never make it back to them with his foot like that. He is drawn and unshaven, his leg immobile in the splint Signora Donati has fashioned from a few pieces of olive wood and torn fabric.

Stella worries whether she should tell her aunt and uncle about the man, but by the time Stella returns upstairs, it seems they already know about him. That evening, through a heating grate that separates the girls' bedroom from her aunt and uncle's, Stella hears an explosive argument. Shards of their conversation travel along with a trail of hot air through the metal grate. What else could they do for the poor man? They can't possibly afford to let him stay here. Their lives on the line. Finally, her uncle raises his voice. "Where will you send him, Angela?"

After that, her aunt and uncle fall silent, and it seems no one has a good answer to this question.

When Stella finally settles alongside Mariasole in bed that evening, the *tramontana* stirs again, spilling its icy blast over the tops of the hills. They cover the windows with the black curtains and hunker down for whatever is to come. She feels grateful for the warmth, but her stomach is uneasy.

As she lies there in the dark, Stella wonders if Sergeant Cakebread has ever flown a plane over Torino.

ONE AFTERNOON, Signor Poggi returns unexpectedly to the Villa Santa Lucia. And with him, more paintings.

With a surge of excitement, Stella watches the trucks huff and heave up the winding road. The drivers jump out, hiking up their pants and unlocking the back doors of the trucks. She runs to find Sandro so he can witness the marvel with her.

Stella recognizes Signor Poggi as he emerges from his fine vehicle. He rubs his hand across his white hair and puts on a gray hat as he climbs the broad staircase to the villa's front doors.

"Get Mister Poggi an *aperitivo*," Zia Angela tells her. Stella goes to the root cellar and removes a dusty bottle of white wine, which feels cool between her palms. Livia helps her twist out the cork and pour a stream of wheat-colored liquid into a small glass.

In the courtyard, Sandro stands dumbfounded as the men bring several enormous canvases through the doors. Next are three giant painted crosses that look like they belong over the altars of three different churches.

Stella's uncles sit once again with Signor Poggi at the great dining table. Signor Poggi takes a quick swig of the drink and nods to Stella in appreciation. "Simple pleasures," he says. "They are in short supply these days."

"How are things in the city?" Zio Stefano asks.

"Unfortunately, we can't afford to keep the paintings in Florence anymore," Signor Poggi says. "The air raids have become more frequent. The Campo di Marte marshaling yards have been devastated and no more trains are running."

"The Duomo . . . and all the monuments . . ." Zio Tino says.

"We've shored up the church portals across the city with sandbags. We had hoped to keep some of the larger pictures in the galleries, but alas, here we are. We've moved out everything we can now."

"Our main problem here is the number of people needing help," Zia Angela says, exchanging a fleeting glance across the table with her husband. "And that our supplies have run dangerously low."

"We have the same problem, signora," Signor Poggi says. "The courtyard of the Palazzo Pitti must have a thousand people living in it. I know things are challenging for you, but I promise you are living in luxury compared to what people are enduring in Florence. You have it much easier here in the country. You can grow and store your own food. In Florence, there are only lines at the food stores and nothing to buy."

For the moment, this proclamation silences Stella's aunt.

"Here we are," Signor Poggi says, producing a stack of paper from his leather briefcase and spreading them across the table. "All fifteen delivery reports. A total of 272 paintings. And now, the most important thing of all."

Stella watches Signor Poggi produce an official-looking letter with stamps on it. "It's a notice from Generalfeldmarschall Kesselring. In German, of course. No German soldier or official is allowed to set foot inside this villa. If anyone tries, you show them this proclamation from their own commander. I can't begin to tell you how difficult it was to procure this letter."

"We'll make sure nothing happens to the pictures." Zio Tino stands and places the letter in one of the dish cabinet drawers, now empty, Sir Harwell's fine porcelain pieces having been walled up in the attic months ago.

"There's no more space in this room, sir." One of the truck men pokes his head in the door. "The crosses . . . they are too big."

"We'll have to put them in the great hall," Zio Tino says. "But only . . . there is no way to lock the door."

"It will have to do," Signor Poggi says. "I'm just relieved to get them out of Florence at all."

Before Signor Poggi leaves the villa, he makes the rounds of the paintings. Stella feels a swell of pride, watching her zio Tino, no longer a driver but a great and respected custodian of what she now realizes are world-famous treasures, walking along with the director of the Uffizi Galleries. Making the same path around the room that Stella and Sandro do with him each evening.

When they reach the large flower painting by Sandro Botticelli, Signor Poggi stops and contemplates it in silence for what feels to Stella like a very long time.

Then Signor Poggi places his hand on Zio Tino's shoulder and squeezes it before he puts on his hat and turns to leave.

At dinner, Stella's aunt unfolds a hastily scrawled note from a neighboring farm. A German tank has stopped, the neighbor says. The soldiers came along with an interpreter. They say they are with a unit in charge of procuring supplies for their troops. They exchanged a handful of lire for a milking goat.

Winter crystallizes around the Villa Santa Lucia. An ancient, abandoned plow freezes into the hillside. The *tramontana* brings sweeping winds across the treeless valleys. In the village, leaves are caught in its whirling grasp, swirling in mini-tornadoes across the cobbles. It buffets the villa and Stella thinks of the countless prisoners and partisans hiding in the woods. She is grateful for the crackling fires inside the great hearths. Sergeant Cakebread stays put in the cantina, immobilized in his splint. Waiting every night for the radio broadcast on the BBC, the volume turned down low.

Leading up to Christmas, the feast of the village's patron saint comes and goes. Father Ramondo goes through the motions, retelling the story of the unfortunate Santa Lucia and her difficult parents, her speared throat and gouged eyes, with as much passion as he can muster. But the day passes with little fanfare and little hope that putting out carrots and coffee for Santa Lucia will save them from their various individual and collective losses, hardships, and misfortunes.

After mass, rumors circulate that the Germans will cut the power lines to the whole area. Stella's uncles and any of the refugee men strong enough to do so split wood and stack it in the woodshed and in piles beyond the olive grove. Stella and her cousins spend an afternoon searching the house for oil lamps and candles from the storage cabinets and the attic. Zia Angela says it is a fruitless labor because they can't buy oil anyway.

Christmas passes with little fanfare. Zio Tino gives Zia Angela a small basket of Jerusalem artichokes he's been cultivating in secret. Stella blushes when she sees Zia Angela grasp both his cheeks and kiss him on the mouth. Later, she roasts the little roots with mushrooms and a few sprigs of thyme.

Shortly after the new year, a rare snowfall brings all the children out to see the wonder of white fluff fall from the sky. They raise their faces to let the fat flakes fall coldly on their tongues. Stella and Sandro, who says he's never seen snow before, hurl snowballs at each other, laughing, before the wan sunbeams melt it all.

"I heard all the furriers and silver shops in Florence have been looted," Livia says.

"Then it's a good thing we put Lady Harwell's furs away when we did," Zia Angela answers.

Stella thinks of the furs safely walled up inside the attic and the pig sties, where no one would think to look for them. She wonders how many men like Sergeant Cakebread there are in the woods. How many might wish they could find any one of those fur coats as the winter winds begin to swirl again around their bare ankles and heads.

"ARE YOU WRITING a letter to your papà?"

In the great hall, Mariasole hops on the fancy settee next to Stella, wedging her small body against her, breathing loudly. Stella can smell the girl's unwashed hair, the sticky jam on her fingers from breakfast. Perhaps in all her preoccupation with the dozens of refugees, Mariasole's mother has forgotten to make her take a bath.

Around them, the three newly arrived enormous painted crosses from the Uffizi are propped along the walls.

"None of your business." Stella folds her paper and stares at the crosses. They stand skewed, with one arm and the bottom of each on the floor. Each pained-looking Jesus toppled sideways. Stella has been trying to sketch each one, just the sideways face of the bleeding Jesus. Trying to get the nose right. Noses are the hardest things to draw, Sandro has told her. More than anything, she wants to show him she can do it. Even a little.

"My papà doesn't even know how to write," Mariasole says. "Barely read."

On a table behind the settee stands a cluster of photographs of the Harwells. One of the photographs shows the fancy Alfa Romeo now sitting dusty, quiet, and without its tires in the carriage house. Sir Harwell is difficult to discern in the photographs; his face is as still and flat-looking as the Christs on the painted crosses. Stella focuses instead on Lady Harwell, who is not beautiful, but still elegant and restrained-looking in a dark coat and hat adorned with a gem-encrusted pin. Stella thinks if she were asked to converse with the lady, she might find herself tongue-tied.

"But I think you should," Mariasole continues. "Write to him, I mean. It's the least you can do when someone you love is far away."

Stella doesn't want to show Mariasole her weak attempt at drawing the bewildered, passive face of the flat Christ.

"But how would you know where to send it? You *do* look like your papà, you know."

"How do you know that?"

"Because I saw a photograph of him. I can show you."

CHAPTER 6

PURGATORIO

Spring 1944

Some days I feel like giving up on this painting. The whole endeavor feels futile. For what value is making art when so many people suffer? When so many lives are lost because of the poor decisions of our leaders? Painting an image of a goddess with flowers seems a folly. A purposeless task in the face of such devastation and human need. For what purpose could art serve in such circumstances?

—FROM THE LOST DIARIES OF SANDRO
BOTTICELLI, FLORENCE, SUMMER 1480

In wartime, art can represent a form of resistance, a way to preserve culture, history, and identity in the face of potential eradication. It can become a way to hold on to the rich tapestry of one's heritage, maintaining a connection to a pre-war world; a way to carry the torch of civilization.

—FROM THE DIARY OF CAPTAIN WALLACE E.
FOSTER, MONUMENTS OFFICER OF THE FIFTH
ARMY IN TUSCANY, AUGUST 1944

The caretaker's cottage lies shuttered on the hillside beyond the olive grove. The front door creaks when Mariasole unlocks it. Even in the darkness, Stella perceives that the cottage is opposite in every way from the spacious villa at the top of the hill. The air stands thick with the must of abandon, of a life paused, of a waiting for the world to turn right side up again. As her eyes adjust to the dimness, Stella sees white sheets draped across several pieces of furniture. In the kitchen nook, one of the cabinets stands open and half-broken on its hinges. She imagines a fleeing soldier or refugee may have forced their way inside to rummage for whatever was left behind.

Up until the Harwells abandoned the villa for Switzerland nearly two years ago now, Mariasole has spent her whole life living in this cottage. Knowing her way by heart, Mariasole runs excitedly through the dark house. She disappears into a room off the single hallway, and Stella hears her cousin begin to creak open the metal bolt on one of the shutters. Light filters in to reveal a simple, dusty bedroom with an ancient armoire and a double bed with the sagging imprint of two bodies. Stella imagines her zio Tino and zia Angela sleeping here every night for as long as Zio Tino has been Sir Harwell's driver.

Mariasole opens a drawer inside the old armoire, pulls out a small wooden box, and removes the lid. Inside is a mismatched stack of old papers and photographs. She spills them out across the bed-spread, a messy jumble of handwritten letters, envelopes, and faded photographs. Stella sits on the edge of the bed and sorts through the clutter of unfamiliar faces. Women in wedding dresses from long ago. Babies swaddled in fancy lace baptismal gowns. A man with a dog and a walking stick and a basketful of truffles. A dour-looking couple surrounded by a brood of eight children.

Mariasole paws through the photographs, discarding most of them back into the box. Instinctively, Stella looks for a photograph or any mention of her mother. She grew up in this town, after all. But she finds no trace of her.

"Here it is!" Mariasole cries finally, and hands one of the bent photographs to Stella.

Stella holds the grainy black-and-white image in her hands. It's a couple propped against a stone wall much like the one that surrounds the base of the Villa Santa Lucia. The woman leans against the man, her arm entwined in his, her face turned up to him. A fleeting, momentary smile, frozen in time.

The man, on the other hand, looks directly out at the camera, his mouth a thin line. His eyes dark and brooding. He is lean, and his ears protrude out beneath his dark hair. Just like Stella's ears. She's constantly brushing her hair over them so it's not so obvious. There is no doubt she is related to the man in this picture. He is so familiar and so strange, all at once.

Mamma says you're the spitting copy of your papà. That's what Mariasole had said on Stella's first day of school.

Lo sputo. Stella imagines her father spitting her out and leaving her behind. Nothing but saliva.

"That's my mamma," Mariasole says.

Stella brings the photograph closer to her face. She didn't realize until now that the woman in the photograph is a younger version of Zia Angela. But as soon as the words are out of Mariasole's mouth, Stella sees it clear as day. The twiglike body in a flowered dress. The sharp jaw. She is younger and fresher and friendlier-looking, Stella thinks. But Zia Angela all the same.

"Come on!" Mariasole cries. "I'll show you where Livia and I used to sleep!" Mariasole piles the photographs back into the box.

But Stella stays seated on the edge of her aunt and uncle's sagging bed, squinting at the old photograph of her zia Angela and Daniele Costa from so long ago. Something in young Zia Angela's expression is distinctly different from now, Stella thinks. In this picture, she looks happy. She looks carefree. Stella thinks she looks like she's in love.

Stella slides the photograph into her dress pocket and leaves the open box of photographs on the bed. Then she follows Mariasole into the darkened room to see where she and her sister used to sleep, before the Harwells had to flee Italy and the whole world seemed to turn upside down.

"How did your parents meet?" Stella asks Livia in the kitchen. The girls are stacking plates on a tray to take to the upper terrace table for the midday meal, where a glint of sunshine has finally broken through the winter gloom.

"Not hard to meet someone here," Livia says, gesturing toward the window, with its view of the hillside leading down to the tiny village.

"Were they in school together?"

Livia nods. "Same schoolhouse where your own mother went. Suppose it's exactly the same now as it was back then." As Stella tries to imagine Zio Tino, Zia Angela, and even her own mother as thirteen-year-olds like herself, facing the same schoolhouse struggles, Livia picks up the tray full of plates and cutlery and leaves the kitchen. Stella follows, careful not to spill the heavy, hot bowl of pasta between her palms.

On the terrace, the adults are talking about the fighting between Axis and Allies drawing closer to Tuscany. Stella doesn't see any signs of either Germans or Americans, but things in their daily lives and in the village have shifted since the joyous, premature celebrations of last autumn. Perhaps Zio Tino was right after all. The switching of sides didn't mean the end of their suffering in Tuscany; in a way, it was the beginning.

Looking back, those celebrations in September seem a fleeting, naïve dream. Now villagers are hunkered down behind their blackout curtains and shuttered windows. The square stands desolate. Only stray birds flit by, pecking at the cracks between the cobbles.

The *maestra* has only had one letter from her husband, and that was months ago. The fruit seller tells Zia Angela they can't get anything from their usual farms. It's not safe to travel on the roads, and any vehicles parked along the village streets gather dust.

In the villa, the routine involves getting from one end of the day to the other with limited resources. With her aunt, Stella fuels the great hearths using logs stacked in the woodshed and olive kernels dried from the autumn harvest. They make do with smaller portions and reluctantly open the last remaining jars of preserved figs. Stella learns how to make coffee from chicory roots. They turn out bread with the scant wheat portions left over from what is required to hand over to the government stores. They make their own honey and cheese, and their own sausages using fatty, low-grade cuts of pork. Adding chopped sundried tomatoes, fennel seeds, and rosemary. Loading everything into the slippery intestine casings and twisting off the ends. Still, Stella sometimes goes to bed feeling hungry.

"You need a brassiere," Mariasole tells her one afternoon while the two of them stand over a boiling pot on the fire near the well. They are making crude soap bars with the residue of kitchen oils, potato peels, and ash. Over the past couple of months, Stella's breasts have bloomed like small flowers. The change makes her feel strange and self-conscious, like she's in someone else's body or about to transform into someone else entirely, like one of the floating, flowered ladies in Botticelli's painting. She covers her chest with as many layers of clothes as she can find.

Those living in the cantina have also had to make do with whatever they have to keep warm. Livia finds some old wool and thread in a storage cabinet; some of the older refugee women know how to undo it and spin it again for stockings and jerseys. Some of the women make children's clothes and shirts from curtain linings. They turn strips of threadbare rugs into slippers and ragged sheets into baby diapers. Soon enough, they run out of material.

Sergeant Cakebread, through roughly translated words, says he's a farmer back in England and he wants to help with the chores, but he can hardly walk and besides, no one will let him dare to be seen outside the wine cellar.

As THE GROUND THAWS and the tracks between the grapevines turn to mud, a few more escaped soldiers—both Italian and British—stop at the villa, asking for shoes and directions. Each of them seems to know the name of Villa Santa Lucia, and Zia Angela worries what the consequences will be now that word has spread about their unwitting hospitality.

"I know how to raise rabbits," one of the men says, and another says he is willing to do any chore they give him. Zio Tino directs them to neighboring farms and doesn't allow them to stay. One of the men tells Zio Tino there are more defected soldiers gathering at makeshift camps in the woods, organizing resistance activities alongside the partisans who are already there.

One night, an Italian man who escaped from a German work camp near Bologna says there is a long chain of helpers in the countryside providing them with money, clothes, blankets, and directions south. He nearly bursts into tears when Zio Stefano gives him a pair of woolen socks they've pulled from one of Sir Harwell's drawers.

The British men ask for directions south so they can rejoin their own troops. The men's arrival buoys Sergeant Cakebread. Whenever English speakers arrive, he hobbles to the door, talks with them excitedly, and shows them the tattered map he keeps stuffed under his thin pallet. Stella can't understand their words, but he looks sad when they leave and she knows he wishes he could go with them.

The saddest of all, Stella thinks, are the newest refugees. After all these months away from home, they have used up everything they brought with them and are destitute. A woman traveling with three young children appears with nothing, only the clothes on their backs. One of the children has bronchitis and looks like a ghost. The others make room for them in the cellar. "There are more Germans now at the checkpoint at Signa," the woman says. "They told us to come here to the big house."

"The Germans know about our house?" Stella asks, but no one has an answer.

In the evenings, Stella's uncles pace the upper terrace, looking out toward the hills as if they are expecting an important guest. Sometimes, Stella sees Zio Tino climb the spiraling, narrow staircase of the watchtower, favoring his trick knee.

As if her uncles summoned them with their nervous pacing, more planes come—and more often. In the evenings, there are more dark shapes in the sky. A relentless roar that makes the air vibrate. Stella, her aunt, uncles, cousins, and everyone in the wine cellar freeze where they are, holding their breath against the distant threats. Waiting for the planes to pass. Pausing in the heavy and relentless silence. The only sound is the geese nervously chittering in their pens.

WITH MORE TALK of increasing and impending threats, school is all of a sudden suspended until further notice. The children's long-anticipated final weeks leading up to the summer pause are simply canceled—along with it, last exams and lessons mid-stride. The weekly routine and disciplined structure are suddenly yanked away, leaving behind a gaping void.

Stella sees the *maestra* walking through the village. Instead of smiling in her white smock at the front of the classroom, she looks deflated in her worn dress, waiting in line with a dozen other women to buy supplies from the grocer's nearly bare shelves. Returning home to her small, empty home with its closed shutters and dusty doorway.

On the day they get the news of the school closing, after she's cleaned up the midday meal, Stella goes out through the garden and to the lower doorway of the wine cellar to look for Sandro. The air has turned warmer, the promise of spring. He's found a spot in the dappled sun and he sits with a sketchbook on his knee overlooking the vast patchwork of gold and new green.

"You must be happy," he says, not lifting pencil from paper.

"About what?"

"That school is canceled," he says, turning his smirking face to her.

"I am," Stella says, crossing her arms. But for the first time, she realizes she's actually a bit disappointed. "I know," she says, her face brightening. "We can have our own school. I'll teach you how to read better. And in return, you'll teach me how to draw."

"Alright," he says. She feels his strong, dry hand as they shake on it. "*Affare fatto.*" They have a deal and Stella smiles. "That means now we can spend all day in the treasure room to look at the pictures," he says. "For our lessons."

AT THE KITCHEN WORKTABLE, Stella rolls out a new ball of dough alongside the ancient metal pasta roller bolted to the wooden tabletop. Stella carefully feeds the flattened dough into the teeth, turning the old wooden crank handle and watching the long strands emerge and tangle on the floured tabletop under the patches of golden light from the window.

Something has been nagging at Stella. Something she wishes with all her might she could ask her mother. Her breasts have budded like flowers, tiny sprouts of pink that seem to swell each day. She is careful to wear printed dresses to cover her chest, but as the weather gets warmer and she leaves her layers behind, she feels self-conscious.

Stella knows there are things her mother would have taught her, if only she were here now. Things only a mother can teach a daughter at times when their bodies betray them, turn into something strange and foreign.

"Zia Angela," Stella says, watching her aunt turn a fresh ball of dough on the table, "I've been wondering . . ." Her voice trails off and the air hangs thick with unspoken words and carefully avoided subjects.

"Make it thinner!" Zia Angela says. They have made the strands as thin as possible, making their store of flour last as long as it will. Their modest midday meals consist of soup thickened with bread or noodles, vegetables or chestnuts, and a glass of wine. Sometimes they have meat, maybe twice a week.

As much as Zia Angela has complained about the people holed up in the wine cellar, Stella has watched her aunt labor with her own hands for months to keep them clothed and fed. She realizes that many complain about cowardice in Italy. But even her aunt, with her prickly demeanor, has taken great risks—even risks of being shot—to share her own food, her own clothing down to the last pair of shoes in the house. She and Stella's uncles have clothed and lodged countless strangers whether Italian or British. All humans with their own shade of suffering. In the wine cellar, the cigarettes are gone. The playing cards are worn down. People are wearing all manner of tattered and shared clothing. But they eke out another day. Through Zia Angela's actions, she has given Stella hope that hidden deep beneath her harsh and sometimes fiery exterior shell lies a generous heart.

"I wanted to ask . . ." Stella tries again.

Zia Angela pauses, her hands on the dough as she meets Stella's hesitant look.

"I was wondering if you knew my parents . . . when they were younger," Stella says. Immediately, an image of the young Zia Angela with Stella's father looms in her mind. A kinder, happier version of her aunt.

Zia Angela presses the heels of her hands into the dough with renewed vigor. The question hangs in the air, a tangible thing between them. For a second, Stella forgets to breathe.

After a few moments of heavy silence, her aunt wipes her brow with her forearm and meets Stella's gaze. "Of course. It's a village. We know more about each other than we might wish."

"Do you know . . . why they left here?" Stella asks tentatively.

Zia Angela's expression hardens. "I suppose we have all made our decisions as we think best. Under the circumstances."

Then she wipes her hands on a towel and brings a plate of fried dough to the cantina, where the scores of people are hungry and waiting.

But she gets nothing more, and her aunt remains as distant and inscrutable as the day Stella arrived.

STELLA BEGINS HER DRAWING LESSONS with Sandro on the first day that promises long, bright days to come. Near the rabbit pen, Mariasole's cat sprawls on a sun-kissed patch of earth where the shoots of green are beginning to emerge from the dirt. He squints at them, his languid authority and orange stripes a blazing tribute to the hint of spring in the air. The promise of revitalization and, just maybe, something new and better to come. A new start.

Sandro sits cross-legged on the cold ground, a worn pencil crooked in his left hand and a blank page of his school notebook in his right. Stella watches him quickly give form to a few basic silhouettes of the landscape before them—a single line for the horizon, the vertical masses of the cypresses, and the rough, tumbledown inner beams of the Martinellis' woodshed and pigsties in the distance. The image materializes effortlessly, a whole world brought to life in a few simple lines. It can't be so hard, Stella thinks.

"We start with something simple," he says, and Stella thinks maybe he will have her draw a hill or a tree. Instead, he says, "A face. You draw my face and I'll draw yours. The head and face are just a series of basic shapes. You start with an oval, like this," he says, watching Stella closely while marking a quick oval on the page. "Then you can add the eyes, nose, and mouth." A few deft strokes later, a form begins to emerge.

Stella draws a rough oval on her page.

"That's it. Keep your lines light at first," he says. "Don't press too hard. You can go back over them later to darken them up. You build it little by little."

"Prepare to be impressed." Stella twirls her pencil between her fingers, then frowns in concentration while she darkens the slowly emerging oval while carefully observing Sandro. It seems strange and a bit wondrous, for both of them to sit face-to-face without talking, carefully observing each other. She notices small details—a few faint freckles across his nose, his long lashes, a slight asymmetry in his smile. She sees the boy she thought she knew through fresh eyes, with a deeper understanding.

Stella becomes acutely aware of Sandro's gaze on her, too. It's gentle but intense, as if he can see below the surface of her skin. The air between them charged. Humming with a newfound electricity. There is a tender nervousness, but she also feels a certain safety and trust under Sandro's careful gaze. A kind of connection that is deeper than words. Stella realizes there's a vulnerability in sitting before an artist, to allow yourself to be seen so closely, with such focused scrutiny. Yet, as she holds his gaze, a deep trust blossoms—trust in his respect, his will to see her more closely, more completely than anyone has before.

"How did you learn to do this?" she asks.

He shrugs. "I just started practicing. My father was a stonemason and he built a few buildings in our town," Sandro says. "He always used to say the worth of a man is not in what he owns, but in the work he leaves behind. I guess I always wanted to make something that would stay here long after I'm gone, just like he did."

In this mention of his father's absence, Stella realizes that she and Sandro share in their longing for their parents, in the loss of the familiar places and people of their childhoods. That no matter how lucky they are to be here in Santa Lucia, Stella sees that she and Sandro were once anchored and now find themselves adrift. The fabric of their lives is now a patchwork of ragged holes and unanswered questions.

When Sandro lifts his pencil from the page at last, he hands the drawing to Stella. Now she sees herself in a new light, too. He's captured her likeness, it is true. But there is more. A face that is unmistakably hers yet somehow fresh and even kind.

But when she finishes, her picture looks nothing like his.

She hands him her weak attempt and he falls over in the dirt. Laughing until he can hardly catch his breath. Luigi gets up from his lounging and comes over to rub his cheek against Sandro's head, his tail wrapping slowly. Squints at Stella with his golden eyes.

THE NEXT DAY, Signor Martinelli walks all the way from his farm, avoiding the main road and taking an ancient footpath through the thicket of forest and across vast hectares of grapevines from his farm to the Villa Santa Lucia. He warns Zio Tino that a truck full of Germans inspected one of their neighbors and found them harboring an escaped British soldier. The Germans marched the soldier—and the farmer who was hiding him—into the wheat field and shot them both dead.

AT NEWS THAT the front lines have crossed into Tuscany, some families send their children to the church and the schoolhouse—in case of what, no one is sure.

After she washes the midday dishes, Stella unlatches the door to the wine cellar and steps down the stairs as the now-familiar cold air and fermenting smell fills her senses. She searches for Sandro among the refugees. Most of the men and women have gone out to the fields to work. Sergeant Cakebread is asleep on his pallet. Stella watches him warily, wondering where they might find another place for him. She has heard one of the men say he calls out in English and cries in his sleep, which must put them all at greater risk.

She finds Sandro outside the cellar door, sketching. "Come on," she says. "Let's go to the schoolhouse."

He slides his pencils into a trouser pocket and the two of them start down the path toward the village. In the sweeping vista over the olive groves to the hills beyond, there are wavering flowers blooming in the light green grass. "Signora Bianchi told me some Red Cross nurses dropped off some kids with Father Ramondo and the *maestra*," he says. "They're from up north like you . . . Torino, Milano, Genova . . ." He doesn't have to tell her these are the places where parents have stayed behind to work in factories while they send their children to the countryside for safety. Meanwhile, air raids decimate entire sections of their cities.

In the village, they pass the bakery, the fruit seller, the cobbler, and all the houses, every shutter battened against the growing heat or the Germans or the Fascists. No one knows which anymore. Everyone is indoors, sharing stories and rumors about approaching threats and new regulations imposed upon them.

As the schoolhouse comes into view, Stella feels a wave of nostalgia rise into her chest. But the locked shutters and hushed atmosphere are not the same place she knew. Sandro pulls on the schoolhouse door handle but finds it locked. A rap on the door produces the *maestra*, who brings Stella and Sandro inside and closes the door quickly behind them. The *maestra* looks different, Stella sees. She's no longer in her white smock, but in an old, worn dress.

She's let her long hair down around her shoulders, and Stella thinks this makes her look even more like a teenager.

Stella realizes that everything about the schoolhouse is different now. The once orderly classroom, with its creaky wooden desks lined up like regiments, has transformed into the same kind of makeshift refugee camp as the cantina of Villa Santa Lucia. Some of the children have brought thin pallets from home, and small bags full of clothes, books, beloved toys, and games. In one corner, two small girls are playing *scopa* with a worn deck of cards. Another girl is erasing the board. Presiding over it all, the *maestra* has become a stand-in mother for this ragged crowd of temporary orphans.

"Come join us." The *maestra* puts on a smile and squeezes Stella's thin shoulders from behind. But as Stella steps inside, she hesitates. Not only does the classroom feel foreign, but the composition and appearance of the students have changed. She recognizes a few familiar faces. There is Giulia Rossi and Bruno Daddi, one of Fabio's stupid friends, slumped at a too-small desk. Stella has heard that his father and brothers have gone, whether to the front lines or the secret camps in the woods, no one knows. Stella thinks he looks small and scared, no longer the big bully he was before when he was part of Fabio's entourage. Fabio, for his part, is missing, no doubt staying inside his father's house, the only one in town whose shutters remain open to the spring sunlight.

Stella thinks of the stories she's invented in her mind about Daniele Costa, somewhere out there fighting the English. Called to the colors, as they say. A hundred times, she's imagined what it would be like if her papà finally comes for her. She's conjured images of him walking up the tree-lined dirt road toward Santa Lucia, handsome and smart in his uniform. Coming to pull her into his embrace, just like she always knew he would. *Cucciola!* he would call to her. As if she is a beloved pet.

More than once, she has even considered cutting out her father's face from the old photograph Mariasole produced. She could discard the part with the young Zia Angela, then wedge her father's likeness into her locket across from the picture of her mother. When she closed it, their faces would be pressed together, almost as if they were kissing.

But as Stella gazes upon the children's weary faces, she feels a surge of guilt for inventing such a romantic story about her own phantom of a father, when there are so many children who have lost their actual fathers. Fathers they knew and adored. Fathers who embraced them and carried them and protected them for as long as they could remember. Fathers who have now been torn away from them, leaving their wives and children behind in a pool of anguish and fear.

Among the familiar faces in the schoolroom, there is a large group of new children. A small, haunted-looking girl hugs a ragged stuffed dog, peering out at Stella from her pallet under a table, and for a moment, Stella forgets to breathe. She feels lucky to still have any family at all. If not, any one of these skinny waifs might have been her.

The children rush forward, talking at once to Stella and Sandro. In their excited chatter, she catches a glimmer of the old schoolhouse and realizes now she misses it.

"Cristoforo's father got taken away by the Germans!" one of the boys says.

"That's because someone ratted him out for being an anti-Fascist," another boy interjects.

Stella watches *maestra*'s face turn grave as she listens to the children. Strategically, she interrupts. "And now . . . what have you two been up to?" she asks Stella.

"We've been—" Stella stops short. She knows she's not supposed to tell anyone about the treasures of the Uffizi hidden inside Sir Harwell's villa. "Well, he's been living in the wine cellar," Stella says, shoving Sandro's shoulder playfully, but immediately she regrets it.

"Sandro, if you like, you can come stay here with us," she says.

On the one hand, Stella hopes he will say yes. After all, Stella thinks, Sandro needs a mother. On the other, selfishly, she hopes he'll say no. If Sandro left the Villa Santa Lucia, it would tear another gaping hole in the fabric of Stella's life.

"It's alright, *maestra*," Sandro says. "I'm fine at the villa."

At that response, Stella feels both happy and selfish at the same time.

"Stella and I are teaching each other," he says. "We have our own school. She helps me with my reading and I am teaching her how to draw." Stella thinks of the pages beginning to pile up in her leather folder, her inadequate attempts to remember her mother's face by drawing it. Sandro has taught her about cross-hatching, a way to create shadows and shape that reveals the white of the paper underneath. To Stella's astonishment, she's discovered that drawing darkness reveals light.

"*Perfetto!*" the *maestra* says. "Making art is important when things get difficult. Sometimes, when you can't find words for what you're going through, making something with your hands can help express what's inside. So keep drawing. Both of you."

THE EARTH WARMS and the cicadas emerge from their dusky cocoons. On the first brilliantly blue day in months, a small glimmer of hope shines through and then a German plane flies overhead, raining white leaflets that flutter to the ground like fallen leaves.

Stella and Sandro sit in their outdoor drawing spot. With his characteristic contented detachment, Luigi takes up his place. A small, lazy tiger in the warm grass, his golden eyes narrowing. Sandro runs to pick up one of the fallen, fluttering pages. With slow deliberation, he makes out the words.

"Whoever knows the place where a band . . . band . . . of rebels is in hiding, and does not immediately inform the German army, will be shot." He looks up briefly at Stella, his brown eyes filled with questioning. "Whoever gives food or shelter to a band or to . . . individual . . . rebels will be shot. Every house in which rebels are found, or in which a rebel has stayed, will be blown up. Also every house from which anyone has fired on German troops. In these cases, Germans will take all stores of food, wheat, straw, cattle. Inhabitants shot. The German army will proceed with justice but inflexible hardness."

The next day, Allied planes drop their own leaflets directed at the people hiding in the woods. *At all costs, refrain from reporting yourselves to the Army. Commit acts of sabotage on the communication lines. Enter into contact with foreigners in the German army. Go on organizing groups. The moment for decisive action is near at hand.*

In the wine cellar, the families cluster together and read these leaflets with a mixture of fear and hope. Most of all, they try to interpret what it means for their own fates. All they want is an end to the interminable suffering, a solution that will bring their husbands and sons and fathers back to them. And they just want to go home.

Stella's eyes search the sky, looking for answers that loom ominously overhead.

ON SUNDAY, the village church is filled to bursting. The usually serene space is now bustling and loud with conversation, full of not only villagers but a good portion of the two hundred or so people who have taken refuge in Sir Harwell's wine cellar and the several dozen children hunkered down in the schoolhouse. As Stella's family kneels in their pew, more people fill the church. Everyone is scared and seeking solace from the new threats. Plus, there is nowhere else for anyone to go.

Father Ramondo rushes around his sanctuary, looking harried, his thin hair sticking up in wisps as he cursorily bows before the main altar and then rushes over to the lectern. Nervously flips pages in his missal.

Before the mass gets started, Stella points up to one of the Santa Lucia frescoes. Leans into Sandro. "You see how the artist was trying to show three-dimensional space?" She repeats something Father Ramondo taught the children, about how for many centuries artists only depicted space with overlapping figures. But then, in the Renaissance, they became more interested in showing depth and giving the viewer a feeling of looking into a real space, even though a painting is a flat, two-dimensional wall.

Watching Sandro's eyes grow round, Stella feels not just proud to impress him with her newfound knowledge, but excited to open his eyes to something wondrous he didn't see before, just as Sandro has done for her in the treasure room. Stella feels the start of something, a twinge of an emotion she's never felt. It feels warm and good to exchange experiences with another person her age, especially to share in the wonder and beauty of something she is only beginning to discover.

As a stirring chorus of disparate voices fills the air, Stella senses a reawakening of solidarity among the people of Santa Lucia. Whether locals or reluctant guests. Whether peasants from the surrounding farms, refugee children, teachers, or runaway soldiers. All have found refuge in this remote corner of the world. They are a ragged group of humanity clustered together in this little place, all experiencing common tribulations and common dreams for brighter days.

AFTER THE MASS, Stella and Sandro trudge up the dirt road toward the villa.

As they approach the great staircase leading to the villa's front door, they see new cars that weren't there before. Two strange-looking motorcycles parked in the dust.

Stella pushes the front door quietly. Through the crack in the door, the sun shines brightly. They step into the courtyard to find Zio Tino. And a half dozen German soldiers in a circle around him.

CHAPTER 7

GUESTS OF HONOR

Summer 1944

Most of my fellow painters would agree that to let art perish is to let the very soul of the artist wither. That is because an original work made by an artist cannot be torn apart from his spirit, and that is not easily replicated. They would say we must stand as guardians of our own legacies. But some days I wonder if I might be better off throwing all of it onto the flames with my own hands.

—FROM THE LOST DIARIES OF SANDRO
BOTTICELLI, FLORENCE, SUMMER 1480

When the final column of Wehrmacht troops came through Tuscany, they knew at last they were on the losing side of the war and there was no mercy . . . They destroyed or stripped whatever they wanted without the slightest regard for the artistic patrimony of Italy. Nor a human life.

—FROM THE DIARY OF CAPTAIN WALLACE E.
FOSTER, MONUMENTS OFFICER OF THE FIFTH
ARMY IN TUSCANY, AUGUST 1944

After all the atrocities they have heard about at the hands of German soldiers, Stella prepares for the worst.

Instead, she thinks, these men only look exhausted. Sunburnt, sweating, hollow-eyed. Their uniforms and faces are streaked with dirt. Stella presses Sandro into the aisle of the courtyard and they duck behind an arch.

Zio Tino stands in the middle of the tall men, his palms upward. "You can't stay here, *signori*. We have nothing for you."

Only German in response. Abrupt and biting words. No understanding.

Stella watches two of the soldiers leave the circle and begin to explore the courtyard. The men wear loose-fitting uniforms, their chests and hips crisscrossed with straps and small equipment bags. Through the open front door, Stella watches two more trucks arrive. A few more Germans disembark and loiter around their vehicles. They remove their tight-fitting helmets to reveal sweating, dust-covered faces.

A broad-shouldered man who looks like he could be in charge approaches Zio Tino. To Stella, his rapid German sounds like a barking dog, and she thinks her uncle looks brave, facing off with this man who is a full head and shoulders taller. A few other men begin strolling around the courtyard, cupping their hands to windows, their eyes scanning the upper galleries and roofline. One of the men passes close to where Stella and Sandro are standing, and they press themselves against the wall. Freeze.

"You are not supposed to enter this building," Zio Tino says, wagging his hands together as if he is praying.

Suddenly, Zia Angela appears at her husband's side. Her battle-ready expression is all too familiar to Stella, her beady, black eyes trained on the newcomers, her lips pursed as if she's sucked on a lemon. She produces the stamped letter from Generalfeldmarschall

Kesselring, which she's procured from the drawer in the dining hall. Stella recognizes the letter Signor Poggi left behind with them.

Zio Tino takes Kesselring's note from his wife and hands it to the man. Stella perceives the smallest tremor in her uncle's hand. "Please," he says. "You must move on from here. You don't have the authority to enter, *signori*."

Stella watches the German slowly unfold the paper and scan it with his eyes. From the shadows of the archway, Stella can see the official-looking stamps and the looping signature of Germany's highest commander in Italy. Surely this will end the standoff, Stella thinks, as soon as the German reads the order. They will soon depart the same way they arrived.

Instead, the German utters a few unintelligible words and flicks the paper away. It flutters and lands on the cobblestones. Then he pulls a cigarette from a crumpled pack in one of his many uniform pockets, and cups his hand around a match. For a few long moments, there is a drawn-out silence and a slow, single exhale of smoke from the man's mouth.

Next, he barks out a loud order and Stella flinches. The other men break from the circle. They fan out, hands on their weapons, poring over every inch of the courtyard. Stella and Sandro press their backs against the stucco wall. One man disappears down a dark corridor toward the old medieval heart of the villa, where two men begin to walk up the stairs. Another heads toward the wing with the kitchen and dining room. Stella wonders where her cousins are, and if they know the Germans are here at all.

"*Aspetta!*" Zia Angela calls. She stomps after one of the men as if she intends to chase him right out of the building herself. Zio Tino grasps her arm and she spins around, stopping, her angry eyes following the men as they begin to crawl across the villa like an army of ants.

At last, an interpreter appears.

The man is tall and lean, with closely cropped blond hair and a struggling mustache. The same uniform as the others, with a few more patches. His Italian isn't perfect, but he makes himself understood. He tells Zio Tino that he's the men's commanding officer and they have explicit instructions to requisition the villa. They have been traveling all the way up from Calabria and no matter what Kesselring's letter says, they have stayed at countless country houses just like this one. They have orders. Also, he says, the men will need beds and food. Some of them need shoes, if they have any to spare. If they don't cooperate willingly, he explains politely, they might be forced instead.

By this time, Zio Stefano has appeared in the courtyard. He comes to stand beside Zio Tino and Zia Angela. The three of them look small and worn in the face of these tall intruders who have suddenly spread out across the house.

"Look! Wait," Zio Tino says. "It would be un-Christian of us to turn you away. You must be weary after all you have endured. *Prego.* You will be our guests."

Zia Angela turns her head slowly, looking at her husband as if seeing him for the first time. As if he has suddenly lost his mind.

"Angela," he says, "fire up the stove. You and Stella will make them a nice plate of pasta. And let's find the *commandante* a bottle of our finest cherry brandy. I'm sure we can make you comfortable, *signori.*" Zio Stefano heads toward the cantina to unearth one of Sir Harwell's treasured bottles.

The German commander nods and yells something in German to the other men left in the courtyard.

"You'd better go," Stella whispers to Sandro. "Tell everyone downstairs what's happening. Lock the doors and tell everyone to stay put. Don't come upstairs or let anyone go outside. Not for anything."

He hesitates.

"Don't worry," she says. "Zio Tino will know what to do."

With trepidation, she watches Sandro slip out the front door and run around the house toward the wine cellar in the waning light. Then she goes to Sir Harwell's kitchen to help her aunt prepare something for the intruders while the men fan out. Searching.

STELLA'S COUSINS FINALLY APPEAR in the courtyard and Zia Angela looks like she will fall over with relief. She pulls all three girls into the kitchen. "Do not leave this room unless I leave it with you."

For the next hour, Zia Angela and the girls cobble together dinner in anxious silence. They know how to make things last, how to make a lot of food with a few ingredients and precious supplies. As they've done all winter and spring for themselves and the dozens of people in the cantina, they prepare a simple dish of hand-rolled pasta with basil and bright green olive oil.

While some of the enlisted men erect tents in the olive grove, Stella's uncles prepare the dining hall for a group of the highest ranking among the Germans. The men take all the seats around the broad table. Stella and her family stay in the kitchen.

Zio Tino stands in the dining hall, a reluctant host to the dozen or so men who remove their hats and take their places at the table. The one man who speaks some Italian says his name is Captain Rolf Bauer. He says he's from Munich but he's been all across Italy and Poland, too. He tells Stella's uncles some of the other men at the table have been in Russia and France, but one of them has already seen combat in three different countries. Most of them haven't been home in more than four years, he says. Stella realizes the men around the table must be much younger than they look. One of them says he's been away from home since he was sixteen.

After the men clean every last crumb on their plates, Zio Stefano produces a bottle of Sir Harwell's brandy. Through the doorway,

Stella watches the men swill the liquid the color of blood in their glasses. Sitting tall and mute like toy soldiers. Captain Bauer says the role of their unit is to go ahead of the front-line soldiers in order to requisition oil, wine, sheep, wheat, and other things the troops may need. Their rations from Germany are not arriving anymore, he says, and they need to procure things locally instead. They will pay them in exchange for supplies, he informs Stella's uncles, showing them a roll of German military payment vouchers attached with a leather strap to his belt.

After the men eat and the girls have cleared the table, Zia Angela lays the strange-looking vouchers out on the wooden block in the kitchen. Stella runs her fingers over the odd bills with their long, indecipherable German words printed on them. She wonders how you could exchange one of these for anything, when there's nothing left to buy anywhere.

"I'd rather them leave this place than take their dirty money," Zia Angela says. But she rolls the vouchers into a small wad and shoves it into the strap of her brassiere anyway.

STELLA KNOWS she's supposed to stay in the kitchen but instead, while Zia Angela is drying the dishes, she slips down to the wine cellar. She descends the dank stairwell and makes her way through the crowds of people, the shadowed outline of barrels and crates, until she finds Sandro on his pallet.

"Are you alright?" she whispers.

He nods, his big brown eyes flashing.

In a dark recess between two barrels, Signora Romano is crying. Her three small daughters huddle beside her, eyes wide. "We don't want to leave now. It took so much out of us just to get here," she says. Stella sees that some of the others have already packed their sparse belongings and are ready to head out to the mine-cratered roads at a moment's notice. Stella dares to consider what might happen when the Germans discover the wine cellar.

"Let me stay in the treasure room," Sandro whispers to Stella, as if reading her mind. "Come on. Surely it's safer. No one will know." Sandro rolls up his blanket and tucks a few notebooks under his arm.

While Stella's uncles work out the details of the Germans' occupation of the house, Stella's aunt and cousins wipe down the table in the dining hall.

Stella and Sandro dart across the dark courtyard. And she lets Sandro into the treasure room and locks the door behind him. Slides the key between the stones.

LONG AFTER THE SUN DISAPPEARS behind the dark green hills, Zia Angela orders the girls to quickly pack their suitcases. Stella and her cousins find Zia Angela stuffing clothing into a suitcase of her own. Whispering to herself.

"I refuse to let the girls stay in that bedroom by themselves," she says to Zio Tino. "We can make room for their mattresses in here. At least for tonight." Stella's aunt has let her hair, thick and streaked with gray, down from its tight bun. It hangs over the shoulders of her worn nightdress. Outside the shuttered window, the sky is moonless and cloaked in black. Her aunt and uncle's makeshift bedchamber is now a claustrophobic crucible of anxiety. Stella can hardly breathe in the stifled air. Zio Tino, in his striped bedclothes, sits on the edge of the bed, his face lined and serious. Sweating.

Stella sets her own worn suitcase on the floor. It's the same one she brought with her all the way from Torino. She unearths a dusty memory of hastily packing a few changes of clothes, a hairbrush and toothbrush. A dress that Stella has already outgrown since she's been here in Tuscany. And a letter for Zio Tino from her mother. Seems a lifetime ago.

"Where are we going, mamma?" Mariasole asks quietly, her eyes wide. She's tossed a stuffed dog and a few mismatched pieces of clothing into her own bag, which she heaves into the room with all her strength.

"If we have to, we can make a run for the woods!" Livia says. "We won't be alone out there."

"I don't know," Zia Angela says, her brow knotted, "but I for one would just as soon leave this minute."

From his perch on the edge of the bed, Zio Tino scratches his head. "Where would we go, Angelina? Every farm around here is just like ours. Sheltering refugees, maybe even partisans and escaped soldiers. Boys who have slipped out of their conscriptions. That in itself is a risk . . . perhaps greater than the one we have on our hands here."

Zia Angela slumps down on the bed beside her husband.

"Besides," he continues, "there are mines on the roads. How would you know how to recognize them?"

Stella thinks of the many people she's seen carrying everything on their backs for days on end. And Sergeant Cakebread in the wine cellar with half his foot blown off. She imagines that could happen to any one of them, too.

"But if we leave," Livia says, "what will happen to the villa?"

Zio Tino's mouth draws into a thin line. "I've heard all the hotels have been turned into clinics or barracks for German soldiers. There is no guarantee of anywhere for us to stay, even if we could get there."

Zia Angela stands abruptly and starts shoving things chaotically into her bag. "I'm leaving," she says again weakly.

"No," Zio Tino says, sighing. "We are better off here with a roof over our heads. Even with our . . . guests."

Zia Angela sits back on the edge of the bed and puts her face in her hands. She takes the strange-looking German payment vouchers out of her skinny bosom, where they unfurl on the bedcover. "They could be here for weeks, months . . ." she continues. "I don't think I can take it." In the dark, she looks like she has aged twenty years in a day.

"At least we hid as many of the Harwells' things as we could," Livia says. "I don't think they'll find anything."

But Zia Angela only shakes her head and bites a ragged thumbnail. "It seemed like such a desperate thing to do," she says. "All that time ago. Burying Lady Harwell's jewelry under some rosemary," she says. "We should have been closing the whole house instead. Now look at us! We are like innkeepers for the worst kinds of unwanted guests. And with that . . . that, that Eng . . . that *man* downstairs! We have to get him out of this house. They will shoot us, Tino."

Zio Tino doesn't respond at first. Stella thinks he looks like he's trying to think of a place to send Sergeant Cakebread. He puts his hand on his wife's back. "I don't think they want to shoot us," Zio Tino says. "Otherwise, how would they manage? They are relying on us to feed them and give them supplies they need. I think they just want a place to stay until they can get home. They need us to cook for them. They want to pay us . . ."

"I don't want their dirty money!" she snaps, brushing the unfurled vouchers off the bed.

"But they look like they've been through Hell. And perhaps they have already lost," he says.

"Zio Tino . . . the paintings," Stella says.

A shadow falls over Zio Tino's face, but he says nothing.

Surely they won't stay. Her aunt's words ring in her head.

But the days tick by and Stella's worn suitcase remains tucked in the corner of her aunt and uncle's bedroom.

The Germans stay. Stella and her cousins, aunt, uncles, and all the refugees stay. Sergeant Cakebread stays.

No one dares to go anywhere.

OVER THE NEXT TWO DAYS, the Germans—paratroopers, Zio Tino says—settle into the villa as if it were a fancy hotel.

"And then they left their filthy boot prints all over the rug in Sir Harwell's bedroom," Zia Angela says, whispering between gritted teeth while she rolls out the pasta. Her hands are rough and caked with flour, the muscles of her forearms stout from the years of repeating this activity countless times. She looks as if she might just as well flatten one of the men as a roll of dough. Below the fabric skirt under the sink, Luigi peers out from the darkness, as if he is hiding, too. His eyes round and glassy, reflecting the light.

"What happens if we refuse to serve them?" Stella whispers back.

"Hmph," her aunt says, looking at her conspiratorially. "Exactly my opinion. But your uncle won't have it. He insists on treating them like guests of honor instead."

Upstairs, the men have taken over all the bedrooms, all except for the one where the girls have dragged their mattresses to sleep under the watchful eye of Zio Tino and Zia Angela.

Bored, the men fan out, opening cabinets and doors, climbing and descending the stairs, taking turns in the watchtower.

Stella and Sandro must abandon their lessons. In the cantina, the refugees stay quiet or go out to work in the fields and outbuildings, keeping their heads down. Zio Tino tells Signora Bianchi to warn Sergeant Cakebread not to open his mouth or move from his cot for any reason.

In the evening, before they turn the lights out to sleep, Stella asks her uncle about the paintings again. She thinks about the beautiful masterpieces sitting in the dark rooms. Her uncles pace day and night in front of the doors, watching.

He runs a thick palm over his stubbled jaw. "We have to reach Signor Poggi," Zio Tino says. Even though he is uneducated, just a driver, Stella thinks her uncle is brave to bear the burden of such a responsibility. He always looks elegant in his dark suit and tie. But now, he seems vulnerable in a white undershirt while he gets ready for bed. "We can't have the pictures here anymore. It's too risky. I've held them off as long as I can but I don't know how much longer we can do so. I just don't know how to reach him."

Stella imagines Sir Harwell returning to an empty villa. Her uncle, if he was still here, would be disgraced. Dismissed.

"Maybe we should send the girls down to the church or the schoolhouse," Zio Tino says. "Get them out of this house. Out of this inn of unwanted guests, as you say."

"No!" Zia Angela blurts, pulling Mariasole to her. The girl's body looks small and slight under her mother's bony grip. "I refuse to let them out of my sight. The girls will stay here with us. Including Stella."

THE GERMAN COMMANDER, Captain Bauer, is tall and lean, with wheat-colored hair and stark blue eyes. His dark mustache looks like it's been enhanced with the same polish used to shine his shoes. He's told Zio Tino that some of the paratroopers were dropped near Chiusi and they are supposed to go ahead of the front lines to secure supplies. Zio Tino's assessment turns out to be correct: they don't want to shoot Stella's family, at least not today; they only want them to put a roof over their heads and supply them with whatever they need.

Still, the way they walk around as if they own the place . . . Stella imagines her aunt and uncles must not be happy about this, after the way they have kept the house meticulous for Sir Harwell. The way they have taken pride in making every surface gleam, everything in its place.

From the corridor near her aunt and uncle's bedroom, she watches the men collect around small tables in the great room. Captain Bauer and several other officers smoke cigarettes, looking up at the painted ceiling while a few other men deal a round of cards for another game.

Stella imagines that German mothers must not teach their children even the most basic of manners. The men leave food and drinks all around. Glasses with the dregs of wine stuck to the bottom lay around for days and Stella can't wash them out. One of the toilets in the upstairs hallway is clogged and reeking. Instead of trying to fix it, the men simply relieve themselves in the garden. Even the hillside closest to the upper terrace now stinks of urine. The men take turns in the tower. Night and day, there are armed men climbing the narrow, winding stair to the top, where they survey the landscape with their binoculars.

Zia Angela has instructed the girls to stay out of their way. To keep their heads down and make themselves invisible. Stella and her cousins are rarely out of sight of Zia Angela. All three girls are resigned to their chores, confined to the kitchen or *lavatoio* for hours per day. So many mouths to feed with so few supplies. School is a distant memory. So is the precious time she and Sandro spent in the treasure room, sharing their own drawing and reading skills. Stella misses all of it.

The saving grace is that Zia Angela no longer complains about or corrects Stella's cooking. Knead until spongy. Roll it out. Cut it with a mezzaluna. Roll it up on your thumb. Put it on a floured board and knead it until there is flour on your arms up to your elbows. Boil the water. Press the tomatoes. Add the salt. Stir the sauce until it coats every ridge and tube in the pasta. Dump the slippery mass of pasta into a bowl and stir. Start again.

ONE MORNING, as long streaks of sunshine dry the puddles of standing water left over after a thunderstorm, Stella enters the kitchen and immediately stops. There is a feeling of tautness, a tension that wasn't there before. Through the doorway to the dining room, she sees Zio Tino and Zia Angela seated at the dining table, their backs upright. Across the table from them are Captain Bauer along with the mayor, Signor Bagnoli, with his bulging middle and flushed cheeks. Alongside his father is Fabio.

Stella hasn't seen Fabio since school was suspended. He looks like he's grown a head taller and a year older in a matter of weeks, Stella thinks. His jaw has become square and taut. He looks like he has already started to shave. He is a miniature version of his father, complete with dark hair slicked back using the same *brillantina*. A cold ripple of unease moves down her spine as she stands just out of view, listening to the conversation. Soon enough, the reason for Mayor Bagnoli's appearance becomes clear. He's trying to ingratiate himself with the Germans, making it clear he's on the side of the German-controlled puppet government commanding the brutal Fascist militias they say are moving northward from Rome.

"Il Duce's new government has declared the formation of a special tribunal," he tells Captain Bauer. "I assure you those who speak against us will be tried. Especially those who have betrayed their faith by switching to the other side and spoken out against the regime." He looks conspiratorially at Captain Bauer, seeming to seek his agreement or approval.

In spite of this impassioned vitriol on the part of the mayor, Stella thinks Captain Bauer looks bored. He rolls the tip of his cigarette in the ashtray. A hushed silence falls over the room, interrupted only by the subtle shuffle of feet. Zia Angela sits rigid in her chair, her arms crossed, looking sidelong at the mayor.

The mayor's gaze sweeps over the room again, locking onto Stella's aunt and uncle. "I trust you are not harboring any Italian defected soldiers among the derelicts in your wine cellar, *signori*?" There is a long, uncomfortable pause. Stella feels her chest clench.

"What do you think, Giorgio?" Zio Tino retorts.

The mayor nods. "Needless to say, it would be inadvisable—"

"We've already checked the cantina," Captain Bauer says.

The mayor nods. "They've already made an example of one of our farmers. The Germans held him hostage until he gave up the soldiers hiding in his pigsties. He's lucky he gave them away. Otherwise he may not have escaped with his life. I wouldn't want to see the same happen to you, my friends. You do not want to find yourselves in trouble."

"Any word from your older son, mayor?" Zia Angela asks. Stella thinks of Alessio, Livia's intended, somewhere out there. Maybe even in Germany.

The mayor is silent for a moment, then says, "I'm afraid not." He stands and Fabio stands with him. The encounter has lasted only minutes, but to Stella it seems like hours have passed since she's been standing just the other side of the doorjamb.

Mariasole races into the kitchen now, tying apron strings behind her back. Immediately, Stella puts her index finger in front of her lips. Mariasole ducks behind the flour-covered table where they roll the pasta shapes. Zia Angela does not say goodbye to Fabio and his father. She only scrapes back her chair, turns her back to the men, and returns to the kitchen, dirty espresso cups clenched in her bony hands.

"Seems we are in trouble enough already," Stella says.

"Not a word." Zia Angela places the cups in the sink and shoots the girls a warning glance. "Get to work on the dough."

Stella rolls the ball of dough onto the table and watches the mayor exit the dining room.

STELLA WALKS TO THE WELL to fill a bucket with water and sees Mayor Bagnoli and Fabio marching back toward the village down the dusty path. The overinflated and ridiculous-looking Fabio following closely alongside his father.

Around the gardens and the grounds of the villa, an oppressive silence hangs in the air. You would never know there are more than two hundred people huddled in the wine cellar. Stella's eyes scan the landscape for Sandro. She expects to see him sitting on his rock, sketching. But there is no one. The old wooden doors to the cellar remain closed, bolted. As far as she knows, he is alone and perhaps even lonely in the treasure room; she can't help but feel envious. She looks for an excuse to dart into the room with him and bask in the quiet splendor of the paintings.

Stella spies one of the German soldiers leaning out one of the upper windows of the villa, a cigarette clutched between his fingers like a claw, looking out at the horizon. He turns his gaze to Stella, studying her while he takes a deep drag on his cigarette. He exhales a swift plume of smoke and half smiles at her. Then winks.

The vision leaves her unsettled to the depth of her gut. Stella quickly fills her bucket and hurries back to the kitchen.

LONG PAST THE DINNER HOUR, the Germans loiter at the table. The once-golden hues of sunset have given way to the soft luminescence of candlelight and a black night sky. Stella's stomach rumbles. The men are drunk and it is late. One has fallen asleep, or passed out, on the table, his arms sprawled across the wood. The dining room reverberates with the discordant melody of foreign voices and laughter.

No one listens to the nightly broadcast anymore because the soldiers have overtaken their evening routine, and Stella and her family are little more than unwitting servants. The crackling airways that used to be the nervous center of the family's evening routine have been silenced, replaced by a cacophony of German chatter and drunken laughter. The men have finished the plates of *pici* that Stella and her cousins and aunt have made, and the table is strewn with dirty plates and glasses. The room filled with cigarette smoke.

At the latest burst of laugher among the men, Stella sees something change in Zio Tino's demeanor, as if he's put on armor. He walks into the dining room, his mouth a thin line. He begins to stack and clear the plates loudly.

"It's our turn to eat now, *signori*," Stella's uncle says. "*Buona notte!*"

Zio Tino begins clearing the mess, stacking dirty plates and clanging together stained wine glasses. The men at the table don't follow his words but they understand soon enough. The ones who haven't already fallen asleep scrape their chairs back from the table. They rouse their drunken friends and stagger out into the courtyard.

Stella thinks Zio Tino sounds full of confidence, but when he returns to the kitchen, his face looks like it's lost all color and the dirty plates rattle as he sets them on the counter next to Zia Angela.

AT THE TOP of the stairs to the wine cellar, Stella pauses to let her eyes adjust to the darkness. She balances a basket of bread on one hip and lets the fingers of her other hand trace the cracked plaster wall as the damp air grows colder with each step along the sagging stair treads. There is the sickly sweet smell of damp fermentation, familiar yet nearly overwhelming every time.

Below, the dim light brings shifting shadows and murmurs. Beyond the cellar door to the hillside, a dark sky has descended, the rain pouring from the roof tiles, splashing the rocks where Stella and Sandro did their lessons. Relentless, like the distant drumbeat of an impending battle.

As Stella reaches the bottom stairs, Ornella Rivelli—a young woman who, strangely, looks to Stella both skinny and pregnant at the same time—appears from the shadows. "There are more of them here," she whispers, and moves her head to the side.

Stella follows the direction of her gaze and sees two men she doesn't recognize, hesitating in the darkness. The older of the two with a salt-and-pepper beard, his face etched with lines. The younger man has raven-black hair and haunted eyes. They shift nervously near the cellar door, seemingly unable to come all the way inside but reticent to go back out into the rain and the dark night. Stella thinks they must be desperate with hunger and exhaustion to enter a building with German trucks and motorcycles parked in the dirt outside.

"They came from Bologna and Verona," Ornella whispers. "They said everyone is running away, no matter whether they are officers or enlisted. They don't dare to board the German trains."

In the corner, Sergeant Cakebread is writing something in a small leather-bound journal, his leg now wrapped and bound in strips of cloth, propped up in front of him. His hat covering his fair hair. Zio Stefano has fashioned a crutch from a couple of tree limbs lashed together with twine. Now, Stella sees it propped against a wine cask. Stella's heart aches to think how homesick he must be, how unable to help himself he is. And how much in danger. There is no way he could flee like these other men.

The room is filled with exhausted souls, each one fighting his or her own battle. Her heart sinks to think of all of them sleeping in the dark cellar, with its dank earthen walls and silvery cobwebs in the corners. On another side of the room, a mother sits nursing a large baby, the woman's hair falling loose around her shoulders. Beside her, her husband stretches out.

And Stella, so fortunate with a warm bed, and a basket of bread on her hip.

Stella approaches the new men and hands them some bread. "You can't stay," she tells them. She fears she sounds harsh and cold like her aunt.

One of the men tears the loaf and chews it like a starving dog. "I'm sorry."

"Don't worry, signorina," the man with the beard says. "We will be out of your way. Thank you for your kindness."

She watches them slip out the cellar door into the pelting rain and she feels sad for them. Says a prayer that they will remember the directions the older men gave them, and be able find their way in the dark.

THE NEXT MORNING, the sun is bright, the wine cellar door stands propped open, and some of the men and women go out to work in the muddy vineyard. Stella is surprised to find Sandro at the edge of the kitchen garden with his sketchbook and pencils. "I slipped out the window when the sun came out," he says.

"Let's go to the treasure room for our lessons." She pulls on Sandro's hand. "Everyone is busy. They won't notice I'm gone for a bit."

Sandro hesitates. "What will your uncles say? They don't want anyone in there."

"How will they know?" Stella sees his eyes sparkle. A streak of mischievousness. "Come on. We already know where the key is. You know that."

Stella thinks if they're caught, her uncle might forgive them but her aunt might beat her back into shape anyway. But looking at Sandro's bright, conspiratorial expression, how can she resist? She is hungry for the spark of friendship and an escape from the laborious monotony of German servitude.

Crouching, Stella and Sandro move swiftly along the massive foundation of the villa, a carpet of olive trees descending steeply down the hillside. Stella searches the windows above, expecting to see one of the Germans leaning out, smoking, looking to the horizon with his binoculars, or at her with a leering gaze. But the villa is quiet. She feels a rush of excitement to be off on a mission together, right under the noses of the soldiers and even her family.

Sandro follows Stella up the terrace staircase, and they slip through a back door into a long, dark corridor. They pass a series of large paintings that were part of Signor Poggi's second delivery, too large to fit in the treasure room. Zio Tino has told Stella they were painted by a man named Fra Angelico, who was a monk as well as an accomplished painter in his monastery in Florence. There is an overwhelming stench of urine in the corridor. The Germans have been using it as a latrine.

"*Che schifo,*" she hears Sandro say behind her. He holds his nose but stops, stupefied by the quiet beauty of an angel's wing painted as if it reflected the light of a heavenly rainbow. Stella wonders why the Germans don't seem to see the paintings in the same way that she and Sandro do.

"Hurry up!" Stella whispers loudly. He turns reluctantly from the beautiful angel wing and follows Stella. They tiptoe quickly along one of the aisles in the main courtyard. Stella fishes in the hiding place for the key and unlocks the door to the treasure room. They dart inside and close the door quietly behind them, locking it. The air is stifling.

"I can't open the shutters," she says. "It's too risky."

With a sense of quiet excitement and reverence, they walk together in the familiar pattern of making their rounds as their eyes adjust to the darkness. At the end, Sandro lowers himself to the ground in front of the enormous painting with the label that says "Sandro Botticelli." He crosses his legs, opens his sketchbook, and begins to run his pencil over the page. She watches him focus on the blindfolded angel who has drawn back its bow, ready to shoot.

Stella tucks her skirt underneath her legs as she sits on the tile floor next to Sandro. All around the room are small stacks of paper, every inch of them covered in Sandro's drawings.

"What do you think the blindfolded baby is doing?" Stella whispers.

"He's shooting an arrow from his bow to make them fall in love."

Stella squints in the dimness, looking at the figure who is about to be shot through with the blindfolded baby's arrow. Not knowing what will happen next. Is that how it feels when you fall in love? Stella wonders. A sudden, sharp stab to the heart that changes everything in an instant?

Stella looks at the lush, green garden, a carpet of flowers. And then at the tall, slender blue man blowing a gust of air from his mouth. Stella thinks he looks like the wind. He blows his visible breath onto a woman who looks like she is on the verge of transforming into a flower. A metamorphosis. Even in the darkness, there is an aura of golden light, an overall sense of serenity.

"You didn't want to go to the schoolhouse with the others?" Stella asks, observing him carefully. Stella thinks that the *maestra* is kind of like a mother, even though she doesn't have any children yet. Stella thinks Sandro needs a mother. Maybe.

But Sandro only shakes his head. "I didn't want to leave here. How could I leave . . ." For a fraction of a second, Stella thinks he will say *how could I leave you* but instead, he says, "How could I leave all this?" His brown eyes scan the room full of wonders.

"Even with all the Germans here?"

He nods. "Even so."

Stella shows Sandro one of the crumpled payment vouchers Captain Bauer left behind on the dining table. The two of them put their heads together and nearly fall over laughing when they try to pronounce the words printed on it.

"So, the most important question . . ." Sandro whispers. "Have you put dirt in their pasta yet?"

Stella giggles, and for a moment everything else falls away. Their heads bent together, it's just the two of them, co-conspirators in a magical universe all their own. Stella thinks it can't get any better than right now. Germans and all.

But then, she remembers what Zio Tino told her.

"Zio Tino says he's looking for a way to get the paintings back to Florence. Back to Signor Poggi." Sandro's face falls and Stella immediately regrets sharing this bit of information. Breaking the spell. "But he can't reach anyone," she says quickly, giving him a weak smile. "Zio Tino says the pictures speak to him."

"They speak to me, too," Sandro says. "They give me hope that there will be life again after all this."

"I won't let the paintings leave," she says. She knows it's a lie, because how could she begin to have any control over what happens to any one of the magical paintings in the treasure room? All the same, he gives her a smile that seems to light him up from the inside out. A small spark that, for the moment, keeps the flicker of wonder alive.

CHAPTER 8

PORTRAIT OF A MAN

Summer 1944

All perfect things in God's creation emerge from darkness. And so I always begin with a wash of black paint. Colors and shapes and forms and distance and motion and balance—everything that is meaningful in a painting—only come into being when they are exposed, bit by bit, to the light.

> —FROM THE LOST DIARIES OF SANDRO
> BOTTICELLI, FLORENCE, SUMMER 1480

The superintendency did everything in its power to protect these masterpieces of human achievement. But by a certain point, it had no more resources, and neither the Italian Fascists nor the German leaders would offer any more trucks or gasoline to transfer the works. Until a new plan could be made, German troops had already requisitioned some of the countryside repositories and there was no controlling what decisions they made of their own accord.

> —FROM THE DIARY OF CAPTAIN WALLACE E.
> FOSTER, MONUMENTS OFFICER OF THE FIFTH
> ARMY IN TUSCANY, AUGUST 1944

Stella is roughly cutting pancetta and rosemary under the same blade when Father Ramondo appears, sweating in his black cassock. Stella hears him talking quietly with her uncles in the courtyard. She is surprised the priest is not afraid to come to the house with the Germans there. Up to now, only the mayor and Fabio—along with a few desperate travelers—have been brave enough to knock on the door.

"Make *padre* a plate." Zia Angela nudges Stella.

Stella has gotten better at getting the sauce right, following her aunt's lead. She has learned how to drain the pasta, then return it to the pan, carefully coating the surfaces and insides of each noodle with the sauce made of rabbit meat, tomato, garlic, and pieces of rosemary growing wild on the hillside. Stella grates a little pecorino and brings it to the cramped table in the kitchen. The family has given up trying to do anything in the dining hall save for serve German soldiers.

"Grazie, *cara*," Father Ramondo says, crossing himself as she sets a steaming plate in front of the old round priest. He mumbles a few quick, garbled words of gratitude to the Lord, and then says to Stella's uncles, "I will write to the archbishop. But I can't guarantee my letter will arrive. Our communications have been all but cut off. I've tried to reach my brothers at San Marco as well. But I haven't gotten a response. Might as well be separated from Florence by an ocean."

Zio Tino nods, digging into his own dish. Zio Stefano piles some of Stella's pasta onto his plate. "Perhaps the archbishop could reach Signor Poggi—or anyone at the Uffizi. We need to get these paintings out of here. No one could have foreseen . . ."

"I understand, but my fear is that the Florentines have too much to worry about right now to bring them back into the city; they have their own problems," Father Ramondo continues. "I had a brief visit from a priest friend on his way out of Florence. He says there are German soldiers swarming all over the city. There is hardly anything to eat. People can do little more than find food and avoid getting shot. All the bridges are mined. And the new Italian SS, no help at all. They say they are modeled on the German system, but mostly it's just a bunch of seventeen-year-old boys playing with guns and hand grenades. The art will have to wait, I'm afraid, my friend. It is far down on their list of priorities. I'm sure they are just glad the paintings are in the countryside at all." He digs back into his dinner plate.

Stella watches Zio Tino's shoulders slump with the weight of this news. "Even if they can't take the paintings back . . . I just would like to reach Signor Poggi somehow. I don't know how else to get a message to him. He must know that the villa is full of Germans now. Surely, if he knew . . ."

"Sounds like he has other things to think about," Stella's aunt says. She flits around the kitchen like a moth trapped inside a lantern, the electric lights harsh and glaring.

Father Ramondo contemplates silently for a moment. "I have an idea," he says finally. "You know a few partisans have come out from the city," he says.

Stella stops wiping a dish with a damp rag.

Father Ramondo's voice lowers. "They've set up camps in the hills not far from here," he continues, gesturing to the window as if they could see them from the kitchen table. "They seem to have an ability to move from one place to another more freely than anyone else. I suspect they have figured out how to circumvent the German checkpoints."

"*Partigiani* . . ." Stella says aloud, but immediately her aunt puts her tight hands on Stella's shoulders and shushes her.

Zio Tino's face looks suddenly grave and he lowers his voice.

"It's not good news," he says. "It will put everyone in the village in greater danger. Best if they move on from here. The last thing we need. It won't take anything to start a gunfight."

Father Ramondo nods. "Yes. I have advised them to stay away from the church. I have refugees staying with me too, you know. In the church and the *canonica*. Innocent people. And also children in the schoolhouse with the *maestra*. We don't want the partisans in town under any circumstances. But perhaps . . . At least they could help us pass a message back into the city."

"I have seen them," Zio Stefano says, and Zia Angela gasps. "We can't keep them away," he adds. "And anyway, don't they deserve our support?"

"Yes, but Stefano is right. We must be careful not to attract attention to ourselves," Zio Tino says.

A German soldier walks by the kitchen door and everyone falls silent. His worn boots scuff across the stone courtyard. His uniform, stained and rumpled, speaks of long days and dust from the road. He shuffles past their field of view, heavy with fatigue. Zio Tino and Father Ramondo return to their plates, eating together in silence apart from the scrapes of forks against plates.

If Signor Poggi and the Florentine superintendents can't get to their paintings, at least, Stella thinks, the Germans seem largely indifferent to the hundreds of masterpieces locked inside the villa's shuttered rooms.

Instead, they ask Stella's uncles for batteries to power their radios. For air filters and tools to fix their trucks and motorcycles. For blankets and socks and ointments for their blistered feet. For cigarettes and endless bottles of brandy. Three officers are on constant rotation, climbing and descending the spiral staircase of the skinny watchtower with binoculars slung around their necks.

But they don't seem to care about the paintings. "What use do they have for such things?" Zia Angela asks, but Stella thinks her zio Tino still looks worried the Germans will disappear with something from the treasure room in one of their dusty vehicles.

Meanwhile, the men play cards and music on the upper terrace, the tables littered with cigarette butts and sticky wine glasses. They hold loud contests in the olive grove to see who can do the greatest number of pushups before falling on their chests in the red dirt while everyone laughs. They give each other haircuts and shave their soapy stubble under the branches of the lemon trees, their undershirts rolled down to their waists, their shoulders red and painful-looking from the relentless sun.

A large metal basin now stands in the olive grove, its surface of water reflecting the clouds and blue sky. The mirage breaks as a man stands, naked, and Stella blushes at the sight of his pale buttocks. Apart from that, Stella has moved past the initial shock of watching grown men strip down to their underclothes.

Snickering behind their hands, Sandro and Stella come up with nicknames for some of the soldiers. *Baffi* becomes the name for a man with a thick, bristly mustache and a mismatched mosaic of teeth. *Salsiccia* for a soldier whose bulging midsection threatens to pop the buttons of his field tunic. *Schnitzelino* is one of their favorites, a sprite of a man whose enormous self-importance translates across any language barrier.

Mostly, Stella discovers, they are polite. As the days progress, the men greet Stella and her cousins cordially, like old acquaintances still kept far apart by their lack of ability to communicate. They pull crinkled, well-worn photographs from their pockets. Faded likenesses of their wives and children, their girlfriends waiting for them back in Berlin and Hamburg. Soft commentary and understanding beneath their unintelligible words. Stella begins to see them not as intimidating enemies but as young men far from home, yearning for the basic comfort of a hot meal and dry socks. The possibility of a kiss or maybe more.

"We are living in a barracks!" her aunt complains. "They put their muddy boots and clothes all over the place!"

"They won't hurt us," says Livia, who seems somehow to have become an expert on Germans. "They just need us to feed them and clean up after them."

"How do you know, Livia?" Mariasole narrows her eyes at her older sister.

From the courtyard, the pacing man on guard lights a cigarette and smiles at Livia in the doorway. She turns her head to the side and twirls her hair. While Stella feels gratefully invisible.

AT THE EVENING MEAL, Stella watches the dozen or so most high-ranking Germans assemble around Sir Harwell's dining table. They are still in their muddy field tunics as they don't seem to have any other clothes. Sir Harwell's wardrobes and trunks are all empty now. Stella's aunt and uncles have passed out socks, shirts, shoes—anything that wasn't hidden or buried in the weeks and months before the Germans came.

The aroma of roasted pork and boiled potatoes, a smell from happier days, fills the room. These are their favorites, Stella's family has learned. And for now at least, potatoes and pork remain relatively available, made palatable by the rosemary that has escaped the confines of the garden and grows wild down the hillside. Steam from the latest pot of boiled potatoes covers the windows, so Stella can't see the view to the Martinellis' distant farm.

When Livia brings out a large serving platter, Stella sees all the men's eyes on her. "*Danke*," a few of the men say as she places plates on the buffet, having not forgotten what their mothers taught them. "*Grazie*," a couple of the men have learned to say.

Livia moves gracefully around the table, her dark curls cascading over her shoulder. Even in her simple, worn dress, she is a picture of youthful beauty. Stella watches the soldiers' eyes follow her, their gazes lingering a touch too long. Their knuckles tapping their neighbors' arms, their whispered comments and laughter.

In turn, Stella sees the lines on either side of her aunt's mouth grow deeper. When Livia returns to the kitchen, Zia Angela orders her to stay put. After the men empty another bottle of wine, she says, "Stella and I will serve them."

Stella steps into the dining hall and places another bottle of wine on the table among the men. Picks up their dirty plates. But they don't look at Stella the way they look at her older cousin.

Late that night in the bedroom, Stella finds Zio Tino writing the letter to Signor Poggi. He finishes a paragraph, then sighs and wads up the page. Starts again. When he steps out to the toilet, Stella picks the crumpled page out of the waste bin.

THE NEXT AFTERNOON, Stella is headed out to the garden to pick the ripened eggplants when she sees Livia leaning against the stone wall, talking with one of the German soldiers.

Livia has abandoned her washing on the rim of the old stone *lavatoio*. The two stand very close together. Livia looks up to the man's face, talking softly. For a fleeting moment, Stella remembers the photograph of her father with Zia Angela, and she thinks Livia looks like the younger version of Zia Angela, smiling and hopeful, gazing up at him. Stella's cousin looks different somehow. It makes her feel strange to watch them, especially because she can't figure out how Livia is talking to him when he doesn't understand Italian. His head is bent forward, closely observing her. The strange interaction makes them seem like old friends.

Stella accidentally steps on a twig, and the sound makes the man turn around.

Now she sees it's Captain Bauer.

IN THE TREASURE ROOM, Sandro and Stella stand before the great painting of the red-haired man on horseback. Sunlight sneaks through the cracks in the shutters and shadows play upon the walls. They each make careful lines in their sketchbooks. Stella is making her first attempt at drawing a horse; it's going badly. The proportions are all wrong and the animal is a travesty, a mismatched amalgamation of eyes and shapes. It looks like something a four-year-old would draw. She sets down her pencil and sighs, then pulls out Zio Tino's crumpled draft letter to Signor Poggi and flattens it out on the tile floor with her palm.

Sandro picks it up. "I'm not so good at reading handwriting," he says, but he squints at the wrinkled page and makes his way haltingly through the words. "He wants . . . someone . . . to come from the Uffizi . . . to take the paintings back to Florence."

Stella nods, watching Sandro's face turn shadowed. "Zio Tino is still trying. He believes they're not safe here anymore. Even though the Germans don't seem interested in the first place. But Father Ramondo says bringing the paintings back to the city is too risky."

"So you think they will stay here?"

Stella shrugs. "I guess it depends if they can reach Signor Poggi at all. Father Ramondo said maybe the letter can be passed to partisans in the woods. That maybe they can get it to the archbishop. I didn't really follow . . ."

"*Partigiani?*" His eyebrows fly up.

She shrugs. "I don't know."

"They're regular people like you and me. Only they stockpile grenades, explosives," he tells her. "They might bomb a train track or a line of trucks."

"How do you know this?"

"They're talking about it downstairs. Plus, we had them back home." He hands the letter back to Stella.

Stella picks up her sketch again. But her horse looks ridiculous, and anyway, she can't focus. She puts it back down on the floor and sighs.

"Horses are difficult to draw," Sandro says, gesturing to another portrait nearby. "Try the dog instead." Stella knows he's just trying to make her feel better.

THE DAYS GROW HOTTER AND LONGER, while the circle of their lives constrains ever more tightly around them.

Every morning, the sun rises to cast its golden glow over the undulating olive groves. Inside the villa, the days roll out with a stifling, repetitive rhythm, each day barely distinguishable from the last. The grand expanse of the world seems to have contracted, wrapping the villa and its occupants in a tight cocoon of blazing isolation. Modern life seems to have slipped away, replaced by a relentless cycle of old-world chores and concerns.

Stella and her family move into a sweltering routine as if they are living in a medieval village cut off from the rest of the world. They make their own honey. Gather their own eggs. Use their own oil, cheese, and wine. They sew their own clothes. Spin and weave their own wool. They teach their own children. Nurse their sick. Shelter strangers. They look out for one another in the face of dangers so real and ever closer. Each day, the men mend tools, patch roofs, or chop wood, sweat beading their foreheads, their backs, glistening under the merciless sun. The women milk goats, make soap, and hang sheets on the line.

The German soldiers, for their part, lounge on the terrace playing cards and smoking cigarettes. Sit on the parched earth in the olive grove and laugh with one another. Wait for the battle to reach them.

ONE EVENING, after serving the Germans dinner, Stella stands back, looking at the mess they've left behind. Food particles scatter across the polished wood, stains from spilled drinks creating a map of carelessness. With a deep sigh, she begins clearing up, the weight of the day settling heavily on her shoulders. School seems a distant dream now—replaced by the relentless rhythm of chores.

As she trudges up the stairs, tiredness tugging at her every step, she catches sight of Livia sitting near the old stone staircase, pulling a needle and thread through drab green fabric. Stella recognizes a German paratrooper's field jacket stretched out in her cousin's lap.

Stella's brow furrows. "What are you doing?"

Livia's hands don't stop, the needle darting in and out. Her voice is soft, almost defensive. "I don't mind." But as she says it, Livia rotates the fabric, hiding her work from view. A protective gesture.

Stella's curiosity gets the better of her. She reaches out and touches the stiff fabric. Across the rip, her cousin has embroidered a small heart in green thread.

"SHE LIKES HIS MUSTACHE," Mariasole says, giggling, pulling the sheet over her head.

Stella has gotten used to sharing a bed with her younger cousin. She always wanted a sister. But now she knows having siblings comes with both bitter and sweet.

When Stella thinks of Captain Bauer's smudge of a mustache, it reminds her of the German führer. Then she only sees cold blue eyes and a lean, hard man. A strict demeanor. "*Che schifo!*" Stella says, giggling. "I wouldn't want to kiss that." She tries to see what her cousin sees, something special, something that sets Captain Bauer apart from the other men beyond his rudimentary Italian language skills. But Stella can't see how any relationship between Livia and Captain Bauer could be possible, no matter what happens at the end of all of this relentless toil and waiting.

"What are you laughing at?" Livia says as she enters the bedroom.

Under the sheets, Mariasole snickers, but Stella falls silent and only feels unsettled. Thinks of how people so unsuited could get together. Of the silly Cupid with his blindfold. Of how people make big mistakes when it comes to choosing a mate.

"THEY ARE USED to eating a much bigger breakfast in Germany," Livia reports to Stella and Mariasole the next morning in the kitchen, suddenly an expert on German culture. "They eat sausages. Cheeses. Jams and honey. Bread." She rummages through the cold storage and pantry, pulling out a dusty jar of marmalade Sir Harwell's servants had brought from England.

Stella knows better than to comment on this. Instead, while she waits for a loaf of bread to cool on a warped metal rack, she prepares for the day's labor: crack the eggs without getting pieces of the shell in them. Use a fork to add the flour into the egg. Press the dough until it's elastic. Cover it for a half hour with a damp rag. Roll it out. Spin it between her floured palms, Stella's favorite part. Go back to the beginning and do it again.

She doesn't tell anyone her perfectly formed loaf on the stovetop is half baked with dirt from the garden where she's seen the men urinate.

But Mariasole is never one to hold back from commenting. "Why do you like him anyway? He'd just as soon kill you as kiss you. Plus, his mustache makes him look ridiculous!" Mariasole giggles loudly and Stella stifles a laugh with the back of her flour-coated hand.

But Livia doesn't seem to take offense. Instead, her eyes, normally so bright and lively, now look distant, almost dreamy. Her fingers fidget with the stem of a ripe apricot on the table. "He's different," she says.

Mariasole's face turns serious. "You're going to be in big trouble if mamma and papà find out."

Livia shrugs. "They can't stop me," she says. "Have you seen his eyes? Blue as the sky."

"His nose is pointy." Mariasole giggles again, shaking her head.

"He's told me everything about Munich," Livia says. "And about his parents and sisters. He showed me pictures of them."

Stella purses her lips. "Livia. Have you forgotten that he's fighting against us? All of us Italians."

Livia folds her arms across her chest. "He's not a cruel or ruthless person. He won't hurt us. He's just caught up in something . . . bigger than himself. Besides, Stella, you don't know the first thing about love."

"You're in *love* with him?" Stella's mouth hangs open. She can't begin to see how two people as different as her cousin and Captain Bauer could have a future together. She considers how the war might have brought together many people across Europe who may have never encountered one another otherwise. All at once, Stella realizes this is also true for her and Sandro. An image of the blindfolded Cupid in Botticelli's *Primavera*, aiming his bow at his intended prey, floats in her head again. Stella thinks you never know when you might be an unsuspecting target, when Cupid's bow might spear you out of the blue.

"Here you go," Stella says, slicing large pieces off the newly cooled loaf of dirt bread and putting them in a basket for Livia to take out to the men who have begun to collect in the dining hall for their breakfast. Stella crosses her arms and half smiles when Livia sets the bread basket down on the table among the hungry, unsuspecting men.

The soldiers scrape their chairs across the floor and greet Livia with smiles and "good mornings" in German and Italian. No one is paying attention to the bread. But Stella feels proud of her freshly baked dirt loaf anyway.

ONE EVENING, as the sun sinks below the silhouette of the spiky trees and purple hills beyond, the rumble of engines disrupts the tranquility. Like a dark wave, a half dozen German tanks advance up the hill. The sun catches on their metallic forms.

New Germans.

From the kitchen garden, Stella watches the new Germans come. When the tanks finally arrive at a standstill in front of the villa and cut their rumbling engines, the men open the hatches and climb out of the top of the machines like ants spilling out of an anthill. Suddenly, there are dozens of exhausted-looking Germans she's never seen before, their postures telling an unspoken tale of the weary journey behind them.

Stella wants to warn Sandro and the others, but then she remembers she's let Sandro into the treasure room, where he's brought a blanket and some sketchbooks. He'll miss it, she thinks, this strange and unsettling sight of the men crawling out of their beastly machines.

Next, a half dozen motorcycles with sidecars pull up alongside them. Their uniforms and helmets are covered in dust and mud. Each man has a rifle and scores of bullets strung like ugly garlands across their bodies. They grab their packs and come clanking along the dirt path, then up the stairs. The first one to reach it raps loudly on the wooden door.

CHAPTER 9

<u>EXILES</u>

Summer 1944

The eye is the highest, the most evolved of all bodily organs to perceive the nature of things—light and dark, color and substance, distance and proximity, motion and static. But no two persons' eyes will perceive these things in the same manner. It is the artist's greatest calling to guide this perception to what he wants the viewer to see.

—FROM THE LOST DIARIES OF SANDRO
BOTTICELLI, FLORENCE, SUMMER 1480

All day, my assistant and I drove through the wrecks of medieval villages and along the rutted roads, increasingly fearful of what we might find the closer we drew to Tuscany. For we already knew what the tank units were capable of and by this point, any optimism we might have felt when we started had long worn thin . . .

—FROM THE DIARY OF CAPTAIN WALLACE E.
FOSTER, MONUMENTS OFFICER OF THE
FIFTH ARMY IN TUSCANY, AUGUST 1944

Stella stands frozen in the kitchen doorway alongside Zia Angela, and feels like she's watching the grainy, flickering loop of a newsreel that's been fed into the machine and restarted from the beginning. She watches her uncles rush into the courtyard. Their voices rise along with the soldiers', a chaos of overlapping shouts in Italian and German.

Zio Tino strides into the midst of the soldiers, with the now crumpled letter from Generalfeldmarschall Kesselring in his hand. Stella thinks her uncle is brave to walk directly into the scuffle. "You have no authority to enter this villa, *Herren*," Zio Tino states to a big man who appears to be in charge of the newly arrived tank men. "And anyway, we are already at capacity."

For a moment, there is a tense silence as the new soldier's gaze travels from Stella's uncles to the piece of paper, then to one of his compatriots, then back again. Her uncle is dwarfed by the tall men around him. For a long, silent moment, Stella reaches for a sliver of hope. Behind a large terracotta planter, Luigi peeks out, his striped tail shuddering slightly.

But the man, who stands a full head and shoulders taller than Zio Tino, hands Kesselring's note back to him dismissively. Then barks a loud order to the men around him.

The momentary peace splinters. Like a trigger, the man's command to the others, who have already grown impatient with this silent letter-reading, makes them spring into action. Walking along an aisle of the courtyard, one of the men suddenly breaks a glass window with the butt of his rifle. The shatter, sharp and piercing, makes Stella's entire body flinch.

At the sound of the breaking glass, Zia Angela screams and runs into the courtyard. There is a steady flow of shouted Italian. Zia Angela bolts into the crowd of soldiers, a whirlwind of rage. Stella thinks she looks as if she will strangle the commanding officer with her bare hands.

Stella knows what it's like to rush in. To act before thinking. To take a chance even when you know it's dangerous.

Zio Tino grasps his wife by the waist to stop her.

THE INITIAL CONFRONTATION with Stella's family does little to slow down the tank men. Instead, pandemonium breaks out between the German paratroopers who have been living in the villa and the men newly arrived in the tanks.

The men share the same language. The same insignia on their uniforms. But between the paratroopers and the tank men, shouting ensues. Stella understands none of their words, but the meaning is clear. The newcomers want to requisition the villa for themselves. Stella can feel the tension in the air, like electricity crackling from one group of men in uniform to the other.

As the disagreement continues between the two units, more paratroopers enter the courtyard from the corridors, lured from the olive groves and the upper terrace, where they've been lounging with their cigarettes and card decks. It's as if they themselves are the owners of the villa, angered by the intrusion of strangers entering their home.

Somehow, Stella thinks, the tank men look more intimidating than the paratroopers. Stella sees their sturdy jackets with rows of buttons and patches, the meaning of which she can't begin to interpret. Giant boots with thick soles that track in mud and ruddy dust from outside the villa. Their ugly rounded steel helmets. One has a long, diagonal red scar across his cheek.

"Where is Captain Bauer?" Stella whispers as Zia Angela finally capitulates and retreats to the kitchen. She only shakes her head. No one wants him there, but maybe now, in this circumstance, Stella thinks, Captain Bauer's calm, commanding presence, his high rank, might be their only hope to smooth over this scuffle. He's been the only mediator, the only person to keep an uneasy balance when things have seemed on the verge of spiraling out of control at any moment. But Stella has not seen him in two days.

The tank commander barks a new order, and his men move across the courtyard. They yank the handles of locked doors. Cup their hands against glass to look in windows. Draw their weapons. Scan the various doors and corridors leading off the courtyard, as if they might face a surprise attacker from any angle. It might even be Stella or her aunt, she thinks.

But now, Zia Angela stands frozen at the sink when there is the sound of boots just outside the kitchen door. Stella and her aunt both pick up wooden spoons from the ceramic container on the kitchen counter. Stella feels a wave of panic rise in her throat. When a large man fills the doorway, Zia Angela yells, "*Stammi lontano!*" at him but he doesn't understand. And anyway, Stella realizes, these men hardly pay attention to their protests.

Stella bolts the door to the cantina and presses her back against it. Wooden spoon in hand like Zia Angela. Doesn't dare blink.

THE NEW MEN FAN OUT, searching the villa. From her position with her back against the door to the cantina, Stella hears a string of violations: rummaging through storage cabinets, flinging open doors, wardrobes, and drawers, leaving them open, tearing out their contents. Turning over furniture, leaving behind a mess that might be impossible to put back together later, if they escape this riot with their lives. Stella imagines the tank men in all the bedrooms, pulling out their lights to look under the beds and behind cabinets. Peering into dark corners and under stairwells, leaving muddy boot prints on the treads of the coiling tower stair.

Zio Tino stays in the courtyard, trying to reason with a group of the men even though they don't understand.

Stella remains frozen against the door to the cantina, hearing the sound of ransacking, of breaking glass. Of ceaseless aggression. Of the screeching of furniture dragged across wooden floors. Of her aunt shouting a stream of obscenities in the direction of the kitchen ceiling. They are deaf to her cries.

From her spot, Stella watches one of the soldiers cross the courtyard and approach the door to the treasure room. He rattles the handle, but the door is locked. He exchanges a fleeting glance with one of his fellow tank men. The friend retrieves a metal bar from his pack and wedges it into the minuscule gap between the door and its jamb, pressing his weight into the lever.

Stella watches in horror as the door shakes under the pressure. Even though she waits for the terrible splinter, the lock holds. But Stella can't help it. Something inside her snaps. She steps away from the door of the cantina and runs out into the courtyard.

"Get away from there!" she yells at the soldier with the crowbar.

"Stella!" Zio Tino yells, watching her run across the courtyard. "Get back to the kitchen!"

But Stella rushes to the door of the treasure room, shouting. Yelling at the men with everything she can muster.

THE SECOND SOLDIER rattles the lock on the shuttered window that leads to the treasure room. He manages to wedge open one of the bolts that holds the window closed. To Stella's horror, he folds back the wooden shutter. Then he turns his rifle around and with one swift motion, smashes the butt of it into the glass. There is a shuddering crash and another scattering of glass shards across the floor. The second soldier steps forward, clearing away the jagged glass with the toe of his boot. He points his rifle into the room, peering into the darkness.

Stella runs after him. "Sandro!" she yells through the ragged opening of broken glass.

AFTER THEY UNLOCK the door to the treasure room, the tank men start dragging paintings out into the daylight, and messily stacking them in the middle of the courtyard. They pile them unceremoniously atop one another, their frames digging into the canvases beneath. Stella sees the masterful landscape with wheat fields she's admired in the shadows dozens of times, now in the brash afternoon sun. Stella recognizes paintings Zio Tino has told her are by famous artists like Filippo Lippi and Andrea del Sarto.

"Sandro!" Stella cries. She can't help herself. She doesn't know where to turn her attention now: to the pictures or to the gaping doorway, through which Sandro is surely hiding inside.

But there is no response from the treasure room.

"Don't touch the pictures!" she cries at the tank men, to no avail.

"Stella, come back here this instant!" Zia Angela yells from the kitchen door.

Stella watches one of the tank men reach into the pocket of his uniform trouser and produce a small wooden box of matches. Strike one to create a small, leaping flame.

"*HALT!*"

The courtyard echoes with the command. Every head turns to find Captain Bauer striding in, his face a cold mask. The other soldiers stop mid-activity and stand at attention. Even though he is a young man, he outranks them.

For a few moments, heavy silence falls. Then Captain Bauer cries out several more commands in German and the men freeze. Stella watches him gesture to the pile of paintings while he speaks.

In the momentary pause, Zio Tino rushes in, picking up a canvas showing a harbor scene from the pile and running it back into the treasure room. Zio Stefano runs behind him, bringing another framed painting with him. Stella rushes in to help her uncles bring the paintings back into the room, a wave of panic and relief all mixed together.

Finally barred from the treasure room, the men file away from Captain Bauer, moving across the courtyard. When she comes back out of the treasure room to pick up another painting, Stella sees one of the men go into the kitchen. He turns the thumb lock on the wine cellar door and flings it open. At the top of the stairwell, the light bulb flickers. The soldier hesitates, then when two others appear, they pull their weapons and disappear down the stairs to the cantina. Stella brings her palms to the sides of her head, thinking of Sergeant Cakebread and all the others, huddled there, hearing the chaos and waiting silently for what happens next.

In that long moment, Stella only hears ringing in her ears. She doesn't know whether she is more panicked for Sandro hidden in the treasure room, or Sergeant Cakebread hidden in the wine cellar, or any of them who have risked everything to hide people and paintings and precious belongings. Either way, the nervous détente, the seemingly unending waiting, is behind them now and the tank men are everywhere at once, flowing through the house like an unstoppable army of boring insects.

AFTER SEVERAL MINUTES that pass like a lifetime, Captain Bauer and the tank commander work out an arrangement.

Captain Bauer explains to Zio Tino and Zio Stefano that both the paratrooper and tank units, confusingly, have orders to requisition their villa and live off its resources. And so, he shrugs and makes a strange apology. They will have to find room in the villa for both units to stay.

After a while, the men slow down the pace of their rampage, disappearing down the dark corridors or returning outside to the olive groves and their tanks, leaving behind a mess of broken glass and ransacked rooms.

Stella rushes into the treasure room, with its broken glass, splintered locks, and disarray. She darts into the narrow tunnels behind the stacked paintings, where they are propped against the walls. Behind the *Primavera*, she finds two wadded blankets, a scattering of papers and pencils. But Sandro is not there.

Stella picks up one of the drawings, a beautiful rendition of one of the women in the picture. She climbs out from behind the painting and brings Sandro's drawing to the light. She recognizes the oval. The diagonal lines to place the eyes and lips. One down the middle to place the nose. The barest emergence of a perfect face.

In the corner he's written "Stellina."

Stella sinks to the floor.

Pages flutter on the tiles.

STELLA FINDS SANDRO standing on the hillside, where the tall grass tickles the backs of their legs.

The tank men have moved on from the wine cellar, and many of the refugees have spilled out the door onto the villa grounds. A few women and children remain crouching in the tall grass down the hillside, just out of view.

"Where were you?!"

"I hid behind the *Primavera*," he says. "And then I slipped out the door while they were tearing everything apart."

Stella imagines him sliding into the narrow sliver of space behind where the painting is propped against the wall, curled on the floor like a rabbit in its dark burrow. She feels a wave of admiration for him and a relief that he's safe.

"What were you thinking?" he says, shaking her shoulders with his palms. "*Sei . . . spericolata!*"

"I know; my aunt says I rush in," she says. "But I was just worried about you."

STELLA AND SANDRO return to the cantina to find the refugees in small, anxious knots.

"I think they were surprised to see how many we are," Signora Donati tells Stella's family when they descend into the dim embrace of the cellar to check on everyone. The air is heavy with a mixture of solidarity and exhaustion.

The tale unfolds, not from one mouth but from many: how someone suggested that Sergeant Cakebread coil up in a small space between some stacked wine barrels, just like Sandro hid behind the giant Botticelli painting. How a group of women and babies formed a shield of their bodies in front of the barrels to conceal his presence. How the Germans realized they were vastly outnumbered, even if the refugees were unarmed. How they left through the cellar door without touching anything or anyone.

As Stella listens to their story, the scene vivid in her mind's eye, her heart swells with pride and admiration for these brave souls whose actions had, once again, united to protect another human. Even a stranger who put everyone's life at risk.

STELLA RETURNS to her precarious duties in the kitchen, where, for the first time since coming to Tuscany, she sees her aunt cry. Zia Angela sits at the kitchen table with her face in her palms. Zio Tino stands with his hand on her shoulder.

"What will Lady Harwell say when she sees this place?" she says. "And Sir Harwell was so proud of his beautiful things. Who would have imagined this? I hope they never have to see such a travesty. They've ruined everything. It's not right. And we have not done our duty."

Stella can see that Zia Angela's words weigh on her husband, but he says, "Angela. We have done well to keep our lives at this point. We cannot think too hard beyond that."

"They are brutes!" she says bitterly. "They expect us to feed them constantly. To clean their plates and their sweaty sheets and their disgusting toilets. I can't do it anymore. I can't."

"If we don't, Angela, we lose what access they have to food and resources. Or worse."

"What about the paintings?" Stella asks.

Zio Tino huffs a large sigh but says nothing. Zia Angela blows her nose loudly into a handkerchief.

Near the kitchen window, Stella pours water into glasses for her family while she watches one of the soldiers urinating in the kitchen garden. She takes note of which rosemary plant she should avoid picking.

Compared to the paratroopers who upended her family's lives upon their arrival weeks before, the tank men have made Captain Bauer and his unit seem unlikely gentlemen. Stella's family feels a deeper dread now, knowing the tank men have the power to take away whatever life remains for them in their isolated world. The air is thick with despair.

"The tank regiment came up from Rome," Livia says.

From the sink, up to her elbows in soapy water, Stella watches Livia twirl a lock of dark hair, self-assured that she knows something they don't, as if having privileged access to the German soldiers is something to be proud of. "The tank men were surprised to find the paratroopers already here. I guess they have their own orders."

"How do you know?" Mariasole says, running a piece of stale bread into a swath of thick tomato sauce on her plate.

"All of *die Bruder* are sick of it and just want to go home. Five years away from their houses and families. They are depressed by the turn of events in Italy and France. Captain Bauer told me that."

Zia Angela stops chewing and her eyes become slits. "Why are you talking about such things with Bauer?"

But Zio Tino ignores the implications of his wife's fishing. "We have to get *him* out of here now," he says, gesturing to the door of the wine cellar. Everyone knows it's high past time to get Cakebread out of the villa. For everyone's sake.

Stella thinks her uncle looks exhausted but nervous energy flickers in his eyes. "And those paintings. Dear God."

FOR A FEW DAYS, a nervous silence overtakes the villa. But then, one afternoon when clouds descend over the valleys like a blanket, two of the tank men demand a car.

Their guns pulled, they force Zio Tino to open the doors of the old carriage house. Inside, there is the sleek silhouette of the old Alfa Romeo Zio Tino battened down months ago. The men speak to him in German but Zio Tino only shrugs. "No tires, *Herren*. And no gas." The men discuss among themselves, then finally click their heels, and return their guns to their places.

Stella has heard Livia say the Germans spread rumors there is an Aston Martin somewhere on the property; they would consider a nice British car with the steering wheel on the other side quite a prize.

But days go by and there is no Aston Martin. No tires appear. Nor any gas. Zio Tino locks up the carriage house again and hides the key.

THE HOUSEHOLD FULL of uninvited guests resumes its weary cadence.

Like the paratroopers, the Panzer men fall into their new routines. Even though she doesn't understand a word of German,

Stella can see that the two units have reached an uneasy accord. Each staking out their parts of the house and the grounds beyond.

The officers of each unit have carved out space inside the villa's upper-floor bedrooms, while their enlisted men fan out into the olive and lemon groves, making their strange quasi-barracks of tents and pallets under the shifting, shadowed tree canopies. Some of them lounge in their trucks like slothful cats. They wash themselves in the *lavatoio*, so that the refugee women find naked Germans in the stone basins when they bring their washing. But the sudden presence of the women doesn't seem to disturb the soldiers. They stand in the tubs in all their glory, then use their green neckerchiefs as makeshift loincloths and return to the olive groves. Stella thinks if she were to witness this sight with Sandro, it might make her face flush red. Instead, Stella and Mariasole giggle together behind their hands, watching the tall men's white asses in the sun.

UNDER THE SHADE of a birch tree, Stella and Sandro try their best to settle back into their drawing and reading lessons. Stella's attempts at sketching Sandro's dark, even features have improved somewhat. Beyond, the olive grove is bathed in the soft hues of twilight, the sun slanting through its silver leaves, shimmering in the gentle breeze. Rows of olive trees stretch out, their gnarled trunks squat and brown in the dimming light. On his own paper, Sandro is working on a revision of the central goddess in the *Primavera*, resketching her pose and the drapery of her layered dress. Stella imagines her skill will never come close to matching his.

Farther down the hill, boisterous laughter breaks out among the soldiers. Soon enough, the object of their hilarity becomes clear. They are watching Livia walking up the hill with her basket of laundry folded from the lines, the sound of their commentary amplified by the evening stillness. Their banter and brazen gazes are universal, piercing the fabric of her dignity.

Stella watches Livia's reaction. There is a certain pride in her stance—upright and unyielding, her chin tilted up in the face of the men's amusement. Her smirk is devoid of humor. But there is also a hint of vulnerability amid the defiance, as if Stella can feel the dress becoming thinner under the scrutiny of the men's appraisal, their open consumption of her as she walks up the hill with her basket.

Sandro, taking in the scene, says, "Your cousin attracts a lot of attention."

When she disappears into the house, shrill laughter and crude remarks linger in the air behind her.

"I don't think she likes it," Stella says.

Sandro hesitates for a moment before saying, "She's like a grown-up version of you."

The words hang in the air, mingling with the scent of olive leaves and the distant laughter. Stella turns to him, eyebrows raised, searching his face. She sees the flush on his cheeks, the nervous dart of his eyes.

"I'm nothing like her," Stella says sharply, returning to her drawing with renewed concentration.

AT SUNSET, in a clearing beyond the olive grove, the tank men gather around a bonfire that reaches to the height of the tallest of the olive trees. Some of the men have dragged a few of Sir Harwell's wooden chairs they've broken apart to add fuel to the bonfire. An intense heat emanates from the blaze, surrounded by German language and laughing. On a spit, they are roasting a whole pig they must have taken from a nearby farm, its charred silhouette hellish against the flames and their voracious appetite for destruction.

Stella goes out to the well to draw some water for the parched kitchen garden. Near the edge of the woods, a dozen fireflies float in the gathering darkness, like a linked series of tiny bulbs flashing their frenzied sequence. Outside the door to the wine cellar, Stella spies Zio Tino pacing back and forth, then talking quietly to Old Giuseppe.

Then, to Stella's surprise, two men suddenly emerge from the dark void of the tree line at the edge of the woods. The fireflies extinguish their flashing lights and vanish. Stella immediately panics and drops to her knees behind the stone arc of the wellhead. Both men are dressed in black from head to toe, dark bags strapped across their midsections. When Zio Tino goes out to meet them, she watches him hand over a slim envelope to one of the men, who slips it into his shirt pocket. Then, the men follow Zio Tino into the wine cellar.

Moments later, the two men in black reemerge. This time, they stand on either side of Sergeant Cakebread, who is hobbling as quickly as he can with his splinted leg and makeshift crutch. Signora Donati rushes out behind them, handing a small bag to Sergeant Cakebread, and Stella imagines there must be food inside. The three men make an awkward dash for the tree line. In a matter of seconds, they disappear into the black. One of the fireflies tentatively returns, an infinitesimal spark, luring the others to join back into the flickering dance as if nothing has happened.

If Cakebread makes it back home, all the way to England, Stella thinks, it will be a miracle made possible thanks to his unlikely friends at Santa Lucia. She feels an immediate and immense relief to see him go. But Stella can't help it. Her eyes well with hot tears of relief and trepidation.

At the cellar door, Stella finds Signora Donati wiping giant tears from her cheeks with the cuff of her sleeve. Stella reaches out and touches her arm softly.

"You've helped him survive," Stella says. "He's going to be alright." Stella has no idea if what she says is true.

Signora Donati wipes her face, nodding, her voice high-pitched and tremored. "I just keep thinking that if we do what we can to help, then maybe, in turn, someone will do the same for my boy."

THE HARWELLS' ONCE-WELCOMING GREAT HALL becomes a makeshift Nazi communications hub. Stella watches the men set up telephone lines, stringing long cords and metallic equipment across the tables. One of the men in charge of this effort has set up his own bedroll on one of Sir Harwell's fancy divans.

The unit's chaplain is also involved with this effort. He is a hard, severe-looking man with a thin nose and pale, icy eyes. Through a few halting Italian words and the translation of Captain Bauer, the chaplain advises Stella's aunt and uncles not to leave out anything of value in the house. They should put away any jewelry or silver, he says. This warning seems comical to Stella and her cousins. The men have no idea the quantity of valuables that have been bricked up behind the wall in the attic and the pigsties, or long buried in the kitchen garden. And if there had been anything at all left out that was portable, the men would have taken it by now. Stella thinks the only thing standing in the way of the men taking away the Uffizi's paintings is their sheer size, which makes them difficult to take away without notice.

Each morning, the men stir and make their way to the dining room. Stella and her aunt make coffee and serve stale bread softened with wine or a bit of milk, sometimes a pinch of sugar from the German rations. Later, in the confined prison of the kitchen, Stella tears pieces of stale bread and cuts them into cubes. She cuts up a tomato and fresh onion. She tears some fresh basil leaves and puts them in a bowl. Then adds olive oil and vinegar. They don't dare unearth their hams, sausages, and other things they have buried or tucked away. They make do with vegetables canned long before Sir and Lady Harwell left, with *panzanella* with stale bread, tomatoes, and basil. They pull rosemary and basil from the weed-filled garden.

But the Germans seem to enjoy even the most cobbled-together meals, gulping them down in seconds. Whenever, out of spite, Stella mixes a handful of red dirt into a loaf of bread, no one even seems to notice.

Livia has learned from Captain Bauer that the tank men are part of a reserve unit that rotates into the battle to relieve the other troops. It means the men have a lot of downtime, which is why they must look so bored, Stella thinks. They spend the day in the dining and living rooms, spreading out maps and smoking cigarettes. Others climb the skinny watch tower with their binoculars, looking southward. They pace back and forth, watching the horizon line on the southern hills. In the olive groves, they lie on the ground and target shoot, making big rivets on the gnarled tree trunks until the silvery leaves shake and the black fruits fall to the hard dirt like small projectiles.

But beneath this façade of normalcy lies an undercurrent of almost unbearable tension. Each day feels like walking on a tightrope, balancing the day's compromises with the fear of what tomorrow will bring. Simmering. Waiting for the next upheaval.

In the field beyond the olives, some of the men tinker with the tank engines. A few of the refugee boys loiter curiously around the tanks. Stella watches one of the soldiers lift up one of the boys and let him turn the tower around.

AT LAST, Stella's aunt and uncle suspect that a nearly unthinkable romance has budded between Livia and Captain Bauer.

Stella watches Livia's face turn a fiery shade of red when her parents call her into the kitchen one morning. "I can't believe you are sending me away!" she cries, arms crossed tightly across her chest.

Zia Angela sets down the spoon she's using to mix dough and

turns to face her daughter. "Livia. We've been over this. It's not safe here anymore for a young lady."

"So you're sending away Stella and Mariasole too, then?" She flings one arm out to gesture toward Stella, who keeps her head down and chops the red onions into tiny pieces smaller than her fingernails, using an old *mezzaluna*. She chops fiercely, bringing a sting to her eyes. Trying to be invisible. The room seems to constrict, the walls inching closer. The only sound in the room now is the loud *chop chop* of her blade.

Her aunt continues. "*Guarda*. I don't want to let you out of my sight for one second. But they are young girls. You, on the other hand, look like a grown woman and you're drawing too much attention from the men."

"Stella has breasts, too!" Livia says.

Her aunt only sighs in response as Stella feels her face turn hot.

"I don't want to go," Livia says, and suddenly, her hard, eggshell exterior looks like it will crack. Her voice wavers. "The schoolhouse is filled with babies! Besides, I'm old enough to make my own choices."

"You are our daughter and it's our job to protect you," Zio Tino says. "Besides, the decision has already been made. The *maestra* is expecting you."

For a moment, her frown grows deep. "You can't make me."

Finally, Zio Tino raises his voice. "That's final, Livia!" One of the Germans at the dining table in the next room turns around and peers into the kitchen.

With one last angry huff, Livia storms out of the kitchen, slamming the door on her way out like a gunshot.

THE NEXT MORNING UNFOLDS like a blank, silver curtain, the sun somewhere absent behind the sobering gloom. Livia's leather bag is packed and her bed stands empty and neatly made.

Her parents walk with her to the schoolhouse. Stella watches them head wordlessly down the dusty path, a triptych of familial bonds and impossible decisions. She thinks about Livia there among the babies, and she remembers she used to feel like that at school, too.

By evening, as the gloom transforms into twilight the color of charcoal, Stella spies Captain Bauer, thin blond hair and serious face, on the high terrace with his binoculars. She wonders if he is searching for Livia.

In a way, Stella feels sorry for him.

CHAPTER 10

SEVEN SORROWS

Summer 1944

Birth and death are partners in a dance . . . A winter and spring of the soul that exist together simultaneously. Only good art transcends this mortal coil. Every stroke of the brush an act of defiance against oblivion, a battle cry before the inevitable and ever-nearing silence. For me, perhaps, it's little more than a vain hope I might create something that would outlast my poor, corroded body. Done correctly, art is a triumph over death.

—FROM THE LOST DIARIES OF SANDRO
BOTTICELLI, FLORENCE, SUMMER 1480

During the Italian Renaissance, incalculable beauty emerged from one of the most brutal periods in the history of the world. Botticelli's famous Primavera stands at the center of this paradox, embodying the strange and wondrous coexistence of darkness and light that characterized the era. A historical stew of events that produced works of art to withstand the test of centuries. It's as if this great artist worked with the precept that his work might give us hope, many years later, in our own times of darkness. Standing before that masterpiece in the most unlikely of places gave me hope for survival after the long months of destruction and despair.

—FROM THE DIARY OF CAPTAIN WALLACE E.
FOSTER, MONUMENTS OFFICER OF THE FIFTH
ARMY IN TUSCANY, AUGUST 1944

At last, there is a letter from Signor Poggi. No one knows how it got to the Villa Santa Lucia, all the way from Florence.

Stella finds Zio Tino in the kitchen, crumpled page between his hands, reading it aloud to his wife. He leans forward, elbows on his knees, sweating. On the table is an empty bowl with the remains of breakfast: an orange peel and a knife. A coffee cup lined with foamy residue. Stella collects ingredients for a simple cake made with ground chestnut flour, pignoli, and rosemary. A few shriveled grapes from the last harvest for garnish.

"He says a man named Cesare Fasola is coming to bring the paintings back to Florence. They must have arranged for the trucks to come back." His voice breaks with relief.

"It's about time somebody came to get those blasted pictures!" Zia Angela says. She chops a fistful of parsley, roughly hacking the herb with a dull knife. Surely everyone has tired of *panzanella*, but stale bread and wild parsley are easy enough to come by at this point. "They have expected us to protect those damn paintings with our lives—and for so long. As if we don't already have enough troubles without trying to keep their dirty hands off those pictures?"

Zio Tino ignores the provocation. "He says this Fasola has worked as a librarian at the Uffizi for many years and we can trust him." He reads from the paper in his hand: "'I want to assure you that you can put your faith in Signor Fasola and it is very important that you cooperate fully with him. He has been entrusted with the safe transport of these priceless works of art and I'm sure I don't need to convince you of the importance of this operation.'"

The gravity of the news settles in Stella's mind as she ties the apron strings behind her back. Her uncle's relief is palpable as he wipes his forehead and emits a long, slow exhale. "Thanks be to God."

Stella knows that for her aunt and uncles, the letter is like a breath of fresh air, a glimmer of hope after a long, grim period of tribulation. She knows she should feel hope, too. And even gratitude that the paintings might be taken to a safer place than the chaotic Villa Santa Lucia.

Instead, trepidation, even sadness, pools in her gut. For Stella, the paintings have been more than a duty. More than a secret. They have been a window to another world that is more wondrous, more colorful, more filled with meaning than anything happening in this one. And connection with another lonely child not so different from her. A shred of hope in a dark time. A lifeline.

AFTER DARK, Stella fishes the key to the treasure room from between the cracks of the stones and unlocks the door. If anyone is to be trusted with being in this room alone, it's Sandro. He loves these pictures more than anyone. Maybe even more than Zio Tino himself. Stella finds Sandro there in the shadows, running his fingers over the pages of a leather-bound book she has pried from one of Sir Harwell's shelves and attempted to help him read.

Closing the door and locking it behind her, Stella feels herself exhale. She takes in the sights and smells of this isolated universe, a haven of peace and solitude in a world of upheaval. A place of retreat, a place of magic. A place of hope. She appreciates it now more than ever before as she imagines the room emptied of its treasures.

Ever since Zio Tino read Signor Poggi's letter aloud in the kitchen, Stella has carried the pang in her gut to think about the works of art leaving the villa. But even more than that, she fears having to tell Sandro they're going away.

"*Ciao!*" he says brightly.

Stella hesitates, her heart heavy with the truth that Signor Fasola will empty this room of the paintings that have become their silent companions. She wonders if she'll be able to muster the courage to tell Sandro. It will mean the loss of their haven, their own space in the world. She knows the paintings have given him hope, too, in a hopeless time. He's said so himself. Surely the truth that they will be gone will be devastating. The paintings have brought together two wayward children of opposite fortunes. They've forged a bond between them that Stella believes can never be broken.

Stella doesn't know what to say. If they lose the pictures, she's afraid Sandro will lose hope. And then what? Stella sits heavily on the tiles with the burden of the secret she carries, weighing her to the floor like a heavy bucket of water carried from the well. She hands Sandro a small kitchen rag. Inside is a hunk of bread with some of the soggy *panzanella* tucked into it.

"Mmm!" he says, taking a bite. His eyebrows rise in elation. "*Che buona.*" Then he examines Stella's face. "*Tutt'apposto?*" His dark eyes flash in the shadows.

She begins to tell him, but the words die on her lips. "Why wouldn't it be?" she says instead, crossing her arms and feigning a close look at Botticelli's masterpiece. She picks up a blank page and a pencil from the floor.

"Did something happen?" he asks.

Stella manages a weak smile and a shrug. She can't bear to see the disappointment on his face. Her stomach hurts.

"Just thinking about what my uncles were talking about . . . The British and Americans are coming this way."

"Some of our friends in the wine cellar saw them, down south."

Stella finds it hard to imagine Americans coming over the dark silhouette of the distant hills. She's never seen an *americano* before. It is all hard to imagine when as far as the eye can see, there are only half-naked Germans, broken trees, muddy tanks, and parched earth.

"You get very far?" she asks, gesturing to the pilfered book.

"Can you just read it out loud to me instead?" He tries to hand her the book.

"Why, *sciocco*? You're the one who's supposed to be practicing your reading. That was the deal we made. Remember?"

For a moment, the two of them sit in silence, looking at the bright colors of the *Primavera* before them.

"I've been keeping a secret," Sandro blurts, suddenly and heavily.

Stella sits dumbfounded. Those should be her words, not his. "Well . . . what is it?"

"Even when it's light," he says. "Even with trying harder . . ." She sees him hesitate. He closes the book and sets it down on the tiles. "Stella, the words have gone blurry. I can't really see them anymore. I'm scared."

"CAN WE TAKE SANDRO to a doctor?" Stella asks Zia Angela in the kitchen. "There's something wrong with his eyes."

"Where would we take him, child?" Zia Angela says, lifting one arm from the sink of dirty dishes and wiping her brow with her forearm. "There's no leaving this place."

Stella knows this, of course. She's already heard the adults say there is no doctor in their village and the *medico* who usually travels from town to town in this area can't get to them at all now. The doctor in the nearest village has been sent to the front along with the latest round of recruitment. There is only one midwife left between here and Pienza. And no one can go to Florence at all.

"I don't want anyone to know about it," Sandro says later, quietly, as they walk down the hill toward the herb garden, a mass of fragrant blossoms and leaves. Stella feels thankful they aren't in school, where the other boys might look for any excuse to ridicule him.

Stella knows he feels embarrassed. She's never seen him look so vulnerable, so afraid. "But you need help," she says. "You don't want to go blind."

Stella searches the landscape for Signora Donati's broad silhouette. If she could help Sergeant Cakebread, Stella reasons, perhaps she has some way to help Sandro, too, as his world becomes more clouded and even more uncertain than before.

They find Signora Donati near the animal pens, where she has gathered up every last chicken, goat, and pig and corralled them into a small enclosure, determined to protect them from the hungry soldiers. When they pose the question about Sandro's vision, her face turns grave. In the dappled light, she brushes Sandro's hair back from his forehead with her bent, earth-stained fingers. She looks deeply into his brown eyes. Sandro tries not to squint.

Stella feels a dull ache spread across her abdomen. It started days ago and has only intensified. But it's nothing, she reasons, compared to what Sandro is experiencing, so she pushes it to the back of her mind.

"I don't see anything wrong," Signora Donati says after a few long seconds. "But I mostly know about bringing babies into the world. I'm afraid eyes are a bit outside of my experience."

STELLA WAKES THE NEXT MORNING with the sheets under her damp and sticky. And a feeling of swelling, pulling at her from the inside. A deep ache. She reaches her hand down and then looks.

She bolts upright. Her sheets—and her nightgown—both have a vivid crimson stain.

"*Aya!*" Stella jumps out of bed. Hot panic streaks through her mind.

Beside her, Mariasole rouses. "You got your things," she states matter-of-factly, leaning on one elbow.

Stella wads the hem of her ruined nightgown between her legs and runs to the *bagno*. Mariasole gets up, too, stumbling behind her. Yawning.

LATER, STELLA CLEANS HERSELF with shaky hands and Zia Angela, frowning, shows Stella how to fold sanitary cloths and fasten a belt to keep them in place.

"You're a woman now," Mariasole says when Stella, burning with embarrassment, bundles her soiled laundry and brings it to the stone basin at the edge of the hill. She prays that no one sees her dump her sheets into the ancient stone vat. Stella knows her aunt must view her new womanhood as another inconvenience. Another burden to her family, now with more sanitary cloths and sheets to scrub in the *lavatoio*.

Stella thinks she ought to feel some connection to the shared experiences of the grown women in the villa. Of women everywhere. A rite of passage that maybe should feel important, even sacred. But Stella doesn't feel like a woman. Or special. Or especially sacred. She just feels uncomfortable. And even though Sandro is her best friend, when she thinks about telling him, her face turns scalding and she resolves not to tell anyone at all.

Before bed, Zia Angela gives her a cup of warm goat's milk.

"It's good for cramps," Mariasole says.

"How would you know?" Stella curls up on her side on the clean sheets and turns her back to her little cousin. The new sanitary cloths bulky and uncomfortable under her nightgown.

That night, Stella squeezes her eyelids shut but can't fall asleep. In the distance is the echo of artillery fire, and Stella can see the night sky behind the hills flash orange. Dark, ominous silhouettes of tanks and men with rifles. She rubs her sore stomach and back, willing it to stop. She thinks of the paintings of the Madonna, the skewered throat of Santa Lucia, and all the toils and troubles

Father Ramondo has recounted about these sacred women. Now, Stella longs for her mother's embrace, a need that feels fresh and more insatiable than even on her first day at Santa Lucia. When she finally sleeps, she dreams of a river of blood and of the saint's gouged eyes on a plate.

THE FAMILY'S LABORS INCREASE.

If they learned anything from last winter, it's that they will need to prepare more food than before. They will need to can more vegetables, preserve more fruits, store more wheat and barley, turn out more sausages and bury them in the ground. Last year, they had so many mouths to feed in the wine cellar alone. But now, the house is also full of soldiers.

Looking down from the upper terrace, Stella sees the soldiers have descended on the villa grounds and neighboring farms like a swarm of locusts. The landscape bears the ugly scars of occupation. The once lush expanse of olives, tall cypresses, and citrus trees lays ravaged, stripped, their branches skeletal silhouettes, like out-stretched arms, bare and twisted. The fields are barren, silent. On the neighboring farms, the sheep and cattle have either been eaten or are being hidden inside whatever structures haven't been pilfered. On the Martinellis' nearby farm, the Germans have burned all their beehives. There is no milk, no sugar, no meat.

In the dim kitchen light that evening, Zio Stefano triumphantly unwraps a package tightly wound in white cloth, one of the sausages buried in the herb garden months ago. A secret stash. Unearthing this little sausage and tasting its salty sustenance, away from the prying eyes of the soldiers, feels like a triumph. A small act of defiance. They huddle around it as if it is a precious treasure.

"Stella is a woman now," Zia Angela says matter-of-factly. Her uncles clink together their glasses.

Stella feels her face flush crimson to hear Zia Angela share this private news with grown men. To think her aunt ordered Zio Stefano to dig up a sausage from the ground so Stella could eat some meat. Or that her blossoming and unbidden womanhood was a cause for celebration at all.

Still, Stella feels grateful. It feels as if, with this skinny little wrapped sausage, Zio Stefano has unearthed a memory of happier times, a secret treasure like unearthing a gem from a hidden mine. The family gathers around the wooden table in the kitchen, tasting the peppery, salty goodness pulled from the cold earth. This simple piece of meat represents a time before the inexplicable series of events, this relentless black cloud, came to hang over them.

Outside the wine cellar, women gather to can vegetables in glass jars. The pepper seeds scatter across the table. The tender squashes sliced into finger-sized pieces. Each jar is a universe, a time capsule, each one holding a sunlit summer day. Stella imagines that when opening a jar in the cold of winter, they will remember the hot day when they didn't know how they would get through the cold months ahead. Zia Angela brings down pots of vinegar and brine that will keep the vegetables edible through the winter. A bittersweet mixture of holding on to the past. Holding on to hope.

These refugee women were once strangers, thrown together by chance, but now their fate is inextricably linked as they work for the future. For their communal survival. "As long as no more come, we should have enough," Signora Donati says at the end of a long day, wiping down the table. Long rows of glass jars filled on the table before them.

But with those words, Stella's sense of hope falters. She realizes her family probably won't taste this goodness this winter. They will need all the food they can make to feed the German soldiers instead. They are only toiling for their uninvited guests. Another stinging testament to the war's unending appetite and their role in feeding it. The pressing need to survive overshadowed by the uncertainty over who will benefit from their hard-earned labor.

BUT TO EVERYONE'S SURPRISE, the paratroopers leave. One morning, the sudden roar of engines shatters the dawn stillness. Stella and Mariasole watch the trucks wind down the roads away from the villa, headed north in a cloud of red dust.

Even Captain Bauer, the one man among them who walked a fine line between friend and enemy, departs without saying goodbye. Stella stands rooted on the high terrace, a mixture of relief, confusion, and apprehension filling her mind.

After they leave, Stella and Mariasole follow Zia Angela, Zio Stefano, and Zio Tino through the house, their steps careful in the unnatural silence that envelops it. Only the tank captains are left behind in some of the bedrooms.

"Where did they go?" Mariasole asks, but none of the adults has an answer. Stella wonders if the men will requisition another villa tonight, farther north of here. If they will intrude on other innocent people's lives. Eat their food. Shit in their hallways. Bare their asses in the olive groves. Strip their trees.

Without answers, all they can do is marvel at the mess they've left behind. The place is a mass of broken furniture, dirty sheets, clogged toilets. The smells and scars of desperate men. The floors are marred and streaked with red mud. Drawers yanked open, their contents strewn haphazardly. Cobwebs stringing across the chandeliers. Graffiti on one of the walls in the medieval stairwell.

Stella's fingers brush over a layer of grime on an ancient sideboard in one of the hallways as her aunt and uncle take stock of the disarray. Her aunt leads the way, hands on her hips and head wagging in disapproval. Taking in the full extent of the devastation for the first time. Stella covers her nose with the sleeve of her dress against the smell of sweat and desperation, the bitter taste of their intrusion into their lives.

Zio Stefano scratches his balding head. "At least they've gone," he says. "And we still have our lives, thanks be to God."

And to her relief, Stella finds the paintings in the treasure room intact. Sandro smiling among them.

Later, Stella leads Sandro to the great hall, where she finds that the paratroopers, even though they haven't said goodbye or thank you, have signed Sir Harwell's guest book in their jagged script.

Now only the tank men are left.

NEAR THE WOODSHED where Stella discovered Sergeant Cakebread, Stella finds Zio Stefano repairing an ancient-looking wooden plow. The sun has barely risen above the distant hills but the air is already oppressive. The tank men have rattled off for their daily misdeeds in their loud contraptions, stirring up red dust clouds that obscure the views of the wildflower fields. Now, the farm stands in a moment of delicate peace. Watching her uncle working on this antiquated wooden contraption meant to be hitched to oxen, Stella imagines what life at Villa Santa Lucia must have been like before the war started and she came here to stay. Her uncle's weathered face breaks into a grin as Stella approaches. He stops and wipes his forehead with the back of his sleeve. "*Ciao*, Stellina."

Stella props herself against an old metal piece of another disused plow, half buried in the ruts of the field. "Zio Stefano, can I ask you something? I've been wondering . . . Do you know why my father had to leave the village? Why he went to Rome?" she asks. "Zio Tino says maybe there was work there for him."

"Mmmm." Zio Stefano removes his work gloves. He nods and stares out at the rows of grapevines, flush with green leaves that lie still in the gathering heat. "Work. Yes, I suppose. But often, for someone to leave home, there must be something pulling and something pushing, too." Zio Stefano comes to stand next to Stella. He smells of sweat and tobacco and freshly tilled soil. "As I recall, your father found himself in a difficult situation here." He looks at her warily, as if judging how much to share.

"What kind of situation?" Stella studies his lined face.

"Some years ago, he entered into a partnership with our farming cooperative. Nothing out of the ordinary; we've been operating with shared resources for a very long time here. Let's say he promised a bit more than he could deliver and he stopped contributing. I suppose we should have known he might have taken on more than he could manage. It ended badly."

"Badly? How?"

"Eh . . ." Stella's uncle gestures animatedly, as if his hands could tell the whole story of Daniele Costa and his failed dealings with the local farmers without any words at all. But after a while, he adds, "I think he felt suffocated in some way by the partnership. He believed he wasn't getting his fair share of the profits, even though the others didn't see it that way. He left a few other farmers in the cooperative in a . . . difficult position. Financially, I mean. And then, there were some personal, family matters . . ." But Stefano stops himself with a wave of his hand. "After that, I guess they felt they didn't want to associate with someone who had broken their trust."

Stella lets the story sink into her mind, understanding better why her father felt he had to leave Santa Lucia. No one trusted him to forge a fruitful relationship. Stella can understand how the farmers must have felt. She herself has felt the pain and disappointment of being let down by both her father's action and inaction, all at the same time.

"But people can change, *capito*?" Zio Stefano says, turning a kind expression toward Stella. "It was a long time ago. Perhaps things are different for him now."

On Sunday, Stella and her family go check on Livia. Many of the refugees also walk into the village to find their children. As they approach, the harmonic resonance of the church bells reverberates through the streets, ringing true and clear, calling the small community to gather in shared faith and hope.

In the village square, they spot Livia standing with her arms crossed in the sun, talking with two other teenaged girls. One of the girls has a cascade of golden curls; the other, sleek, black hair to her trim waist. Just like Livia, Stella imagines their fathers must have had good reasons to send them away, too.

"She got her period!" Mariasole yells across the square. Stella feels her face ignite, a rush of heat flooding her cheeks.

Stella sees one side of Livia's mouth turn up at this loud proclamation. "I suppose she told you about—"

"I told her everything!" Mariasole calls. "Like she can't touch raw meat or make sauce while she's got her things or it will go off."

Livia's dark-haired friend laughs, bringing her hand to her mouth. "That's a myth, silly. Some old lady made that up so she wouldn't have to work so hard in the kitchen."

"You can do everything you want on your period," Livia's other friend says. "Well, mostly."

"Captain Bauer is gone!" Mariasole now informs them loudly, mercifully changing the subject and drawing everyone's attention away from Stella. "He didn't even say goodbye."

Livia's smile dissipates. *Poor Livia*, Stella thinks. *Two bad boyfriends, come and gone.* Stella thinks she and her cousins have a lot to learn about relations between grown-ups. As far as she can tell, they are as precarious and fragile as wartime itself, when each day can bring circumstances you could never have imagined before.

OUTSIDE THE CHURCH, while the children's conversations revolve around periods and boyfriends, the adults, instead, share news of nearby atrocities. The refugees have come from unimaginable terror. In Stia, every member of the male population has been shot. In Val di Chiana at San Pancrazio, the village has been burned to the ground. At San Godenzo, women have been raped and a child killed. In another town, people were gunned down inside the church. Stella wonders if it was a good idea for them to come into the village at all. Everywhere, farms have been plundered and burned.

Everyone moves inside the small church for mass, and Stella's family finds a pew along with another group of villagers. The air is thick with history, a comforting smell of cool dampness and incense ash and the flames of a hundred candles. They find a spot among the whispering, the occasional cough, and the soft rustle of everyone's clothing against the wooden benches.

A man turns to shake Zio Tino's hand from the pew in front of them. He leans his head close to Zio Tino's ear and speaks quietly to him. "There is a new group of partisans from Florence—in the birch thicket near my farm," he whispers. Stella feels the few simple words hang heavy in the air, a strange portent of potential allies and unforeseeable threats.

Father Ramondo takes his place at the front of the church, confident in his age-old role. He bows before the altar, then begins the rhythms and rituals of centuries. His voice is a steady rock in a sea of turmoil, an unfurling, seemingly unending call for safety, for peace, for unity in trying times. His voice echoes through the space, a collective heartbeat of a community resilient against the ever-shifting tide.

Zio Tino takes his wife's bony hand and clasps it between his knees while he hangs his head in prayer.

IN THE AFTERNOON, Sandro and Stella bring their drawings outside in the oppressive, late-summer air. They have left the books in the treasure room. Stella doesn't want to make Sandro feel any worse about not being able to see the words. And especially about his dwindling fragments of vision. Stella feels powerless to help him.

Several German soldiers mill about as Stella and Sandro get started on their drawings. They see the man they call Baffi come to the edge of the hill and unfasten his trousers. Stella has grown immune to the sight of the men urinating anywhere they choose. They have mostly abandoned the toilets inside the villa, most of which are clogged or in other states of disrepair. They try to ignore the sound of a steady stream of urine beating on the dried earth.

Suddenly, there is a rustle of dried leaves in the bush. A few seconds seem to unfold in slow motion.

First, a disheveled figure emerges from the depth of the undergrowth near where they are drawing. Stella sees a ragged black sleeve, a pair of desperate eyes. And then a pistol, reflecting the sun.

There is a blast. A flash. The deafening echo of a gunshot, cutting through the serenity of the woods. A flock of birds takes sudden flight, a thousand fluttering wingbeats creating a chaotic percussion above their heads. Then the forest falls silent. Stella hears the thud of the urinating German's body as it hits the dirt. A dark stain blooms on the back of Baffi's dirty white undershirt.

Stella instinctively reaches for Sandro's hand. "Come on," she whispers. They jog back to the villa as a group of Germans comes running toward the sound of the gunshot. Two of the men squat down beside their fallen *Bruder* while the others rush into the trees to find the gunman.

IN THE VILLAGE, the reprisals begin at dawn the next day.

The Germans start at the mayor's house and then go door to door, threatening retribution if people don't give up the locations of the local partisans or flush out anyone hidden in their homes. Their bodies covered in grenades and belts of bullets. Banging on every door until they nearly break. Shouting orders and prodding everyone, hands up, out of their homes at gunpoint.

They drag every man from their bed and collect them in a circle around the fountain in the center of the square. Ragged in their bedclothes. If they don't reveal the whereabouts of partisans, they will be shot. If they are partisans themselves, they will be shot.

When they search the *maestra*'s house, they find three men hiding in her attic. The Germans demand to know whose house it is. From the schoolhouse, they pull her by her thin arms into the circle with the ragged-looking men she's let stay in her empty house for the better part of a month.

From the villa, Stella and her family hear the echoing rounds of four gunshots.

IN THE WAKE of the massacre in the village square, Zio Tino rushes to the schoolhouse to bring Livia back home. The least they can do is watch her with their own eyes, Zia Angela says, even with the Germans in the villa. In the meantime, no one in Santa Lucia dares leave their house, and rumors circulate that even Mayor

Bagnoli is hiding inside the *municipio*. Stella and her family are left with the tank men, without Captain Bauer as a moderate force who might help smooth things over, at least enough to get them through the day.

Watching the men patrol the edges of Sir Harwell's property, weapons slack and smoking cigarettes, Stella feels an uncontrollable wave of hatred well up inside. She wants to scream and yell and hit them as hard as she can for taking the life of the one person in Santa Lucia who believed in her from the start, without question. The teacher with a pure heart who believed in all of her students. Who was brave enough to hide innocent men in her own home. Stella tightens her fists, her knuckles turning white, her mind searching for a way to put things back to the way they were before this horrible, irreversible tragedy. She feels the familiar ache radiating from within, a deep, gnawing emptiness that presses so heavily on her chest she feels she might stop breathing.

But Stella hardly has time to process what has happened because that very afternoon, Ornella Rivelli's water breaks while she's picking tomatoes in the garden.

The poor woman's wails begin with that water breaking, and they don't stop. The men retreat from the wine cellar while all the women rush in, making a circle around Ornella. Zia Angela orders Stella and her cousins to boil water and fetch clean sheets and cloths. There is no midwife.

Stella brings clean linens from the cupboard as they make a makeshift birthing room, a thin mattress surrounded by women. They bring water and diluted wine for Ornella, but she doesn't drink. Only sweats and calls out to the Madonna and every saint who comes to her mind while one of the women wipes her brow. In the dusky light, a circle of frantic but determined faces gathers around her, ready to bring a new life into the chaotic world outside, even if Ornella herself doesn't at all look like she's ready. Twilight descends around the villa. The men busy themselves with chores outside, in a kind of nervous frenzy. Even the Germans fall silent. The wine cellar transforms into a canvas of flickering light and shadow, of sweat and blood, of a kind of metallic undertone of animal fear. Stella watches the older women run their fingers over rosary beads, their prayers ardent and unceasing.

As darkness falls, Signora Donati and Zia Angela squat along-side Ornella, murmuring encouragements and instructions in the flickering gaslight. Ornella carries the weight of the world in her frightened eyes and scrawny body, as each contraction gathers force like a wave in a storm. Unstoppable. Her hair is sweaty and stuck to her head. Her face red with effort. Contractions and pains over-taking her in agony beyond her control. The wails of the woman's tears and cries, her calling on the Madonna, on the saints, echo through the vaulted room.

Stella has never witnessed a birth, and even though she imagines she should feel awe and anticipation about this event, instead she feels as if she herself is drowning in the chaos of contortions and blood and sweat. She can't pull herself away, as much as she would like to, from the mesmerizing, terrifying waves of Ornella's physical anguish. In that moment, Stella makes a vow that she will never have children and that the birth of any healthy child must be a miracle.

At last, long after midnight, a shrill cry pierces the room as the slippery baby is handed over to Ornella, who is wrung out as a wet rag. A tiny creature with crimson fists and a knotted face. Stella sees Ornella's tears illuminated in the flickering gaslight, a beacon of hope and heartbreak all at once. A new life in the vast darkness and unknown of this world.

Stella can't help it. When the mother lays eyes on her baby and her face twists with relief, Stella darts up the stairwell as a stream of her own tears erupts, a river unleashed. She sits on the top stair and lets her stinging tears come. It's a purely physical thing that happens, as violent and uncontrollable as the birth itself. Her tears come not just for the safe arrival of this baby girl. But for her suffering mother. For the unknown whereabouts of Ornella's husband. For the loss of the *maestra*. For Sandro's failing vision and Torino and her own betraying body. For her own mother and father, who, for their own reasons, have vanished. For her past life in the schoolhouse, which now stands dark and empty in the center of the village. For all the things beyond her ability to change.

For everything.

EVEN AFTER THE VIOLENCE in the village square, Stella is surprised to find a new wave of refugees arriving at the villa. There are only women and children now. To Stella, they look different from those who arrived in the past. They are not only skinny and hungry, begging for shelter and any food that can be spared, they look haunted, their eyes sunken and ringed in black. They carry nothing with them.

At the wine cellar door, they share horror stories that Stella can hardly believe are true. They say all the men in their villages have been rounded up and killed. Their husbands and sons shot mercilessly. Their houses set on fire. Their centuries-old villages nothing but a pile of charred ruins. In one town, they say, the Germans opened fire on more than two hundred villagers during mass. They look more haunted than anyone Stella has ever seen.

When the newly arrived people realize there are Germans staying in the house, they don't dare enter. Everyone advises them to go to the schoolhouse or the church. "Right before they leave here," one of the women warns her aunt and uncle, "at a minimum, they will strip your trees and eat your animals. Maybe burn all of your crops. If that's all they do to you, consider yourselves fortunate."

Beyond the village, there is a new section made in the ancient cemetery for the freshly dug graves.

CHAPTER 11

THE LIBRARIAN

Summer 1944

Across the surface, there are strawberries and cornflowers and roses and carnations and periwinkles and daisies and purple irises. Each one a story, a world unto itself.
—FROM THE LOST DIARIES OF SANDRO
BOTTICELLI, FLORENCE, SUMMER 1480

You can destroy a whole village. You can burn their farms and homes and churches to the ground and somehow, they will find a way to rebuild. But if you destroy their culture, their history, then you destroy their achievements. You destroy their soul. How could they be expected to come back from such an affront? It would be as if they never existed at all.
—FROM THE DIARY OF CAPTAIN WALLACE E.
FOSTER, MONUMENTS OFFICER OF THE FIFTH
ARMY IN TUSCANY, AUGUST 1944

Stella imagines that when the librarian of the Uffizi Galleries finally arrives, things will be like they were when the pictures were brought to the Villa Santa Lucia, all those months ago. There will be trucks and men. Wrapping and crates. Everything will be packed up and then all the paintings will be loaded into the backs of trucks for their safe return to Florence.

But that's not what happens.

Instead, the librarian arrives alone. On foot.

Stella finds her uncles greeting him in the dining hall. Signor Fasola is short and unassuming, dressed in a dark suit like Zio Tino and most other men his age. Sweating profusely. His black, round glasses look too large for his face. Thin wisps of dark hair lie flat against his balding head.

Stella places a glass of water from the well in front of Signor Fasola and he drinks it down in a single gulp.

"Stella, make Signor Fasola something to eat," Zia Angela says. "He must be famished after such a journey."

Stella arranges a plate with cured eggplant and peppers in oil, pulled from the stash of goods they put away when they thought they would have to feed the paratroopers all winter long. She pairs them with some of last year's olives, a hunk of pecorino cut from a half-wheel, and a basket of bread. Zio Tino uncorks a dusty bottle from Sir Harwell's stash of table wine they've been hiding in a bedroom cupboard.

"I couldn't get any trucks," Signor Fasola says, dabbing his brow with a handkerchief. "It's a wonder I made it here at all."

Zio Tino and Zia Angela exchange worried glances. "But . . . how will you remove the paintings?" Zia Angela says.

Signor Fasola sighs deeply. "I had been promised two trucks. But then the museum had no way to procure them. The Germans have control over all the motorized vehicles in Florence. Anyway, even if they had found one, there is no gasoline to be had anywhere, neither for us nor for them. And perhaps it's for the best. The roadsides are mined. I traveled as best I could through the fields . . . away from the roads."

"So the pictures . . ." Stella says. She can't help butting in.

"They're not going anywhere," Signor Fasola says. "At least not for now. I'm afraid we have no choice."

Stella feels immense relief at this news, but she sees it has the opposite effect on Zio Tino, whose hand is shaking as he lifts his glass of water.

"Please . . ." Zio Stefano says, "give us some good news from Florence."

"You have no idea how I wish I could, *signore*," Signor Fasola says, his face grave. "People are desperate for food and supplies. Many parts of the city have already suffered damage. Everything is sandbagged, of course, but it seems such a small act. Some are saying Florence will remain an open city. That there are agreements to protect it on both sides. But I don't see it."

Zio Tino nods. "We are isolated here. It's not easy to understand what is happening beyond our little universe."

"The biggest problem you seem to have here in the country-side is looting," Signor Fasola says. "Before I got here, I stopped at two of the other repositories where we have more stashes of hidden paintings. Montagnana and Oliveto."

Stella's mind reels. *There are other hiding places like Villa Santa Lucia?*

"We've had several hundred other paintings stored there since forty-three. Just like here. I almost don't want to tell you what I found there, *signori*. Most of it gone."

"Gone!" Stella says. Her mind can hardly imagine other villas like this one, filled with paintings. Her mind spools out as if she could see all the villas across Tuscany in a single view, each filled with hundreds of paintings. It is nearly impossible to comprehend.

"Only a few kilometers from here," Signor Fasola says, piling a few pieces of pickled eggplant on a hunk of bread. "I'm sorry to say that we are missing important works from the Pitti and the Uffizi . . . Several altarpieces by Filippo Lippi and five paintings by Piero di Cosimo . . . The *Bacchus* by Caravaggio, which I'm sure you must know. Several tremendous pictures by Pontormo. Even a *Pallas and the Centaur* by Sandro Botticelli."

At the mention of Sandro Botticelli, Stella almost drops the slippery pitcher of water.

Signor Fasola continues. "What a mess," he says, setting down his bread. "They smashed furniture in the villa and there were human feces in most of the rooms."

Zio Tino rubs his forehead. "Then we must do everything we can to make sure that doesn't happen here. After all this time and all we have risked already . . . we can't let them fall into the wrong hands."

"Exactly." Signor Fasola nods. "Back when we brought the paintings here, all of us thought it was the right decision. We couldn't have known that your villas out here would be occupied. We couldn't have known that Florence might be a safer bet than these more isolated locations . . ."

Stella watches Signor Fasola's lips tremble at the weight of this responsibility on his shoulders.

"You and Signor Poggi and all the others did what you thought was right at the time," Zio Tino says. "I know that's little consolation. You can rest assured that we've had surveillance here twenty-four hours a day."

"Even though we have had many other things to worry about," Zia Angela interjects.

"I understand, *signora*," Signor Fasola says. "But the reason the paintings disappeared from the other repositories is that the custodians feared the German troops so much that they abandoned their posts and went into hiding. So, constant surveillance—and even defiance, if needed—is the only way to have any chance of protecting paintings," Signor Fasola says. "Otherwise, I fear your own villa will be next. And these are the jewels of our collection— the jewels of our heritage. How could we live with ourselves if something happened to them? That's why I did whatever I could to get here."

THEY MAKE SPACE for Signor Fasola in the bedroom that Captain Bauer vacated. Stella and Mariasole help Zia Angela mop the red tiles and change the sheets. Stella thinks of all the soldiers taking up the bedrooms, sweating on the sagging mattresses. Zia Angela curses under her breath, a picture of exhaustion from the months of relentless labor and anxiety of the unwanted guests under her care.

Stella's uncles give Signor Fasola a tour of the treasure room. Stella wishes with all her might that she could go, too, but she follows her aunt upstairs.

Outside the window, there is a sudden clatter of gunfire. Stella, her aunt, and cousin go to their knees by instinct. But then, there is only laughter and friendly banter in German. When Stella finally dares to look out the window, she sees the bored soldiers with their shirts rolled and stripped down to their waists, their chests bare. They are using one of the old olive trees for target practice. A friendly competition.

"*Dio!*" her aunt exclaims, then closes the shutters. The room falls dim as the girls resume their chores.

"Maybe they will leave soon, *zia*, just like the paratroopers did," Stella says. "They can't stay here forever."

Zia Angela wipes her brow. "Feels like they already have been here for all time."

AFTER SERVING the German tank officers their dinner in the dining hall, Stella and her family crowd into the kitchen and close the door so they don't have to witness the sight of the men. Stella's aunt and uncles sit at the small table with Signor Fasola while the girls stand at the worktable. They speak in hushed voices as Stella spoons hot *ribollita* with white beans and wilting vegetables into small bowls.

"One of the farmers who helped me along the way here told me they've spotted Americans near Montepulciano," Signor Fasola says. He stops, gauging the reaction at the table. "Some are still expecting an Allied landing at Grosseto, but who could say?" A big shrug.

"We have heard the same," Zio Tino says, nodding, "but we have heard so many things over the months . . . They keep saying the Allies will land in Tuscany, but then, nothing."

"I know it's precarious with these men here, but whatever you do, do not leave this villa, *capito*?" Signor Fasola says. "The roads are covered in mines and Germans. I have only sympathy for those trying to stay out of their line of sight. There are corpses everywhere. And there are also escaped Allied soldiers," he continues. "I came across a few on the way here. Most of them are headed toward Bolsena and are smart enough to avoid the main roads." Stella thinks about Sergeant Cakebread and wonders how far he's gotten in the woods with his crooked leg and ravaged foot. She wonders if any of the *partigiani* she's heard about have come to his aid at all.

"We've seen them," Zia Angela says, and Stella sees Signor Fasola's expression turn grim.

"They're not here now," Zio Tino interjects quickly.

Signor Fasola says, "You cannot harbor soldiers—or partisans—under any circumstances."

"We know that," Zia Angela says, and for a while, the room falls silent.

"The good news . . ." Signor Fasola says. "There is a long chain of courageous, brave, and generous people who help them to go south and rejoin their troops. Or to head north to Switzerland and escape the whole thing. They give them clothing and food, new shoes, medicine, whatever they need. But they risk being arrested or shot."

When Signor Fasola hesitates, Stella realizes he must count her own family among this long string of helpers.

"You can see, *signori*," Signor Fasola says, "why moving the pictures now is out of the question."

Stella knows the museum professionals see this as bad news, but Stella is just relieved the paintings are still here. But she knows for sure now that no one is coming to take the paintings out of the Villa Santa Lucia. And no one is coming to help *them*. They are truly on their own.

"Stay as long as you like, my friend," Zio Tino says, standing and patting the still rattled-looking Signor Fasola on the shoulder.

Stella finishes her chores and goes to look for Sandro to tell him the news. The paintings won't be leaving the villa after all. She is certain he will feel just as relieved as she does.

THE NEXT DAY after the midday meal, Zio Tino allows Stella and Sandro to follow Signor Fasola as he makes a new round of the treasure room to inspect the condition of the paintings.

With a loud clatter, Zio Tino opens all the shutters for the first time in months. A golden light bathes the room. They haven't seen the paintings like this since the day Signor Poggi's men brought them here. Haven't dared to. But something about Signor Fasola's calm, unassuming authority gives them the confidence to bring a bright light to the room for the first time in so long.

The paintings suddenly take on a different aspect. Stella imagines this is how people must see them when they go to view them in the Uffizi Galleries. They are more than just objects of beauty and worth. Bathed in the soft sunlight, they seem to hold a magic beyond words.

"You can see a lot of thought went into which pictures to bring here," Signor Fasola says. "Not only from the Uffizi but from the Pitti Palace, the Accademia Gallery." Fasola is a humble man, but it's clear that the paintings are like old friends. After he surveyed them all stacked together in this single room, his whole demeanor has shifted. His shoulders are back, and for the first time, the shadows dissipate from his face and he smiles.

"A labor of love, no doubt," Zio Tino says.

Signor Fasola raises himself up, standing straighter. "I'm glad you feel that way. It's been a difficult task, but knowing these pictures are safe here in this temporary haven, and God willing, will be around long after we are gone, makes it worthwhile."

Stella and Sandro trail behind Stella's uncle and the Uffizi's librarian with an excitement they haven't felt since the first time they visited the treasure room.

"If any one of them was lost or destroyed, we'd lose a fragment of ourselves, no? It's amazing to think about the cultural legacy that these paintings represent. Each one tells a story about our past—and about who we are. Any one of these paintings—from any of the fifty hiding places."

"There are *fifty* hiding places?!" Stella blurts.

Signor Fasola nods. "Across all of Italy, yes. More or less. Nearly forty of them in Tuscany alone," he says. "That should give you an idea of our rich heritage here in our own region, *signorina*."

Stella's mind races with the idea of fifty places like this one, spread out across the whole of the Italian peninsula. Now Stella can't help but feel a sense of pride at her family's role in helping to protect Italy's cultural legacy during such a tumultuous time.

The paintings take on a new importance, and Stella feels moved by the gravity of their beauty and presence.

"They are all villas like this one?" Sandro asks.

Signor Fasola nods. "Some of them, yes. But also monasteries, churches . . . Plus other places you might not guess. Even train tunnels."

"It's an honor that we can make a small contribution," Zio Tino says. "I can assure you Sir Harwell feels the same."

"An important contribution, yes," Signor Fasola says. "With any luck, these paintings will be treasured for generations to come."

Signor Fasola picks up a piece of paper from the old table, the one where Sandro has sketched the outlines of the three dancing women.

"Who drew this?" he asks.

Sandro looks suddenly shy. "I did."

"*La Primavera,*" Signor Fasola says, taking a deep breath. His eyes now go from Sandro Botticelli's tremendous flower painting to Sandro's small sketch of the same subject. "One of the jewels of the world."

He taps Sandro's drawing lightly with the back of his hand. "*Che bravo.*"

To everyone's surprise and dismay, another group of Germans arrives. This time, it's a small group of medical corps. They don't attempt to terrorize the family, to everyone's immense relief. Stella and Sandro watch the new men set up a makeshift infirmary. Protected from the rain but open to the fresh air, the space lies inside the covered loggia sheltered beneath the villa's upper terrace.

Stella and Sandro watch the men line up cots and unpack their medical supplies. The sharp smell of astringent fills the air, mingling with the sweet fragrance of flowers blooming in the garden in spite of the complete lack of tending. Beyond, in one of the olive groves, they erect a tattered tent as weary as the men now inside it.

The man in charge of the new medical team is a broad-shouldered doctor with fine blond hair who speaks decent Italian. Stella wishes he could have been here for the birth of Ornella's baby, or maybe he could even have saved the *maestra's* life if he was the least bit inclined to do either. But he's arrived too late for any of this.

When the doctor spies Stella and Sandro sketching near the rear terrace, he calls out to them to collect the citrus trees' last remaining lemons. "Bring me as many of them as you can," he says in halting Italian, "even if they are rotted. They will make good disinfectant."

Stella and Sandro go into the grove and pick up the half-spoiled fruits from the ground. They smell of a long-lost past before anyone thought a war might reach them here. Of rot and rebirth. Of the eternal cycle of the Tuscan countryside that continues to turn no matter what else happens around them. They smell of life.

Sandro peels one, wrinkling his nose as he bites into its sour flesh.

AT THE SAME TIME the medical corps arrives, the reserve tank men finally get called up for battle. Zio Stefano says this means the fighting is drawing close.

One day during the next week, some of the reserve tank men leave, their packs full. Sandro and Stella watch the German they call Salsiccia squeeze his bulk into a truck and roll off into the distance. In the evening, he comes back covered in red dirt and blood. One of his friends returns on a stretcher. The newly arrived soldiers treat them under the terrace and in the ragged tent. Those who come back in one piece fall in heaps of exhaustion into their cots under the trees.

"One of them got his leg amputated!" Mariasole informs them loudly, running into the courtyard. "They buried it down by the olive press."

At night, Stella and Mariasole lie in bed and from their window, they hear the man groaning for morphine.

EVERY DAY, Sandro and Stella do whatever they can to be sure they are present for Signor Fasola and Zio Tino's daily round of the paintings in the treasure room. Stella makes sure she gets her kitchen chores done quickly, and Sandro runs inside from helping Zio Stefano in the vineyards.

"What is this painting about?" Sandro asks when they come to stand before the *Primavera*.

"Ah! We believe it was painted to celebrate a marriage," Signor Fasola says, lacing his fingers behind his back. He begins to pace back and forth in front of the painting, which dwarfs him. Stella, Sandro, and Zio Tino stand nearby, looking at the painting with new eyes. "Lorenzo di Pierfrancesco de' Medici was a cousin to Lorenzo the Magnificent. He married a noblewoman named Semiramide Appiano in the 1480s. Not many people know this, but Semiramide was the niece of Simonetta Vespucci, who was considered the most beautiful woman in Florence and perhaps even Botticelli's muse."

Stella's mind reels at the amount of information Signor Fasola has rattled off about the painting in mere seconds. She holds her breath, waiting for what's next.

"Quite a wedding gift, if you ask me," Zio Tino says.

"*Infatti!*" Signor Fasola says. "We believe the painting was meant for a villa much like this one. The Villa de Castello, not so far outside the city. Lorenzo probably commissioned Sandro Botticelli to paint this picture upon his marriage, when he was decorating the villa for his new wife. The sixteenth-century art historian Giorgio Vasari saw it there himself and wrote about it. In fact, several visitors from these early centuries mention seeing Botticelli's work in that villa."

"The artist worked for the Medici?" Sandro asks.

"Yes. Botticelli was already well known for painting mythological scenes. You might know the *Birth of Venus*. It's another very famous painting, probably made for the same Lorenzo and for the same villa."

Stella nods. She feels embarrassed to tell Signor Fasola she has no idea what he's talking about. In fact, the more she learns about this painting, the more she thinks she hardly understands anything at all.

IT'S SANDRO WHO IS BOLD ENOUGH to admit he needs more help to understand Botticelli's painting.

"Well, typically we read things like books from left to right," Signor Fasola says, "but instead, Botticelli invites us to read this painting from the opposite direction—from right to left. The blue man on the right is Zephyrus, or the spring wind. He is embracing a nymph named Chloris. He plans to kidnap her and then marry her."

"*Che pazzo!*" Stella interjects. "Why would you agree to marry someone who kidnapped you?" She thinks about the story of Santa Lucia, whose eyes were plucked out and throat speared, too, just because she refused to marry. Stella realizes that, time and again, history has been unkind to women when it comes to selecting husbands.

"It gets more interesting," Signor Fasola says. "Notice, the trees above Zephyrus don't have any fruit on them. Next, we see Chloris transformed into Flora, the goddess of spring. Now she is spreading the flowers that have gathered in her dress. This transformation is indicated by the blossoms flowing out of Chloris's mouth; a symbol of springtime and fertility."

Sandro was right, she realizes. The woman on the right is the same as the next one to the left, just at a later time. The scene unfolds like the illustrated children's publications Stella used to see in the newsstands back in Torino. Only in reverse.

"So, who's the lady in the center?" Sandro asks.

"Ah! Venus herself, the goddess of love and beauty. You see how the figures in the foreground create a frame around her. Even the trees part around her body, and the sky forms a kind of a halo so your eye is drawn to her."

"I told you," Sandro says.

"Like a Madonna," Stella says.

"*Brava*," Signor Fasola continues. "The blindfolded Cupid at the top of the painting is her son. Sometimes he's called *Amor*. He's about to fire his arrow of love. Then the dancing ladies are the Three Graces, goddesses who symbolize chastity, beauty, and love. They are dancing in a circle with pearls on their heads, symbolizing purity. Just like you drew it, Sandro."

Sandro says, "The three dancing women are the same figure seen from different angles all at once." Stella wouldn't have seen this before. But Sandro makes everything seem so obvious.

"I never saw that before, but you are exactly right, my friend," Signor Fasola says. "And finally, on the left, we have Mercury, the messenger of the gods. We know it's Mercury because of his helmet, the winged sandals, and the caduceus, which is kind of a magic wand. Sometimes you can identify a character in a painting by their attributes—things they wear or carry."

"Just like we know Santa Lucia from her speared neck and her eyes on a plate," Stella says.

"*Brava!*" Signor Fasola says again.

But Stella doesn't feel smart. Instead, she feels dumbfounded. She never could have made up a story like this.

"YOU HAVE TALENT, young man," Signor Fasola tells Sandro.

"I couldn't make anything close to *that*," he says, gesturing to the *Primavera*.

"But you have every right to trust in your talent," Signor Fasola tells Sandro. "Besides, even if you don't make a masterpiece for all time like this one, the small act of drawing has a way of opening up something bigger than ourselves. I myself have experienced this, as I've walked through our galleries in Florence with my sketchbook. Attempting to replicate a great work of art helps us see things we hadn't seen before, and to see it in ways we hadn't before as well."

Stella finds herself absorbed in Signor Fasola's words. All this while, she'd marveled at the distant, mysterious beauty of the paintings hidden in the treasure room and had even attempted to sketch some of them herself, yet she'd never grasped that trying to draw them might allow you to see something you didn't see before, and to interact with them in a more deeply personal way.

"For our museum visitors who bring along a piece of paper and a pencil, drawing can help them make sense of their own experiences. I have seen these paintings have the power to heal—especially when the wounds are deeply emotional or at least below the surface. I think it's because drawing and making art can be a way to purge things like despair or grief that we can't find words for. It helps us say what is buried deep inside," he says, touching his heart. "Also, drawing can give you a feeling of control or accomplishment; at a minimum, it can be a distracting activity that allows people to temporarily set aside their pain and focus on something else."

A shift occurs in Stella's perception. The paintings around her suddenly feel a bit less distant, a bit less impenetrable; instead, she sees each one as a possible way to navigate the labyrinth of the inner mind, if only she will take the time to try to replicate it on the page. And even when her own picture turns out lacking, she may have seen something new about the painting—or about what's locked inside her own heart and mind.

Stella turns to share this revelation with Sandro, but stops. He stands very close to Botticelli's masterpiece, straining to see the intricate details of its blanket of flowers. It seems that he cannot see more, but less. His proximity to the canvas and the tight squinting of his eyes reveal a sad truth. Stella can hardly comprehend the tragedy of his gradual loss in his ability to see clearly, the cruel paradox of her own ability to begin to see the paintings in a new light, while Sandro's light grows ever dimmer.

FOR STELLA, preparing food and washing dishes for the innumerable people living in the villa has become the metronome of her days. Each meal is an anchor, a predictable routine and a cadence that allows them all to make it from one moment to the next in a world where the ground seems to shift beneath them, everything a precarious truce that might shatter at any moment. They adhere to a strict meal schedule so everyone knows what to expect without too much discussion.

But all day long, Stella searches for a moment when she and Sandro might escape again to the magic of the treasure room, the only break from their monotonous, endless toils. Where they might stand before the *Primavera* and feel some sliver of hope for a springtime and a chance to begin again. Where they might sketch the figures that Signor Fasola has helped them see in a new light: the flower-crowned Venus, the Roman goddess of love. The winged Mercury. The Three Graces. Where—even if they fail to capture it with their pencils—the mere act of reaching for eternal love and the wonders of nature might allow them to forget the grim reality that awaits them as soon as they have to leave the wondrous solitude of the room again.

The summer days unfold under cerulean skies. The Germans continue to rotate in and out of the villa as the days pulsate with an alternating pattern of exhaustion and reprieve. They leave in the mornings in their drab trucks and tanks, and stagger back in the evenings like weary chess pieces, beat down and muddy.

One evening, one of the soldiers produces a violin—from where, Stella has no idea—and the Germans gather around it. As the sound of the violin begins to fill the air, Sandro and Stella tiptoe up the back stairs to the upper terrace, which has transformed into a magical realm against the glow of the setting sun. The men sit on the stones and rest, listening to the squeaking, eerie refrains. Suddenly, a deep voice rises to meet it. The singer has an even, sonorous voice, and for the first time, Stella thinks, their language sounds at the same time sorrowful and beautiful.

A few of the refugees emerge, coming up from the wine cellar, just out of view. They loiter alongside the villa's stone wall to listen to this strange impromptu concert, a moment of light as the night gathers.

After a few melancholy songs, they turn to German folk tunes and all the soldiers join in, raising their voices in the night air. A round of cannon fire in the distance serves as a bass drum. Stella sees that the soldiers, too, are just humans trying to forge a moment of beauty and relief from the endless hours of mounting tension that hang over them while the tide of war finally begins to wash onto their shores. They too reach for something to break the grim reality and tension of the days that tick by with their relentless, unceasing darkness.

The next morning, a new fleet of trucks appears, bearing large metal cannons. They park alongside the main road, and the *die Bruder* come out of the villa to meet the new men.

THE GERMAN DOCTOR in charge of the makeshift infirmary is an intelligent-looking middle-aged man. He listens intently as Stella explains Sandro's condition.

"And then he said he couldn't see very well in the dark," she says quickly. Sandro sits on the examining table in his white undershirt. Looking sheepish.

The doctor frowns. "Look to the side." He points to the left and Stella closely watches Sandro. He shines a battery-powered light toward Sandro's face and squints through his small, wire-framed glasses. He speaks Italian haltingly, with a heavy accent. But he's one of the only ones who understand them at all. Stella watches the doctor, his pale face very close to Sandro's, looking carefully. "And to the other," he says.

After a long while of having Sandro look in all sorts of directions, the doctor puts down his light and wipes his hand on a rag. "I'm not an ophthalmologist," he says, pushing his glasses up farther on his nose. He speaks slowly, deliberately. Mispronouncing some words. "What I can tell you is you may have a condition with the retina that is causing your vision to deteriorate bit by bit, over a period of time. Rare in a person of your age. But I've heard of it."

"What can we do about it?" Stella leans forward and peers into Sandro's brown eyes. He blinks, his eyes red and watery from the doctor's evaluation. "Does he need glasses?"

The doctor sighs. "Glasses may not help in this case. Under normal times, he might be a candidate for surgery," he says. "But these are not normal times. I'm afraid there is nothing we can do for the moment. Perhaps . . . when this is all over . . . you could find an eye specialist in Florence or another city closer to your home."

Stella feels her heart sink. She doesn't know what a retina is, but she knows surgery is serious. Sandro stares down at his toes, and she knows he's scared even if he won't say it to the doctor.

"Surgery could be complicated," the doctor continues, as if he could read Stella's mind. "And risky. But left untreated, I imagine . . . it might get worse. But slowly."

They sit stunned. From his cot, one of the men calls in a weak voice to the doctor for morphine. The doctor is momentarily distracted, but then he turns back to Sandro and squeezes his arm with a measure of compassion.

"But as I said, this is beyond my capability. I wish I could tell you more, my friend. I'm sorry."

Then he turns to the patient in the bed.

EARLY ONE MORNING, the most delicious, sticky-sweet smell wafts from the villa's kitchen, drawing Stella and Sandro to the door.

The kitchen is mostly the domain of Stella and her aunt. But to their surprise, Stella and Sandro enter the kitchen to find one of the German soldiers there. Cooking. They freeze in the doorway. He's put one of Zia Angela's aprons over his drab uniform and he's frying dough in a pan over a small flame. The soldiers don't normally venture into the kitchen at all. Stella's only seen them with guns, not spatulas. Her aunt and uncles are nowhere to be seen, so she doesn't know what to do. Suddenly, Mariasole races up to them, drawn by the enticing smell. The aroma of frying dough brings a memory flooding back in Stella's mind, of her mother making *bignole* at carnival time, tiny puffs of dough filled with cream. A pang of nostalgia alongside loss.

The man turns and looks at them. He grins slightly, uttering a few words in German. They watch blankly. Not blinking. Not understanding. Stella and Sandro share a fleeting, wordless exchange. The soldier keeps talking to them anyway. He mimes eating something delicious, then rubs his stomach with pleasure. Stella wonders how he managed to get the sugar he's sprinkled across the fried dough.

As he moves the sizzling fried dough to a plate, he wags a sugar-dusted finger at them. Slowly, back and forth. A prohibition.

"He doesn't want us to eat them," Mariasole says.

"Must be the best baker in Berlin or something," Sandro says.

Stella's mouth waters at the sticky-sweet smell. Before leaving the kitchen, the soldier places the plate of round, fried dough in a cabinet, hangs Zia Angela's apron back on its hook, and leaves, wagging his finger at them once more. Chuckling to himself.

"WHAT KIND OF PAINTS did they use? Oil?"

In the treasure room, Sandro's questions for Signor Fasola are detailed and never-ending. It would not have occurred to Stella to ask this. Signor Fasola stations himself outside the door to the treasure room all day. Zio Tino seems relieved to have this backup vigilance. For now, the Germans don't seem interested in the paintings. They are just looking for food and a place to rest while they rotate in and out of the fray.

Signor Fasola's bushy eyebrows fly up. "Ah, no! Artists in Italy only began to use oil paints in a widespread way after Botticelli's death. No. Sandro Botticelli would have painted mostly with tempera. They ground their own pigments in the workshop and used egg yolks as a binder. Then they used soft brushes made of the fur of animals like weasel."

Stella tries to imagine what it was like to be an artist hundreds of years ago. An image of an artist's workshop where they ground their own colors, broke eggs, and made paints grows in Stella's mind. Signor Fasola has begun to enumerate titles for all the paintings in the room and the names of all the artists, which, to Stella's astonishment, he rattles off from memory, without even consulting a book or a single piece of paper: Rubens and Fra Bartolommeo and Lorenzo di Credi and Paolo Uccello and some just called "Florentine school." So many more that Stella's head spins. And, they learn, several more paintings in the room are by Sandro Botticelli.

"What about all the flowers?" Sandro asks next.

"The flowers and fruit!" Signor Fasola says. "One of the most interesting parts of this painting, in my view. There are a variety of orange and laurel trees. Both trees are symbols of the Medici family. Did you know there are more than five hundred individual plant species depicted here? He has made the whole thing look like tapestry—very similar, in fact, to what we find in northern Europe at the time."

"And Sandro Botticelli knew about all these things?" Stella asks, incredulous.

"Good question. No doubt he had someone helping him. A priest named Marsilio Ficino was a spiritual adviser to the Medici around the time Botticelli painted this. He was the first translator of Plato's works into Latin; he had a tremendous influence on Renaissance thought. So he could have provided input on Botticelli's subject matter here. Neoplatonic philosophers saw Venus ruling over earthly and divine love; she is the classical equivalent of the Virgin Mary."

Stella is already distracted. "So, at Montagnana, the other villa, the soldiers took away even huge paintings like this?"

In the gentle glow of sunlight piercing a single crack in the shutter, Signor Fasola's face is grave. "Yes. It was a privately owned villa like this one. Maybe not as large or elegant. But they still took more than two hundred paintings out of it."

Stella is dumbfounded and feels relief that the Germans billeting at Santa Lucia haven't taken anything yet. "Where do you think they took them?"

Signor Fasola scratches his forehead. "No idea. Northward."

"And what happened to the people inside the villa?" Sandro asks. Stella feels sheepish for not asking this question first. "Was the family there?"

"No," Signor Fasola says. "The owners believed Florence might be safer than the countryside, so they went to their apartment there and left a caretaker behind in the villa. But when their caretaker saw all the German tanks and trucks arrive, he decided to run to the village church for safety. So, he saved his life perhaps by leaving the paintings behind. But unfortunately, it meant no one was there to guard them when the Germans came."

"Then we must not leave this place," Stella says.

"I won't leave here, as much as I wish I could," Signor Fasola says.

"You mean we risk our lives to save the paintings," Sandro says.

Signor Fasola stands silent for a long time. "Yes. That is the reality of it. But we can't let them take or destroy whatever they want."

"But . . . why us?" Sandro asks.

"Why not us?" Signor Fasola says, the twin frames of his glasses reflecting the glowing light. "If we don't take some action—any one of us—then who will?"

THREE DAYS GO BY, and they don't see the German pastry chef anymore, even though the tanks return at dusk as usual.

"You think he's dead? The best baker in Berlin?" Sandro asks.

Stella imagines the man lying in a ditch on the side of the road.

Stella and Sandro look at each other for a long moment, then run to the cupboard where the donuts are stored. They are still there in the darkness.

They take the sugary pastries into the treasure room and eat them, sitting on the floor in front of Sandro Botticelli's vision of beauty, joy, and rebirth. The pastries stale and sticky and delicious in their hands.

"You are a better cook than he was," Sandro says, licking his fingers. "Even your dirt cake was better."

This makes Stella laugh.

MORE AMERICAN PLANES COME.

Great steel birds, glinting in the sun, swoop overhead. Each roar resonates like rolling thunder. Stella and Sandro tent their hands over their eyes, watching them trace streaks across the blue sky. Below, the very earth seems to hold its breath with each pass.

"Here we go again," Signora Donati says, reluctantly abandoning her chores to hunker down in the wine cellar until the noise of the planes subsides.

At this point, the small children in the cantina, all returned from the schoolhouse, feel immune to any threats. As soon as the swooping planes are out of sight, they rush out into the garden, re-suming their games. Stella watches them start an impromptu sack race down the hillside, using grain sacks left over from the autumn harvest. Stella watches them fall over with laughter, tumbling into the tall, hot grass.

IN THE WINE CELLAR, many of the refugees are making contin-gency plans. Old Giuseppe tells Zio Tino he and another man have gone out to see the partisans in the woods. They say the partisans have begun to dig deep trenches near a creek in case they all need to make a run for it. If everyone needs to abandon the house at a split-second's notice, he says, they should make a bolt for the tree line. That's in case those planes open their bellies and release bombs on them. Surely the villa appears like a small fortress from the air, Old Giuseppe says. An easy target.

But seeing how fast the planes come, Stella can't imagine how any one of them could run from the villa to the woods fast enough. Much less how they would have time to go to their bedchamber first and fetch their still-packed suitcases. And what would happen to Villa Santa Lucia, Stella wonders, to everything in the villa—especially the paintings—if they had to abandon it?

"I won't leave, no matter what," Stella hears Signor Fasola tell her aunt and uncles. "I won't leave the paintings." Stella imagines Signor Fasola as the captain of a sinking ship. Going down willingly and valiantly with his doomed vessel. "And if these were my own children, *signori*," Signor Fasola tells Zia Angela and Zio Tino, "I would consider sending them to safety in the church—especially if the situation deteriorates."

But Stella doesn't want to think about leaving now. Villa Santa Lucia is no longer a novel wonderland for her. A safe place in the countryside. Or even an unfamiliar place she's trying to escape.

Instead, even with the fear and desperation that has filled her days since she arrived in Tuscany, Villa Santa Lucia feels like home.

"No," Zia Angela says. "I won't let the girls out of my sight."

ONE AFTERNOON, Stella finds Signor Fasola in the great hall among the sideways Tuscan crosses, writing a letter.

"You've found a way to mail something?" Stella asks, hopeful.

"Sadly, no," he says. "But I write to my wife every day all the same. I write what I've done each day. I fold it up, address the letter, and then . . ." His mouth forms a line. "Well, I hang on to it. Perhaps I'll find a way to get word to her before too long."

Stella sits on the matching sofa opposite him. The fabric feels slippery and expensive under her legs. She pulls out a page from her own notebook and wonders if she should try writing to her mother again.

Signor Fasola reaches into his jacket pocket and produces a small black-and-white photograph from his wallet. "See?" he says. "My wife, Giusta."

Stella takes the tiny photograph in her hand. Two faces side by side. Signor and Signora. Giusta's face is narrow and drawn, her lips puckered. Glasses just like her husband's. They look like identical lovebirds now separated from their perch, neither of whom can imagine life apart from each other.

"The letters have become more of a diary for me, I suppose," he says when Stella hands the photograph back to him. "A chronicle of this strange place where I've been marooned." A tight smile.

"I tried writing for a while, too. To my mother," Stella says. "But now I mostly try to draw instead." She removes a page from her notebook and musters the nerve to hand it to Signor Fasola. It's a rough outline of the blue man with wind flowing from his mouth. Zephyrus, she now knows.

Signor Fasola holds the unfolded paper in his hands and purses his lips, just like his wife in the photograph.

"It's not as good as Sandro's," she says.

"It's a valiant attempt," Signor Fasola says. She watches a tender smile emerge. He hands it back to her with kindness in his eyes. "The important thing is to express yourself. And to keep doing it over and over."

Signor Fasola stands now and walks over to one of the tables where a great, round painting lies horizontally on the tabletop. "You have seen the Ghirlandaio?" he asks. Stella comes to stand next to him, peering down at the image of the three magi coming to visit the Christ Child among a fantastical landscape with ruined ancient arches and columns. "It's a *tondo*. That means it's a round . . ."

Suddenly, outside the open window, there is the sound of loud commands in German and the scrape of metal. Stella and Signor Fasola quickly move to the window.

The olive trees provide no shade on the hot, cracked earth. Around the edge of the villa, a group of soldiers has cobbled together a collection of shovels and tools from the olive press and storage buildings around the property. A few of the men retrieve shovels and other tools from their tanks. More yelling in German.

"You think it's true that . . . the Americans are coming soon?"

"I hope so." Signor Fasola shrugs. "These men . . . they've been here for way too long."

"But they can't be here forever. At least that's what my uncles say."

"Yes, but they are a formidable enemy. It will take courage and firepower to defeat them."

"Some in the cantina think the Americans might destroy everything instead . . ." Her statement comes out like a question.

Signor Fasola's face grows grim. "All I know is no matter what, we have to protect our lives—and these pictures."

The next sight out the window makes Stella's heart drop to her feet. The soldiers have rounded up the young boys and old men from the wine cellar. A long line of males emerges from around the stone wall. The men and boys straggle out into the bright sunlight. There are rough shouts and clanking metal. Germans marching up and down the line, urging them to take their places. Fear in the men's eyes as they form a ragged line around the base of the villa.

Stella feels her breath catch in her chest. Sandro is among them, stumbling forward into the blinding light.

CHAPTER 12

THE BATTLE OF SAN ROMANO

Summer 1944

The poet tells a story that we must imagine in our mind's eye; while the painter presents an image that the viewer must put into words. On both counts, we can fail at this most basic of attempts to convey what is in our God-given imaginations.
—FROM THE LOST DIARIES OF SANDRO
BOTTICELLI, FLORENCE, WINTER 1480

When we opened the doors, to our surprise, we found a repository of hidden paintings representative of every Italian artist you could name. That single room encapsulated the entire history of Italian art.
—FROM THE DIARY OF CAPTAIN WALLACE E.
FOSTER, MONUMENTS OFFICER OF THE FIFTH
ARMY IN TUSCANY, AUGUST 1944

The unforgiving sun casts long, harsh shadows on the parched earth. From Stella's vantage point at the window, she sees the Germans have corralled not only Zio Stefano and Sandro but all the old men and boys from the wine cellar. They have also rounded up old men from the village, making them walk up the hill. She recognizes the mayor's son Fabio, with his familiar trudging gait and his cowlick. Even Old Giuseppe is among them.

With twisted relief, Stella sees they are not being lined up to be shot outright like the *maestra* and the men in the village square. Instead, they are being pushed into forced labor. Their plan soon becomes clear: the males are being coerced into digging holes in which to place the newly arrived cannons. The Germans hand the men and boys shovels and other tools, barking orders. There is no understanding of the words, but their objective is painfully obvious: to dig holes deep enough to house the looming, dark iron cannons that stand as sentinels nearby.

Sandro, his face streaked with dirt, stumbles under the weight of a heavy shovel. His worn-out shoes slip on the ground, causing him to falter. A large German soldier takes notice. He strides over and roughly grabs Sandro by the collar, lifting him off the ground, barks a string of threatening words. Sandro, trying to maintain some semblance of dignity, doesn't respond. Stella watches him stare back, a mixture of fear and defiance in his eyes.

Stella feels a surge of anger. Her fingers curl into fists, the nails digging into her palms. She wants to scream, to shout from the window, to do something to help her friend. But she is acutely aware of the loaded guns slung over the soldiers' shoulders, the weight of the danger freezing her in place. Beside her at the window, Signor Fasola utters a few indignant words under his breath.

The soldier's face inches toward Sandro's and barks another order, throwing Sandro back toward the hole. He scrambles to his feet, retrieving the shovel and resuming his work.

All Stella wants to do is shove the big man into the hole with her own hands. In fact, she's mad at herself for not doing so.

"Stop pushing him!" she yells from the window. Sandro and the German look up. Immediately, Signor Fasola pulls Stella by her shoulders, away from the window.

"Stella! *Che diavolo?!*" Zia Angela suddenly appears at the door, her fists balled and her expression as if she has summoned the very devil himself with her words.

ALL DAY, the old men and boys labor under the unrelenting sun and the shouts of the armed soldiers. No one is under the illusion they won't be immediately shot if they stop. Sweat pours down the faces and shirts of every boy and man. Their hands blister to the point of bleeding. They glance at one another, their eyes filled with fear and a common hatred toward their oppressors.

Stella's mind feels like a boiling pot, but Zia Angela forbids the girls to step outside and do anything for the boys and men. Stella and her cousins are not allowed to go outside under any circumstances. Stella feels generalized anger toward everything: her aunt, the Germans, and all the wrongs foisted upon them. But mostly, she's mad at herself for not finding some way to stand up to this injustice.

When the sun sets and the cannons are placed in their new positions in the freshly dug dirt, the Germans finally disband and return to their respective places in the villa and the olive grove. Stella and her aunt and cousins run out to bring water to their old men and boys. Some of them lie down in the dirt and stay there, seemingly unable to move. Sandro gratefully takes a glass of water from her hands. For the first time, Fabio looks humbled and beaten. Too exhausted to move another inch. Their bodies aching, their hands bloody, their spirits broken.

By dusk, the newly placed cannons around the newly fortified Villa Santa Lucia glint in the fading gilded light, like a metal necklace of defense around a medieval fortress. Ready for the battle to come.

THE NEXT DAY, Stella winds her way down the hillside to the animal pens. A soldier looks out at her from one of the villa's high windows. Stella draws herself up, trying to make herself look confident. She refuses to run or cower.

At the gate to the goat pen, she finds Signora Donati sitting like a centurion, guarding her beloved geese, rabbits, goats, and cats with the same vigilance with which Signor Fasola guards the paintings. With a fierce look in her eyes, she stations herself at the door of the outbuilding, ready to defend her charges with every ounce of her strength. Signora Donati doesn't seem to care that she is just one elderly woman, or that the soldiers are armed and dangerous. She will not let them harm a single one of her beloved animals. Her hand stays tight around a wooden pitchfork, her eyes never leaving the gate. In the silent shed, she stands a guardian of the innocent, a protector.

Stella pulls up a milking stool next to the old woman.

"Seems their labors are done for now," Signora Donati says, looking out to the newly placed cannons.

Stella nods. "Zia Angela wouldn't let me go out to give the boys water while they were working. I guess I still feel a bit angry about that."

Signora Donati smiles and the crinkles around her eyes grow deeper. "Never a bad thing to be fearless," she says. "Your aunt"—she shakes her head—"she is a tough woman and I'm afraid there is no changing her. Your mother was tough, too—in her own way."

They sit in silence for a few long seconds as Stella tries to imagine her mother as a girl. A tough girl.

"Did you know my father, too?" Stella asks.

Here, Signora Donati falls silent for a moment, though her hand continues to make a gesture like pleading. "I did," she says finally. "He wasn't a bad man. He just . . . made a lot of mistakes. He was unreliable, I would say. He burned some bridges in this town."

"Is that why Zia Angela wants nothing to do with him?"

"Well . . ." Signora Donati seems to struggle for the answer. Finally, she says, "Your mother and your aunt used to be best friends in school. The very schoolhouse in the village where you used to go. About the same age as you are now, I would say. There was no separating those two. They did everything together. I remember it well."

Stella sits stunned, unable to visualize her mother as friends with Zia Angela, both younger versions of themselves. One of the geese pecks the dirt around them. Beyond, the sun glistens on the yellowish undersides of the olive leaves.

"The trouble started when your father arrived," she says. "He came with his parents from another village near Pienza, so he was the new student in school. You know what that's like."

Stella struggles to think of her father as a new kid at school, just the same as she was.

"For a while, it was a game," Signora Donati says. "Your aunt wanted nothing more than to marry Daniele Costa. But in the end, it was your mother who stole his heart. She had this quality of . . . being soft and bold at the same time. A combination I think most men find difficult to resist."

"That's why they went to live in Torino?" Stella asks. "My mother and Zia Angela didn't want to live in the same town?"

Her aunt nods. "Not even in the same region, I'm afraid."

"But Zia Angela went on to marry my mother's brother anyway?"

"*Eh!*" Signora Donati gestures dramatically again with one hand. "Some things in life cannot be reasoned. Especially when it comes to ways in which men and women get together."

The big white goose comes over and leans its long neck along her skirt. Signora Donati strokes the animal as if it were a dog.

"And then, children complicate things," she says. "They are at the same time life's greatest reward and a knife in your gut. And you . . ." she says. "You look like your father. I think it bothers Angela. It reminds her of a painful time. You are the stamp of him."

Stella thinks now about being a stamp rather than spit. At that moment, the sky turns bright and blue, and for the first time, Stella sees things clearly.

THAT NIGHT, Stella views her aunt through a new lens. One that is clearer than before.

When she approaches the bedroom, she finds her zia Angela hunched over, sitting on the edge of the bed next to Zio Tino. A rare moment of vulnerability.

After they extinguish the lanterns, she hears her aunt and uncle speaking softly in bed. Zia Angela whispering and worrying about what the future will be like. How will they earn any money at all? Will there ever be peace again? What will the world be like for their daughters if the Germans win?

"Everything will turn out right in the end, Angelina," Zio Tino says, but his voice sounds small and tired, and Stella thinks he may not believe it himself anymore.

"YOU GOT IN TROUBLE AGAIN for sticking up for me." Sandro sits on a stone stair tread alongside the upper terrace, dashing pebbles at the ground.

"Seems my lot in life." Stella pulls the back of her skirt under her legs and sits next to him, overlooking the ripe fields of alfalfa waving in the golden light. "It's nothing compared to what the *tedeschi* might have done to me."

"I know. But you are . . . *pazzesca*! I don't want you to do that again. Stick up for me." His face is creased with concern.

Stella shrugs. "A girl can be brave. Besides, why shouldn't I stick up for you? We're friends."

"You may be brave—but still crazy."

"No I'm not. You are." But Stella doesn't know which is worse: counting on a person who is cruel and unpredictable, or having no one to count on at all.

Silence stretches out between them. The past months had brought so much darkness. The saving grace is that if there had been no war, she would never have met Sandro.

"At least now I have a bit more insight about why my aunt doesn't like me."

"And why is that?"

"It has to do with my father. I guess I look like him. And my aunt sees him when she sees me."

"You think he's alright—your papà? Still alive, I mean?"

Stella looks between her worn shoes at the red dirt littering the ancient stair tread. "I have a confession to make," she says finally. She pulls the now-wrinkled photograph of her father with the young Zia Angela from her dress pocket. "I made up that story about my father fighting at the front. The truth is he might be in Rome, but I don't know. I don't remember him at all." Sandro takes the photograph between his dusty fingers, listening carefully as Stella tells him everything she knows—and doesn't know—about Daniele Costa. The more she talks, the more weight Stella feels lifted from her chest.

"So, I have no idea if he's alive," she says finally. "I only know my mother isn't. I would've heard from her a long time ago if she was." She feels a fresh pang of loss, of the gaping void that's been her constant companion since the last moment she heard from her mother.

"We are alone together then," he says with a tight grin, and for the first time, Stella realizes Sandro might also feel the same engulfing sense that something fundamental, something vital is missing.

Stella sighs loudly in response to Sandro's assessment, which feels somehow painful and comforting all at the same time.

"And my father . . . When I heard he was still out there, maybe in Rome, I thought there was a chance he would come for me. But I guess he's not as reliable a person as I thought . . . So I don't think so now."

"But that's *his* choice, not yours," Sandro says. "There's nothing you could have done to change his mind."

Sandro's words are simple but they ring grave and true, and Stella knows he's right. She doesn't know why she didn't see it before. In some ways, she thinks, she's the one groping in the half darkness most of the time. And Sandro sees more brightly, more insightfully than anyone.

OVER THE COURSE of the next few days, the Germans put the old men and boys to hard labor again. This time, they make their unwitting workers cut down tree branches from the edge of the woods to cover their cannons so they can't be easily seen from the air. The grounds around the villa begin to look hacked. Stripped of their beauty. In the hottest part of the day, the Germans nap under the thickets and in their trucks, also covered with stacks of felled cypresses.

Stella imagines that from the air, everything dangerous will look green rather than like a target for a bomb. At least, she thinks, they might avoid taking a direct hit from an Allied pilot who has no idea they are sheltering hundreds of innocent people and some of the most famous works of art in history.

In the evenings, the soldiers test out the new arrangement of cannons. Stella sees her uncles, Sandro, and the other men and boys collect around the edges of the olive grove, putting their fingers in their ears. Stella holds on to the lip of the kitchen sink when the great cannons boom so loudly the whole villa shakes.

Later, Sandro and Stella sit together in the treasure room and push their fingers into their ears, feeling the reverberations on the tiles. The building trembles with each thunderous blast. They contemplate the implications of these new additions, and Stella understands why her uncle continues his daily vigil with his rosary before Giotto's great golden Madonna.

A feeling of hopelessness washes over her as she watches these stark and relentless preparations for violence. She thinks her aunt's questions are valid. How will peace ever be restored to this place? For now, all they can do is brace themselves against the rattle of the ancient walls.

ALL DAY, British and American airplanes fly over the area. There are small, swift-flying groups of six or seven fighters. Later, there are big formations of two dozen or more. They fly over even at night now—if there is enough moonlight—their hulking forms making rushing, silvery shadows on the ground as they pass. Signor Fasola says they may be heading to bomb train yards or bridges, and he worries whether they are heading to Florence. Stella knows he is thinking of his beloved Giusta, who must be worried to death about him while holed up in their apartment. Waiting for any one of the letters he's stacked on the desk in his bedroom.

The main road to the village is now strewn with leaflets dropped from the Allied planes. They wheel into the fields, tempting the

German soldiers to surrender. In four languages, the messages say all they have to do is wave one of these little leaflets in the air like a flag. In return, they'll get humane treatment. Food. Medical attention. But Stella doesn't see any one of the tank men take them up on the offer. The Germans ignore the little pages that flutter through the olive groves and lie motionless in the freshly dug pits around the cannons. Stella and Sandro collect them for sketch paper.

Another round of Allied leaflets informs partisans hiding in the woods that ammunition will be supplied to them from the air. They should light a bonfire at midnight to let them know exactly where to drop it.

When Father Ramondo comes up for dinner, he is grinning from ear to ear. He blesses the long, tender *pici* Stella has prepared and swirls it neatly onto his fork. He whispers to Stella's family gathered around the small table that the partisans are now indisputably in charge of the woods around all the farms. Even the formerly Fascist-run carabinieri have joined them. Fabio and his father have left in the night, and now the *municipio* stands empty and dark on the square. The Germans have no one left on their side.

That night, from the terrace, they watch Allied light bombers sweep down on the roads, where some of the German convoys are heading northward. Then, over the trees, Stella imagines them dropping ammunition and supplies rather than bombs.

IN THE EVENING, a scuffle breaks out in the great hall.

Stella peers around the doorjamb, just out of view. As they do most evenings, the Germans, soiled and tired, collect around the small tables, surrounded by the sideways Tuscan crosses and other masterpieces that were too large and numerous to fit inside the treasure room. The men largely ignore these works, preoccupied instead with their drinks, cigarettes, and card games. Tonight, they've been drinking heavily, their banter and laughter echoing across the large room.

The scuffle breaks out among a group of men seated at the round table where the tondo by Ghirlandaio lies horizontally on its surface. The men have placed their bottles on the canvas and deal a new hand of cards. Stella watches the men collect their glasses and bottles on the painting, making rings. She feels her blood begin to boil.

Suddenly, the argument over the card game escalates. One of the soldiers tries to stand but stumbles forward drunkenly. The man across from him yells something, then draws a sheath knife from a pocket along his thigh. Two men try to separate them, but he flicks the knife, and it lands on the canvas with a thunk, tearing through Ghirlandaio's canvas. She watches the handle of the knife shudder while the soldiers around the room break into laughter.

For Stella, this is the breaking point. She has had enough of their ruthlessness and cruelty.

"How dare you!" Stella steps out from the corridor and stands framed in the doorway. All at once, the men's eyes are on her. She feels her voice quaver. There is silence. The men look at her, baffled, a young girl who dares to yell at them. She locks eyes with Schnitzelino, whose usual bravado seems to waver. Having silenced them, her courage grows and she continues.

"That painting is a masterpiece." She points with one finger to the slashed canvas on the table. "Created by a great artist. It is worth more . . . more than all of you put together!"

She knows they don't understand her words. But with any luck, her meaning is clear.

One of the men begins to chuckle and a few exchange words. She turns to the man they call Salsiccia. "You have no right to come into my family's home and destroy everything that is precious to us."

She wags a finger at the man who threw the sheath knife, feeling a pulse at her temple.

One soldier stands now, a tall, slim man with a clenched fist. He says something to her in German. She feels her face turn hot, but she doesn't flinch. The soldier who tossed his sheath knife and slashed the painting stands now, too. And a few others.

But Stella's eyes only blaze with anger. "You have no respect for what is ours! You may have the power now, but one day not too long from now, we will get our house back. That's not just a picture, you know, it's part of our history. Part of our culture. You have no right to touch it! I'll make you leave! I'll make you pay! I'll—"

"Stella!"

Suddenly, Zio Tino appears behind her. "Come at once. Please excuse us, *signori*," he says to the men. Stella feels the clutch of her uncle's hand on her shoulder.

Zio Tino guides her out of the room and closes the door behind him. Swiftly, they make their way down the corridor. She hears laughter and joking behind her, but she holds her chin high. Even if it was a small face-off, she feels strong in standing up against their tyranny.

"What are you thinking, girl?" Zio Tino whispers, but he doesn't sound so mad.

Zia Angela, on the other hand, flies into a fit of rage when she gets wind of what Stella has done.

Her face is twisted in anger and Stella flinches under her aunt's scrutiny. "I didn't plan to . . ." she begins. But she knows it's fruitless.

"Didn't plan to what? Play with fire? Put yourself in the middle of an impossible situation where you could get yourself and all of us shot dead?"

Stella shrinks back under her aunt's wrath as the lean woman approaches her, her finger pointed in accusation.

"What foolishness!" she continues. "I've a mind to lock you up until you understand the gravity of what you've done. You're lucky to have escaped with your life. Anyway, protecting those pictures is Signor Fasola's and your uncle's job. Not yours. *Capito*?" Suddenly, Stella thinks, her aunt looks more exhausted than angry.

Stella swallows, realizing she may have indeed endangered all of them by getting involved, by lashing out at the Germans. But she can't shake the feeling that she was justified in doing so all the same.

"That's enough, Angela," Zio Tino says.

"She has caused nothing but problems ever since she got here," Zia Angela says.

"But you know I was right, *zia*!" Stella fires back. "And if you had seen what I saw, you might have done the same!"

This time, her aunt backs down.

OVER THE FOLLOWING DAYS, fighting in the area intensifies, with the distant rumble of cannons and cracks of gunfire at any hour of the day or night. After dark, the sky lights up orange and it sounds as if the house—a house that to Stella, the first time she saw it, seemed an impenetrable fortress—will tumble down to a pile of rubble.

"The women are bringing their little ones down to the village," Zia Angela tells Zio Tino before bed. She doesn't know Stella is listening. "They believe we are at greater risk with so many German soldiers here, so they are betting on the church."

"Some might say we are safer because of having the Germans here," he says.

"Yes, but now, with those blasted cannons . . . Father Ramondo has his hands full already but—"

"You want to go to the church . . . or send the girls?"

But Zia Angela shakes her head vehemently. "I'm not sending my children away again. No."

Stella doesn't know if Zia Angela includes her in this category.

"Besides," she says, "we cannot let those brutes have this house. The minute we leave, we won't have the opportunity to come back."

Zio Tino nods. "But Sandro should go down to Father Ramondo with the other children. I worry about that boy."

"I DON'T WANT TO LEAVE," Sandro says, sitting on his blanket with his knees under his chin.

"It's for the best," Stella says, even though the last thing she wants is for him to leave the villa. "You can come back when it's all over. Zio Tino only wants to keep you safe."

"But you don't know if the Americans will be any better than the Germans . . ."

"I won't let anything happen to the paintings," Stella says, but of course they both know Stella has no control over what happens next.

IN THE VILLAGE, every shop and house is battened shut. Fabio's family has fled to relatives near Prato; the *municipio* stands dark and hollow, its shutters locked. Now the building awaits the arrival of the next mayor, who, rumor has it, will be the old *maestra*'s widower, who has returned from fighting in an anguishing swirl of grief and resolve. The local carabinieri nowhere in sight. There is no electricity and no water running. The sewer lines leading into town have been blown. There is a large hole in the schoolhouse roof, letting in light, rain, and pigeons.

Zio Tino and Signor Fasola stay behind in the villa, standing guard at the door to the treasure room while Zio Stefano, Zia Angela, and the girls help the mothers and their children bundle their things and walk down to the village church in small knots. Sandro carries his scant belongings in a sack slung across his body.

Stella's stomach flip-flops when they enter the church. In the candlelight, the air is cool and damp, and the smell of burning candles fills her nose. It's much the same crowd as in the school-house, back when the *maestra* was caring for many of the village children. Boys and men on one side, girls and women on the other. Stella recognizes many of her former classmates and some of their parents among them, their eyes now hollow-looking and haunted. Everyone has brought blankets, lining them up along the nave and side aisles, where banks of candles blaze with offerings and prayers lifted up in the face of raw uncertainty. The Santa Lucia frescoes dance in brilliant hues above the flickering light. The great statue of Santa Lucia presides over everything, looking distant and passive from her place at the high altar.

Now there is only Father Ramondo in his dusty cassock to watch over everyone. He welcomes the new children from the villa and shows them to the crowded nave where they will be sleeping. Rows of pews have been pushed to the side chapels to make way for makeshift pallets of blankets and piles of clothing.

When Stella sees her former schoolmates, a pang of sadness wells up through her ribs. Now she wishes she hadn't taken it all for granted in the time before, which now seems very far away. Sandro steps through the men's crowded side aisle, hunting for a place to settle.

"They say there could be Allied forces near the village as early as tomorrow," Father Ramondo whispers to Zia Angela, taking her bony hands in his. "The children will be safer here. I trust in God. Plus, there are partisans watching the church. They won't let any-thing happen. You're sure you don't want to let your girls stay?"

Zia Angela only shakes her head, but Stella thinks she looks more uncertain than before.

Other parents sheltering in the church say there are now partisans guarding most of the roads in the area, and the carabinieri aren't quick to fire on their fellow Italians anyway. One man says that if the Fascist government makes them wear the same uniforms as the militias, they will defect and go join the partisans in the woods.

From one of the side aisles, Stella recognizes Giulia Rossi, whom she hasn't seen since they were last in school together. "Isn't your papà coming to get you?" she asks.

Mariasole jumps in before Stella has a chance to formulate an answer. "He just hasn't gotten here yet."

But Stella no longer believes he will come. And she's not sure she wants him to.

Perhaps Father Ramondo's words should make her feel more encouraged, but instead, in the church there is an overall feel of impossibility tinged with despair. She surveys the scene around her, which would have seemed so unlikely only months ago. Dozens of people from near and far, adults and children, all crowded together in this squat, ancient church. The plaster walls, the wax candles, the flickering frescoes and whispered prayers, the sweat across Father Ramondo's brow. All of it, closing in.

Stella sees Sandro finally settle into a small corner in the side aisle. Nearby, a cluster of boys turns and looks at him, then whispers among themselves. He sits there with his back against the stone wall, squinting up at the dark frescoes of Santa Lucia and her own strange and tragic story. Reaching for redemption even if it comes with sacrifice. For any sliver of hope. For those things that lie beyond understanding. Beyond seeing.

WHEN STELLA LEAVES THE CHURCH with her cousins and Zia Angela, a persistent drizzle begins to fall. Small, pelting sprays on the red dirt.

Stella's eyes scan the tree line for the partisans Father Ramondo mentioned. She wonders if the trenches they dug are filling with water, and she can't imagine sleeping in such a place. If they have anything to eat. And if Sergeant Cakebread is still out there with them or if he's somehow making his way back to England by now. She doesn't want to think about the possibility that the Germans may have found him.

When they arrive at the villa, Stella goes immediately to the treasure room, where everything is in order under the watchful eye of Signor Fasola. She is filled with relief.

That night, she lies in bed with her eyes wide open, listening to the relentless rain and thinking of the men hiding in the woods, soaked through to their skin. She thinks about Sandro and the other children in the church, crowded together on their blankets. And she realizes that even now, she feels guilty for having it so good that her aunt and uncle counted her part of their family. And that this wrecked villa is as good and safe a place as any right now, Germans and all.

THE NEXT MORNING, the sun rises behind the hills with a blood orange glow. When Stella goes out to the well, she inhales its cold, earthy aroma and surveys the view. The grounds, so perfectly groomed when Stella arrived, are now a ragged patchwork of hacked-down sections and overgrown, neglected shrubs. The fruit and olive trees have been picked clean. The once-immaculate grounds of the villa lie disheveled and untended.

At the front door, a German paces back and forth, his rifle slack on its strap around his midsection. He smokes cigarette after cigarette, flicking each long trail of ash and crunching each stub under his boot. Stella thinks he looks bored. Under a tree, a group of soldiers is smoking and chatting over a card game. Stella recalls her outburst in the great room and she bristles. Part of her thinks she might be tempted to do it again. One of the men looks up from the table. He senses her movement in the orange light. None of the men has said anything to her since she yelled at them. She dares to think she may have gained a bit of respect among them.

Stella ducks through a side door and moves across the court-yard. The door to the treasure room is ajar. She tiptoes across the courtyard in the gathering shadows as the clatter of gunfire is heard in the distance. In the dark, Stella finds Zio Tino standing before the Madonna. This time, he works the beads of an ancient rosary between his fingers. Whispering to himself. She joins him and sends up a silent prayer for Sandro and the other children in the church.

She feels her uncle's hand on her shoulder and listens to the distant rumbling and the German words. The moaning from the infirmary below the windows. Her uncle's whispered pleas to the Madonna. The cicadas.

THE HOURS TICK slowly by that day, and the cannon and gun-fire grow louder than it's ever been before. Great clattering and booming from the distant hills. The Germans set up tripods with machine guns along the railing of the upper terrace, pacing back and forth to check their placement and load their rounds of ammu-nition. Stella watches a few of the men place mines along the dirt road leading to the village below and realizes they are now cut off from even their closest friends and family. The mothers in the cantina cut off from their own babies in the village church. Stella now separated from Sandro as if an ocean lay between them.

If Stella and her family could climb to the top of the skinny watchtower, she imagines they might see an entire army coming over the top of the hill like some ancient Roman regiment. But there's no going up the tower stair.

Instead, they go to the wine cellar.

When the rumbles and planes grow deafening, Zio Tino says

it's time for them all to take cover. Stella, her uncles, aunt, cousins—even Signor Fasola—retreat down the stairs into the wine cellar with those who are left. Zio Stefano says that at last, the front must have reached them.

The wine cellar is a mass of moldy grapes and unwashed bodies and stale breath. A few members of the Sabatini and Martinelli families have come to join them from their nearby farms. They have abandoned their properties for the big house; in the darkness, their faces are drawn and terrified, bearing witness to everything they have endured. In the corner, Ornella bounces her infant girl on her shoulder, her young, narrow face etched with lines. Signora Romano, who has taken her three girls to the church, now sits empty-handed and terrified on her cot. Stella thinks of Sandro and all the others in the church, who must be listening to the horrible rumbling and rattle of ammunition outside.

As everyone gathers together in the darkness, Stella realizes no one is watching the treasure room. She watches Signor Fasola's pursed lips, his glasses reflecting the dim light. Stella realizes they have finally reached the moment when human lives are put before the paintings.

As THE SUN GROWS LOWER on the horizon, the Germans send the doctor to the door of the wine cellar. He's the only one who speaks Italian. He tells Zio Tino that there is a lull in the fighting now and they don't expect anything else will happen before midnight. Then he asks if they will please make the officers something to eat. Stella and her family venture up the stairs to the kitchen.

Stella dares to peer out the kitchen window. Distant smoke against the infernal orange dusk. Battered tanks parked sideways in the dirt, under sagging, hacked cypresses. A soldier hurries by, flicking a cigarette butt to the ground. A few barks of German under the window.

Zia Angela's bony, worn hands tremble as she instructs Stella and her cousins to cobble together some plates of cold cuts, vegetables, and stale bread. They leave everything out on the table in the dining hall. Then they make a pot of hot barley coffee and some bread and warm milk to take to the wine cellar as the shelling starts up again. It sounds very close now and Stella sees Livia flinch, her eyes wide and shining.

When a shell whizzes by the kitchen window, they abandon the food on the worktable and return to the cellar.

ALL NIGHT LONG, cannon fire rattles the foundations of the villa. The room is damp and dark, thick with the scent of rotted grapes and earth. Stella thinks of snails. The only light comes in flashes from the crack around the old oak doors leading out to the hillside. Mariasole's eyes are wide as saucers as she clings to Luigi, his bright orange form a beacon in the darkness. The rumbles come in waves, like the growl of a great beast beyond the horizon. Then the sound grows more intense. The hidden bottles of wine rattle behind the stone walls.

Suddenly, there is a deafening blast that shakes the foundations of the building. Stella holds her breath, waiting to see if the next one will bring the ceiling crashing down on them. She and Livia cling to each other in the dark.

Then the whistle of shells as they fly through the air, and the ear-splitting crash as they strike the ground. A symphony of destruction that sounds like it is sure to find them. White dust dislodges and falls like snow across their hair.

When the sounds of artillery and cannon fire grow deafening, the frail light bulb flickers and goes black. More dust rains from the ceiling. A group of women huddle together, calling out to Santa Lucia and the patron saints of their own home villages. Stella imagines what the village must be like. She clasps her hands and sends up a prayer for Sandro and the other children in the church. She imagines Father Ramondo praying over them, and she can only hope to believe in his confidence about their safety.

They lose track of time. Stella has no idea if they've been in the cantina for a few minutes or a few hours. Or the whole night. Another battery fires from a distant hill. They listen to shells scream across the valley.

Surely the paintings will be stolen or destroyed now, Stella thinks, wishing there was some way they could have brought them underground along with the people in the cantina.

As the sounds of the raging battle continue, Stella sits there in the darkness and, strangely, thinks of her old life in Torino. Her mother pulling a thread through a hole in Stella's sock. The smell of roasting meat and the sound of their neighbor in the upstairs apartment practicing scales on his piano. The view of pigeons flocking above the belltower at Saint John the Baptist. Crouching in the underground shelter where the scene was not much different from this one. Wondering if her father might come for her one day. She wonders now still.

She watches Signor Fasola sitting nearby, lips pursed, listening to the machine-gun fire and distant rumbling, his eyeglasses large and reflective like the great, wise eyes of an owl in the darkness.

LONG AFTER THE SHELLING SUBSIDES, no one dares move. Everyone huddles together in the gathering silence. The only sound is that of Signora Romano, softly crying and praying aloud for her girls in the village church. Stella can hardly breathe in the stifling air, which presses down on them like a steel helmet. She feels a drop of sweat trickle from the nape of her neck down her back. No one dares climb the stairs to the kitchen.

After what seems like an interminable amount of time, Old Giuseppe dares to open the cellar door to the hillside just a crack.

A golden stream of light pierces the melancholy, illuminating his wrinkled hand and the dust particles suspended in the air. Another day has dawned. A hesitant, fragile light. The need for fresh air outweighs the fear of what might await on the other side. Stella watches Luigi slip out, unafraid, his sleek cat body liquid through the small opening.

About the time the adults take a breath and begin to break their frozen poses, the fleeting peace is shattered as a series of loud gunshots breaks out. Everyone ducks instinctively. There is the sound of a scuffle upstairs and yelling in German erupts. The abruptness sends a wave of panic through the crowd. A surge of fear. Old Giuseppe pulls the cellar door closed again and Signora Romano cries more loudly now. "We will die!" she wails. Above their heads, there is the sound of more yelling and gunshots and confusion and violence.

Stella realizes the sounds are very close now. They are inside the house.

CHAPTER 13

THE CENTER OF THE WORLD

Summer 1944

Even in seemingly total darkness, there is light. It is one of the best weapons in the artist's arsenal, to make the viewer see that there is no such thing as complete blackness . . .
—FROM THE LOST DIARIES OF SANDRO
BOTTICELLI, FLORENCE, WINTER 1480

The key to understanding Botticelli's Primavera is a passage from the classical poet Lucretius' De Rerum Natura, penned in the first century before Christ:

"Spring goes on her way and Venus, and before them treads Venus' winged harbinger; and following close on the steps of Zephyrus, mother Flora strews and fills all the way before them with glorious colors and scents . . . Thou, goddess, thou dost turn to flight the winds and clouds of heaven, thou at thy coming; for thee earth, the quaint artificer, puts forth her sweet-scented flowers; for thee the levels of ocean smile, and the sky, its anger past, gleams with spreading light. (V 737–740; 1.6–9)"
—FROM THE DIARY OF CAPTAIN WALLACE E.
FOSTER, MONUMENTS OFFICER OF THE FIFTH
ARMY IN TUSCANY, AUGUST 1944

Above her head, Stella hears footsteps and the familiar scrape of chairs against the stone floor. Someone—more than one—is in the kitchen.

There is muffled conversation, a jumble of speaking just the other side of the door at the top of the stairs.

Stella's uncles, then gradually everyone in the wine cellar, stand and turn their faces to the ceiling. Listening intently.

It doesn't sound like German.

But it's not Italian either.

WHEN ZIO TINO TELLS THEM it's safe to come out at last, Stella and her family emerge from the underground gloom and into the light streaming through the kitchen windows. Zio Stefano's stooped frame is silhouetted in the door to the bright courtyard.

"Stay here," Zio Tino says to his wife and the girls. He steps out into the courtyard.

But Stella can't stand it. She goes to the kitchen doorway and looks out into the bright courtyard, which is covered in debris and the gray dust that hangs in the air. Stella's uncles are talking with the newly arrived men. Signor Fasola hurries out to meet them. They are speaking excitedly to one of the newcomers, who seems to understand them.

A short man in baggy, belted trousers steps forward to talk with Signor Fasola and Stella's uncles. His wide-brimmed helmet looks different from the German turtle shells, but the men wear the same mud-caked boots. The same faces streaked with sweat and grime. The same battle-weary expression.

While the men talk, two of the newcomers, their faces etched with grim determination, drag a hulking, lifeless form across the stones, bringing it out to the main door. A dead body. In a German uniform. A smudge of blood trailing across the stones.

Stella gasps. It's Salsiccia.

Stella feels a lump well up in her chest and then her throat. She does her best to stifle it. She doesn't know if it will be a laugh or a cry, and anyway, neither one makes sense in this situation.

For Zio Tino and Signor Fasola, Stella realizes, it matters little whether the new guests are from Germany or the other side of the world. Their presence equals a deep-seated duty, an unwavering commitment to protect the silent treasures behind the door—the paintings that are remnants of a world that once embodied beauty and tranquility, a world that now seems so far away, so increasingly distant and inaccessible. Their responsibility remains the same—to protect the villa's treasures with every last sliver of their lives.

Stella watches Signor Fasola and Zio Tino go through the same explanation they carried out before with the German regiments. This time, the commander, who says he's from New Zealand, listens while the two Italian men gesture wildly at the door to the treasure room, explaining what's behind it and why his men may not go inside under any circumstances. Stella watches Zio Tino place his body in front of the door as if he will take a bullet in his chest before he will agree to open it.

Stella feels sad not to be able to go in where the pictures are, to sit in the quiet splendor while the troubled world outside falls apart. For the rest of the day, Signor Fasola and Zio Stefano take turns pacing back and forth, standing at the door. Guarding it with their lives while the New Zealanders fan out across the villa and send their men to the top of the skinny watchtower to see where all the Germans have gone.

Signor Fasola can speak a little English and the commander of the New Zealanders speaks a bit of Italian. Together, they make themselves and their agendas understood. Stella, her aunt, and cousins begin to cobble together food for the men while Zio Stefano shows them around the villa's grounds. Zio Tino paces back and forth before the door to the treasure room, a nervous sentinel. Signor Fasola handwrites some signs and posts them on the doors, showing them to the Kiwi commander.

IN A SCRAMBLED MIXTURE of Italian and English, the New Zealanders paint a picture of progress. The Allies, they say, have cut a rugged, hard-won path up the Italian peninsula. They aren't here to conquer, like the Germans. Instead, they intend to restore Italy to the hands of the Italians. They want to return to their native land and their families just as badly as anyone. As soon as possible, they say, they want to go home.

For the first time, the impossible dream of Italy back in the hands of Italians feels a small bit palpable. It's a vision that takes everyone's breath away—a vision of a life beyond what anyone could imagine over the past five long years.

"I don't mind dying now," Signora Donati tells Zia Angela as her aunt presses the heels of her hands into a fresh ball of dough. "Now that I've lived to see them come." Stella watches Signora Donati's bulky form head out to check on the animals locked in their pens. Swaying with a new pep in her waddle.

As the golden hues of the sky give way to a soft blanket of a new twilight, Zio Tino unearths four of the last remaining bottles of Sir Harwell's prized cherry brandy. The New Zealander officers produce cigarettes in strange, colorful packages and offer them to Stella's uncles, something the Germans never did. In the kitchen, Stella and her cousins roll out what's left from their stores of flour, doing their best to create a feast from their deficient supplies.

"Best add some egg . . ." Zia Angela begins.

"You don't have to tell me how to do it," Stella says.

"Hmmph," Zia Angela responds, then leaves Stella behind in the kitchen while she goes to locate some candles and bring them up to the terrace.

Later, when Stella brings up the large plate of pasta, the terrace is magically transformed. The candles cast a warm ambience over the table. The abandoned machine gun tripods and empty shells, the dust and debris that litter the terrace fall away, out of view in the dark shadows at the edge of the candles' glow.

Down the hillside of olives, the German trucks are gone except for one that wouldn't start, leaving behind rutted tracks. The cedars they used to conceal them are spread and broken around the decimated countryside. In the distance, fires burn. There is an occasional, distant sound of gunfire.

As the New Zealanders dig into the meal, one of the men tells them some of the Italian partisans in their woods have killed German soldiers who were hiding in the shrubs around the villa. Stella thinks of the partisans and wonders where they are now.

In the distance, the village lies in quiet darkness. Stella wishes with all her might she could run down to the church. She only wants to go find Sandro. To tell him about the dead tank men and the strange New Zealanders and the paintings that are still here. To assure him everything is safe. And to make sure he is safe, too. To bring him back to the treasure room, where they can sit together in the quiet splendor and rest assured that there is hope. Hope that things might be different at last.

To STELLA's IMMENSE RELIEF, the New Zealanders don't seem to care about the paintings. Instead, they spend the day at the dining table with their pungent cigarettes and chicory coffee. After negotiating the terms of their requisition of the villa with Zio Tino, they settle into the bedrooms the Germans vacated. With any luck, sir, they tell him, we won't be here in your house for too long. We'll keep heading north to the front lines.

Some of the men rattle off in their trucks in the mornings and come back at night filthy and beat down, just like the Germans before them. Others rest on the high terrace, observing the landscape with their binoculars. The women bring them coffee and water with lemons from the trees. The men climb the tall, skinny tower and watch the silhouette of the distant hills and their olive-green trucks standing crooked and haphazard along the dirt road leading to the villa. Others carefully discharge and remove the explosives along the roadside. A few set up tents in the olive groves, spilling out along the grounds. They pilfer what's left of the infirmary, its tattered awning flapping over a scattering of makeshift cots, bandages, and empty iodine bottles.

From the terrace ledge, Stella watches Signora Donati let the animals out of the pens where they've been locked up for so long. The goats bounce out, stumbling across the rocks into the sunlight. Bleating happily.

But, Stella thinks, there's a familiarity in the soldiers' habits and disregard. They, too, urinate in the herb garden. Their tents spring up among the stripped olive trees. And they leave their muddy boot prints, just like the Germans did, on the stone floor hallway, where Zia Angela curses at them while she shifts her mop back and forth.

In spite of their friendly faces and varied uniforms, to Stella, there isn't much difference. The dining table, once a haven for family and connection, continues to be a place for endless smoky debates, unfurled maps, and strategizing. Muddy boot prints and messy tables and the detritus of cobbled-together meals.

STELLA'S FAMILY WALKS together through the villa with the Kiwi commander, a short man with a suntanned face, weary eyes, and a sympathetic smile. It's the first time Stella and her aunt have been able to take stock of the rooms the Germans left behind.

The villa bears the scars of the brutal occupation. There is one large shell hole in the garden-side façade and several on the roof. The grounds are pocked with shell holes and trenches for cannons and machine guns. The ground is strewn with leaflets dropped from planes, with letters written in German, with discarded sleeping bags and cigarette butts, a crumpled photograph of a pin-up girl. The geese and chickens mill about.

For the first time, Stella's aunt and uncles walk through all the rooms of the villa to survey the damage without fear of German retribution. Inside the great hall, where Stella yelled at the drunken Germans with their sheath knives, the tables stand in the aftermath of a drunken repast; empty wine bottles and smashed glasses and fluttering card decks everywhere. There is overturned furniture and books with pages ripped out. In the bedchambers, there is a nauseating mixture of tobacco, decay, mold, and feces. Dead insects and dripping faucets. Lavatories filled to the brim, with filth and flies everywhere. There is no running water and no light. Abandoned gas masks and tattered maps litter the dirty floors. There is a shattered mirror in the hallway. For Zia Angela, every injustice feels like a personal blow. Stella hears a string of obscenities flow out as a whisper, and her face turns red.

"None of it matters, Angelina," Zio Tino says. "We should be grateful to have our lives."

Outside, Livia and Mariasole scrub sheets in the *lavatoio* and hang them on the line, the scent of their harsh, homemade soap heavy in the hot air. Mosquitoes float everywhere.

In the wine cellar, the farmers have departed to check on their own properties. Stella watches Signora Bianchi packing up her radio and clothing in a small bag. Other brave refugees start to pack their things.

"I'm going to the church," Signora Romano says, collecting outside the cantina door with the other parents.

"May I go down to the church too, to check on the children?" Stella asks Zio Stefano, who is talking with a couple of the refugee men.

The adults are so distracted by the scope of the work to be done that all it takes is a half nod from her uncle and Stella slips out the door. Then she runs fast down the hillside before anyone can stop her.

WHEN STELLA RETURNS with Sandro to the Villa Santa Lucia, they stand in the hot sun and watch the refugees pack up their sad belongings. Many of the refugees have made plans to return home. They retrieve their children from the village church, holding and hugging them until the children struggle and run off into the tall grass. They review the tattered maps, debating what routes they could possibly take through the countryside south of here, which they hear is a mass of blown bridges, cratered hillsides, and mined roads.

Stella watches the women fold blankets and wash out their pots. One of the men burns a soiled mattress not worth transporting. While the baby naps, Ornella folds clothes with frayed edges, stacking them neatly inside a pillowcase. Old Giuseppe packs up his mandolin inside an ancient-looking, battered case. Zio Stefano gives the old man a small packet of prized squash seeds from his garden.

Stella helps one of the old women who is trying to fold a blanket with arthritic hands. Sandro helps another family pack a few belongings and their small children into the back of a handheld cart that looks like it should carry a stack of firewood. Most of the refugees, Stella realizes, are wearing the same clothes they wore when they arrived.

"Don't forget that many of the roads are mined," Zio Stefano reminds them.

"We'll stay off the main roads, but we're taking our chances," one man says. "We just want to go home."

In the afternoon, Sandro finds among the olives a discarded pack of the New Zealanders' cigarettes in a crushed package.

Sandro and Stella sit out on a boulder, their backs touching, and try the New Zealanders' cigarettes. For Stella, the first inhale is an assault—a harsh, raw flavor like burning paper that trails down her throat. Bitter and smoky. She coughs abruptly, doubled over. Sandro laughs while trying to suppress his own coughing fit.

"Why do they like these so much?" he says.

They see Father Ramondo coming up the dusty road. Waddling in his cassock.

Sandro and Stella quickly stub out their cigarettes on the rock, then dive down the hillside. Stella watches Sandro blow a cloud of smoke in the air. They smile at each other.

STELLA SERVES FATHER RAMONDO a cup of chicory coffee on the terrace. In the shade of a tree and among the empty bullet shells, shrapnel, and other detritus scattered across paving stones, he shares the latest rumors.

"The German forces are still holding Florence," he says. "The archbishop has sent letters to all of us in the diocese. He says they've put charges around the bridges."

Father Ramondo goes on to share the many scattered shards of information he's gathered from travelers who stop by the church for help, solace, prayers, or just a momentary respite from the chaos. A mine has exploded on an oxcart, killing the oxen and smashing the drivers' legs—and surely there will be more sad accidents like this, he says. The countryside is strewn with unburied corpses of men and cattle. Flies everywhere, bringing disease. No medicines in the hospital and clinics.

"One of my priest friends from Montagnana walked here with his sister," Father Ramondo says. "Their rectory took a direct hit so they stayed with us for a few days until it was safe to go back."

"It's the same place I was telling you about," Signor Fasola says to Stella's uncles, "where all the paintings were looted."

In turn, Stella's uncles tell Father Ramondo about the refugees preparing to leave the wine cellar.

"I'm afraid it will not be an easy prospect for them to get home," Father Ramondo says, wiping his plate clean with a torn hunk of bread. "For some of them, there will be nothing left when they get back."

"Maybe they will find a new place to live," Stella says. She herself has found a new place to call home, and she hopes the others will be able to do the same.

Father Ramondo nods. "You should be proud of what your family has done for them. You have provided them shelter and sustenance during a crisis. That's no small thing."

Stella stops to think about it. She guesses that the Villa Santa Lucia has made a difference in their lives, cellar and all, and perhaps that's something to be proud of.

"None of us can go back to the way things were," Zio Stefano says. Suffering and sorrow have engraved themselves on people's lives. This experience has left its mark on everyone. No one will be the same as they were before the war.

Before returning to the church, Father Ramondo circulates among the ragged group of refugees left in the wine cellar and the grounds beyond. Stella watches him lay his hands on Old Giuseppe's shoulders and pray with the family for safe passage back home, all those hundreds of kilometers south of here.

THE NEXT DAY, two fugitive German soldiers turn up in the woodshed. Zio Stefano finds one of them hunched over, foraging among the crooked elbows of the squash in the vegetable garden.

"They weren't part of the tank regiment," he says. "I've never seen them before."

Zio Stefano says the men spoke some Italian and were polite and grateful for Zio Stefano's hospitality. "They were carrying their uniforms in a bag in case they got the chance to jump on a German train headed north," he says.

Stella thinks the men will be shot if the partisans in the woods discover them.

But Zio Stefano says he felt sorry for *die Bruder*, so he let them take some carrots from the earth and he pointed them northward.

"Everyone just wants to go home," he says, shrugging.

IN THE EVENING, Zia Angela digs up a few of the sausages stored in the garden dirt and brings them to a wooden table outside. The New Zealanders quickly gobble up the cool, fatty slices of salty meat, incessantly thanking them and telling them how they're the best cold cuts they've had in all of Italy.

In the distance, Stella watches Sandro navigate along a terrace wall, trailing his fingers over the rocks. He trips over a wooden bench and sits on the ground, rubbing his shin.

In broken Italian, the New Zealander asks Zia Angela, "What's wrong with the boy?"

STELLA GOES TO THE WELL and watches a few more families begin to shuffle out of the damp wine cellar, clutching their belongings wrapped in tattered cloth or stuffed into sacks. The musty air carries the weight of their stories—tales of loss, hardship, loved ones killed or missing, homes destroyed. Stella thinks she should feel relief and maybe even excitement for them, but mixed with hope is also her own sadness to see them go.

Stella turns to see Sandro sitting on the same boulder where she first found him drawing, looking out over the panorama of Tuscan hills as if he could see far into the distance. Stella realizes that amid this great displacement of people and families, Sandro has nowhere to go.

"Can't we let Sandro move into one of the bedrooms?" Stella asks her aunt and uncle that evening. "He has no one to take him back home."

When they say yes, Stella goes out to the clothesline to unpin some clean sheets for him.

AT THE FIRST POSSIBLE OPPORTUNITY, Sandro and Stella return to the oasis of the treasure room.

Sandro's hand feels firm and sure as she leads him across the threshold, into the familiar stillness and smells of aged wood and canvas. For Stella, it's a scent rich with history and the spirits of the artists who made these masterpieces that, incredulously, have survived unimaginable circumstances.

To Stella's relief, everything is as they found it before. The pictures lie in the shadows, untouched, gathering dust. Stella huffs in relief as she walks around the room looking at the legacy of Sandro Botticelli and Paolo Uccello and Fra Bartolommeo and Filippo Lippi and all the others.

But when she turns around, she sees Sandro's face. He stands before the *Primavera*, and a tear runs down his cheek.

He doesn't have to tell her what's wrong.

The tears tell Stella what his voice cannot. That even though there is a glimmer of hope to stand before this magnificent, colorful painting, Sandro is trapped inside a world that is ever darkening.

IN THE VILLAGE, people begin to emerge from their homes with an air of caution. They are not about to jump to conclusions this time.

Stella remembers the day last year when people poured into the square with horns blaring and their voices raised in song, assuming the nightmare was over. They've been down this road before, hearts swelling with premature joy, only to be met with the iron fist of reality. The last round of communal celebration was instead the beginning of unimaginable hardships and terror they could never have envisioned that day.

But now a tentative resurgence begins. A few children, having abandoned their pallets in the church, run through the streets like the goats that Signora Donati released from the pens. Doors to cellars and outbuildings are flung open on their hinges. Attics and storage closets stand empty. Saplings emerge from great cracks between the cobblestones. Left untended, they would become trees.

In the square and at the Bar dell'Angolo, rumors circulate. The Germans hold on to the half of the Italian peninsula that lies to the north. But in their little universe, the steep narrow streets are filled with people, coming out to greet the New Zealanders. Stella sees an old woman walk up to one of the soldiers with her hands clasped, praying to him as if he were a great archangel. The fruit seller's wife embraces one of the soldiers and puts a bottle of wine in his hands. From the bakery ovens, the smell of bread wafts into the air for the first time in months. Livia and a few friends put on their best dresses. Arm in arm, they walk to the bakery, but mostly they glance at the New Zealanders over their shoulders and smile, whispering to themselves.

The celebrations are cautious at first, but they begin to bloom and take form. Doors begin to swing open and it seems as if the village itself releases a long-held breath. Men come out to survey the pockmarks on their buildings. Sweep the dust-filled streets littered with debris and notes dropped from planes. Many of the adults keep their eyes on the sky, a habit gained over the past months that Stella thinks may never go away as long as they live.

In the distant hills, an occasional rumble breaks out, but no one pays attention anymore. By the next day, the rumbles cease altogether.

STELLA IS PITTING OLIVES when, by some means that no one understands, a letter arrives at Villa Santa Lucia.

Livia hands it to Zio Tino as he enters the kitchen. He cautiously opens the telegram. The paper is crumpled and dirty, as if it's months old.

"*O Dio,*" Zio Tino cries. He sits heavily on the chair and drops his head toward his knees.

"What is it?!" Zia Angela rushes over to her husband.

His shoulders heave up and down with the weight of his grief. He says nothing. Only hands his wife the telegram.

Stella feels her throat clench. Is it her mother? Her father?

"It's Sir Harwell!" Zio Tino cries. "God rest his soul."

The atmosphere in the room shifts and grows heavy with the magnitude of the loss. Stella feels a certain detachment from the grief, having never met Sir Harwell. But she knows he was an important man. A rich man who's been waiting all this time in Switzerland to come back home. A man who treated his staff with kindness and respect, who saw to their education. A man kind enough to his staff to make a grown man weep like a child.

Stella's aunt says the letter is weeks old. It's a mystery how it arrived here at all.

Zio Tino pulls a handkerchief from his jacket pocket and wipes his face. Then he stands and goes to the window. Blows his nose loudly. She watches his stooped silhouette, looking out over the cypresses.

It's only later, in their bedroom, that the implications of Sir Harwell's death begin to take shape in Stella's mind.

Stella asks her cousins, "What will happen to the villa? And where will you all go? How will your father make a living now?"

But no one has an answer.

And anyway, Stella thinks, even if Sir Harwell's family were to come back, they wouldn't find any of their clothing, coats, socks, or shoes.

JUST ABOUT THE TIME Stella thinks the New Zealanders have settled into the villa enough to stay awhile, they pack up their trucks, thank Stella's uncles and aunt, and depart northward. A day passes with such tranquility in the villa that it feels surreal. Stella stands in the middle of the empty courtyard and deeply inhales, listening to the sound of birdsong amid the silence.

Later, Sandro and Stella settle in their usual drawing spot. Sandro hands his sketchbook to Stella and begins to give her instructions for drawing the pointy cypress trees. With a pang like an arrow to her heart, she realizes he doesn't feel confident enough to draw an example himself because he can't see the page well enough anymore.

Stella begins to sketch what Sandro's told her when a distant roar of tank engines overtakes the din of cicadas. Stella squints into the rays of the sun. Up the main road, she sees two tanks approaching. Stella stands and brushes dirt from the back of her dress.

"What is it?" Sandro stands.

"More tanks," she says. "But they look different."

The tanks slow and the top of one of them opens like the lid of a jar. A man with a dusty helmet pops his head up.

"*Buongiorno!*" the man calls from the tank, in heavily accented Italian that sounds flat and nasal. "You live here?"

Stella nods warily.

"You think we could use your tower? We heard there were some Germans still here in the area."

Stella hesitates.

"*Siamo canadesi,*" the man says.

"Canadians!" Sandro cries. "Let them in, Stella."

"Alright," she says. "But I have to ask my uncle."

Stella grasps Sandro's hand and they head inside while the newly arrived soldiers cut their tank engines and climb out.

When Stella and Sandro open the door to the villa and step inside the courtyard, Stella's aunt looks at them with alarm.

"They're Canadians!" Stella cries. "They want to use the tower."

Zio Tino appears now, wiping his hands. He shakes one of the men's hands, and a half dozen Canadian soldiers enter the building. Zio Tino leads the way to the tower stair. Stella follows the men. Sandro hangs on to the waistband of Stella's skirt as they make their way down the hallway.

"Just here, *signori*," Stella says.

One of the men, with curly brown hair, hesitates, his eyes lingering on Stella for what seems like a few seconds too long. He makes her feel strange and unsettled, as a feeling of unease grips her. She feels the weight of his intrusive, predatory stare down to her skin. As if he could see her without her dress on.

"*Grazie, bambola,*" the man says, winking at her.

Stella darts away, a rush of anxiety with the sudden acknowledgment of her changing body. She has trouble shaking the feeling of the soldier's eyes as they washed over her, and she's glad Sandro doesn't notice the way the men look at her in the same way they look at Livia.

Then the men disappear up the narrow stairwell with their binoculars and guns.

AFTER THEY FAIL TO SEE German soldiers from the watchtower, the Canadians leave the villa as quickly as they came. But the next day, more men arrive at the villa, the tower drawing them like an ancient beacon.

A new set of tanks and trucks amass outside the villa, and a group of uniformed men arrive. Stella has never seen a group of men with skin so dark. Their officers, who are British, tell Stella's family the regiment is from India, and they promptly negotiate a deal to make the villa their headquarters. Stella thinks Zio Tino looks mildly excited about the prospect of the Villa Santa Lucia as the heart of British operations for as far as the eye can see.

But Zia Angela only sighs deeply and shakes her head. They have barely gotten the sheets washed and hung on the line. "What's next, Vikings?" she asks. "Samurai? Gladiators?"

Stella and Mariasole giggle and run out to the kitchen garden to salvage whatever they can find.

STELLA IS FILLED with wonder at the Mahratta soldiers' neat khaki uniforms, their thick black sideburns and mustaches. A few of the men wear turbans. In contrast to the muddy, exhausted-looking men who have rotated through the villa so far, these soldiers look somehow regal and steadfast, even though they have been through the same horrors. One of the men is limping, but paces as he stands guard at the villa's front door all day long, for hours on end.

To her astonishment, Zio Tino and Signor Fasola bring the captain of the Mahrattas through the treasure room, letting Stella and Sandro trail behind. Signor Fasola tells Stella's uncles that the captain has a deep knowledge of Italian art. Signor Fasola speaks enough English to explain the paintings.

When the Indian captain stands before Botticelli's *Primavera*, he weeps openly. Stella feels a chill ripple across her arms, recognizing that he knows the painting from all the way across the world. Stella feels a deep awe that a man from across the globe might love this painting enough to weep before it, and she feels a new sense of pride that her family has managed to preserve this masterpiece up to this point. Here is a soldier, from a land she knows little about, deeply familiar with the art of her country. She had always pigeon-holed soldiers into a single mold—tough, battle-hardened. Now she sees them as multifaceted, with passions and knowledge extending beyond the battlefield. And she sees her homeland through the eyes of someone from the other side of the world.

"They make a mess all the same," Zia Angela says, drawing herself up with indignation as she watches them from the kitchen doorway, squeezing out her ragged mop.

But Stella feels a new sense of pride in her adopted home. Before, the Villa Santa Lucia seemed a remote outpost where no one could find them. Now it seems they have become the center of the world.

BUT THE NEXT VISITORS to Villa Santa Lucia aren't Vikings or gladiators at all. Instead, they are radio men—two Englishmen who say they work for the BBC. One of the men, Major Linklater, says he met Sir Harwell once, years ago in London. He gives Zio Tino his condolences.

The reporters say their job is to document everything at and around the front lines; they are eager to interview the Indians and even Stella's uncles. Stella can't help but feel a sense of foreboding as she watches the radio reporters set up their strange equipment in the villa's courtyard. It brings back images of the Germans assembling their radios and electrical cords in the great room and dining hall, just before the blasts and violence reached them.

Instead of newspaper or radio reports that seem far away and disembodied like the old voices on the wireless, these men have seen the fighting, and everything and everyone in its wake, with their own eyes. And now Stella's family has become something to report upon.

But Stella can see that Zio Tino and Signor Fasola only let the men into the treasure room reluctantly. Before the broadcasters load into their Jeep, Stella watches Major Linklater write OUT OF BOUNDS in chalk on the cracked, pockmarked façade of the villa. She imagines Zio Tino is glad Sir Harwell won't have to see his villa in such bad shape.

After the reporters leave, Signor Fasola's face is drawn and puckered. "I heard them report about the paintings into their radio microphone. I fear they will bring even more of the world to us. We don't know what the consequences could be."

CHAPTER 14

TWO SANDROS

Summer 1944

This morning, I ate two eggs and a few radicchio leaves while I gathered the courage to show my work to His Excellency at last. I have done everything I know to fulfill all his requests, but there is always a wavering, an unknowing that goes along with showing your work for the first time. After so many months of self-doubt, I had hoped that the feeling would lift as I put the final strokes on the painting. But I should know by now that such insecurity never disappears.

—FROM THE LOST DIARIES OF SANDRO
BOTTICELLI, FLORENCE, WINTER 1480

The Primavera is a complex allegory that brings together the elegance and decorative beauty of the International Gothic style, combined with the humanistic narrative of the Italian Renaissance. I would consider the painting itself to be a kind of poetry. A poetic coalescence of flower and flesh, which Sandro Botticelli brought into the world in his singular fashion.

—FROM THE DIARY OF CAPTAIN WALLACE E.
FOSTER, MONUMENTS OFFICER OF THE FIFTH
ARMY IN TUSCANY, AUGUST 1944

S tella is sitting under an olive tree, trying to draw the Three Graces from memory, when the Americans arrive.

She looks up from her sketch when she hears the puttering of an engine. A Jeep rolls up the drive, coated in mud and dirt. A tall, lean man with round glasses and a dark green uniform gets out. Removes his helmet.

From the passenger seat, a woman steps out with a case and a leather bag that looks heavy with stacks of paper. She is wearing a uniform that looks identical to the driver's, except she wears a skirt instead of trousers.

THE AMERICAN SOLDIER speaks better Italian than anyone who's come through the villa so far. Speaking quickly and fluidly, he tells Zio Tino and Signor Fasola that his name is Captain Foster and he's something called a Monuments officer, part of a special Allied unit tasked with preserving and restituting artworks recovered in war zones.

Signor Fasola says it's about time someone like him showed up.

Captain Foster says he learned about the Villa Santa Lucia from someone who heard about it on the BBC, saying there are valuable paintings hidden here. He introduces the woman to everyone, saying her name is Miss Evans. She is his assistant and has also traveled all the way from America. Stella sees that Miss Evans speaks a little Italian, too.

"Seems the BBC reports have made you famous," Captain Foster says, asking for permission to view the paintings with a certain anxious expression Stella hasn't seen on anyone else's face. She marvels at this, thinking about their villa being reported about on the airwaves across the world.

When they open the doors to the treasure room, Zio Tino slowly begins to fold back the shutters. Stella watches the American remove his helmet and run his hand across the stubble on his head as he takes in the stacks of dozens of paintings. Then he moves his hand to his heart and slowly makes his way around the room. The wonder on his face reminds Stella of the first time she shared the treasure room with Sandro.

When he gets to the *Primavera*, Captain Foster sinks to his knees.

LATER, CAPTAIN FOSTER and Miss Evans spread dozens of pages across the large table in the middle of the treasure room. Stella sees handwritten lists of what must be thousands of paintings and sculptures.

"What you've managed to preserve here is beyond words, beyond an ability to quantify," he tells Stella's uncles. "It's what we've been looking for since we left the United States! We landed in North Africa and have been trying to make our way up here for more than a year. I was afraid of what we might find."

Miss Evans, who has told Stella and Sandro they can call her Josie, sets up a strange-looking metal contraption on the table. It looks something like a miniature typewriter, and her hands fly rapidly across it, producing a long, unfurling roll of thin paper.

"These cultural treasures are not just important for Italy," Captain Foster goes on, "they are part of our shared human history. They deserve to be treated with the utmost care and protection." As Captain Foster talks, Stella watches Sandro's face brighten. Then he tells us he teaches at a famous university in America and he's written two books about Italian art that teachers in the United States use in university classrooms.

"Your *Primavera* is in them, of course," he says, smiling from ear to ear.

Later, Captain Foster says it's not possible to reach Florence.

That the roads are cratered and mined, and there are many Germans between here and there. The Allies are fighting their way northward, but the Germans still hold the city.

For now, Zia Angela and Zio Tino tell Captain Foster he can stay in Sir Harwell's big bedroom, just above the treasure room. Stella helps put clean sheets on the bed and wipe down the large desk with its ornate scrollwork, buffing away hints of grime the Germans have left behind. She runs a damp rag over it until all traces of the tank men have been erased.

Then she opens the shutters to a vista of lilac-colored hills and massed cypresses, their tips pointy against the bright blue. She takes a deep breath.

OVER DINNER and a bottle of wine on the terrace, Captain Foster tells everyone he's not the only Monuments officer out there. "We are men and women from many nations, spread out across Europe, Asia. All the theaters of war. You must realize that during times of war, many cultural treasures are destroyed or stolen," he tells them. "It's our job to protect them from damage, and if they've been moved or stolen, to find them and get them back where they belong." Stella sits in stunned silence, trying to imagine the vast scale of work Captain Foster has described.

As he slowly twirls the long, narrow *pici* Stella made onto his fork, Captain Foster goes on to explain how, during the Great War, the Germans stole countless paintings, sculptures, books, archives, and other works of cultural significance. "But no one," he says, "could have anticipated the scale and scope of Adolf Hitler's looting plan."

Stella is stunned to think about this. "Why does he want these things?" she asks. "Doesn't he have other things to do during a war?"

"Good question," the captain says, leaning forward. He goes on to paint a picture of a man obsessed with acquiring works of art and objects that tell a story of Aryan supremacy and Germanic superiority. Stella is stunned to learn the scope of one man's twisted ambitions, and the far-reaching consequences of it.

"That's why the Monuments, Fine Arts, and Archives program was created," Captain Foster says. "We work to protect important works of art and architecture from being lost forever."

"Then I guess we were lucky the German soldiers left without taking anything," Stella says.

"You were fortunate," Josie Evans says. "We have seen much worse on our way here."

After dinner, in broken Italian, Josie gestures to Zio Tino. "Your father is a hero, you know," she tells Stella.

"He's *my* papà, not hers," Mariasole says. "She's waiting on *her* papà to come get her."

But Stella's given up hope that her papà will ever come back here. And even if he did, she thinks she doesn't want him to take her away. The Villa Santa Lucia feels like home.

AFTER RECOVERING from his initial emotion at seeing the *Primavera*, Captain Foster walks through the treasure room each day, speaking excitedly about each picture with Stella and her uncles, Sandro, and anyone who will listen. He tells them more than they could ever have imagined about the paintings they've been looking at so closely for all these months.

"The *Primavera* was meant to be seen much like it is here," he says. "In a Tuscan villa. In private contemplation by a small audience who understood all the complicated references in it. Its patrons were part of a very small circle associated with the Medici family. They were educated humanists, interested in mythology and symbolism and the study of antiquity. Lorenzo, the patron, lived in a sophisticated court culture where people would have spent a lot of time studying these things."

Stella tries her best to follow and grasp the flood of Captain Foster's knowledge of the painting. His Italian is fluid, a continuous stream of knowledge and passion. She feels enveloped by the whirlpool of information and insight as Captain Foster tells them more about Botticelli's masterpiece.

"It's a complicated subject, though," he says. "No single source mentions this particular group of figures together. Instead, the painting shows knowledge of various ancient texts. But a first-century poem by the philosopher Lucretius might have served as its primary source."

But as he delves into the history and wider context of the painting, Captain Foster embarks on the more allegorical meanings, and Stella finds her mind wandering away. The names and terms are unfamiliar. She realizes that, as much as she and Sandro have spent time looking at this painting, and as much as Signor Fasola has told them already, there is a rich tapestry of historical and artistic references that form an intricate maze where she loses her way. She is left with the lingering feeling of being out of her depth, a girl standing before an expansive ocean of knowledge that is rich and profound, yet inaccessible. Stella's mind is left in a swirl of awe and frustration. But it stirs within her a desire to grasp the rich histories and deep meanings encapsulated in these paintings. Someday. The grandeur of art and a beacon of the deep well she might one day understand, inspired by Captain Foster's vibrant, infectious enthusiasm.

Each night, she finds the American captain sitting on the high terrace until the darkness envelops the villa, sipping a glass of dark red wine and writing in his diary.

ONE NIGHT, the surprising sound of artillery fire fills the air, a deafening roar that shakes the floor beneath Stella's feet. The sound of explosions echoes across the valley and the air is thick with the smell of gunpowder. Stella expects that everyone will need to run to the wine cellar again, but that doesn't happen. Instead, the fire dies down and life resumes. Everyone is used to almost being blown up now.

The next day, another handful of art experts from Florence arrives, along with a British general.

TWO OF THE MEN, newly arrived in a small car from Florence, are colleagues of Signor Fasola. Signor Fasola introduces them as a curator and a conservator from the Uffizi and the Pitti Palace; they say they have come to assess the condition of the artworks. They are serious-looking middle-aged men, dressed in tailored suits and shiny shoes, carrying large leather-bound ledgers and notebooks. They get to work immediately, shaking hands and inspecting the paintings and taking detailed notes. Sandro and Stella stand by and watch them with curiosity.

One of the men, introduced as Signor Conti, examines each painting with intense focus, leaning in close with a magnifying glass and a light, occasionally running his fingers lightly over the surfaces. He begins applying small bits of white gauzy paper to places where paint has begun to flake.

To Stella, the man's observation is a revelation. She's never imagined such a job existed, that someone could spend their whole days preserving art for the future.

"Do you have to be an artist to be a conservator?" Sandro asks, trailing him around the room. Something about the man's gentle smile and voice makes him seem approachable.

He laughs. "Not at all. You can be, I suppose, but I, for one, have no artistic talent. I just do my best to preserve and restore the original artist's vision."

Stella's mind expands, thinking of the various people who dedicate their time and efforts to preserving art. Stella's uncle, who was brave enough to accept Signor Poggi's request. Captain Foster, who has traveled across the world and risked his life along the embattled countryside, all the way from North Africa. Signor Poggi and the other curators who found places to hide the paintings. Signor Fasola, who walked many kilometers across cratered roads. A long chain of people who cared enough to risk their lives, to devote their whole careers, to preserving the things that matter. Artist or no artist.

The men spend the day cataloging each painting and making notes about its condition. They work tirelessly, moving from one painting to the next with a sense of purpose and dedication. Stella feels a sense of connection to these men, who seem equally intent on studying and learning more about these same paintings Stella has grown to love. When the men complete their inventory and assessment of the paintings, they begin making plans to move them back to the Florence museums. Stella imagines they will be carefully packed into crates and loaded onto trucks, ready to be transported back to their rightful place.

But Signor Conti tells Zio Tino, "We can't move them yet. You have done a fine job of protecting the museum's treasures. I have no reservations about leaving them here for now. They are in excellent hands. Now we have to see if we can get to some of the other repositories."

When they turn to leave, Signor Conti says to Zio Tino, "You have a remarkable young man and woman here." He tips his hat to Sandro and Stella.

As she watches the men disappear down the road, Stella feels a renewed sense of hope that the paintings might stay safe, that Zio

Tino is just one of many people who will cherish and protect these treasures for generations to come. And she sees herself for the first time as "a young woman."

But when she turns, she sees Zio Tino slumped and looking exhausted, sitting in a small chair pulled up to the table. She sees for the first time that his once iron-black hair has begun to turn silver. In the time Stella has been here, she may have turned into a young woman. But Stella's zio Tino has turned into an old man.

WHEN CAPTAIN FOSTER LEADS General Harold Alexander of the British Eighth Army through the treasure room, he speaks quickly and excitedly in English. He switches briefly to Italian to introduce Stella's family, who are lined up in the courtyard to receive this important visitor. The general spends a very long time standing in front of the *Primavera* before he returns to his entourage and his truck, and departs in a cloud of red dust.

Afterward, Stella describes in detail everything she's seen to Sandro. The general's short pants and long socks over his skinny legs. His field jacket covered in colored insignia. Captain Foster's proud and impassioned tour in English. Zia Angela bowing awkwardly toward the general and not knowing what to do with her hands.

"I GUESS SOME PEOPLE are just born artists," Stella says to Captain Foster in the treasure room. He is seated across from Miss Evans at the central table, she at her strange machine and he handwriting annotations in his inventories.

"Yes," he says, "I would say many artists are born with natural talent. It's difficult to teach someone to be an accomplished artist if they don't already have a natural ability inside them."

"That's for sure," Stella says, deflated.

"But . . ." he continues, "just because someone isn't an artistic genius doesn't mean they can't become an artist. Even Michelangelo and Botticelli had to practice and study to perfect their craft. Perhaps they even doubted themselves," he says, even though Stella can't imagine this. "And," he adds, "just because someone isn't an artist doesn't mean they can't contribute meaningfully in the world of art. I work with many people at the museum—curators, art historians, art restorers—who are not artists. Look at me; I can hardly draw a straight line."

"How did you become . . . ?" she begins, realizing now she doesn't really know what he is.

Captain Foster sits back and laces his fingers behind his head. "An art historian? For one, I was in school for a very long time. Back in America. But ever since I've been on this side of the ocean, I haven't had access to libraries and photographs and other resources like I have back home. That's been a bit of a problem, but we've managed."

He leans over and pulls from his bag a copy of an ancient paperback guidebook to Italy, the kind you might buy in a bookshop. The pages are tattered and dog-eared, as if the book itself has been through a war. He pushes it across the desk to Stella. She picks it up and thumbs through the pages, looking at all the images of churches, museums, countless treasures across the country.

"Been relying on that quite a bit," he says, laughing. "Kind of sad, really. But coming up from the south, we've had to make sure we know what monuments we need to check on. That's the best we could do, I'm afraid."

When she flips through the pages dedicated to Florence and its museums, there is an image of Sandro Botticelli's *Primavera* that fills a whole page. Stella gasps.

"Now that I'm here," Captain Foster says, "I don't need that book anymore. I have everything I need right here in this room. You can keep it."

"Really? You don't need it?"

"I'm sure."

Stella's first reaction is to handle it as carefully and delicately as she would an important painting.

"For some people, it seems strange to be focused on art at a time like this. It's something we hear a lot. But it's more important than just about anything." He looks at her carefully. "You seem like you already have an appreciation for that."

Stella nods. "I guess I have Sandro to thank for that."

"Sandro is an old soul," Captain Foster says, his expression softening. "And Stella, you do something important for him, too."

"What is that?"

"You help him see."

"No," she says. "He may have lost his ability to see clearly, yes. But he's the one who has helped *me* see things I wouldn't have seen before. The stories and the beauty in these paintings. Without him, I might not have been able to see that each one of these paintings is a whole world."

"I understand," Captain Foster says. "There is always more than meets the eye."

"You're going to take the pictures back to Florence?" Stella asks.

Captain Foster sighs deeply. "I don't know. Hopefully, it will be safe to do so at some point. Right now, Florence is still a dangerous place and the Germans have looted the homes along the Arno. They still hold the northern bank, and so we can't go anywhere."

Stella feels a wave of sadness even though she's never seen Florence with her own eyes. Now she knows how important the city is to her country and to the world. How important it is for the history of art. She knows how worried everyone has been about what will happen to the city. She has heard rumors of looting and destruction. She has seen the worry of Signor Poggi, of Father Ramondo, even of people from the opposite side of the globe like Captain Foster.

Everyone prays for the city to be spared, but all they hear are reports of destruction and suffering.

"Anyway," Captain Foster says, standing, putting his hands on his hips, and surveying the treasure room. "The paintings are in a good spot here. It's safer in the countryside," he says.

Now Stella thinks this might be true.

IN THE EVENING, Stella and Sandro sit cross-legged on the floor in the treasure room, just like old times, and Stella reads from the guidebook Captain Foster gave her. Sandro hangs on every word as she turns the tattered pages.

"'*La Primavera* is one of the earliest examples in Renaissance painting of a non-religious scene,'" she reads. "'Botticelli has replaced the more common Virgin Mary with Venus, a pagan symbol, in a natural yet mythic environment. The painting is one of the first large-scale European paintings to tell a story that was not Christian. It is not a sermon, not a lecture, but a depiction of rebirth and earthly pleasures.'"

Sandro listens intently as Stella turns each page dedicated to the Uffizi's collection and reads it aloud.

"Sandro!" she cries. "Look!" She immediately regrets saying the word. But Stella is mesmerized by the figure of a goddess rising from the sea in a giant seashell, surrounded by more strange and beautiful mythological figures. "There's another one . . . *The Birth of Venus*, it says. By Sandro Botticelli! There is another painting like this one. Just as beautiful. Maybe just as big."

AFTER WEEKS OF ANXIETY AND TERROR in the crowded villa, Stella awakes at first light to the peaceful sound of birdsong in the quiet. It's eerie, like the calm before the storm. Stella steps outside to the upper terrace. In the growing light, she looks beyond the vineyards where the Germans and others had set up their tents. Now, she thinks, no one would believe that just a few weeks ago, Germans, tanks, and trucks littered this hillside and olive grove.

Now, Stella realizes, she's not alone. She sees Miss Evans sitting at the table on the terrace, writing something in her notebook.

So far, Stella has only seen men involved with art. But now she sees a woman can play a role, too. Stella is drawn to Miss Evans with a sense of wonder and curiosity. A foreign woman. A woman in uniform. A woman who operates a strange machine and works with art.

"*Buongiorno,*" Miss Evans says, raising her hand. Stella comes over and takes a seat next to her. "It's beautiful here," she says. "I like to get up early so I can see the sunrise."

"Are you glad you came here?" Stella asks. "You're far away from home."

She nods. "Yes, some parts of being here have been difficult. But . . . I have come to love your country." She hesitates. "My mother died a few months ago, back home in Connecticut. She was really all I had. And so now I'm not in a hurry to go home. I'll stay as long as they need me."

Stella's breath catches in her throat to have found another person, so different from her, to be similarly shaped by the war.

"I lost my mamma, too," she says tentatively. "Back in Torino."

Miss Evans' face grows shadowed. She reaches for Stella's hand and squeezes it. "Oh, I'm sorry."

"How did you start working with Captain Foster?"

In halting Italian, she tries to explain. "I didn't choose it. I just signed up for the Women's Army Corps." She laughs. "A friend dared me to do it."

"Were you in school for a long time like Captain Foster? To learn about art?"

She quickly shakes her head. "Not at all. I left school as soon as it was allowed, and I knew nothing about art before I came here.

I've learned a few things just by following the Monuments officers, all the way up from North Africa. Before I came here, I was just a typist. But . . . being here has given me the chance to do a lot of things I never thought I would do before."

Stella leans in, full of admiration and wonder for this woman of art, so far from home. A woman who has found a way not only to work with art but to be brave all at the same time.

"But it has been difficult at times," she says, and Stella imagines that Miss Evans might have seen some of the same injustices Stella's family has.

"I didn't know women could do that kind of work," Stella says. "I've only seen men here. Maybe it's different in America."

Miss Evans laughs. "Maybe. But you can do anything you set your mind to. You seem like a smart girl. Why not?"

THE NEXT DAY, the news breaks that the Germans have exploded every historic bridge in Florence except for the Ponte Vecchio. There are fragmentary, urgent whispers of smoldering ruins, hunks of stones washed away in the Arno. Families on the north and south banks separated from one another as if by an ocean.

In the afternoon, Stella winds down a narrow path to the olive grove. She spies Captain Foster all alone, sitting on the hard ground. Elbows on his bony knees. Weeping into his palms, his back racked with sobs.

CHAPTER 15

SIGHTLINES

Summer 1944

*When I handed over this Primavera to His Excellency, it was
I who felt reborn. It felt the beginning of a new season, setting
aside the many months I contemplated, tried and failed, tried
again to create a world, an ode to spring, to the ceaseless dance
of nature and divinity.*

—FROM THE LOST DIARIES OF SANDRO
BOTTICELLI, FLORENCE, WINTER 1480

*Ultimately, the fate of the most significant works of art in
history lay in the hands of just a few individuals. It was their
own courage, their own actions, that would dictate the future
of the culture of Italy. And even children . . . they were not
just passive observers. They learned to see, to appreciate the deep
wells of human emotion and history encapsulated in the brush
strokes and pigments, becoming a part of the unbroken chain of
passing down stories and wisdom through art.*

—FROM THE DIARY OF CAPTAIN WALLACE E.
FOSTER, MONUMENTS OFFICER OF THE FIFTH
ARMY IN TUSCANY, AUGUST 1944

When news finally comes that the Allies have pushed the Germans north of Florence's city limits, the last of the refugees living in the cantina prepare to depart. They pack up their ragged dolls and copper pans and worn rosary beads and faded photographs. They leave with a mixture of hope and trepidation, wondering what they will find when they get home, and how they will begin to put back into place what is left of their lives. Those who depart clutch at the hope their homes and villages will still be standing. That their neighbors and loved ones might be there to greet them when they get there.

Ornella shuffles out of the cool dampness with her newborn baby girl on her shoulder. She will travel with a small group of women headed to their hometowns on the outskirts of Rome. They leave the wine cellar, the place they've called home for more than a year, the place where they have all huddled together, where they have lost and regained hope in the midst of unimaginable circumstances. Stella hands them a few jars of squash they canned months ago, back when they thought the Germans would eat them instead.

Stella watches the small group of women start off on foot together, carrying bundles under their arms. They look exhausted already, Stella thinks, their faces creased with worry. She thinks of all the meals, games, and stories they have shared together. She feels a pang of sadness to think she may never see them again, a feeling mixed with a sense of joy that they can finally leave this place and begin anew. It is bittersweet, Stella thinks, like tasting honey and vinegar from the same spoon. She reaches for the baby's hand, and she relaxes her tight little fist around Stella's finger.

"*Addio!*" Zio Stefano calls. "They'll be alright," he says softly, coming to stand beside Stella and putting a hand on her shoulder as she feels a lump grow in her throat. "They have each other."

Stella watches one of the old women, her back bent, shuffle with a slow gait, leaning heavily on her walking stick. Stella thinks she looks like she will make it home no matter what. Stella runs and waves until the women disappear out of sight down the dusty road toward the village and to the unknown dangers that lie south of here. She waves and waves until the golden landscape swallows them.

When Stella returns to the wine cellar, it stands cavernous and silent as a tomb. Dust motes hang suspended in the weak light. The smell of humanity lingers in the air and Stella imagines it will be there long after they are gone.

Stella thinks about Sergeant Cakebread, the dozens of fugitive soldiers and the other individuals who have crossed paths here. Signora Romano, who wept over being separated from her daughters by the mined roads. Old Giuseppe, who played his mandolin to lift everyone's spirits. The children in their mismatched, ragged clothing who continued their games even as the planes flew frighteningly low and artillery fire lit up the hills in silhouettes. Their shared moments of despair and flares of hope, the meals cobbled together over a single fire, the whispered worries and cries in the dark. The night when they all huddled together as the cannons fired, and then everything changed.

Now there are only two people in the villa whose future is uncertain. Two refugees left with nowhere to go.

Stella and Sandro.

For a while, the only topic of conversation in the whole region of Santa Lucia is the liberation of Florence. Father Ramondo, flushed and jittery with nervous energy, comes up for the evening meal on the warm terrace. Among the adults, there is talk of the blown bridges and the Allies' dramatic entry into the city, driving German forces north at last.

Captain Foster says he and Miss Evans will depart immediately so they can find their colleagues and begin assessing the damage in the city. Signor Fasola says he will depart with them. He is beyond eager to get home to his wife and he feels confident now that the works of art are in good hands.

"Seems all your guests are leaving," Father Ramondo says to Zio Tino as Stella puts a basket of freshly baked bread in front of the priest.

"Yes," Zio Tino says. "I'm sure they will be relieved to be home, and God willing, they can make it there."

"*Caspita*, this is the best *pici* I've ever tasted!" Father Ramondo exclaims. "I hope you're not planning to go anywhere, Stella . . ." Then he hesitates. "I mean . . . well, you are fortunate to have a family to shelter you through this time." His eyes are filled with compassion. But then he seems to second-guess himself. "Still not possible to go north . . ." he says, his voice trailing off awkwardly.

"She will stay with us for now," Zia Angela says. Stella feels her aunt's bony fingers on her shoulders. She flinches at first, but she senses a warmth in her aunt's skeletal grip. Comforting and discomforting all at the same time.

"FATHER RAMONDO!" Stella runs down the dusty path as the priest makes his waddling descent back down to the village. He stops and turns back. Alongside the road, the weeds grow tall and the countryside lies in peace and silence.

"I was hoping you could help. We have to do something . . ."

Stella thinks that of anyone, Father Ramondo might have an answer to what Sandro can do, now that he is stranded here just the same as Stella.

"It's Sandro," she says. "He can barely see anymore, Father. And he's on his own. Everyone who's been staying in the wine cellar has left. Even the family who brought Sandro here left months ago. His family . . . He doesn't have anywhere to go. He needs a doctor and . . ." Stella's voice trails off. She doesn't have words to convey the breadth of her worry for her friend.

"I see." The priest's face turns grave. For what seems a long time, he tents his fingers in silent contemplation under his lips. "The Lord always provides," he says finally, raising a finger. But then he wavers. "But even if he doesn't, well . . . Give me a little time, child," he says. "I have an idea."

ON THE NIGHT BEFORE Captain Foster, Miss Evans, and Signor Fasola leave for Florence, they gather around the dinner table. The family moves back into the formal dining room for the first time since soldiers from every corner of the globe commandeered it for their own. The men take their places at the large table while the women bring everything out to it. Stella notes that Miss Evans is the only woman sitting at the table with the men.

Stella serves Captain Foster and Miss Evans rabbit with stewed tomatoes and olives, the aroma of fresh rosemary rising from the serving dish. During the meal, Captain Foster thanks Stella's family for their hospitality. He says they will load their Jeep at dawn and will make their way into Florence with one of the Florentine partisans as their guide. These men, he says, know how to navigate the pockmarked, mined roads well enough to get them into the city, all the way to the south bank of the Arno. Stella thinks Miss Evans looks excited, expectant, even though Stella imagines she must be scared at the same time.

Amid the tension of their impending departure, they enjoy their last conversations along with the food Stella has prepared. The time and shared experience have brought down any walls of culture, of language, of other barriers. Stella thinks Captain Foster and her uncle look like old friends assembled around the table.

Captain Foster shares a BBC report that mentions the Villa Santa

Lucia for a second time. The reporters say the American and British Monuments officers have discovered some of the most valuable and important paintings in the world in this unknown villa.

Stella watches Signor Fasola bristle. "Discovered! Discovered? But then you are taking credit for finding things that were never lost," he says. "We . . . we Italian custodians have known where they were the whole time. They were never *lost* at any time. Just hidden."

"Of course you are right, my friend," Captain Foster says, putting his hand on Signor Fasola's shoulder. "And I'd be the last one to dispute that you have risked your life to save these treasures."

Captain Foster now turns to Zio Tino. "How much has the superintendency been paying you?"

Zia Angela casts her husband a wary glance.

Zio Tino clears his throat roughly. "Seventeen lire per day." Then he crosses his arms. The silence stretches out between the two men and Stella thinks her uncle suddenly looks a bit duped. "And twelve for Stefano."

Captain Foster only shakes his head. "Do you know how much these works of art are worth, my friend?"

Stella thinks it's a good thing Zio Stefano wasn't around to hear Captain Foster's assessment. Then she thinks about all the German vouchers her aunt has been hiding in her brassiere and under her mattress, and she wonders if those bills have any value at all now.

A FEW DAYS AFTER the Americans and Signor Fasola leave for Florence, Stella watches Father Ramondo come up to the villa. He spends a long time talking with Zia Angela and Zio Tino in the kitchen with the door closed.

THAT NIGHT, in the treasure room, Stella breaks the news to Sandro of everything she's overheard when she eavesdropped on the conversation between Father Ramondo and her aunt and uncle. They keep the shutters partly open all the time now, and a golden light floods the room, reflecting off the red tiles and illuminating the painted surfaces in all their colors and gilded splendor.

"It's a special school for blind kids," Stella says as they sit splayed on the floor in the sunlight. "In Pistoia. You can live there and they'll take care of everything for you."

She studies Sandro's face for any shift in his expression. She tries to be as tender as she can. A school for blind children . . . Stella never knew such a place existed. She watches the news transform Sandro's face. He is silent, but scratches his nose roughly as if trying to tear it off. A nervous gesture.

"Father Ramondo says they have special eye doctors there—and a lot of teachers. They will show you a new way of reading—with your hands instead of your eyes."

Stella goes on to explain how Father Ramondo has said they will teach Sandro how to navigate with a special kind of walking stick. He will have the chance to sing and learn a musical instrument. He will even be able to do sports. And even if his vision doesn't come back, he will be able to learn a trade so he can make a living.

In her heart, Stella knows it's the right thing for Sandro. She can't imagine how else he could possibly manage. And she knows Father Ramondo's assessment is correct: it will be the only way Sandro can move forward and he should not be denied such an opportunity. All the same, Stella's heart sinks to think about him leaving the villa. Her only friend in the world.

She waits for him to look at her. To cry or cheer or hug her. But he is just silent for a long time. Outside, a few clouds gather and soft shadows fall over the room. Sandro's continued silence makes a pain spread across her midsection. It means that her promises ring hollow. Finally, she realizes why.

There is only one thing in life Sandro wants. He doesn't care about the walking stick or the sports or the doctors. He may be able to enjoy many of the things Father Ramondo has so wonderfully described.

But his dream will be lost to fate. Sandro will not be the one thing he wanted more than anything in life.

An artist.

ON THE DAY Sandro is to leave Santa Lucia, he and Stella walk through the treasure room one last time. The paintings stand as quiet witnesses to the impending shift in the universe. For Stella, this is much more than a hushed farewell. It's a final communion.

For a few long minutes, they walk through the room, perusing the pictures together in the silent dimness, the space like a church, a hallowed sanctuary beyond words.

Sandro breaks the silence. "I have something for you." He hands her a small package, a rectangle wrapped in a sheet of yellowed newspaper left behind in the wine cellar.

"You didn't have to give me anything . . ."

He shrugs. "I know." He seems to teeter on the edge of embarrassment, his face flushing, suddenly demure in giving her a gift.

Stella unwraps the paper. Inside is Sandro's most prized possession: his leather-bound folio full of finished sketches, the one he showed to the *maestra* on his first day of school all those months ago. "Guess I don't need it anymore."

"Sandro," she says. By instinct, Stella clutches the folio close to her heart. She wants to say more but words fail her. She knows that book has been so important for him. She recognizes that he's given her his most prized possession, the only thing in the world that really matters to him. And that he won't need it anymore.

"Don't let it fall into the wrong hands," he says, grinning.

Stella feels her cheeks flush and lowers her head, knowing that this is why she loves Sandro—he always knows the right words to say.

"You don't have to give me anything now because you've already given me something I'll keep inside me forever," she tells him. "Just by teaching me to draw." She takes his free hand in hers and holds it. "I wouldn't have been able to do that without you. Even though I'm terrible at it."

Sandro smiles, the sparkle of the morning sun in his dark eyes. "Well, I learned something from you, too. Guess I won't be able to do that anymore either."

Stella feels pain in her chest. "You learned how to read once. You'll learn again. With your hands this time."

In the courtyard, there is movement and then Zio Tino's silhouette darkens the doorway. "They're here for you, Sandro," he says.

Sandro and Stella pause before Botticelli's magnificent *Primavera* one last time. Stella watches Sandro run his fingers lightly over the paint, over the long centuries of care along with injustice and endurance. Stella watches his fingers linger softly over the surface of the crackled, brilliant colors as if searing the image into his mind's eye forevermore.

When Sandro leaves the Villa Santa Lucia, it's with two nuns in a horse-drawn wagon.

"First-class transportation," Father Ramondo says as Stella and Sandro walk out the front door of the villa. Sunlight filters through the leaves of ancient olive trees, casting dappled shadows on the dusty ground.

"This is Sister Teresa." Father Ramondo places his hands on Sandro's shoulders. "She will help you get settled at your new school."

"Should take most of the day to get there this way," the other nun says from the driver's seat of the cart. "But we won't find much traffic."

Stella feels a sudden stinging in the back of her throat. She pushes it down with a hard swallow.

At that moment, Signora Donati emerges from the villa, openly sobbing. Great tears pouring down her cheeks. She fans her face with her palms. "*O Dio*," she calls to Sandro. "What a sad day for all of us. But what a blessing for you, my child."

Zio Tino brings Sandro's meager pack and lifts it into the back of the cart. Inside, Stella knows, is a change of clothes, a toothbrush, and a few notebooks and pencils.

"Stella . . ." Sandro says, his face searching.

"I'm here," she says, taking his hand. He faces her but says nothing. He is speechless.

"It's not goodbye," Stella says. "It's see you later."

Sandro reaches out both hands now and does something he's never done before: he touches her face. Stella feels his rough palms on her cheeks, run over her forehead, her lips. She closes her eyes and for a moment, experiences Sandro the same way he experiences her: through the magic of human touch.

When she opens her eyes, he is smiling. Small divots in his tanned cheeks. His brown, nearly unseeing eyes sparkling in the sun.

"*Ci vediamo*, Stellina," he says.

Zio Tino helps Sandro's foot find the mount and he sits up between the two nuns in the seat. One of the nuns gives a gentle tap of the reins, and they set off.

"*Ci vediamo*, Sandro," Stella calls. "See you."

When the wagon starts down the dirt path, Stella closes her eyes. She feels the sun's golden light, warm on her eyelids. That way, she figures, she doesn't have to see him go.

ON THE DAY the village schoolhouse reopens, Stella is the first to arrive. She marches down the dirt road to the village just as the sun rises over the hills.

"*Aspetta!*" Mariasole calls out as she scrambles to keep up, her leather satchel slapping on her hip.

In the distance, Stella sees Signora De Luca, the new *maestra*, open the wide door. Signora is a broad-chested, stern-looking woman with a swirl of silver hair. Approaching the schoolhouse, Stella thinks the building looks small now. Not intimidating like it did when she first came here. She thinks about the first time she walked into the building. And the day when she brought Sandro with her to meet the *maestra*. A day filled with uncertainty, with the focus on things that hardly seem to matter anymore.

The stone façade is riddled with pockmarks made by shrapnel and one of the windows is shattered. But Signora De Luca says they should get the school back up and running so the village children don't fall too far behind and so that families can return their lives to normal as soon as possible.

Inside, Signora De Luca has done her best to get the room back into shape for the first day. The desks and chairs are put back into neat rows and the stone floor is swept and mopped. The chaos of makeshift pallets, tattered stuffed animals, and sad belongings has ended. A few children straggle into the building.

As she walks down the empty aisles between the desks, Stella smells the chalk and hears the sound of children's voices outside. Just a year ago, she thinks, this room was a place of fear and obligation. A place she was intent on leaving behind as quickly as possible.

But then, the schoolhouse turned into a refuge for so many children. A place where they could grieve and seek shelter from the chaos outside—until that grim day that no one in the village will ever forget. But even now, the schoolhouse no longer seems like a place Stella dreads; instead, it feels like a place where she belongs.

The long months of having school unavailable have made the

children hunger for their routine, for the familiarity of the school hours and the opportunity to learn, denied to them by the violence and volatility of the months of German occupation. In the faces of the other children entering the schoolhouse, Stella sees excitement and eagerness to get back to normal. To learn again. To see opportunity in the things they once took for granted until it was lost. Each child has lost something—a parent, a sibling, their own innocence during the long months of tribulation.

Stella slides into her place at her old desk, which suddenly feels small and creaky. The desk behind her, Fabio's spot, remains empty. She thinks of him now. He, too, forced to forge a new life, and she wonders how the war has changed him.

She remembers Sandro's first day, too, when he showed the *maestra* his own drawing. Stella has begun writing Sandro letters every few days. She posts them in the old post box in the village square, but she doesn't know if they will ever arrive in Pistoia. She only hopes that if they do make it that far, someone will be able to read them to him.

Signora De Luca takes her place at the front of the room amid a loud din of conversation among the excited children. Stella remembers how the old *maestra* used to clap her hands to bring the children to order. By instinct, Stella claps the pattern loudly and the children follow suit. The loud chattering quiets immediately.

"Thank you, Stella," Signora De Luca says. "I'm glad to know this trick! Would you like to come up and read the first chapter of our new book?"

When Stella stands at the front of the class, she looks out upon the sea of young faces and realizes she's not the new kid anymore. Also, she's the oldest in the class.

When Stella finishes the reading and retakes her seat, she looks up and sees that someone has taken down the photograph of Benito Mussolini that, for decades, hung above the *lavagna* of every schoolroom across Italy. The wall retains a light-colored rectangle in the stucco as a reminder not only of the ill-fated era of Il Duce but of everything that has unfolded in the past few months to change their village forever.

Later, Stella hears some of the boys have taken the picture into the woods and shot at it.

WHEN STELLA AND MARIASOLE walk up the dirt road toward the Villa Santa Lucia at midday, Stella realizes that for the first time in months, she feels a spark of hope. The first day of school has opened a new chapter. As much as Sandro's departure has left a void in her heart, she feels relief that he will get the help he needs at last. Both of them with new beginnings.

When they arrive at the villa, they find the doors of the empty wine cellar flung open. Stella's uncles are in the garden, digging up the hidden things: Lady Harwell's jewelry, the Harwells' most-prized bottles of wine, and a myriad of stored food. The smell of roasted meat and onions fills the air from the open kitchen window.

"Maybe they have forgotten where everything is buried," Stella says.

"I hope they found more sausages, at least," Mariasole says. "I'm hungry!" She jogs around the bulk of the old building to the crumbling stone stairs that lead to the upper terrace. The girls climb to the terrace, where the day has turned hot. Two large beech trees shade tables where the German soldiers once gathered.

Now there is a new man sitting at one of the tables. From behind, Stella thinks, he looks skinny and disheveled in a ragged shirt and dirty trousers. Another escaped soldier who's stashed his uniform somewhere in the woods? They haven't seen one in weeks. The poor man must be very lost or perhaps hasn't heard that the Germans are no longer pursuing him in these parts.

From the house, Signora Donati emerges with a glass of water in one hand and wine in the other. Luigi and her favorite goose follow closely behind her skirts. When Signora Donati catches sight of Stella, her mouth suddenly forms a thin line. Stella feels a wave of unease wash over her. Signora Donati places a glass of cold wine in front of the man and says, "*Ecco ci qua, signore.* Something to tide you over. We'll have food ready for you soon."

Stella hears Signora Donati try to make her voice sound light and high-pitched. Something in Stella's mind shifts. Awakens.

The man in the ragged clothes seems to sense the tension, and he turns now to the girls. His eyes flit back and forth between Stella and Mariasole for a few seconds. Then his eyes rest on Stella.

"*Ciao cucciola,*" the man says. He pushes his chair back and stands.

All at once, the myriad facets of Stella's past and present life shift, reorganize themselves, and then click together like shards of glass in a kaleidoscope. Her mind begins to match up his various physical aspects with the jagged shards of memory contained in the now-crumpled photograph: the dark, slick hair; the particular geometry of his face; the ears that protrude out a bit more than average, just like hers. He looks different from the photograph, and different from the mythic father she's concocted in her head all these years. Stella realizes she wouldn't have recognized her own flesh and blood if she had passed him on the street.

All the same, Stella's hope, the long-held dream she let go of months ago, has come true at last.

Her papà has come for her.

"Look at you!" Stella's father exclaims, turning up his palms. He hesitates, and the space between them seems to yawn. Electrify. For a long, awkward moment, he doesn't seem to know what to do with his hands. Should he embrace her or keep a respectful distance? Stella thinks he can't decide, and at last, he puts them in his pockets and rocks back and forth on his heels. "A young lady. All grown up."

Stella feels herself grow suddenly shy. Last time her father saw her, she was a baby, not a teenaged girl with her period and a brassiere handed down from her older cousin.

"I guess," Stella says.

But in the years since that photograph was taken alongside Zia Angela, Daniele Costa has changed, too. Deep crevices have formed across his brow and his unshaven face. He is gaunt, haggard, and hollow-eyed, his face dark and rugged as if he's toiled outside for a very long time in the sun like Zio Stefano.

The space between them is filled with erratic energy, some kind of force like two identical magnets that pull together or repel, depending on which way you turn them.

LATER, WHEN THE WHOLE FAMILY assembles at the table on the terrace, there are many questions for Daniele Costa. To Stella's astonishment, the story she invented about her father fighting at the front turns out to be true. He has been in uniform for most of the past three years. Even at the front lines.

From her place at the table, Stella carefully observes him. He devours the plate of *cacio e pepe* in seconds, like a stray dog who hasn't eaten in weeks. He wipes the plate clean with a hunk of bread. While he eats, his eyes flicker among them—back and forth to Zia Angela, then to Stella's uncles and cousins and Signora Donati.

"You've been in Lazio or Tuscany the whole time?" Zio Stefano asks, a certain formality and politeness coloring his voice.

Her papà shakes his head. "Neither. Ever since I had to register, I've been in Emilia-Romagna for the most part," he says. He goes on to explain how his regiment disbanded when the armistice was announced last year. He set off on foot along with several other men. They hid in the woods whenever a German truck went by. But then, the Germans became too numerous. They took him prisoner and at first, he thought he was being taken to Germany, but they brought him to a forced labor camp near Modena, where, after a while, he managed to escape.

Here, his voice falters and Stella sees his eyes seem very far away, as if he's watching a newsreel unfurling inside his own head.

"I'm not proud," he says finally, "to admit that I stole a horse and wagon from a farm in the middle of the night. And some clothes. That's how I finally got rid of the uniform." He shrugs. "But that's what it took to get me here." For about a week, he says, he managed to pass himself off as a *fattore*, keeping to the farm roads heading southward. He says he abandoned the cart and horse nearby when he was within walking distance of Villa Santa Lucia.

"And here I am," he says. "I thought you might let me stay." Her father directs this statement to Zio Tino. "I didn't know where else to go and I thought . . ." Stella's papà stalls, his eyes flickering to Zia Angela for a split second.

Zio Tino jumps in. "*Senz'altro*," he says. "If you can't turn to your family in such times, then who could you turn to?" Zio Tino stands and gives Stella's father a handshake and then a bear hug. Stella watches her father stand as the two men slap each other's back.

Stella's aunt doesn't say anything. She puts down her fork and crosses her arms. Pushes her chair back from the table.

STELLA WONDERS if her aunt will make her papà sleep on the wine cellar floor or out in the olive grove, like every other unwelcome guest. Instead, she makes up a bed for him with clean sheets unpinned from the line.

Zio Tino unearths one of Sir Harwell's fine suits from one of the trunks in the attic. After her father bathes and changes into it, he emerges from the bathroom like an English lord. Except for the too-long pants that drag on the ground and the belt holding them up around his skinny waist.

"No one in this town will hire him so he's better off going back to Rome," Mariasole whispers to Stella. "That's what mamma said."

From the corridor, they watch Stella's papà fumble with the cuff links of Sir Harwell's shirt as if it's the first time he's ever handled such a thing.

LATER, IN THEIR BEDCHAMBER, Stella hears her aunt and uncle arguing in hushed tones. She stands just out of view, at the edge of the doorway.

"He can't just show up out of nowhere and take her!" Zia Angela's voice. "How could we trust him?"

"He's her father, Angela," Zio Tino says, more quietly than his wife. "He has the right to take his own daughter to Rome with him if that is what he decides."

"He is a stranger to her, Tino. Besides, he didn't even write one letter. Not to us. Not to her."

"You know that was beyond his control."

For a few seconds, there is silence. "She is better off here with us," Zia Angela insists.

"She's nearly fourteen, Angela. Surely she's outgrown the village schoolhouse. You know as well as I do that there is . . . no one . . . waiting for her back in Torino."

Stella feels a sharp pang in her gut to hear her worst fear spoken out loud, even if Zio Tino doesn't say her mother's name directly.

"Anyway, what else are you going to do with her?" she hears Zio Tino continue. "She's a smart girl. She could . . ."

"But he . . . he can't even take care of himself, much less an adolescent girl who needs more guidance. He's completely unreliable. His behavior was already erratic before. But now . . ."

After that, their voices grow too low to hear.

OVER THE NEXT FEW DAYS, Stella and her family do their best to care for her father. Stella prepares her *pici*, careful to make sure the simple ragù has the right balance of salt and sugar. Zio Tino hands over a pair of his own trousers that fit her father's short frame better than those of the Englishman.

Signora Donati retrieves some antiseptic and a bandage left behind from the Germans' infirmary, and dresses a wound on the bottom side of her father's left foot that looks red and angry. He says it's been causing him pain for nearly two weeks and it's the reason he had to steal a horse and cart.

But as the days pass, Stella begins to realize that her father's wounds go deeper than the painful-looking, infected lesion on his left foot. She looks for an opportunity to ask him about her mother and what happened between the two of them, but as the days pass, broaching the subject of her mother with Daniele Costa becomes an ever-widening chasm that eventually grows too great to bridge.

Sometimes, he sits under the olive trees, smoking for a long time, or with his head hanging in the crook of his elbow. One day, he doesn't rise from his bed at all. In the middle of the night, through the walls of their bedroom, she hears him cry out as if some unseen force is torturing him.

"WHY DON'T YOU give your father a tour of the paintings?" Zio Tino asks one afternoon.

She hesitates. For both Stella and her father, their first few attempts at conversation have proved awkward and strained, the silences between them a testament to the gaping void of time that has separated them.

"I hear you've learned a thing or two about art," he says as they enter the treasure room.

For Stella, the opportunity to show her father the paintings—

to relay everything she's learned about the *Primavera* and the other treasures from Signor Poggi and Signor Fasola, from Zio Tino and even Sandro—gives Stella something sturdy to hang on to, something to talk about that means she doesn't have to enter into another awkward conversation with Daniele Costa. Instead, it gives her a chance to reach again for these works of art that have given her comfort, hope, and refuge during the greatest time of uncertainty in her young life.

After she's completed her tour of all the paintings, she dares to look at her father's face for the first time since they entered the treasure room. "*Brava,*" he says, looking satisfied. "Your mamma would have been proud of you . . . You look like her, you know, now that you're grown."

Stella thinks about the times people have said she's the spit of him instead. For a long time, silence stretches out and Stella runs her old locket back and forth across its silver chain. A shadow falls over her father's face when she only nods in response.

"I guess we have a lot to catch up on," he says.

"Almost fourteen years' worth," Stella says with as much light-heartedness as she can muster. But they both know too much time has passed to recapture all the past fourteen years has brought.

He doesn't respond at first. Only purses his lips and nods slowly. "Well," he says, "you heard what I've been doing recently. But before I joined the army, I was working in Rome. I was selling flowers in Trastevere, but then, well . . . I was out of work for a bit. Then I got a job as a porter at the Stazione Centrale. Maybe when the train lines are running again, I could go back to it . . ."

Stella imagines her father cobbling together a string of jobs in the big city, or maybe going without for a time. The years of eking out a living, one day to the next. It all seems distant, as if her father's life in Rome sits on the other side of a canyon that might be too wide to cross.

"But what about you . . . ?" he asks. "Tell me what you've been doing here in Santa Lucia all this time."

Stella is struck mute. For how can she find the words to describe Sandro, the Germans, the New Zealanders, the Indians, everything she has learned about Botticelli's *Primavera* and Italian Renaissance art, and everything that's happened since the moment her mother put her in a Red Cross car headed to Pisa? The words bind to the lump in her throat and she can't seem to get them out.

Instead, she stares at the toes of her scuffed shoes and shrugs.

"I don't know," she says finally. "I guess I've learned to make pasta."

AFTER THE SUN GOES DOWN, Stella sits at the rickety desk in the bedroom, sketching in one of the pages of her notebook. Alongside, she opens a spread of pages that Sandro left behind. She does her best to copy the sinuous lines of a horse's back. So simple. So difficult.

From the rumpled bed they share, Mariasole says, "My papà says you are old enough to work now. Maybe you'll find a job in Rome when your papà takes you. Like in a bakery or a laundry."

Stella carefully drags the pencil on the page, doing her best to mimic what Sandro has drawn. She tries to imagine herself cobbling together a precarious string of jobs alongside her father.

When she doesn't answer Mariasole, the girl tries again. "Well? Maybe you could find a job in a restaurant? You know how to make pasta now."

"Maybe," Stella says, only to silence her cousin.

But Stella doesn't want to work in a restaurant or a laundry or a bakery, she realizes. She only wants to find a way to stay in school. To find a way to do something bigger than herself. To find a way to stay in the presence of great works of art. After all, Miss Evans taught her that she could do something daring and important; that she could do anything she wants. Miss Evans was just a typist, but look at everything she's accomplished now. Stella holds on to the belief that maybe she could do something like that, too.

Stella realizes that, when she arrived at Villa Santa Lucia, her biggest dream was that her mother might follow her to this wondrous new world on a Tuscan farm. And that her mythic father might return from war, scoop both of them up in his arms and complete their family circle, whisk them away to a new and perfect life.

But now she sees the truth: her mother is gone and her father is incapable of whisking her away to a perfect life, even if he wanted to. Stella has her father back. It's the thing she thought would make her normal, just like all the other kids in Santa Lucia. But she is more on her own than ever before.

CHAPTER 16

A WOMAN OF ART

Summer 1944

To think of it: a painting that might outlast me. Making art is the only way a human being can achieve immortality.
—FROM THE LOST DIARIES OF SANDRO
BOTTICELLI, FLORENCE, WINTER 1480

Even before we arrived at our respective posts, we compiled exhaustive inventories and maps that indicated historic monuments and collections of irreplaceable works of art. Each one of us Monuments officers around the world is committed to the belief that if we have done our jobs, then the art will outlive us all.
—FROM THE DIARY OF CAPTAIN WALLACE E.
FOSTER, MONUMENTS OFFICER OF THE
FIFTH ARMY IN TUSCANY, JULY 1944

On the day Giovanni Poggi returns to the Villa Santa Lucia, Stella is working in the vegetable garden, harvesting the many tomatoes that seem to have ripened all together at once. Each red fruit feels warm and heavy in her palm. She gently twists each stem, just as Zia Angela has shown her. If the fruit comes off easily, it means it's ready to pick and Stella places it in her basket. She watches Signor Poggi's long black car come to a stop before the villa.

This time, Signor Poggi has brought two men with him. She watches them emerge from the vehicle as a swirl of unanswered questions rushes into her mind. She abandons her basket of warm tomatoes on the ground and rushes to the house.

When Stella enters the treasure room, Zio Tino is exchanging firm handshakes with the newly arrived visitors. She recognizes one of the men as Signor Conti, the paintings conservator from the Pitti Palace who placed white gauze on the flaking paint during his last visit.

Livia and Mariasole come jogging through the courtyard, their curiosity matching Stella's. "Are they taking the paintings?" Mariasole whispers to Stella as they enter the room. Stella only shrugs.

"Signor Conti is our most senior conservator," Signor Poggi is telling Zio Tino. Stella sees that Signor Conti is already leaning in close to Paolo Uccello's *Battle of San Romano*, checking the gauze he had placed on the surface of the paint as Zio Tino flips back sections of the wooden shutters and light fills the room.

Stella comes to stand beside him. "Is the paint still flaking?" she asks.

He chuckles. "Hopefully not, at least if I have done my job. But unfortunately, it's inevitable, especially when paintings are stored in less-than-ideal conditions. You have a wonderful space for storing them, under the circumstances. But many of the paintings prior to the fifteenth century were painted on wooden panels. They are very sensitive to changes in temperature and humidity. As the wood expands and contracts, the paint can become cracked, and sometimes it flakes off in small pieces."

Stella feels her heart plummet to think of the paintings sustaining damage, just by sitting here in the treasure room. Especially after everything they have done to keep them from harm. "But what can be done about it?" she asks.

"That's my job," he says, grinning. "I spend all day thinking about how to prevent paintings from being damaged in the first place. And those of us in the conservation studio can then work together to repair damage when it occurs."

Stella's mind expands with the possibility of working in such a wondrous place as a conservation studio. She is captivated with the idea of being able to work surrounded by art all day.

"You're taking the paintings back with you?" Mariasole asks.

"Not today, I'm afraid, *cara*," Signor Poggi says. "It will be some time before we're ready to bring the paintings back to the city. For one, we have a giant hole in the roof of the museum. And all the window glass is smashed along the Vasari Corridor."

Signor Poggi goes on to enumerate the nearly unfathomable injustices the city has endured. The medieval tower houses are great piles of rubble along the banks of the Arno. There is incalculable damage to churches and historic buildings across the city. Refugees are still milling about in the courtyard of the Pitti Palace. Not to mention all the things they haven't been able to account for yet.

"I know you all have been through Hell, especially with the Germans here. And I know you're anxious for us to take them back," Signor Poggi says. "But ultimately, we were right to bring the paintings here. It could have been much worse for them in Florence. You've been beyond courageous," he says to Stella's uncles.

Mariasole butts in. "But Stella's the one who yelled at them for throwing the knife into that round painting!"

Signor Poggi's eyebrows fly up and he turns to Stella. "Then you've all been brave. Thanks to people like you," he says, placing a hand on Stella's shoulder, "with any luck, these treasures will still exist long after we are gone."

LATER, STELLA WATCHES Signor Conti place new strips of white gauzy fabric on specific spots on several pictures.

"What will you do in those areas?" she asks.

"Each painting will tell us what it needs. We'll need to do quite a bit of conservation work," he says. "Of course, it's impossible to do it here. But once we get the paintings back to the museum, I'll be able to bring them into my conservation studio and fix the places where paint is flaking. In the meantime, these little strips will help stabilize the bad spots."

Stella watches Signor Conti make notations in his ledger, filled with terms and words she has never heard before. Its own kind of language. The idea of saving art, of preserving it, of holding the essence of the past in your hands, begins to stir something in her.

"How did you learn to do that?" she asks.

"Oh, we have several good conservation schools in Florence. And many opportunities for conservation apprenticeships in our various museums. That's what I did."

"A school just for saving art?" Stella is incredulous.

He smiles. "Yes! A wondrous place. But you have to come to Florence to go to one of them."

Stella has never imagined such a path. The first step of a journey she never knew existed but now yearns for. She is captivated by the idea of having the chance to somehow spend your days taking the wrongs of the past and making them right again.

"*PERMESSO.*"

Stella's father stands in the kitchen doorway early the next morning. Sir Harwell's clothing loose and baggy on his slight frame.

Angela halts the rhythm of her chopping. A mere second of silence seems to yawn between them. "Come in," she says at last, frowning.

"*Ciao, cucciola.*" Stella feels her father's palm brush over the top of her head, a lingering touch that yearns for affection beyond salvage.

"You want something to eat?" Stella asks brightly, trying to ease the tension that has begun knitting its way through the room.

"There are *biscotti* in the bread box," Zia Angela says.

"I'll make more coffee," Stella says, wiping her hands on her apron and picking up the steel pot from the stove.

"*Grazie, cara,*" he says, leaning against the counter and watching them. For a few long seconds, the air thickens again, becomes palpable, as if they could touch it. Stella lights the stove and fills the small container with black, pungent grounds.

Her father walks across the kitchen, navigating the tight space between the counter and Angela. Zia Angela appears to freeze, a barely visible reaction that seems to carry the weight of moments lost and regrets unvoiced.

Her father fumbles with the latch on the bread box, a slight tremor in his hand. He pulls out one of the pieces of hard, stale bread. "Going to be a nice day," he says at last.

Stella's aunt glances at the window, where the morning sky has turned amber and soft pink. "I'm afraid it's going to be infernal again," she says. Her chopping resumes, a kind of violent, striking rhythm of the knife that makes thin slashes against the wood. The room fills again with heavy silence.

Stella realizes a very long time has passed since the idea crossed her aunt's mind that she may one day marry Daniele Costa. Stella knows that after so long, it is difficult—maybe impossible—to bridge the gulf of years and feelings that time has laid between two people who shared something important that was lost. Sometimes, it's too late to put words together that can bridge such a gaping hole in someone's history. Besides, Stella knows what it's like to be on the wrong end of her aunt's good graces. She turns the idea around in her head that if her father and Zia Angela had married, Stella herself wouldn't even have had the privilege of being born.

The coffee carafe breaks the silence with its bubbles and hisses. Stella turns off the flame and pours the dark stream into a cup. Her father takes a seat at the small table and she places it in front of him. He dips the stale, hard bread into the steaming liquid.

"I'm going to check the tomatoes," Zia Angela says abruptly. She lays her knife on the table and heads toward the door leading out to the vegetable garden.

When she walks out of the kitchen, it's as if the room itself exhales.

BEFORE SIGNOR POGGI LEAVES again for Florence, he makes a point to find Stella in the kitchen.

"I have something just for you, Stella," he says, placing his leather case on the table. "A little gift." Stella sees his eyes sparkle. "A gift for a girl brave enough to stand up to a soldier with a knife. Brave enough to save a Ghirlandaio."

From his bag, he produces a small red notebook tied together with a red string. On the cover is a beautiful image of the Madonna and Child inside a gilded oval. The book fits neatly in Stella's hand. She flips open the cover to find a stack of postcards made from heavy paper, each one looped into the binding with a red cord. Each one has a painting on it from the Uffizi Galleries. On the back of each card is the name of the artist, the title, and more details about the painting.

"Oh!" Stella pulls the precious collection of bound postcards to her heart. "Thank you. I will spend a lot of time looking at them."

"It's not much, I'm afraid," he says, "especially in exchange for such bravery. But perhaps you can study it until the joyous day when every painting is back in the museum and you can come visit us in Florence and see everything in person."

"I can't wait for that day," she says.

"Nor can I."

"Do you have another postcard book like this?" she asks.

"I have a whole collection!" he says, pulling a second postcard book from his case.

"Thank you. I know someone else who would love one. A friend."

"My pleasure. Will you stay here at Villa Santa Lucia? Or are you headed home?"

Home. The question pools in her mind. Stella knows she could stay at the Villa Santa Lucia. As much as she has been an outsider and had difficulty with her aunt, she knows Zia Angela and Zio Tino would let her stay. But where the villa once seemed like a fantasy land where nothing bad could reach her, it has now grown small. She longs for a place where she can do more. Where she can reach for things that are bigger than herself. She misses being in a city.

But when she thinks of going to Rome with her father, a dull throb spreads across her middle, like the ache of an old wound.

A feeling of uncertainty. Will they be able to find equilibrium, maybe even happiness, if they go together to Italy's capital? Will her father take care of her? Or will she have to take care of him instead? Will he prove as unreliable as Signora Donati said? She knows she is the spit of him. But they are nothing alike.

"I . . . I don't know yet."

"Well," Signor Poggi says, looking as if he regrets having asked a question that made Stella pause for so long, "if you come to Florence when the Uffizi is open again, I can show you the collection—and the conservation lab, since that interests you. I'm sure Signor Conti would be happy to show you, too. Maybe your zio Tino will drive you in that fancy car."

"Thank you . . ." Stella begins, but then she is at a loss for words. The idea of seeing the conservation lab at the Uffizi in Florence lights a spark of an idea, of a possibility she could never dream would be a reality. She only wishes Sandro could be there to see it, too.

FOR THE NEXT FEW DAYS, Signor Poggi's question about home weighs heavily on Stella's mind. She cannot shake the uneasy feeling that has settled in her heart. The uncertainty of it. With all her might, she wishes Sandro were here to talk it through with her, to sit in the treasure room together and see things for what they are. To know the direction that will start the next chapter of her life.

From the high terrace, Stella watches her father pace back and forth among the olive trees. Chain-smoking. Talking to himself. From here, Stella thinks, he looks small and broken.

The right thing to do, Stella decides, is to go to Signora Donati, the one person who has given her good information and guidance through this rocky chapter in her life. Maybe she will be able to help Stella know what to do next.

But the next day, Signora Donati's heart stops while she's feeding the goats. Zia Angela finds the old woman flat on her back, eyes staring blankly up at the robin's-egg-blue sky. Bucket in hand with the orange cat swirling around her and the goose nestled peacefully in the crook of her arm.

The following day, Stella turns fourteen.

Signora Donati's funeral mass draws all the villagers into the church. Under the ancient frescoes of Santa Lucia, Father Ramondo says a few nice things about the woman who was a constant in the village for as long as anyone could recall.

When the villagers watch Daniele Costa walk down the center aisle of the church and take a seat in a pew next to Stella, they nod at him in recognition. Some of them whisper among themselves. Stella thinks he looks uncomfortable with all those curious people he knew so long ago, maybe even some of the farmers he left in a difficult position, now making him the center of attention.

Signora Donati is buried in the small cemetery on the hill outside the village, not so far away from the *maestra* and the few Germans who have lost their lives while in Santa Lucia. Their graves all marked with small white crosses.

That evening, Zia Angela, Livia, and Mariasole make a simple flourless almond cake. On the terrace, everyone begins a round of *tanti auguri* while Stella smiles and her father, his face glowing in the candlelight, sings louder than everyone. His eyes are lined and crinkling, and she feels the gentle tug of time, the weight of memory of all the years before now when he wasn't there to see her turn a year older. Among the chatter and singing, the tender and fragile threads that bind the past and present unfurl in Stella's mind.

"*Tanti auguri a te!*" Everyone finishes the final round and Stella blows out the flame.

"You don't have to go to school anymore!" Mariasole exclaims, bouncing in her seat and clapping her hands.

ON THE NEARBY FARMS, the relentless cycle of work returns to its eternal rhythms, and life reemerges in the village.

Courageous laborers begin clearing the mines from the roads between Florence and Siena. One train line begins to run from the main station in Lucca. Neighbors begin repairing holes in their roofs, replastering bullet holes in their walls. The fruit sellers and the cobbler reopen their shops. Sweep their stoops and hang out new signs. Some of the nearby farmers bring a bounty of tomatoes to the vegetable seller's baskets.

In the schoolhouse, Stella stands in front of the chalkboard and shows her classmates two things: the tattered guidebook that Captain Foster gave her, along with the beautifully bound postcard book that Signor Poggi placed in her hand. Stella does her best to tell the children everything she knows about Sandro Botticelli and his beautiful paintings. About why it's important to know about art and to preserve it. About how art can have hidden symbols and complex meanings and mysterious elements you could never understand. About how it can give you hope in times of darkness.

When she's finished, Signora De Luca smiles and nods. "Well done, Stella. Perhaps you will be an artist."

"Not me," Stella says, feeling heat rise to her cheeks. "I don't have the talent that some others have." She thinks of the precious sketchbook Sandro left behind for her.

"Well then," the *maestra* says, "perhaps a teacher or a curator of some sort."

Stella's lungs fill with air, with hope and possibility for a purpose larger than herself.

ONE DAY, Fabio's older brother Alessio returns from a liberated German work camp near Bologna. He finds the old *maestra*'s husband, newly elected as mayor of Santa Lucia, in his father's former office in the *municipio*. The villagers inform Alessio he'll find the rest of his family in Prato.

When Alessio knocks on the door of the Villa Santa Lucia, he is still in uniform and he holds his hat in his hand. But Livia instructs Mariasole to tell him she is not home.

From the window, Stella watches as Alessio returns to the village down the winding path while Livia sits on her bed with her arms crossed. Watching her sitting like that, sullen in her flowered dress, Stella thinks Livia looks an awful lot like her mother.

AS SOON AS THE RADIO BROADCASTS return and the mail starts running again, even if erratically, there is a telegram from Switzerland. Lady Harwell is returning to England, but the Harwells' grown children say they will come back to claim their ownership of Villa Santa Lucia, now that they are no longer considered enemies of the state. But no one knows how soon they will be able to safely cross northern Italy, which is still occupied by Germans.

"It means we'll be moving back to the caretaker's house," Mariasole informs Stella while they wash dishes. The era of the young countesses in the villa is finished, Stella reckons.

In the attic, Zia Angela is a knot of anxiety as she unpacks the silver and other valuables they hid all those months ago. Two laborers from the village have come up to demolish the brick wall they created to hide everything. In the wine cellar, Zio Stefano is putting everything back in place and sweeping the dust out of the crevices.

In the evening, they dig up the last of Lady Harwell's jewelry.

"The last thing I want Sir Harwell's children to see when they get here is their mother's baubles in the dirt. That's the entire reason they are still here, of course. But they wouldn't understand what we have endured."

But Zio Tino says there is no rush. All of northern Italy is still swarming with Germans and it might be a while before the Harwell children can return to their parents' haven in the Tuscan countryside.

A FEW DAYS LATER, there is a letter from the United Kingdom. Stella takes the nearly weightless paper from the messenger's hands and runs her finger across the foreign-looking stamp before running it under the adhesive flap.

At first, she thinks it's another letter from the Harwells. Instead, she reads the return address. John Cakebread of Hallgarth Street, Durham, England. There are several lines handwritten in beautiful looping script. Stella squints and tries to understand anything at all, but the only words she recognizes are the two at the end of the letter.

Thank you.

FROM THE HIGH TERRACE, Stella watches her father and Zio Stefano walk up and down the neat rows of grapevines. Zio Stefano squeezes the ripening fruits between his fingers, showing them to Stella's papà.

Stella is only fourteen, but she realizes she has already experienced the loss of nearly everyone she has cared for in her life—her mother, her favorite teacher, Sandro, Signora Donati, her friends in the wine cellar, and her father—sort of.

As she weighs her options, she knows that if she's learned one thing from all this loss, it's that she will need to be self-sufficient in the world. Like her mother. Strong and capable. But, Stella thinks, she's still a girl and she has a lot to learn about being independent.

Watching her papà and Zio Stefano among the vines, Stella realizes that *home* isn't really about choosing a place like Torino or Tuscany or Rome. Rather, *home* is choosing the people you want to be with. What matters most, Stella realizes, is not to choose where to go, but who to be with when she becomes who she wants to be. At the same time, Stella knows she can't rely on any one person. If she is to become an independent and capable woman, she will have to learn to rely on herself. *At least I know how to cook*, she thinks.

Having lost so many people who are important to her, Stella knows now that choosing someone to be your family is a privilege and a decision you can't make lightly, without a lot of consideration. Up until now, Stella never considered that family could be a decision you make. A choice rather than a matter of fate.

She watches two men who have shaped her into the woman she is becoming. Her father, God bless him, flawed in every way. She hangs on to the belief that he cares for her still, in his own fashion.

And Zio Stefano, who has not had any obligation to do anything for Stella at all. And yet he has done everything in his power to keep her safe and help her. Still does. He has been more like a real father than the one who made her. He has been a steadfast keeper of lost art and a stabilizing force during a tumultuous chapter of Stella's life.

For the first time, Stella realizes she might have a choice in the matter. A measure of control over her own fate that wasn't there before.

STELLA WRITES ANOTHER LETTER to Sandro from the small, rickety desk in the room she shares with Mariasole and Livia. She hopes someone at the school for the blind will read it to him.

This one is longer than the others. She tells him about how

the new *maestra* asked Stella to teach the younger children more lessons about art and about how the village has come back to life. After she writes the letter, Stella attaches a crude sketch she's made of the central figure of the *Primavera*. She knows it will never measure up to anything Sandro might have drawn, but that's alright. Then she includes the second book of postcards that Signor Poggi gave her, describing to him in detail what's in it. She knows he won't be able to see the cards well, but at least he will have something real and tangible to hold in his hands as a memento of the time the two of them sat together in the treasure room. She addresses it to the school in Pistoia and she hopes he will have a way to write her back.

Stella takes a deep breath and observes the quiet, hot landscape out the window. She marvels at how new relationships were forged that wouldn't have been otherwise. Built between a boy and a girl from different villages, from people of different nationalities and from all corners of the globe. How regular people can do extraordinary things in the face of adversity.

In the last part of her letter, Stella tells Sandro all that's happened in recent weeks. Signora Donati's death; the recent visit of Signor Poggi. And all about the conservation school in Florence.

Finally, she tells him she's made a decision. She's not going to Rome with her father after all. She's decided to stay in Tuscany instead.

IN HER MIND, Stella practices how she will deliver the news to her papà. As much as she knows it's the right decision not to follow him to Rome, she doesn't want to hurt his feelings. After all, he has been tender with her even if he hasn't really known what to do with a half-grown daughter who is more or less a stranger.

She doesn't want to tell him she's let go of the illusion that he's come back just for her. That he will whisk her away to the new and perfect life she had once imagined. Admitting that might hurt his feelings.

Instead, she reasons, she'll tell him she wants to stay in Tuscany. That he can come visit any time he'd like. That she's growing up now. She knows how to take care of herself and she doesn't want to be a burden on him, when she knows he has so many things to figure out. Maybe, Stella thinks, they'll finally have time and a chance to talk about what happened all those years ago. That she'll finally be ready to hear the real story of how her father and mother were together and then they weren't. About why.

But first, Stella will tell him she wants to stay in school and continue her education. She's heard about a special school in Florence where they teach you how to preserve and restore paintings. When things are back to normal, she wants to go to Florence to visit it and learn how to start.

Stella dreads seeing her father's face, his disappointment. She dreads breaking his heart.

It is not only safe in the countryside, it has become home for her.

But when she wakes up the next morning, he is gone.

"I TOLD YOU SO!" Stella hears her aunt whisper to Zio Tino as she hesitates just outside the kitchen door. "I told you he was unreliable. And now look what's happened. He has broken that girl's heart again."

Stella feels a surge of defense for her father, in spite of her better judgment. He is far from perfect and has his own inner struggles. She supposes he's done the best he can.

"It's alright," Stella says, coming into the kitchen. "I didn't want to go with him anyway." But she feels her throat constrict all the same.

"You can stay here with us," her aunt says, coming around the worktable and circling her arm around Stella's waist. Stella feels the unique imprint of her aunt, strong and sure and brittle, all at once.

"I know," she says. "Thank you."

She feels her zio Tino's warm, fatherly palms on her shoulders. "This girl can take care of herself, Angelina," he says. "She's a fighter."

CHAPTER 17

PRIMAVERA

Spring 1945

Art can give you hope in a time of despair.
—FROM THE LOST DIARIES OF SANDRO
BOTTICELLI, FLORENCE, SPRING 1481

Art can give you hope in a time of despair.
—FROM THE DIARY OF CAPTAIN WALLACE E.
FOSTER, MONUMENTS OFFICER OF THE
FIFTH ARMY IN TUSCANY, MAY 1945

On Stella's last day of school in the village, she and Mariasole walk together down the road in the brilliant spring sunshine. The hillside between the Villa Santa Lucia and the village below is a carpet of red poppies.

In the square, the celebrations began a week ago and are still on-going. The nightly broadcast and the newspapers have confirmed everything they have heard. Mussolini and Hitler are dead; the Führer by his own hand and Il Duce by the hands of his enemies. Across Italy, people are flooding into the streets, cheering and singing. Celebrating the liberation of the country after six years under the clench of an iron fist of terror and heartbreak. The whole world feels like a different place now, a shift in the universe that began on that hot day last summer when Stella's father disappeared from her life for the second time.

Stella reaches down among the wildflowers growing along the roadside and picks a bright red bloom to give to Signora De Luca. Looking at the panorama of wildflowers and the blooming fields beyond, she thinks of Botticelli's vision of the spring as a time of a thousand vibrant flowers and a beautiful, floating goddess orchestrating a new season to come.

BEFORE SHE LEAVES FOR FLORENCE, Stella makes a final round of the treasure room, standing in front of the *Primavera* for a very long span, just like Sandro did all those months ago. Then she climbs the tall, skinny watchtower of the Villa Santa Lucia one last time.

Her feet find the worn treads as she winds up the coiling stair-case, looking out the narrow, slit-like windows to the sky hanging with weightless clouds. There are new buds on the trees and on the grapevines. The tall grass is turning from burnished gold to light green as the new growth crops up on the hills as far as the eye can see. Zio Stefano is feeding the piglets they've brought from a nearby farm. The babies root loudly for bits of grain in the dirt. Beyond the Martinellis' tumbledown farm, there is a blazing field of red poppies stretching to the farthest hillside.

From the top of the tower, Stella can see that Zio Tino has pulled Sir Harwell's old roadster out of the carriage house where he has stored it for so long. The car is now spotless and the tires have been put back on. Zio Tino is running a rag over the headlights one more time. Stella knows he's getting it ready for the Harwells' children.

But first, he and Stella are going on an important trip. For a day, Zio Tino will be not just a wealthy Englishman's driver. He will be *her* driver.

Stella takes a deep inhale of the spring air, tinged with the smell of freshly tilled soil and new growth on the vines. She touches the pocket of her dress, which holds Sandro's latest letter. He's found a way to write to her, to have his letters transcribed by people at the school for the blind. In his letters, he tells her he's found friends and sports and books he can read with his hands. Everything Father Ramondo promised and more. One of the teachers has even taken on the challenge of helping him continue to draw. And best of all, his older brothers have returned from fighting to salvage their lives and their village far south of here.

Stella thinks she will write Sandro a letter from Florence and tell him the whole story. The story about how Signor Poggi placed a telephone call to Zio Tino that has changed the course of Stella's life: he's secured a place for her in one of the city's conservation schools. A school where she can begin at the beginning to learn how to care for and fix old paintings. A place that may lead to an apprenticeship and even work in a museum one day. He's even found a place for her in a convent that takes orphans who are apprenticed to studios across town.

In her letter, Stella will assure Sandro that Botticelli's *Primavera* and all the other paintings are still safely stored in the treasure room. About how Signor Poggi promises that they'll go back to the Uffizi just as soon as the museum building has been repaired and is ready to receive them. And about some of the best news of all: Signor Poggi's assurance that the paintings stolen from Montagnana have been discovered in two different hiding places near the Austrian border and will eventually return to Florence. Maybe, she thinks, one day she and Sandro can walk through the Florentine museums together and Stella can describe everything she sees.

In her letter, Stella will describe for Sandro the latest things happening in the Villa Santa Lucia. She knows he loves to hear about everything so he can picture it in his head. Stella will tell him how Zio Tino, Zia Angela, Mariasole, and Livia are moving their things back to the caretaker's cottage now that the Harwell children will be able to come back soon. About the beauty of the pink buds on the trees and the baby goats just born. About the cleared roads and life returning to the village.

And she will tell him about the things she sees, thanks to the gift of vision and new light: How the countryside around Santa Lucia feels reborn into a new era, a place where all their tribulations prepared them for something better and bigger than they knew existed. A place where the sun shines brighter, and all the winding roads leading to Florence have been cleared. The fields are once again a carpet of wildflowers. A spring. A flush of renewal after a long season of darkness. A whole world of possibility and rebirth unfurling to the horizon. As far as the eye can see.

AUTHOR'S NOTE

At first glance, the field of art history is about beautiful objects. But after four decades of studying this ever-fascinating subject, I believe art history is as much about stories and people as it is about paintings, sculpture, ceramics, wood, metalwork, or glass. I spend my days playing at the intersection of material objects and their stories—a place where my fiction and nonfiction halves weave together in ways I still don't fully understand. Writing historical fiction involves pulling apart and then knitting back together the known and the unknowable, marrying evidence with imagination to fill ragged holes in the patchwork of history.

Often, the seed of a historical novel takes root when I find a story from art history that seems too incredible to be real. Studying what happens to works of art in wartime, it's easy to find stories you couldn't make up. *The Keeper of Lost Art* is inspired by one of these strange but true tales: masterpieces of Western civilization, hidden away in a Tuscan villa when German soldiers came to call. To my mind, this story begged to be brought to life through historical fiction.

In some of my other historical novels and art history programs, I've explored the evacuation of the Florentine art collections on the eve of the Second World War. The operation unfolded alongside other such museum evacuations across Europe, in the face of an unstoppable tide of German troops and the increasingly clear intent of art looting. Even in 1942, few could have grasped the staggering scope of Hitler's ambition to strip Europe of its artistic heritage and appropriate great works of art for his own gain. But art professionals across Europe had learned during the First World War that artistic masterpieces might be as much victims of war as human lives, and they set about to save their precious collections from theft and from destruction, whether intentional or accidental.

The beautiful countryside surrounding Florence seemed perfect for hiding works of art in the face of these impending threats. Villas, farms, and castles—whether owned by the state or held in private hands—became quiet repositories. The staff of the Florentine museums decided to spread their collections across various locations in order to avoid the risk of storing many important works in the same place, where they might be targeted or accidentally damaged. Across the Italian peninsula, there were some fifty hiding places— villas, monasteries, castles, wine cellars, train tunnels, and other unlikely places. Of these, thirty-nine were located in Tuscany, a testament to the incomparably rich artistic heritage of the region. Over the course of just a few weeks, curators and regional super- intendents of monuments sent thousands of paintings, sculptures, fragile porcelains, metal objects, enormous ancient marble sculp- tures, and many other objects for safekeeping to these countryside depots. Florentine art officials saw the Tuscan repositories as remote enough to protect their museum treasures, yet close enough to Florence to access them if needed. On both counts, they turned out to be mostly wrong.

The real-life drama behind *The Keeper of Lost Art* unfolded inside one of these hiding places, a privately owned villa in a place called Montegufoni, today little more than a half-hour's drive southwest from Florence. Montegufoni lies nestled in a beautiful swath of agriculture, along with several other secret hiding spots just a few miles away. I discovered the story while researching my historical novel *The Last Masterpiece*. The circumstances at Montegufoni and other repositories in the Tuscan countryside were more than I could fit into my work in progress at the time; instead, the tale deserved its own book. As I finished one project, I followed the thread into the next one.

In the fall of 1942, a humble driver named Guido Masti was guarding this quiet, beautiful Tuscan villa—Castello di Montegufoni—recently vacated by its exiled English owner, Sir George Sitwell, when there was an unexpected knock on the door. Giovanni Poggi, director of the Florentine Galleries, was scouting locations to safeguard some of the city's museum collections. Among the priceless masterpieces on his list: Sandro Botticelli's famous *Primavera*. A quick agreement was reached: a daily pittance for Guido Masti and his brother-in-law in exchange for their twenty-four-hour surveillance of some of the most important works of art in the world. A hastily signed IOU was exchanged for several truckloads of medieval and Renaissance paintings. Eventually, nearly 250 masterpieces from the Uffizi and the Palatine Galleries, the Accademia, and the Museo di San Marco in Florence would fall under Masti's care.

All went according to plan until the following summer, when another unexpected knock on the door produced battle-weary German regiments who requisitioned the villa for their own use. The summer of 1943 also ushered in the beginning of the end of Mussolini's regime, the arrival of Allied forces on Italian soil, and eventually, Italy's dramatic about-face. It was also the start of a brutal German fight to hold their occupied territories, a battle that would soon reach Tuscany, other hiding places nearby, and finally, Montegufoni itself.

But in the tiny universe of this Tuscan villa, Masti and his family had to face more pressing daily challenges: housing German soldiers, not to mention sheltering several hundred refugees who had set up camp in the wine cellar and on the grounds, all the while keeping

everyone away from the Florentine treasures. It was this conflu-
ence of improbable events—all within the microcosm of a country
home—that sparked my interest in pursuing this story as the basis
for a historical novel.

When writing historical fiction, my preference is usually to de-
velop a fictional protagonist, then place them in a setting and a
set of historical circumstances that are as real as I can make them.
Most of the specific events and circumstances described in this book
are true to the historical timeline and context. These include the
strange interactions between Italian citizens and German soldiers,
which ranged from cordial to brutal; the evacuation of artworks
and children from the cities; the difficulties of travel and communication; the relentless waves of the agricultural cycle, which carried
on in spite of the war; the hard-won victories of the *partigiani*; and
the orders—often ignored—signed by top brass on both the Allied
and Axis sides to not touch works of art. Also true is the breath-
taking bravery of individuals; the plundering of artworks; the
hiding of Allied soldiers in the countryside; the random execution
of civilians; and the fractured loyalties of townspeople and families
among the Fascists, puppet governments, resistance fighters, and
other groups. My Italian friends have told me stories about family
members being afraid to reveal their true loyalties during this precarious period of 1942–1944. Some felt they couldn't trust anyone;
others, that they had to take things into their own hands. Sadly,
the looting of some three hundred priceless works hidden at the
Villa Bossi-Pucci in Montagnana is also true.

Among the more amazing true events that unfolded at Montegufoni include Masti's effective distraction of the German soldiers
with choice bottles of Sir Sitwell's wine and brandy, an official but
largely ineffective signed order from Generalfeldmarschall Albert
Kesselring, and damage to Ghirlandaio's beautiful *Adoration of the
Magi* with a sheath knife during a rowdy card game. The villa saw a

revolving cast of Indian, New Zealander, Canadian, and American troops, whose presence must have been a once-in-a-lifetime experience for people who had never ventured beyond their little villages. It is also true that the paintings stayed at the villa while Florence was nearly brought to its knees in the first few days of August 1944, all its bridges blown up except for the Ponte Vecchio, and for a year afterward, until they could be returned safely to Florence.

Just as during the Italian Renaissance, war in Italy in the 1940s saw the unlikely coexistence of unthinkable brutality alongside incredible beauty. And in both periods, art served as a beacon of hope when things seemed dark or even hopeless. It's hard to imagine a work of art that might inspire more hope for brighter days than Sandro Botticelli's meditation on spring, his *Primavera*. This tremendous painting stayed hidden in the shadows in a large room of the main courtyard at Montegufoni. It's mind-boggling to imagine what it must have been like to shelter such an icon of Western civilization under your own roof—and to be responsible for its safety when everything seemed on the brink of ruin.

Botticelli's *Primavera* invites us to unravel one of the most exquisite and enigmatic allegories of the Italian Renaissance. This single painting and its complicated history across five centuries deserves many hours of exploration. For example, we could take a deep dive into the different theories about the circumstances of this work's creation, and how the Medici family may have commissioned Botticelli to create it to mark the marriage of Lorenzo di Pierfrancesco deli Medici to Semiramide Appiano in 1482. We could explore the Villa di Castello, on the outskirts of Florence, which once displayed not only the *Primavera* but one of Botticelli's other masterpieces—*The Birth of Venus*, similar in size and style—perhaps even in the same room. We might spend hours considering the unusual allegorical subject matter that makes the *Primavera* one of the most hotly debated paintings in the history of art. There have been many theories, for example, about the identity of the figures, their allegorical references, and their inspiration in ancient myth. We could fall deep down the rabbit hole of the several hundred individual plant species that have been identified in this single painting, not to mention the symbolism of each one for a fifteenth-century viewer. In the summer of 2022, while I was busy writing this story, climate activists entered the Uffizi as visitors and glued themselves to the protective glass covering this painting. The act reminded me that Botticelli's *Primavera* is not some dusty vestige of centuries past, but remains very much alive today in our minds as an icon of Western civilization.

We could delve into Botticelli himself, a fascinating character in the panorama of Italian Renaissance giants. Among other claims to fame, Botticelli, according to the sixteenth-century art historian Giorgio Vasari, destroyed some of his own paintings in the famous Bonfire of the Vanities in February 1497, when Florence was in the grip of the fire-and-brimstone Dominican friar Girolamo Savonarola. Thankfully, *The Birth of Venus* and the *Primavera* were likely already hanging safely on the walls of the Villa di Castello at that time and already out of the artist's hands.

My students always want to know more about the personal lives and psychology of these Renaissance artists (I do, too), but unfortunately, we are always left wanting. Botticelli left behind no writings to explain anything about his personal life or beliefs, which is why the lost diaries became such a compelling framework for me in writing this story. To my mind, creating such a body of artistic work might have emerged from a person who could hold both high-flying ambition and crippling self-doubt in their heart simultaneously. That is the mark of so many great creators, whether visual artists, performers, or writers.

In thinking about how to approach the construction of this

novel, the biggest question was who might be in the best, or perhaps in the most unique, position to tell this story. I was pleasantly surprised when, out of nowhere, my subconscious produced a preteen girl named Stella. At first, I worried that writing such a young and inexperienced protagonist might be a risk. After all, in my previous historical novels, I have tended to choose protagonists who are art professionals—or those who become art professionals over the course of the story. But this book seemed to demand something different. It made me want to see what such a sophisticated and complex icon of Western civilization might look like through the eyes of someone relatively naïve, someone who found herself coming of age during wartime, under unthinkable circumstances.

Because Stella and Sandro's story quickly grew beyond the bounds of real history to take on a life of its own, I felt it was important to fictionalize some of the setting and other characters as well. Out of respect for the brave real-life individuals who navigated these horrific events in what is relatively recent history, I want to be clear that Santa Lucia is fictional and only loosely based on Montegufoni. The villa itself, the nearby village, church, schoolhouse, and other places are figments of my imagination. Zio Tino is loosely inspired by Guido Masti, but I don't pretend to project any of Tino's specific qualities on Masti, who in real life had the good sense to send his daughters to a nearby church when the Germans came. Zia Angela, Zio Stefano, Sandro, the teachers and kids at school, and the refugee families are also fictional.

Apart from Stella and her extended family and friends, a few of the characters in this story are based on real people who are true heroes of art preservation. In these cases, I have done my utmost to follow the historical record and timeline as faithfully as possible. Giovanni Poggi, then the superintendent of the Florentine Galleries, was partly responsible for orchestrating the complex evacuation of these treasures to the countryside. The Uffizi's librarian, Cesare Fasola, walked over bomb-cratered roads to the Tuscan depots, putting his life on the line to make sure the works remained safe. These Florentines were immensely proud of their heritage, believed in its essential role in the future of humanity. They risked their lives and their jobs and their families and so much more to preserve these works of art for the future—for us. I hope to have done their stories at least a small bit of justice in this book.

Captain Wallace Foster and his assistant, Josie Evans, will be familiar to those who have read my novel *The Last Masterpiece*. These characters are inspired by the heroic Monuments Men and Women, who, like their Italian counterparts, made an indelible contribution to the preservation of works of art that might not otherwise have been saved after the war. In particular, the contributions in Italy of real-life Monuments Men Lieutenant Frederick Hartt and Captain Deane Keller are difficult to overstate. I highly recommend reading more about their lives and incredible legacies for the history of art in Italy. And for a memorable real-life account of what it was like to live in a Tuscan villa along with refugee children like Stella, who were evacuated from northern Italian cities during the air raids, be sure to read Iris Origo's amazing diary, *War in Val d'Orcia*, which helped me imagine better the daily struggles of Stella's family.

The panorama of the war in Italy during these months is, of course, much bigger than this small story of a single villa and its role in hiding some of the masterpieces of Western civilization. But I believe bringing into focus one location and one painting can give us a perspective that's a bit different from the history books, and different from some of the more sweeping historical novels set during World War II, including my own. By bringing this small world to life, I hope it might help you see things differently, too.

To the many people in Italy who, during the course of research, generously shared their knowledge and personal access to places and things I would never have seen otherwise, I am forever indebted. In particular, I am grateful to Guido Masti's grandson, Andrea Pestelli, who grew up at Montegufoni and has been so generous with his time, research, and personal experience with this story. While walking through Montegufoni with Mr. Pestelli, I was able to experience the villa through the eyes of a child, through the eyes of someone who didn't know the first thing about art or war. Someone who was simply trying to make sense of the complicated world of adults while growing up in wartime and its aftermath, in the unlikely presence of great works of art. Growing up, by chance, in the crosshairs of history. Mr. Pestelli's story helped breathe life into Stella's, and for that I am immensely grateful.

In Italy, I am grateful to Elena Fulceri, Marco Paoletti, Simona Pasquinucci, Attilio Tori, Francesca Bozzetto, and Corinna Maria Carrara for setting the stage for my understanding of the area's World War II history. They helped me experience Florence and its surrounding countryside in ways I had not before, even on many trips to the area.

On the home front, I am grateful to my editor, Tessa Woodward, and to my literary agent, Jenny Bent, who have paved the way for my books to come forth into the world with expertise and sure-handed support. Thank you to the copyeditors, proofreaders, typesetters, book designers, and marketing and sales staff at HarperCollins for working your magic, for assembling this book into something more than the sum of its parts. Thank you to Jessica Hatch and my other first readers, who review my early drafts and pull apart the *bello* from the *bruto* with such care and expertise. Thank you to my early morning text champions, who kept me honest and on task while revising this manuscript. And to my late-night commiserators, who keep me laughing. Writer friends are the best.

Most of all, my undying gratitude goes to my husband and children and mother, who cheer for whatever I write. They love me enduringly, in spite of my living with my head in the clouds most of the time, especially when on deadline.

For book club questions and more research, images, videos, notes, and other stories behind *The Keeper of Lost Art*, visit: lauramorelli.com/lostart

MEET LAURA MORELLI

LAURA MORELLI holds a PhD in art history from Yale University and is a *USA Today* bestselling author of historical fiction. Laura has taught art history students in the United States and in Italy, and teaches art history at lauramorelli.com. Laura's Made in Italy guidebook series has been leading travelers off the beaten path for nearly three decades. She has been a columnist for *National Geographic Traveler* and *Italy Magazine*, and has produced educational programs for Ted-Ed.

As a historical novelist, Laura's passion is bringing little-known stories of art history to life. Her novels have earned starred reviews and editors' picks in *Publishers Weekly*, *Library Journal*, and the *Historical Novels Review*, as well as numerous awards. Her fiction includes *The Night Portrait*, *The Gondola Maker*, *The Last Masterpiece*, and other books.

More at
lauramorelli.com

MORE FROM
LAURA MORELLI

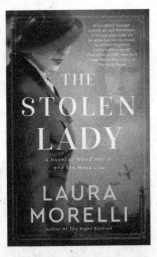

From the acclaimed author of *The Night Portrait* comes a stunning historical novel about two women, separated by five hundred years, who each hides Leonardo da Vinci's *Mona Lisa*—with unintended consequences.

When art and war collide, Leonardo da Vinci, his beautiful subject Lisa, and the portrait find themselves in the crosshairs of history.

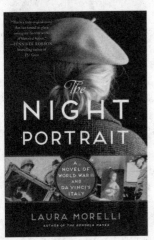

An exciting dual-timeline historical-fiction novel about one of da Vinci's most famous paintings, *Lady with an Ermine*, and the woman who saved it from Nazi destruction in World War II